A Tangled Web

by

Suzanne Rossi

This is a work of fiction. Names, characters, places, and incidents either are the product of the author's imagination or are used fictitiously, and any resemblance to actual persons living or dead, business establishments, events, or locales, is entirely coincidental.

A Tangled Web

Cover Art by *Kim Mendoza*

The Wild Rose Press
PO Box 708
Adams Basin, NY 14410-0706
Visit us at www.thewildrosepress.com

Publishing History
First Crimson Rose Edition, 2010
Print ISBN 1-60154-795-1

Published in the United States of America

"I can't believe I came back. I must be going senile," she muttered.

"I think you have a conscience."

"I think I'm a sap." Vicky closed her eyes, weariness stamped on her face.

A slow heat burned in the pit of his stomach, radiating outward until engulfing his body. His breath quickened, and before he stopped to think, strode toward her. He grasped her shoulders and pulled her upright into his arms. Trevor didn't hesitate, but covered her lips with his.

The burning sensations exploded into a full blown fire. Her lips parted, and he tasted the sweetness of her tongue. His heart hammered in his ears. He tightened his arms when she moaned deep in her throat. His hand slipped beneath her sweater to caress her breast. Even through her bra, he felt the erect nipple.

Her arms snaked around his neck, her fingers tangling in his hair. When she let her head fall back exposing her white throat, he took advantage of the opportunity to nibble the delicate tendon to her collarbone.

She gasped, and while the temptation to throw her on the sofa was strong, he was also cognizant of where they were and of Halston just down the hall. He backed away.

Vicky stared with glazed eyes, trembling from head to foot. He wanted her—bad—but it was the wrong place and certainly the wrong time.

He ran his thumb down the line of her jaw, and then kissed her chin.

"Go to bed, Vicky. We'll talk tomorrow."

Dedication

My husband, Bruce, would rather die than
be caught reading a romance novel.
However, that does not prevent him from
encouraging me to write one.
In the seven years I have pursued my ambition,
he's always been there making dinner
or doing housework,
when the muse refused to let me abandon the
keyboard.
He never complained
and listened to me moan and groan about plot lines
and writer's block without rolling his eyes.
So, honey, this one's for you.
And I promise, when you need me, I'll be there.
Love ya!

Prologue

The man stared at the fireplace poker in his hand with fascinated horror as the blood crept down the weapon where it gathered at the tip, ballooned, hung, and then fell with a soft plop onto the body lying at his feet.

Panic pressed against his lungs, threatening to suffocate him. Fear clogged his throat. He swallowed hard. The poker fell from suddenly flaccid fingers. He was sobering up fast.

Oh my God, oh my God. The words slammed through his head. He'd never killed anyone before. He was a thief, not a murderer.

The killer wiped the sweat from his forehead with the sleeve of his jacket. The weight of several bundled stacks of money stuffed in the pocket slapped against his ribs, reminding him he needed to get the hell out.

Pulling out a handkerchief, he wiped his fingerprints from the poker, then stepped over the body and did the same to the open safe, not bothering to close it. After all, this was a robbery. In spite of his fear, he remembered to whisk the cloth over the picture frame and safe door. His prints anywhere else in the room wouldn't be suspicious given the time he'd spent in the house.

Finished, the man made his way to the desk, glancing at the open bottom drawer and the empty cigar box it contained.

He patted his pockets reassuring himself the bundles were safe, and grabbed a stack of folders from the desktop. He clutched them in a sweat-drenched hand and hurried across the room, giving the still warm body a wide berth. He paused in the doorway looking back over his shoulder.

Now that the deed was done, the panic increased. For a moment, his legs shook and his knees wobbled. Blood pounded in his ears, and his breath rasped in and out. He flipped off the light, ran through the foyer, and out the front door, stumbling down the porch steps to his car. His trembling fingers twisted the key in the ignition. He didn't bother with the seat belt, but jammed the car into gear and peeled down the driveway.

He had no idea what to do next. Instinct screamed run. He drove fast, putting distance between himself and the body.

Go! Get out! Now! His foot pressed the accelerator further toward the floor as he fled into the darkness.

Chapter One

Ed Williams smiled from across the dinner table at Chez Paul's, while waving a check under Victoria Denton's nose like a treat. "Twenty-five thousand dollars, Vicky, just like I promised."

She allowed her eyes to fill with tears, sniffing as though overwhelmed, and squeezed his hand.

"Oh, Ed...I...I can't tell you how much this means to me. I would never have asked, but the economy has left my finances in a mess. The bank is about to foreclose on Mother's condo." Vicky blinked the tears away and quivered her chin, a skill she'd learned in childhood. "I'll pay you back. I swear it."

"Take your time, darling." He raised her hand to his lips. "Get your mother's situation under control first."

She extricated her hand from his, accepted the check and slipped it into her evening bag. "I'll put this in the bank tomorrow morning, contact her lawyer, and by Friday the whole mess will disappear." She batted her eyes. "You are so supportive. No wonder I love you."

Ed laughed and winked. "I feel the need for champagne. Waiter!" he called out over a band tuning up behind the dance floor.

Chez Paul sat smack in the middle of the Miami South Beach district. With a five star rating and an eclectic menu, it shouted elegance. The artic white tablecloths and napkins impressed her. Chandeliers, the muted lighting tumbling through crystal beads, enhanced the glow from the tabletop candles. Even on a week night, the place was packed. Reservations for the average Joe who could afford it were hard to come by.

The waiter stopped beside their table. While Ed ordered, Vicky's mind slipped into high gear. *The old goat came through. Now, I need to get out of here.*

Vicky let Ed talk, making all the right responses while thinking at the same time. She'd put the check in the bank, wait until it cleared, transfer the funds to her account in the Caymans, and then head for another city. Ed represented her second Miami scam in six months, which was one too many. Hit 'em and move on had always been her motto. She needed to lie low for a while. Maybe she'd join her brother if he was still in Vegas. Rod had split for greener pastures after the Jordan con. Vicky hadn't seen or heard from him in a year.

The waiter brought the champagne, filled their glasses, and left. Ed lifted his in a toast.

"To us and the good times we're going to have," he said, winking again.

Vicky knew what he meant. Since he'd forked over twenty-five grand, he expected something in return. *Probably has high expectations and took a double dose of Viagra.*

She'd find another excuse to avoid sleeping with him. Ed was all right. He looked years younger than his admitted sixty, although she suspected he dyed his hair to maintain the illusion.

She sipped the French wine, glancing at the menu beside her plate. The cheapest entrée was forty bucks. The lobster thermidor carried a hefty hundred twenty-five dollar price tag. She'd have that.

God knows, old Ed can afford it. Maybe, I should've asked for fifty thousand. No, don't get greedy. Rod's greed with Jordan had her escaping steps ahead of the bunko squad.

The band, finished with the preliminaries, swung into an old tune, *Isn't It Romantic.*

Damn, even the music in this place is elegant.

"Ah, darling, they're playing our song." Ed rose, his hand extended.

Vicky accepted, and they joined several other couples on the dance floor. A good dancer, Ed twirled her around, but her thoughts remained on her imminent departure.

First and foremost, she had to dodge Ed until the check cleared. A reservation at a non-beachside hotel under her real name should do the trick.

Next, get out of the condo she'd used for two months. Her brief stint as a receptionist for a cleaning company had given her access to numerous addresses of snowbird homes. And with the crews turning in the condo keys at the end of the day, it had been simple to duplicate a set, move in, and cancel the service. But this was October. The owners would soon return.

"Vicky! Imagine finding you here!"

A masculine voice ripped her mind away from escape plans. She stumbled to a stop, and jerked her head toward a tall, good-looking man standing next to them, a wide smile on his face.

Do I know this guy? Her mind suspected the worst. *God, was he a mark? No, he wouldn't be smiling if I conned him.*

Pretending not to know him wasn't an option. He'd used her name in front of Ed. Wary and suspicious, she played along. "Good grief, what are you doing here?"

"Business." The stranger turned toward Ed. "Hi, I'm Vicky's cousin. Mind if I cut in?"

He didn't give her date a chance to refuse, but gathered her into his arms and swept her across the floor, leaving Ed with a confused look on his face.

"Who the hell are you?" she demanded.

"Name's Trevor Sloane. I take it your companion is your latest mark. I saw him hand you a check. Tell me, are you using an alias or sticking with Denton? No, you wouldn't use your real name. How about Sedgwick? Or maybe Grayson?"

Vicky stumbled again as shock raced through her. Sloane tightened his grip around her waist. A strange pulse throbbed in the pit of her stomach. Her breath caught in her chest. Years of practice clicked into place.

"I have no idea what you're talking about. Let me go or I'll call security. You are *seriously* unbalanced."

Her partner laughed. "You're good, I'll give you that. We're gonna talk, but not on the dance floor. Now, here's the plan. You'll introduce me to the sucker as your cousin from California. Then explain how you hope he understands, but due to my short time in Miami, you just have to spend the rest of the evening with me. We have family matters to discuss."

"I'll do no such thing." Her gaze met his hard, unrelenting brown eyes. A shiver slithered up her spine.

"If you don't, I'll be forced to bring Ed, the chump, up to date on your activities of the last few months. Shall I begin with the Olivers, who still aren't convinced they've been had? How about the guy in Naples, Florida? And let's not forget Aaron Jordan in Houston. The man's pissed. He wants your head on a platter, and your half-brother's family jewels as a trophy on the wall behind his desk. He doesn't know I've located you yet. Be a good girl, and maybe I won't tell him."

Vicky struggled to breathe. Her worst nightmare had come true. She was caught. Her gaze swept the room, seeking a way out. Sloane's hand squeezed hers hard. She gasped and flinched.

"There's no way out."

"Who the hell are you? A cop?"

"No, I'm a private investigator from Los Angeles. I've been on your trail for six months. Took me five to track your activities, find you, and another few weeks of observation."

"What do you want?"

"Later."

The music ended and he steered her back toward the table. Ed rose as they approached.

"Remember, the name is Trevor Sloane," he whispered in her ear.

"Vicky?" Ed asked with raised eyebrows.

Could she bluff her way out of this? A public scene might work. Sloane's fingers bit into her waist. She got the hint. *I'll deal with him later.*

"Um, Ed, I'd like you to meet Trevor Sloane, my cousin from Los Angeles. Trevor, Ed Williams."

Trevor smiled and offered his hand. "A pleasure. Sorry if I butted in, but I couldn't believe it when I saw Vicky on the dance floor. Would you believe I've been looking for her?"

"How coincidental," she replied through stiff lips.

"Won't you join us?" Ed asked, his expression far from pleased. His questioning gaze flicked to her face.

"Ed, I'm...I'm sure you'll understand if I leave. Trevor is flying out tomorrow afternoon, and we have family matters to discuss."

Ed frowned and looked at Trevor with narrowed eyes. "Your mother? But I've taken care of that."

"Vicky told me, and I appreciate what you've done," Trevor said. "However, the problem goes deeper than Vicky knew."

"Yes, apparently there are some major health

issues involved. Mother wanted to spare me. We can have dinner tomorrow night, can't we?"

The waver in her voice wasn't all acting. Given the greeting on the dance floor, the excuse sounded hollow and contrived.

Ed's eyebrows drew together, but he accepted the lame explanation. "I suppose. Here again at eight o'clock?"

"That sounds wonderful, darling." She kissed his lips. "Thank you for understanding. I'm afraid my cousin's news has upset me. I'd have made a lousy dining companion. I'll bring you up to date tomorrow night."

Trevor shook hands with Ed and once again apologized before cupping her elbow and guiding her toward the doors.

"I can't believe he bought that load of crap," he murmured. "What an idiot."

Vicky agreed, but Ed Williams's gullibility was the least of her problems at the moment.

Outside, her captor handed the valet his parking ticket. Neither of them spoke until the car arrived.

Settled into the passenger's seat, Vicky stared straight ahead, asking, "What's this all about?"

"Let's talk at the condo you've usurped. Any idea when the owners are due back?"

"How do you know so much about me?"

"It's my job. Any idea when the Conways are due to take possession of their winter home?"

"Go to hell."

He laughed. "This is mid-October. My guess is you'll have to vacate within the next couple of weeks. That's cutting it close. What fairy tale did you spin the condo association for your presence?"

Vicky glanced at him, wanting to smack the self-satisfied smirk off his face. *I should've gotten out of town after taking the Olivers.*

Sloane laughed again. "Not talking, huh? Never

mind, I can guess. You're the niece who's looking after the place during the summer."

She averted her face. Miami Beach flashed passed the passenger side window. How the hell had he guessed? "Mr. Sloane, what do you want from me?"

"Retribution, my lovely little con artist. Retribution."

They drove the rest of the way in silence. Vicky unlocked the door to her purloined living quarters with shaky fingers, entering with Sloane close on her heels.

Retribution? What kind of retribution? Money? If she conned him at some point of her life, she didn't remember. Had a pissed off mark hired this guy to track her down? She racked her brain. Who had she conned six months ago before coming to South Florida.

Kravitz? No, he was the man in Naples Sloane had mentioned. Kravitz with his toupee, dentures, and constant gifts of jewelry probably still had no clue he'd been conned.

She'd pulled little scams along the way from Reno to finance her journey. No way could she remember them all. If he didn't want money, what did he want? Would he turn her over to the police after extracting his pound of flesh?

She caught her lower lip between her teeth. Whatever Sloane wanted, it wouldn't be pleasant. Her heart hadn't ceased its heavy beating since his revelations on the dance floor. She'd never been caught before—well, not like this. Cash Marriott had scared the crap out of her when he'd discovered her and Rod rifling his safe.

Forget about Marriott. He's dead. Sloane is your problem now. Get rid of him, and then get the hell out of Dodge.

The object of her thoughts sauntered through

the living room toward the bar. "Nice place. Mind if I pour myself a drink?"

"Go ahead. It's not my liquor."

He walked behind the polished oak counter and read the labels on the bottles before selecting one. Vicky slapped her purse on the bar top, slid onto a stool, and stared as he grabbed a glass, pouring scotch a third of the way up the crystal.

If not for the situation, she decided Trevor Sloane had possibilities. On the dance floor, she'd fit nicely in his arms, the top of her head level with his mouth. She estimated his height as around six-three.

Her gaze settled on his face. Not handsome, but more in the line of rugged good looks. A small scar on his right cheekbone and another above his left eyebrow told her he'd been in his fair share of fights.

Even scared, she'd found being in his arms for a few minutes not an unpleasant experience. A tug she didn't often feel plucked her awareness.

Get the train off that track. You're in big trouble.

"You?" Sloane said, gesturing with the bottle.

"No. What kind of retribution?"

"Do you remember Roland Richardson?"

"Not offhand."

"Roland was the heir to a mining fortune in Colorado. He hated the business, preferring travel and books. And that's what he and his wife, Helen, did when a conglomerate offered big bucks for Richardson Mining." He paused and sipped the scotch, eyebrows raised. "Damned good stuff. At least you picked a condo whose owners have good taste."

"Yeah, whatever. Get on with it."

His dark gaze bored into her. "Roland loved stories about the American west, so he and Helen bought a winter house in Palm Springs. They traveled to places like Tombstone and Santa Fe.

Ring any bells yet?"

The name meant nothing, but Palm Springs tickled her memory. She'd been there several times. Had she conned someone? She didn't remember.

"No." A wave of nausea clenched her stomach. This conversation had a purpose. She changed her mind about the drink. "Hand me a glass."

Sloane slid one toward her. She caught it, tilted the bottle, poured, and gulped. The fiery liquor flamed down her throat to settle in her dinnerless stomach, erasing the sickness and sending waves of heat outward.

"But Roland had one weakness. He was a sucker for old legends. One winter, Helen left him alone for a few weeks to visit her sister in Los Angeles. Roland decided to search for the Lost Dutchman Mine."

Oh, shit! Now, she remembered. The Lost Dutchman was her brother's action. He'd called her in to keep the pigeon distracted.

"I had nothing to do with that. I was hired for my secretarial skills and assisted with research."

"Your brother, Roderick Halston, under the alias, Robert Harrison, did most of the work convincing Roland he knew the mine's location. I imagine you forwarded every piece of information back to your brother. By the way, you used the Victoria Sedgwick alias. Am I right so far? Of course, I am. I've seen the canceled paychecks."

Vicky bolted the rest of the scotch in a single swift movement, ignoring the burn. She set the glass back on the bar. Damn Rod anyway. She no longer recalled how much they'd taken the old boy for, but did remember the wife's imminent return from California had prompted a fast exit on both their parts—Rod to Vegas and she to her Aunt Iris's in Phoenix.

"What's all this got to do with you? That

happened years ago."

"Six to be exact."

"And he's just now decided to track me down?"

Sloane finished his scotch and pinned his gaze on her again, making her feel like an insect in a display.

"Roland was my uncle by marriage. Helen is my late mother's sister. That's who Helen visited those few weeks. My aunt's a smart woman. She knew Roland had been up to something. My uncle died a year later, but it wasn't until eight months ago she discovered some papers in an old file cabinet in the attic. Aunt Helen found the canceled checks, her husband's notes on the Lost Dutchman, and an inventory of the equipment his partner was supposed to have bought. You and your brother cleaned him for over a hundred grand."

"A hundred grand!" Anger bubbled in her chest. That scum-sucking, lying, son of a bitch Rod had told her fifty. She'd wondered at his generosity when he gave her half. *Never trust a relative.*

"I see by the look on your face there is no honor among thieves. I take it that's more than you thought," he said with a laugh.

"Go to hell, and if you expect me to pay it back, you're out of luck. I haven't got that kind of money."

"Maybe not in the States, but I'm sure you have an offshore account."

"Why come after me? Go find my slick half-brother."

"Already did."

Vicky didn't like the smooth tone of his voice. The other shoe was about to drop. Her stomach churned again from the liquor, nerves, and lack of food.

"I take it Rod doesn't have any money either."

"This isn't about money. It's about paying the price. Aunt Helen's madder than hell. Called me the minute she realized what had gone down. She knew her husband had been conned. So did he. It was in his notes."

"What's Rod's reaction to all this?"

"He doesn't know yet."

"You found him first."

"Through you. The name Victoria Sedgwick rang a bell. I researched old case files. You used that name when you stole a supposed treasure map from Cash Marriott. His grandson contacted me to dig up more about you. Did I mention Quinn Rafferty was once my partner in the PI business?"

Vicky propped her elbows on the bar and leaned her forehead on the heels of her palms. *Quinn!* Memories of Guatemala slashed through her mind. Until now, that whole fiasco had been the low point of her life.

"And I suppose as a refresher, you called Quinn who gave you chapter and verse about Rod and me."

"Of course. Guatemala was one of the few times the two of you used your real names. You couldn't take a chance on an alias with a passport involved. Your brother used his because he worked at Alex Rafferty's antique store. Unlike you, he doesn't have several different social security numbers—just aliases."

"Rod never worked a day in his life. If he couldn't steal it or con it, he borrowed it, usually from me. *And* never paid it back." She raised her head. "Is Rod next on your list?"

"Helen's taking care of him."

"How?"

"I found him in Las Vegas. Helen got a suite at the same hotel and struck up an acquaintance in the bar. Flashed a lot of money and jewels. Your brother homed in like a missile. He jumped at the invitation to join her in Granite Springs. He's there now, convinced he's about to score big."

"Where the hell is Granite Springs?"

"Colorado, and the last stop on our journey. Go pack your bags. We're leaving. But first..." Sloane picked up her evening bag, opened it, and extracted the check. "...some unfinished business." He also removed her credit cards and two hundred dollars in cash. "You won't be needing these either."

He walked over to a desk in the corner, found an envelope, addressed it, slipped the check inside, then sealed and stamped it.

"I'll pop this into the mail on our way out of town. I'm sure Mr. Williams will understand. Better hurry. We have a plane to catch."

Vicky clutched the bag and slid from the stool, her legs shaking. Airports were crowded. She'd wait, lull him into a false sense of security, and then make a run for it. He hadn't mentioned her other two aliases. *Maybe he doesn't know them.*

Dinner represented another avenue of escape. She'd insist on stopping to eat, then head for the ladies room. The restrooms were always down a dim hallway not far from the kitchen. And kitchens had back doors.

If she didn't ditch this guy, Granite Springs would be the end of the line for her.

In the bedroom, Vicky changed clothes and packed. The endeavor didn't take long. She traveled light—her clothing, jewelry, and a few toiletries. A handbag, the one she carried when not out on the town, sat on the dresser.

With a glance toward the living room, she picked it up, entered the bathroom, closed the door behind her, and whipping out her cell phone, dialed. When voice mail picked up, she left a message, snapped the phone shut and exited.

Outwardly calm, she hauled the suitcases into the living room where Sloane talked on his cell.

"That's right, the Oceanside Condominiums.

We'll be out front." He ended the call and dialed again. "Jerry, Trevor. I'm about ready to leave. The keys are under the front seat...Yes, both cars. Your payment is over the visor...Nice doing business with you, too." He hung up and turned toward her. "I need the car keys."

"Why?"

"Because it's rented, and I'm not running out on the rental agreement. Some friends will come by in the morning to return yours and mine." He wiggled his fingers. "Condo keys, too. You won't need them anymore."

She unclipped the items from a sterling silver key ring, tossing them onto the coffee table while her mind shifted into high gear, visualizing restaurants and airports.

"Ready?" Sloane asked.

"Yes, I travel light."

"Except for your wallet. That's usually stuffed to the brim with ill-gotten gains."

"Not this time. Thanks to you, I'm broke."

"Thanks to me, Ed Williams is a richer and wiser man." He picked up her wheeled case and extended the handle. "You can carry the other."

Irritation bubbled in her chest, and she bit back a scathing reply. Instead, she hefted the smaller, non-wheeled bag.

Sloane opened the door with a mocking smile. "Ladies first."

Her fingers itched to slap his face, but keeping her composure, walked past him into the hallway. He closed the door, locked it, and then pocketed the key.

Be cool. When the time comes, act cowed. Squeeze out a tear or two along the way.

"I'm hungry. You interrupted my dinner. Can we stop to eat before you haul me off to Bumfuck, Idaho, or wherever?"

"Granite Springs, Colorado. We'll grab something at the airport."

Good. Better than a restaurant. I'll lose myself at the airport. He can't watch me every second. A moment's inattention and I'm gone.

****

Trevor hated Miami International Airport. Big and sprawling, the terminals covered acres of ground. *Stay close. Don't trust her for a moment. Keep her in sight.*

At the check-in counter, he heaved their luggage onto the scales.

"What about that one?" he asked, pointing at the bag she carried.

"This contains my jewelry. I'll carry it on."

He nodded, and they both produced ID for the agent, who issued boarding passes.

"I'm hungry," she said.

"Sure, no problem." He bypassed several decent restaurants before stopping in front of a busy kiosk.

"Burger Biggie?" Victoria's blue eyes stared in disbelief.

"Hey, you're not gonna take me for a two hundred dollar dinner."

Her eyes narrowed and her lips compressed into a thin line. Damn, Quinn had been right. Even pissed off and probably scared, she was beautiful. Dressed in tan slacks and a cream-colored blouse, she presented a striking picture. Her hair was piled on top of her head in an elegant upsweep. The jewelry from her anticipated dinner and score from Williams still graced her ears and fingers. Gifts from a smitten mark? He wondered if the diamonds and sapphires were real.

"What'll you have?" he asked, enjoying her obvious irritation.

"I want lobster thermidor, rice pilaf, asparagus with hollandaise sauce, and several glasses of

16

champagne."

"Right." He turned to the woman behind the counter. "Two cheeseburgers with everything, fries, and two colas, one diet."

He paid for the food, carried the tray to a table against the back wall, and sat.

"Come on, might as well eat. It's all you'll get."

Victoria jerked out the chair, sat, and unwrapped the burger. Grease oozed, soaking the bun. "You know, all I have to do is scream, claim this is an attempted kidnapping, and you'll be in police custody before I can say 'two all beef patties.'"

"True," Trevor replied, taking a bite of the sandwich. How could a burger be greasy and dry at the same time? He ripped open a package of mayonnaise, spreading it on the bun. "But then, I'd be obliged to explain my uncle, the Olivers, Ed Williams, and who's that jerk in Naples? Kravitz? You don't want me to do that. The cops will check out my story, contact those people, and when your marks learn you've been caught, they'll line up to throw stones, baby. I'll contact Jordan when my aunt's done with you. I can't wait to see his reaction."

He shoved a limp fry into his mouth. It tasted rancid. Burger Biggie obviously wasn't concerned with changing the fryer oil. Trevor chewed, amused when Victoria's expression changed from angry to frightened. Damn, she *was* good.

"Eat up, Vicky. You don't mind if I call you Vicky, do you? I feel like we're old friends."

She dropped the burger on the wrapper. Her chin quivered and tears filled her eyes. Laying her fingers on his hand, she said, "Vicky's fine...Trevor. Look, I had nothing to do with your uncle getting scammed. It was Rod's idea. He asked me to keep the man distracted with a little flirting. Yes, I passed on information, but that's all. I swear. My brother gave me a few thousand bucks for my time. When Roland mentioned his wife was returning, Rod decided it was time to split." A tear trickled down her cheek.

Trevor crammed the remains of the worst burger and fries he'd ever eaten into the wrapper, took a long swallow of his watered down drink, and then laughed.

"You are championship material, lady. That was convincing. I like the single tear. Reminds me of a TV commercial years ago with an Indian chief. If I hadn't talked to Quinn or read Uncle Roland's notes, I might've believed you."

The chin ceased quivering, and the tears disappeared. An angry expression crossed her face.

"Are you finished?" he asked.

"Yes." Her sharp reply told him she was furious. If he was in her shoes, he'd feel the same. Trevor bet it wasn't often her charms went unappreciated.

He dumped the half-eaten meal into the trash, and cupping her elbow with his hand, headed for the security check-through. Fifteen minutes later, they walked down the concourse toward the gate.

"Excuse me, but I have to use the facilities," she said, veering to the right.

"Don't take forever. Boarding begins soon. I'll wait here."

Vicky nodded and followed a short, dumpy woman wearing a light blue raincoat and floppy hat through the entryway.

Trevor wasn't worried she'd slip out a back door. The restrooms were located on an interior wall. But he wondered if she'd stay inside until they missed the plane. He'd give her ten minutes before hauling her out.

He waited, pacing while his mind jumped ahead to their arrival in Granite Springs. His aunt didn't figure on recovering one thin dime of her husband's money, nor was she interested in jail time for the pair. The statute of limitations had run out, but he doubted Vicky or Rod knew that. No, his aunt wanted an apology, along with a few other things.

The woman in the blue raincoat left the restroom. Trevor glanced at his watch. Vicky had been dallying for seven minutes. *Three more and I'm in there.*

Waiting and tapping his foot, a gut feeling not all was right washed over him.

He was about to charge through the door when a short woman emerged. She held her right hand in front of her, admiring a large diamond ring. Her ears sported the sapphire and diamond earrings his captive had worn a few minutes earlier. *Oh, no!*

The lady looked up as he approached. "You must be the jealous boyfriend."

"No, I'm not." He shifted his gaze to the earrings and silently swore. "She traded the jewelry, didn't she?"

"For my coat and hat. Said she had second thoughts about going off with…"

Trevor whirled. Tired and preoccupied, he didn't notice the woman leaving was taller than the one who'd entered. He looked up and down the concourse. The thick crowd obscured his line of sight. He saw no woman in a blue raincoat and floppy hat. Victoria Denton had disappeared. If she made it to the front doors, he'd never find her.

"Dammit to hell!" He took off at a run.

Chapter Two

The idea popped into Vicky's head as she followed the woman into the restroom. Putting on her best frightened woman act, she accosted the stranger.

"Ma'am, please help me." She called up the tears again, allowing a couple to slide down her cheeks. "I'm supposed to be going to New York with my boyfriend, but I've changed my mind. He's waiting outside the door. If I tell him I don't want to go, he'll think there's another man. He's very jealous, and I...I'm scared."

"How can I help?"

"Your coat and hat. I'll wear them out, and he'll never notice."

"Are you kidding? I'm going to St. Louis. It's cold there. I can't just show up with no coat. Besides, this thing cost me a hundred bucks. What do I get out of it?"

Vicky gritted her teeth at the avarice on the woman's face, and then pulled the earrings Kravitz had given her from her ears.

"Take these."

"Are those real stones?"

"Yes."

Vicky lied. The first thing she'd done had been to sell the gems and replace them with paste. The same went for the five-carat engagement ring on her finger. She yanked it off.

20

"You can have this, too, but please, give me the coat and hat."

The woman held the items up to the light and smiled. "Lady, you've got a deal. How much are these worth?"

"Uh, I'm not sure. They were gifts, but I imagine quite a lot." Paste copies of a bracelet and a necklace were in the case at her feet, but to offer those sounded like overkill.

"You must really be scared."

"I am."

Tossing the hat toward Vicky, the woman jammed the ring on her finger, then slipped the earrings on, and shucked out of the coat.

The coat was mid-calf length on the woman, but hit Vicky at the knees. It was also a couple of sizes too large, but fooling Sloane for five minutes was the objective. She arranged the hat over the curls on the crown of her head, pulling the brim low.

"Thanks, you're a life saver. Give me five minutes head start, that's all I ask."

"Yeah, sure, whatever." The woman wiggled her fingers and tossed her head watching the light catch the blue and white stones in the mirror.

Vicky picked up her case and peeked around the wall of the exit. Sloane paced fifteen feet away. Taking a deep breath, she pulled the brim lower on the right side of her face, waited until his back was turned, and hurried past him, fighting the urge to run.

No one runs to claim luggage. Walk like any other passenger from an incoming flight. Don't call attention to yourself.

She figured the woman inside wouldn't wait the full five—a minute, two at the most. That's all before Sloane would realize she'd bolted.

The walk took forever. Once free, she'd grab a cab to the Ft. Lauderdale airport and book a flight to

Phoenix. The lack of funds didn't present a problem. She'd lift someone's wallet at the busy Miami baggage claim first.

The checkpoint loomed ahead as did another restroom.

Get rid of the coat and hat. They stand out. Sloane will question the TSA people.

She slipped into the ladies room, entered a stall, hung the coat and hat on a hook, and left. Another hundred feet and she'd be in the clear.

Quickening her pace, Vicky approached the concourse exit, when a hand grasped her arm and pulled her around. She stared into Sloane's angry face.

"Try that again, and I'll handcuff you."

Dammit! A glance over her shoulder showed she'd been a lousy forty feet from freedom.

"You gave me no choice. Did you really expect me to follow like a sheep?"

"It's a mistake I won't make again. Hurry up. The flight's due to board in a few minutes."

His fingers tightened on her elbow. Sickness churned, and her much vaunted coolness slipped a notch toward panic. The thought of jail scared the hell out of her.

"Please don't make me go. I said I was sorry. It's been six years, for crissakes. If your uncle was so outraged, why didn't he come after me sooner?" Her voice rose in desperation.

"Lower your voice, and Uncle Roland was embarrassed. He didn't realize your part in the scam. You, sweet cheeks, are a bonus. My aunt's a smart investor. She loves dividends."

They passed the boarding area for the St. Louis plane. The woman from the ladies room sat in a seat still admiring the ring.

"Wanna reclaim your jewelry?"

"Go to hell, Sloane."

He laughed. "Not real, huh? I love it. Desperate to escape, you still conned."

"She was greedy and deserves to find out it's worth twenty bucks." She pulled against his grip. "Let me go."

"No way." They arrived at their gate where he pulled her into a seat. "For once in your life, you're gonna face the music."

Vicky bit her lip, rocking back and forth. If she got on that plane, she was as good as behind bars. She had to take a chance—make a break for it. She tensed. Sloane's arm snaked around her shoulders.

"Don't even think about it. Handcuffs. Remember?"

Before she could answer, the loudspeaker blared. "Good evening, ladies and gentlemen. Trans-Continental Airlines flight four fifty-two, non-stop to Denver is ready for boarding. We will take all pre-boarding and first class passengers now. Please have your boarding pass ready. Thank you for flying Trans-Continental and have a pleasant flight."

Sloane rose pulling her with him. "Come on."

"First class?" she asked with surprise.

"Courtesy of Aunt Helen."

"Then you could have bought me a decent dinner."

"I could have, but why should I?"

"Because I'm hungry."

"Get over it."

She raised her foot to stomp on his instep. He deftly blocked the move, escorted her to the agent collecting the passes, and then down the jetway. They entered the aircraft, where Sloane nodded a response to the flight attendant's cheerful greeting.

"Seats four A and B. You take the window," he instructed.

"I need to use the lavatory."

He pushed her into the seat. "How stupid do you

think I am?"

"You tell me," she shot back.

"You can go when we're thirty-five thousand feet up. I also suggest you get some sleep. Granite Springs is several hours drive from Denver over mountainous terrain."

Vicky shoved the carry-on under the seat in front of her and fastened her seat belt. She sat back, her hands clutching the armrests, fear gnawing in her stomach. It looked like she was going to Colorado.

****

Trevor fastened his seatbelt. It had been a close call. Intent on scanning the crowd for a woman in blue, he'd almost missed her coming out of the john. Then recognition had set in, and with a burst of speed, nailed her. Until they got to Granite Springs, he'd stick to her like a lover.

A lover? Why use that analogy? Why not glue?

He spared his companion a glance. She stared out the window. White-knuckled hands clutching the armrests showed anger and fear. Her body was tense, like a coiled spring. He'd felt it when his arm had contacted her shoulders. Several blonde curls escaped the elaborate hairdo to hang beside her face. Color splotched smooth alabaster cheeks. Dark circles beneath her eyes suggested vulnerability. The urge to protect rose strong, which was silly given all the time he'd spent tracking and capturing her.

His gaze slipped to her breasts, and then back up again. Nice. A slim waist and hips presented a damned fine package. He'd observed her on the beach one day, the bikini she'd worn leaving little to the imagination. Certainly, Ed Williams had noticed. Trevor had had a brief fantasy of her long legs wrapped around *his* waist before coming to his senses. Even knowing what she was, his body stirred.

Knock it off, dimwit. So, she's gorgeous. So what? She knows it and will use it. Ask Quinn. She bamboozled him. Don't trust her.

The door closed and the engines started, then the plane was pushed back from the gate. He heaved a sigh of relief. In a few minutes they'd be airborne, and he could get some sleep. Still, he'd have to keep an eye on her part of the time. He wouldn't put it past the vixen to turn on the tears, telling the flight attendants a tale of fearing for her life. But no money or credit cards limited her options. He'd cut up the plastic while she'd packed and dumped the shards in a trash receptacle near the security checkpoint along with the condo key.

Vicky's head swiveled, her eyes narrowed and her forehead furrowed. "How did you get handcuffs past security? I didn't see them in any tray."

"What handcuffs?"

She breathed deeply, nostrils flaring. "Bastard."

If looks could kill, he'd be a dead man. He laughed anyway. "Hey, I object on my late mother's behalf. I was very legal."

"Go to hell, Sloane."

"Aw, I thought we'd gotten to Trevor and Vicky."

She glared and crossed her arms over her chest. "What's going to happen in this place you're taking me?"

"You'll find out when we get there. This is my Aunt's show. I'm just the delivery boy."

The plane taxied to the end of the runway, made the turn, and then rolled, picking up speed. A few seconds later the bumping of the concrete stopped as the aircraft lifted into the night sky. Trevor hoped his aunt knew what she was doing.

****

Vicky caught her lower lip between her teeth and tried to quell the rising panic as the plane gained altitude.

Damn! All I needed was another twelve hours to deposit the check. All I needed was another forty feet and I'd be gone. All I needed was a break. But nothing went right.

She should have listened to her logical mind that told her to get out of Miami three months ago. But greed overrode logic. Now, she was stuck with Trevor Sloane going God knew where in Colorado to face the widow of an angry mark. *Dammit, I counted on getting away. Calling Rod was a mistake, too.*

Maybe he wouldn't listen to her message. Rod was like that in major con mode. E-mail and voice messages slid for days. She hoped he followed that pattern. At least then, she wouldn't be alone. Her sniveling half-brother would also have to account for his actions. That almost made this mess worthwhile.

Even if she ditched her captor in Denver, with no money or credit cards she'd still be stranded. Although not her favorite way of getting richer, picking pockets held promise.

Wait a minute. Did he get my ATM card, too? She opened her purse and took out the wallet, thumbing through the slots.

"No use. I got the ATM card, too," he commented, echoing her thoughts while turning a page in the onboard magazine.

She snapped the wallet shut, jamming it back into her purse. "Don't talk to me."

He shrugged. "Fine. I hate chattering females."

For a brief moment, she contemplated spinning a lie for the flight attendant so he'd get arrested in Denver, then shoved the idea aside. He'd made his point earlier. The cops would haul her into custody, too. She'd keep her eyes open for an opportunity on the drive from Denver to this Granite Something place.

The throb of the engines changed pitch, and then the pilot came on the intercom.

"Good evening, ladies and gentlemen. We've reached our cruising altitude of 35,000 feet and expect to arrive in Denver on time. We should have a calm ride, and you'll note I've turned off the seatbelt sign. Flight attendants will be by offering refreshments soon. On behalf of my co-pilot and the rest of the flight crew, thank you for flying Trans-Continental, and we hope you have a pleasant ride."

Vicky tapped Trevor on the arm. "Excuse me, but do you mind if I use the facilities now?"

He grinned, unfastened his seatbelt, and rose to stand in the aisle.

She ignored the grin and slid past him. In the lavatory, Vicky pulled the pins out of her hair, allowing the strands to tumble around her shoulders, and then massaged her scalp. A headache formed behind her eyes. It was going to be a long night.

Trevor stood again when she returned. "Welcome back. Nowhere to run, huh?"

She slipped into her seat. "Is that supposed to be funny?"

"I'm considered witty, or so I've been told." He sat refastening his seatbelt.

"Whoever told you that lied."

A flight attendant stopped beside Trevor. "May I get you something to drink?"

"Scotch on the rocks. How about you, my dear?"

Vicky wanted to belt him in his smartass mouth, but said, "Scotch is fine."

She opened her purse and rummaged until she found a bottle of aspirin.

"Headache?"

"What do you think? It's late, I'm tired, and that shitty burger you called dinner has left me starving."

"I'm sure they've got some peanuts or pretzels on board."

"You'd better be prepared to buy me one hell of a

breakfast or so help me God, I'll hurt you."

He gave her a slow half smile, the kind that lifted one corner of his mouth and crinkled his eyes.

"You really are gorgeous when you're pissed."

For some reason, she couldn't take her gaze off his lips. They fascinated her. Not full, but not thin either. Her mind played with the image of them on hers, kissing her breathless. His smile widened into a grin showing even white teeth.

"Like what you see?"

Realizing she'd been caught staring, she shifted her gaze to the bottle in her hand.

"I don't know what you're talking about."

He chuckled. "Okay, have it your way."

He lowered his seat tray, resting the magazine on it until the flight attendant brought their drinks.

Vicky popped two aspirins in her mouth and chased it with the scotch, finishing in a single gulp. The liquor burned a trail of fire down her throat, but helped settle her shaky nerves. She set the empty glass on his tray.

"Now, if you don't mind, I'm going to sleep."

"Be my guest." He sipped his drink and resumed reading the magazine.

She reclined the seat a few inches and settled into a more comfortable position, her arm brushing his on the armrest. Her breath caught in a silent hiccup. Vicky wouldn't describe the feeling as a tingle or a jolt—nothing so clichéd, but more of a warm glow that burned in the pit of her stomach. Her mind drifted back to the few minutes they'd shared on the dance floor, and once again awareness plucked at her.

Don't be an ass. Your stomach burns because you haven't had anything to eat, just took two aspirin, and drank a large shot of scotch. The thought of seducing him skipped through her mind. *Forget it. He's probably immune, like a machine. He'd give you some rope and watch while you hanged yourself. Don't trust him—not a single inch. Get some sleep. You're gonna need all the rest you can get.*

She closed her eyes. God only knew what awaited her in Colorado.

****

Vicky stared through the windshield at the sun inching its way over the distant mountain in front of her. The rays tinted the snowcapped peaks deep purple, then lavender, and finally pink before cresting the top to dazzle her eyes with icy white brilliance.

"Good heavens," she said, fishing in her purse for a pair of sunglasses.

"Magnificent aren't they? Ever been in the mountains before?"

"Tahoe a few times. Same with Reno, but I can assure you I was never awake to see the sunrise."

"I can believe that."

"When are we going to eat? I'm starving."

"Hey, I bought you something before we left Denver."

"I don't consider a bag of chips and a soft drink as anything more than a cheap snack."

"There's a nice restaurant up the road. I'll buy you a real breakfast."

"About time."

She held her breath and eyed the guardrail next to her door as Trevor negotiated another sharp curve on the twisting roadway. Blackness, as yet untouched by the rising sun, yawned below. A quick glance at the dashboard clock told her they'd been driving for three hours.

To her surprise, Vicky slept most of the way to Denver. Groggy and confused with the time change, she'd followed Trevor to baggage claim, then the rental car place with little more than a resigned sigh. On the road, she'd taken catnaps until about forty minutes ago.

They descended into a valley. She removed the sunglasses. Daylight had not yet arrived here. Around another bend, Trevor slowed when they entered a small town. Ahead a neon sign flashed "Grandma's Kitchen" in a welcoming blue. Her chauffeur turned in. Light spilled from the windows. Inside, patrons ate, read the paper, and chatted. He pulled into a parking spot not far from the door.

"This better not be Grandma's version of Burger Biggie."

He grinned. "This is primo cooking. Cross my heart. I've eaten here before, and the cook really is a grandmother. Don't you remember your grandmother's cooking?"

"I don't remember a grandmother, and my mother ordered in or we ate out."

"Trust me, you're gonna love it." He exited the car and walked around to the passenger side, opening her door.

At least he possessed some manners. She shivered in the cold morning air.

"Cold?"

"Yes. Ten hours ago I was in Miami."

"Shame you don't have a coat."

"Oh, shut up."

He laughed, flinging his arm around her shoulders. Instant warmth flooded her from the inside out. If he didn't remove his arm soon, she'd break into a sweat. Yet, she didn't shake him off. She liked his arm where it was along with the accompanying warmth. Vicky didn't know whether to be disgusted or explore the sensations further. They had possibilities.

Trevor shoved the door open, and they entered a cheerful room. A third of the tables had occupants. He removed his arm as an older lady bustled up.

"Welcome to Grandma's. Two? Booth or table?"

"Booth," he answered.

The lady nodded, leading them to a window seat. She laid the menus on the shiny Formica topped table, and said, "Annie will be by with coffee in a minute. Enjoy."

Vicky slid onto the blue vinyl bench and glanced around the cozy restaurant. A counter ran along the back wall with the kitchen behind it. Plates of pancakes and eggs sat on a shelf awaiting pick up. Blue and white décor gave the place a homey feel.

A waitress balancing four plates on a heavy tray passed by. "Be with you in a second."

The aromas of pancakes, syrup, and coffee made her mouth water and her stomach ache, reminding her how long it had been since she'd eaten a substantial meal.

The girl returned with a coffee pot and two mugs. "Hi, I'm Annie. Coffee?"

"I'll say," Trevor replied. "It's been a long drive. Give us a couple of minutes, and then we'll order."

Vicky pulled two fake sugars from the condiment rack, added them to the steaming cup, and then further diluted the contents with thick cream from a small pitcher. She stirred, blew on it, and sipped.

"Like it?"

She swallowed and licked her lips. "It's delicious."

"Told you. What're you going to have?"

"I want orange juice, blueberry pancakes with blueberry syrup, lots of butter, those little link sausages, and an order of hash browns."

Trevor's eyebrows rose. "Pancakes *and* hash brown potatoes?"

"I'm hungry. You starved me, remember?"

He chuckled and blew across the liquid in his mug before taking a sip. When Annie returned a few minutes later, he placed her order along with a three

31

egg cheese omelet, bacon, and homemade biscuits for himself.

Vicky turned her gaze from his face to the windows. Outside, the shadows lightened as daylight rolled down the mountainside into town.

"Tell me, how did you get involved with conning? Quinn said you're a damned good secretary. Why cheat and steal?"

She took another sip of the excellent brew. "If you researched me, you must know my stepfather's name."

"Harry Halston, Rod's father, but that doesn't answer my question."

"My father died when I was a baby. When I was four my mother married Harry. A year later, Rod was born."

"Did she know what Harry did for a living?"

"She loved him and ignored it. Mom died when I was ten. Harry, never the best of fathers, put Rod and me to work. At first, it was the old Bible scam. I assume you've heard of it."

Trevor nodded. "Scan the obituaries, find the address in the phone book, show up on the doorstep with a cock and bull story about the recently deceased having ordered a special Bible for the lady of the house. I imagine with two blue-eyed cherubs in tow, Harry made out like a bandit—pardon the pun."

"He taught us how to pick pockets and con maids into unlocking hotel rooms claiming we didn't have a key and couldn't find our parents. Rod would dance around crying he had to go to the bathroom while I did the talking, and then we'd nab any cash or jewelry lying around.

"As we grew older, the cons got more sophisticated. I was the bait in an outraged father scam. I'd lure a man into a compromising situation, and then Harry would burst through the door threatening to call the cops on the guy for fooling around with a minor. The idiots always paid."

Trevor snorted and curled his lip. "A variation of the old badger game. He was a real prize. How old were you?"

"Fourteen, fifteen. I looked older."

His gaze bored a hole in her. "You hated it, didn't you?"

She shrugged, refusing to meet his eyes. "It was the only life I knew. Actually, the Bible one was fun. Harry explained we did the grieving widows a favor to let them believe their husbands had cared."

"And if they happened to fork over money in return, that was all right?"

"I was too young to understand the explanation was bullshit."

"How could he do that to a couple of kids?"

She bit her lip and shrugged again. "It put food on the table and clothes on my back. That's all I knew."

"What about school? Didn't the authorities wonder why you and your brother weren't attending?"

"We moved a lot. Whenever Harry did a con where children weren't needed, he'd stuff us in a boarding school for a few months. We learned the necessities—reading, writing, and math."

"Especially math. Had to count all that money."

"Give it a rest. It's too early for sarcasm."

The waitress arrived with their food. Vicky was grateful for the break. She didn't like talking about those days. Trevor was right when he guessed she'd hated her life, but she'd had nowhere else to live, except with her father's sister, Iris, and no way would Harry allow that. Blonde and beautiful brought in too much money.

She shoved unpleasant reminiscences into the back of her mind, poured the syrup, and dug into her

33

pancakes. Light and fluffy, they melted in her mouth. The sausages had just the right amount of spice, and the hash browns held a hint of onion beneath the crispy crust.

They ate in silence. Thirty minutes, and a couple of coffees to go later, Trevor turned the car toward the southwest for the final leg of the journey.

"How much farther?" she asked, trying to keep the tremor from her voice.

"Two hours, less if the traffic's right."

"What's going to happen when we get there?"

"My aunt will tell you. She has a plan."

"Care to let me in on it?"

"Nope."

Her nerves tightened, stretching with every hill and curve they traversed. She stared out the window, not seeing the scenery. Would Helen Richardson have her arrested? Probably. Why go to all this trouble unless jail time was at the end?

She willed time to stand still. It didn't, and they eventually passed a sign stating "Welcome to Granite Springs, population 22,457." Fear stuck in her throat.

Trevor drove through the town before stopping at a red light. Her heart rate accelerated and Vicky couldn't hide the tremors dancing up and down her body. Begging wasn't in her vocabulary, but she'd give that a try first, provided the woman was in a listening mood.

"Relax, Aunt Helen isn't a monster. She won't draw and quarter you, although I wouldn't blame her if she did. Visualize your brother when he sees you walking through the door. Should amuse you."

"I just want this over. How much farther?" she said through clenched teeth.

"She lives on the far side of town in a crenellated monstrosity Roland's great-grandfather built at the turn of the twentieth century. It's a cross between an

English castle and a Victorian nightmare." He halted at a four way stop before proceeding. "It's at the top of the hill around the next bend."

Vicky closed her eyes, clasped her hands in her lap, and inhaled a shaky breath. She'd never faced a mark post-con.

She suppressed the panic bubbling beneath her breastbone as her mind groped for an out. *A small town. Check out the lay of the land. Unless Helen Richardson chains me to a stake in the yard, there might be an avenue of escape. There's always a way.*

Proving the case in court would be tough. A lot of time had passed, witnesses didn't exist, and Vicky was a whiz at lying. With any luck, the jury would acquit her.

"What the hell is this?" Trevor jammed on the brakes.

She opened her eyes as the seatbelt caught her. The driveway was crammed with police cars. Oh, my God, the old lady *was* going to have her arrested. Then Vicky spied the yellow tape strung around the porch pillars. A cop ran down to the car.

"I'm sorry, sir, but you can't come in here. This is a crime scene."

"What the hell are you talking about? My name's Trevor Sloane. Helen Richardson's my aunt. She's expecting me."

Another policeman walked up. "Trevor, sorry you came home to this."

"What?" he shouted in a hoarse voice.

"Your aunt was murdered last night."

Chapter Three

Trevor stared at Sheriff Al Singleton, too shocked to move. Beside him, Vicky emitted a soft gasp. He gripped the steering wheel until his knuckles showed white.

"How? Any suspects?"

The officer shook his head. "None yet, but her car is missing. According to the housekeeper, so is her houseguest, Mr. Harvey."

Anger slashed through his chest. Grief would come later. Furious, he exited the car.

"Give me the details." His voice had a cold, hard edge. "Stay put," he snapped at his passenger when she attempted to get out. "I'll deal with you later."

The sheriff eyed him and Vicky with a frown. At the moment Trevor didn't care how his words had sounded.

"We don't know much yet. Only that it happened sometime after eight o'clock last night. Coroner says rigor is full and lividity set."

"Who found her?"

"The housekeeper, Rosa Ramirez. She came at six-thirty this morning to fix breakfast. When Mrs. Richardson didn't come downstairs by seven-fifteen, the housekeeper went to check, found the bed cold, but slept in, and searched room to room. Discovered the body a few minutes later in the study. Called us immediately."

Trevor took several deep breaths. "Cause of

death?"

"Preliminary shows a blow to the head, probably by the fireplace poker lying next to her. The safe was open, but empty. Did your aunt keep a lot of cash in the house?"

Trevor ran hand through his hair, sickness churning his stomach. "About ten grand in the safe and maybe another two thousand in a cigar box in one of the desk drawers."

The sheriff's jaw dropped. "A cigar box?"

"Aunt Helen always said a thief would find it right off and not bother searching for more."

Another empty safe. Not hard to guess who did this. It's Cash Marriott all over again.

He wanted to yank Victoria Denton from the car and shake her. In Trevor's mind, Rod Halston was the guilty party. Since the murdering bastard wasn't available, guilt by association worked.

"What about the houseguest?" he asked.

"According to Mrs. Ramirez, he and Helen had dinner early last night. Afterward, he went out. The housekeeper left at eight."

"I assume you're searching for him."

"Don't be sarcastic, Trevor. I know you're upset, but we're doing the best we can, and yes, we have an APB out on him. If he's within a three hundred mile radius, we'll get him." The sheriff took off his hat and mopped his forehead with a bandana pulled from his pocket. "I'm sorry to ask this, but where were you last evening between eight and midnight?"

"I was in Miami and on a flight to Denver. We landed about two o'clock. I rented a car and drove down."

"I'll need the details. Drop by the office later with them."

"When can I get into the house?"

"Not sure yet. Whenever forensics is finished."

Another car screeched to a halt at the end of the

semi-circular driveway. A man exited and ran up the slope. Trevor recognized Elliot Corwin, his aunt's lawyer and investment counselor.

"Good God, I just heard the news down at the diner! Is it true? Helen was murdered?"

"Yes," Trevor answered in a clipped tone. He didn't have much use for Corwin. The guy was slick, and he'd offered to investigate the attorney for his aunt on several occasions over the last year.

"This is a tragedy. Helen was the kindest woman I knew. Sharp as a tack, too. Never signed anything before reading it. Wish half my clients were as conscientious." He turned worried gray eyes to Trevor and ran a shaking hand through his blond hair. "If there's anything I can do, let me know. You have my full cooperation."

Trevor nodded, while the sheriff replied, "Thank you, Mr. Corwin. I may stop by your office sometime in the next couple of days."

"Yes, yes, of course, any time. How did it happen? Any idea who killed her? What about that guest of hers."

"We're working on it. What do you know about Mr. Harvey?"

"Not a lot. I met him when Helen invited me to dinner three or four nights ago. Lavished attention on her. Picked him up in Las Vegas. Called himself an investment counselor. Hinted she might invest with him. When we were alone, I told her she was acting like a fool. The guy was obviously a fraud after her money."

"How did you know that?" Trevor asked.

"Something in his manner didn't gel. What kind of investment counselor takes up residence in his client's home? Didn't make sense."

"I'll be in touch soon," the sheriff said.

Corwin nodded, turned, and trotted down the hill to his car and drove away.

"An investment broker? Would your aunt hand over a large amount of cash to someone she just met?" the officer inquired.

Trevor balled his fists at his side. The man named Ryan Harvey was no investment guru. He knew he should come clean to the sheriff about his aunt's scheme along with his part in it. However, he needed answers from Vicky regarding her brother and his habits. Halston wouldn't get far. Helen's blue Mercedes convertible with the license plate LUVSLIFE was distinctive.

He smacked his fists against his thighs hard enough to bruise. His aunt *had* loved life, and for that to be taken away before her sixty-fifth birthday was unacceptable. He'd track Rod Halston to the ends of the earth if necessary.

****

Vicky sat frozen in the front seat, her mind racing while Trevor and the sheriff talked. Now what? And where was Rod? Had he gotten her message? Did he have anything to do with the woman's death, or had he simply smelled a rat and stolen the car? By now, he'd probably switched license plates and was halfway to Vegas.

Trevor slipped back behind the wheel, his face set in grim, angry lines. She shivered. God help Rod if he was guilty.

The sheriff leaned toward the open window. "Morning, ma'am."

"Good morning, officer."

The lawman shifted his gaze to Trevor with a raised eyebrow. He drew in a deep breath and made the introduction.

"Please to meet you, ma'am."

Vicky needed to throw a roadblock in front of Trevor if he had thoughts of turning her in.

"Same here. I guess this means I'm out of a job."

"A job, ma'am?"

39

"Yes, I was hired as a secretary last week by Mrs. Richardson."

"Oh, really?"

Trevor replied in a flat tone. "I met Vicky in Miami, knew my aunt needed a secretary, and suggested her." He started the car. "If you need us, Al, we'll be at the Night's Rest Inn."

"I'll want to talk to both of you later." He stepped back touching his fingers to his hat brim. Trevor nodded, put the car in gear, and backed down the drive.

"Hired as a secretary?" he shot at her in a hard tone. "If you think you're off the hook, think again. After we check into the motel, we're gonna talk about your brother."

The motel was less than a mile from the Richardson home. While Trevor checked them in, Vicky did some fast thinking.

She was out of the woods for the murder, but the excuse concocted for the sheriff set the stage for deception. Sloane didn't want her true colors flown in front of the law any more than she. Nor did he mention the retribution scheme. Such an admission would blow Rod's cover. So, what was his angle?

Trevor returned, handing her a key. "I've got the room next to you. When the house is released, we'll move in there. Dump the bags. We'll, chat at the Foothills Diner."

"Diner? We just ate a couple of hours ago." She didn't want to discuss anything with him, let alone Rod. She needed to figure out his part in this.

"Then we'll drink coffee until lunchtime, and you'll tell me all about your brother. I'm mad enough to kill, and so help me God, if you don't come up with answers, I'll tell the sheriff the whole ugly story."

Left with no choice, Vicky entered the utilitarian room and slung her bags onto the bed. She wanted a long, hot shower, but washed up instead, put on a new layer of make-up, and then clipped her hair back with a large barrette in the nape of her neck. Fresh clothing helped. She had barely finished when someone knocked on the door.

"You ready to talk?" Trevor asked when she opened up.

"I can't tell you much of anything."

"Sure you can. Let's go."

She closed the door and shivered in the chilly mountain air. The morning sun warmed the temperature, but not by much.

"May I have my credit cards back?"

"Can't. Destroyed them."

"Thanks a lot. I need a coat and warmer clothing if you plan on keeping me here longer than today."

"You'll stay until your brother's captured and in jail for my aunt's murder. Call the credit card company and say they were stolen. They'll send new ones."

"Then give me the money you took."

He reached into his back pocket and removed a wallet, handing her the two hundred dollars. "There, happy?"

"No." She meant it. With the sheriff knowing her real name, she couldn't even grab the first bus out of town.

"Never mind. Just get in the car."

The Foothills Diner was located in the heart of downtown Granite Springs. He guided her to a booth in the back corner, ordered coffee for two and remained silent until served.

He ignored the steaming mug and gripped the edge of the table until his fingertips turned white. "Where's your brother?"

"I have no idea."

"Don't give me that bullshit. He's your brother. Where would he go?" His eyes, hard as river stones, glared.

41

She doctored her coffee, took a sip, and then leaned forward. "Look, Rod is a lot of things, but he's no killer. He doesn't have the guts."

"Tell that to Cash Marriott and Quinn Rafferty."

"That was an accident. Ask Quinn. His grandfather had a heart attack and fell, hitting his head on the hearth. Rod and I were scared to death."

"He had a heart attack because he and Halston were fighting. Now, where would the little son of a bitch go?"

His voice matched his eyes. She believed he'd confess everything to the sheriff if she didn't tell him something useful. Could she be charged as an accessory in a long ago scam? Given what she did for a living, her knowledge of the law was surprisingly shaky. But then, she'd never been caught before.

"You're assuming he killed her. I think he may have become suspicious and took off." *Or listened to his voice mail.* She drank a sizeable portion from her mug, needing the caffeine high.

"Suspicious of what? I talked to Aunt Helen yesterday morning and told her we'd arrive today. She said things were under control."

"She could have been wrong. Rod's a sneaky little rat. He may have overheard the call and decided to cut and run. And who was that guy who showed up at the house? The one who suspected Rod?"

"Elliot Corwin. He's Aunt Helen's lawyer and investment advisor." He drank his coffee in several gulps, and then gestured for a refill.

"Rod knows when to get out of a con. Sounds like he was using the investment counselor angle again. Finding the real thing on the doorstep might have prompted him to bail out." Her tone turned challenging. "I heard the sheriff say the safe was rifled. How would Rod know about a safe? Surely, your aunt wasn't dumb enough to show him."

Trevor waited to answer until the waitress filled both their mugs and left.

"You said he's a sneaky little rat. He may have spied on her. He was there for almost a week."

"And how would he know the combination?"

"How did you discover the combination to Cash Marriott's safe? Rod could do the same."

"Maybe the lawyer knew. Same with the housekeeper. Any other servants? How about relatives? Who inherits?"

He rubbed the stubble on his cheeks, closed his eyes, and sighed. He looked dog dead tired. She had the most absurd urge to comfort him, to tell him everything would be all right, and then shook it off. Why feel compassion? He wanted her in jail.

"I don't know how her will is set up. Roland has a younger brother, Walter. He and his son, Adam, more or less run the company. Walter suggested years ago my uncle step down and let him take control of Richardson Mining. Roland finally agreed. I imagine Aunt Helen didn't discourage the decision. She didn't like her brother-in-law and wanted to spend more time with her husband."

"Anyone else?"

"My Uncle Ray, my aunt's younger brother. He's a photographer working out of San Diego. Travels all over the country taking pictures for those big expensive books people have lying around."

"Did she see him a lot?" Vicky finished her coffee and stared into the empty mug.

"Not really. Last time was four or five years ago. His son had just been accepted at the University of Nevada at Las Vegas. He also has a daughter."

"Anyone else?" she repeated.

"That's the end of the relative list."

"What do you know about her friends?"

He glared, his forehead furrowed. "Suppose we get back to you answering the questions? Where would your brother go? Back to Vegas?"

Vicky shrugged, but couldn't lie under his cold stare. "Probably. He'd switch plates on the car, and then sell it."

"Guess I'd better mention that to the sheriff."

"Mention what to the sheriff?" a voice said.

Vicky looked up, her heart sinking. Sheriff Singleton stood next to the table.

Thinking fast, she blurted, "I came here for a job. Now that it's gone, I need to move on. You don't need me to hang around, do you?"

The sheriff flung his hat on the table and slid in next to Trevor. "I'd like you to stay for a couple of days, until I get a few answers."

Her heart lurched, and she swallowed. "What answers? I had nothing to do with the poor woman's death."

"Why would Mrs. Richardson need a secretary?" The waitress paused next to the table. "Just coffee, darlin'."

Trevor jumped in. "My aunt wanted to write her memoirs. For that, she needed someone who could type and take dictation."

"When did you last talk to her?"

"A couple of weeks ago."

"Why were you in Miami?"

"Business."

The waitress brought his coffee and refilled the other two. Singleton sipped the scalding brew, and then set the mug on the table. "What kind of business?"

"Private detective business."

"Got a name for me to check?"

Vicky eyed Trevor's impassive face wondering how he'd answer.

"Come on, Al. You know that's confidential. I can't tell you."

The sheriff smiled drinking more coffee. "Yeah, I

know." He turned his gaze back onto Vicky. "So, Mrs. Richardson needed a secretary and Trevor just happened to know one?"

"That's it," she replied tightening her grasp on the mug to hide the tremor skipping through her fingers.

Al's eyes homed in on the movement. "Nervous?"

"Just upset at Mrs. Richardson's death."

"You didn't know her, did you?" he asked.

"No, but I need the job. I interviewed over the phone."

"Look, what difference does it make?" Trevor said in an exasperated voice. "Instead of questioning us, you should be looking for Rod."

Vicky sucked in a startled breath and leaned back.

"Who's Rod?" the sheriff asked in a calm voice.

Trevor lowered his gaze to the contents of his mug. "The guy who was living with her—the one who disappeared with her car."

"You mean Ryan. Ryan Harvey."

"Yeah, whatever his name is. He could be anywhere by now."

"Relax, Trevor, we'll get him sooner or later." The sheriff drank again, shoved his half-empty cup away, and rose. "Guess I'd better be going. Stop by later and give me the flight number and where you stayed in Miami. I'll need the same from you, miss."

He clapped his hat on his head and strode toward the doors.

"He doesn't believe us," Vicky said.

"He might believe our story, but has nothing better to go on at the moment."

"He'll be suspicious when he finds out Ryan Harvey's real name is Rod. Can't believe you did that."

"I'm tired and pissed. I'll worry about details later."

"Details should be worked out first."

Trevor's eyebrow rose. "Tips from the master?"

Vicky stared into her mug. "Details have tripped up even the best of us. Harry was fanatical when it came to details. It's the one thing I learned from him that was useful in real life. Harry never did jail time. Neither did I, and to the best of my knowledge, Rod is clean, too."

"What a recommendation."

"Do we have to argue?"

"No." Trevor signaled the waitress who stopped by and slapped the check on the table. He slid out of the seat. Vicky followed.

"What's next?" she asked.

"I'm going to visit Elliot Corwin. You can either come with me or go back to the motel."

"Why do you want to see Corwin?"

"He's got a copy of Aunt Helen's will, and I want to hear more about his dinner with them last week."

"If I know my brother, he spread the charm around, made a few correct references regarding investments, and let Helen do the talking. Corwin said Rod was dancing attendance on her. He may have been suspicious, but Rod wouldn't let much slip at a first meeting."

"I don't think your brother's all that bright, and from what Quinn told me, he's got an ego the size of a mountain. He could have said something he shouldn't." He pushed open the door, allowing her to go through first.

Trevor had a point. Rod's ego often got in the way of business, changing a great con, into a minor league money-maker. He often underestimated his marks, Guatemala being a case in point. He'd dismissed Alex Montgomery as a lightweight. She'd proven him wrong.

Vicky needed to think. With Rod on the lam in a stolen car, he'd soon be caught. Her situation was in flux. Trevor had no reason to hang onto her once their stories checked out—unless he told the truth. And what would he do once her brother was in custody? How long would it take for the police to make the brother-sister connection? Not long if Rod broke and told them.

Damn Rod to hell and back. He's always screwing me over. She needed a plan—one that would get her out of town fast when Rod was arrested.

She paused before opening the car door. "I'd rather go back to the motel, grab a shower, and just stroll around town. Corwin doesn't interest me."

"Suit yourself. I'll meet up with you at the motel later this afternoon."

Vicky entered her room, locking the door behind her, then jerked the cell phone from her purse, and punched in her brother's number. After six rings, voice mail answered.

She left another message. "Rod, you little weasel, you've gotten us both in hot water. Helen Richardson is dead and the cops are looking for you, but since you've disappeared, I assume you already know that. Get back to Granite Springs *right now* with an explanation of why you're driving her car, and where you've been. An alibi for after eight o'clock last night would be a nice touch, too. With luck, we both might get out of this. I have a plan."

Vicky headed for the bathroom and turned the shower on full blast, a bubble of satisfaction growing in her chest. Rod would get the message, panic, and return. She'd lied about having a plan. The instant he set foot in Granite Springs, the sheriff would nail him. When the cell door slammed shut, she was gone like yesterday. She felt no remorse at setting up her brother. He'd do the same to her.

Just one big happy family.

****

Trevor settled deeper into the plush leather chair in front of Elliot Corwin's desk. The shadow words *Elliot Corwin, Attorney at Law* were emblazoned on the carpet thanks to the late morning sun slanting through the picture window overlooking Main Street.

The lawyer frowned at the document in his hand. "I called the court first thing and began the probate process. As a rule, the heirs wait until after the funeral before demanding to know the will's contents."

Trevor clenched his jaw, but kept his tone civil. "I don't give a rat's ass who inherits Aunt Helen's money. My responsibility is to make sure her killer's in jail for a damned long time. I think this Harvey guy is on the hook for it, but a huge estate could be a powerful inducement to hasten a death. It's happened before."

Corwin laid the will on the blotter and rubbed his forehead. "I agree with you about the killer, but it's Sheriff Singleton's responsibility to bring him to justice."

"Maybe so, but what's it going to hurt if I get a head start on other possible suspects? I'm a private investigator. Helen was my aunt, and this is my case."

"Are you licensed in the state of Colorado?"

Trevor inhaled a deep breath controlling the urge to lunge across the mahogany desk. He visualized his hands wrapped around the attorney's throat.

"She was my aunt," he repeated.

Corwin sighed. "I guess it can't hurt. It'll be public knowledge soon anyway. Besides, she named you as the executor."

Trevor sat back in amazement. "She what? When the hell did she do that?"

"A few weeks ago." He picked the thick sheaf of

papers up again. "It's a very simple will. Helen left Rosa Ramirez, her housekeeper, a sizable sum."

"How sizable?"

"I shouldn't be telling you any of this, but a hundred thousand dollars. That's a lot of money for a housekeeper."

"Rosa's been with my aunt for close to fifteen years," he replied, a slight rebuke in his voice.

Corwin didn't respond. "There are also large bequests to various charities. The majority of the estate is split between her brother, Ray Hamilton, along with small trusts set up for his son, Jason and his daughter, Caroline."

"That makes sense. Who else?"

"You."

Trevor waved his hand in dismissal. "I expected that. Who else?"

"That's it, except for a tiny bit of stock in Richardson Mining to Walter Richardson and his son, Adam."

"That's all?"

"Roland's will took care of them. He retained some Richardson Mining stock after selling to the conglomerate. When he died those shares went to Helen who sold most of them back to Walter. The rest of his estate went to her to do with as she pleased"

"And how did she please?"

"Roland had a lot of investments. Helen kept most of them intact. She didn't move things around much."

"How much is her estate?"

"Ten million, more or less."

"That's a lot of motive. Do Walter and son know Helen stiffed them?"

"I wouldn't put it that way," the attorney protested.

"Yes, but do they know?"

"I have no idea, but as a nephew, Adam may have expectations."

"You're Aunt Helen's financial advisor, too, right?"

"Yes. Your uncle was my client, and she saw no reason to change."

"So, you handled all investment transactions? When was the last audit?"

Corwin's eyes narrowed. "What are you getting at, Sloane?"

"Don't get on your high horse. I'm not suggesting anything is wrong."

"I gave your aunt quarterly, and then yearly reports in time for tax season."

"And she never changed her investments?" Trevor found that hard to believe. His aunt liked to have her hand in the mix.

Elliot shifted in his chair and frowned. "No, I wouldn't say that. She always had her eyes open for new investment opportunities, although..."

"Although what?"

"About four years ago, I personally got involved with a development firm seeking investors. They bought up a hundred acres south of town with the intent to build a mall. Something along the lines of a couple of anchor stores and boutiques. I suggested she might want to get in on it, but she refused. Then, two years ago, she came to me and wanted in. By that time, the real estate market had soured and I advised against it."

"I didn't see any mall around," Trevor said.

"The market turned before the developer could get all his ducks in a row. The land was sold last year at a loss."

"How much did you lose?"

"Very little, thank God. I pulled out before the market tanked completely. Others weren't so lucky."

All Trevor's dislike of the smooth lawyer rose to

the top. Helen was smart, but didn't micromanage her portfolio. Her trust in Elliot Corwin had always rankled. He'd suggested an independent audit months ago. She'd pooh-poohed the idea. A smooth operator like Corwin could use that trust to his advantage.

And if he did, why mention anything? Because of a traceable paper trail? Talking about it now might indicate honesty at a later date.

Trevor squinted out the window into the bright sunshine to quell his rising irritation. He had no reason to suspect Elliot Corwin of anything. *And therein lies the rub.*

He wasn't even sure why he disliked the man. Jealousy because Helen put so much stock in her attorney? Maybe. He couldn't put his finger on it, but he didn't trust his aunt's lawyer. He couldn't give a reason. That was just the way it was.

The phone ringing in the outer office brought him out of his contemplations.

"Tell me about this Ryan Harvey. You said you met him the other night at Aunt Helen's."

Corwin's lip curled. "I smelled a rat the instant he strolled into the room. Blond hair, blue eyes, and oozing affection. Getting her drinks, giving her little hugs. Disgusting. Around thirty, I'd say, young enough to be her son. Called himself an investment counselor. Then Helen suggested she wanted to transfer some of her funds to him. Later, I begged her to let me check this guy out before she handed over a hundred grand to him."

Trevor knew Helen had no intention of doing any such thing, so why make such a statement?

"That's a hell of a chunk of money."

"That's what I said. She told me she knew what she was doing and to mind my own business. Called for an appointment yesterday morning. Said we needed to talk. I assumed it was about the transfer

51

and stalled. She was supposed to come in tomorrow."

Why would his aunt make an appointment knowing no transfer would take place? Trevor's gut told him something wasn't right. Either Corwin was lying, or Helen had been up to something on her own. He rose and held out his hand.

"Thanks for your help, Elliot. Would it be possible for me to get the audits from the last five years? I'd also like to audit this year as soon as possible."

Elliot also stood and shook his hand. "Sure, I'll have them sent as soon as possible. Probate may take a while."

Out in the street, Trevor paused, pulled out his cell phone, and dialed.

"Sloane Investigations, how may I help you?"

"Hi, Pam, it's me."

"Trevor, are you still in Miami?"

"No, I'm in Granite Springs. Look there's been a development." He told his secretary about his aunt, Vicky, and the missing Rod.

"Oh, my God, Trevor, I'm so sorry."

"I'm going to be here for a while. Who's available to do a little digging for me?"

"Marylou finished her assignment last night. She caught the husband on film with his pants down and his anatomy up in a motel with his receptionist."

"Good, I need her expertise. I want her to check out Elliot Corwin." He spelled the name. "He's an attorney and investment advisor here in Granite Springs. I want everything she can find on this guy—financial, personal, and professional. This takes priority over anyone else."

"Got it, and we still need at least one more operative. Business has been booming."

"I'll work on it when I get back. Have Marylou contact me when she gets something."

"Will do. Where do I send the flowers?"

Her question confused him. "What flowers?"

"For the funeral."

Instant guilt swamped him. He'd forgotten about a funeral. He swallowed the lump in his throat. *Time for grief when Rod Halston is behind bars.*

"I'll let you know."

He hung up and turned toward the police station. He'd give Al the information he wanted, grab a quick lunch, and then head back to the motel for a shower and maybe a nap before dinner.

He quickened his steps toward the police station. Marylou was a damned good operative. She combined the tenacity of a bulldog, and the discipline of a headmistress. She rarely failed. If Elliot Corwin had anything to hide, she'd find it.

Chapter Four

Vicky pulled the navy blue sweater over her head and fluffed her hair, the wavy strands falling past her shoulders. Trevor had knocked on her door, saying, "I'm hungry. I'll pick you up in an hour. Campbell's Steakhouse has a full menu and bar. I need a drink."

I wouldn't mind a good, stiff belt either. She wielded the mascara wand and eyed the results, then added a hint of blush.

She'd notified the banks of her destroyed ATM and credit cards. A simple 'I lost my purse' worked. The replacements should arrive tomorrow or the next day.

Second on her agenda had been clothing. Most of her wardrobe consisted of summer wear for Miami. With only two hundred dollars to work with, she'd been forced to look for bargains. A small boutique catering to skiers in nearby resorts yielded several items from the sale rack. She found a lightweight trench coat in a thrift store, and blew the remainder of the money on a pair of boots.

Vicky had also mapped out the town in her head as she shopped. The business district, while not thriving, wasn't dead either. She noted Elliot Corwin's office and the police station. The jail sat opposite on the corner. The court house, its old-fashioned clock tower soaring past the tree tops, occupied the town square. When Rod showed, this would be the focus of attention. Once re-armed with credit and money, she'd split as soon as possible.

She daubed her lips with a rosy-beige lipstick, and stepped back to view the effect when someone knocked.

"You ready?" Trevor asked when she opened the door.

"Yes, let me get my coat." She turned, picking up the trench coat and her purse from the chair near the door.

"I see you spent the money already."

She shrugged into the coat. "Had to if I didn't want to freeze."

Trevor walked her to the passenger side of the car. "Maybe you can trade up in the ladies room at the restaurant."

"Don't start. Any news yet on Rod?"

"Not that I know of. Sheriff'll notify me when he's caught."

"Did you learn anything from Corwin?"

"Some. I'll tell you later."

His terse answers suggested he wasn't in a talkative mood, so she remained silent until they entered the restaurant.

Campbell's Steakhouse surprised her. It boasted an elegant atmosphere. Subdued lighting, black linen tablecloths and napkins, and hardwood floors gave the place an ambiance not unlike sophisticated restaurants in Los Angeles or Miami.

A hostess showed them to a table along the far wall. Large windows held a panoramic view of lights twinkling in the valley and the mountains silhouetted black against a starlit sky. A huge circular fireplace in the center of the room burned, chasing away any lingering chill.

A waiter stopped next to the table. Trevor ordered scotch on the rocks. Vicky did the same, and then turned her attention to her reticent dining companion. Lines grooved from his nose to his mouth, and his lips had thinned to a hard line. From necessity, she'd learned to read people, and right now, Trevor Sloane was still pissed.

"Are you going to sit in silence the entire night?"

He shifted his gaze from the tablecloth to her face. "I'm not in a chatty mood."

"Well, I am. What did you learn from Corwin?"

He sighed, telling her the results of his interview, pausing only when their drinks arrived.

"So, this brother-in-law she doesn't like and her nephew get next to nothing? Everything is essentially split between you and your uncle?" She sipped the scotch letting the smooth liquor warm her stomach.

"The housekeeper gets some along with various charities."

"How much do you trust your uncle and his family?"

"Uncle Ray is one of those free spirits who bloomed in the sixties. He embraced peace, love, and brotherhood until reality set in and he had to make a living. Lucky for him he was a whiz with a camera. He finally made a name for himself and settled down."

"Yes, but do you trust him?"

"Of course, I trust him," Trevor snapped.

"What about this housekeeper?"

"A hundred grand is not enough to kill over."

Vicky snorted and sipped her drink again. "It's all relative. A hundred thousand to someone who stands to inherit millions might not seem worthwhile, but to someone poor, it's a fortune."

"Would you kill for it?"

"I wouldn't kill for any amount of money—and neither would my brother."

Trevor drained his glass. "I'm not in the mood to discuss your brother. He did it. Let's move on to something else."

"I agree. I'm not in a mood to argue." She stared into the amber liquid in her glass, and sipped again. "Do you buy Corwin's explanation of the investment thing?"

He shifted in his seat. "I just find it odd that Aunt Helen would bother with *any* explanation."

"I know. Just say Rod is her house guest and leave it at that. She had him in her snare, and you were on my trail. It would all be over shortly. Why bring in a third party, especially a lawyer and financial advisor, with a story about transferring money?"

"Didn't make much sense to me either."

The waiter arrived. Trevor requested another drink before ordering a New York strip, medium rare, with baked potato, and a salad. Vicky declined another scotch, but asked for a glass of cabernet with her filet, cooked medium, with the rest the same as Trevor.

After the man left, she fiddled with her silverware for a moment before asking, "What was your aunt's plan for Rod and me?"

"What you mean is how her death affects you now."

She shrugged and finished her drink. "It's only human nature. I can't see how any revenge on me is relevant to what happened six years ago."

Trevor shook his head and laughed with little mirth. "Boy, how fast rats desert a sinking ship. You're only concerned with yourself. You don't give a damn about your brother."

Vicky bit her lip. "It's true. I'm not overly fond of Rod. The sooner he's caught, the sooner I'm out of here. He'll concoct some kind of story for the cops. If he did something to land himself in jail, I wouldn't lift a finger to help him. On the other hand, I won't stand by and allow him to be railroaded if he's innocent."

"You're not going anywhere for a while. I may take up my aunt's plans."

"Which were?"

"Helen didn't care about jail time for you two. She wanted an apology and some services."

"Services?"

"She really was planning on writing a book. A novel set in a mining town at the turn of the twentieth century. You would be her unpaid secretary for a year."

"Are you kidding? She wanted my secretarial skills for free? How did Rod fit in?"

"Gardener and maintenance man. He'd cut the grass, trim the bushes, weed the flower beds, and do simple repairs."

Vicky burst out laughing. "You've got to be joking! Rod would cut off his foot with the lawn mower, kill the bushes, yank out all the flowers, and do more damage than repairing."

"Nevertheless, that was the plan. You'd live in a small cottage on the property. All credit cards, checkbooks, and cell phones would be confiscated. She'd supply food and set up charge accounts limited to a hundred dollars a month at various stores for personal items like toothpaste and clothing."

The waiter brought Trevor's drink and her wine.

"And you went along with this?" she asked.

Trevor hesitated and gulped half the scotch. "No. I thought it was screwy. Told her the two of you were smarter than you looked, and would find a way out of town. I wanted to give you enough rope for a con, nail you, and send you to jail. That was *my* plan."

Her heart sank at the determined look on his face. "Is jail still what you have in mind?"

"Haven't decided yet."

The salads arrived as Vicky's appetite fled. As

soon as the bank cards came and her brother was behind bars, she was gone. She'd use one of the aliases Trevor didn't know, then head for a large city and a legitimate job for a while. Rod could take care of himself. He always did.

"Trevor, is that you?"

Vicky looked up. A tall man with graying hair, wearing a western styled suit and cowboy boots, stood next to the table. Another man, younger but in similar clothing and carrying a Stetson, was behind him. Facial features told her they were related.

"Hello, Walt, Adam."

So, this was the brother-in-law and nephew. The son stared at her with a smile on his fleshy lips. Trevor's voice had held no enthusiasm nor did he ask the newcomers to join them.

"We came down as soon as we heard about Helen. Is it true she was killed by some gigolo she picked up in Vegas?" the older man said.

"That's what the police think."

The son smiled staring at Vicky's chest. "Do I know you, ma'am?"

She didn't like his looks and could see why the murdered woman hadn't liked either of them.

"No, I don't think so." She popped a forkful of lettuce into her mouth.

The man stuck out his hand anyway. "I'm Adam Richardson. This is my father, Walter."

Wanting to be rude, but not sure of her footing, Vicky laid her fork on the edge of the plate, wiped her lips, and shook his hand. Why squander an opportunity? These two could be allies.

"How do you do. I'm Victoria Denton."

Trevor scowled and offered an explanation. "Miss Denton was to be Aunt Helen's secretary."

"Oh, really? Helen's husband, Roland, was my older brother," Walter explained.

"You got down here fast," Trevor said.

"Elliot called with the news. We figured you might need some help with the arrangements once the coroner is finished. How did it happen?"

"Rosa found her in the study this morning. Her head was bashed in with the fireplace poker. You talked to the sheriff yet?"

"Some on the phone. We just got in. Planned on staying at the house, but it's all roped off. We're at the Night's Rest Inn."

"So are we. We'll be moving in as soon as the house is released." Trevor's tone indicated the Richardsons were not welcome. Walter raised his eyebrows, while Adam's face flushed.

The son cast a glance at Vicky. "We?"

"That's right. Vicky and I," Trevor said in a smooth voice.

His lover-like smile made her feel cheap. She decided to set the record straight.

"Yes, Mr. Sloane and I met in Miami a few weeks ago. His aunt needed a secretary, and I needed a job. I've offered to help with the arrangements and any unfinished business Mrs. Richardson may have had. I won't stay long."

Walter ignored her, and stared at Trevor. "We need to see Elliot about the will, too. This could have consequences for the mine."

"Don't see why. Roland's will took care of that. Aunt Helen had nothing to do with Richardson Mining."

Adam frowned at Trevor's words and started to speak. His father cut him off in a smooth move.

"Well, you never know. She may have changed a few things since Roland's death. What about her brother?"

"I called Ray and informed him this afternoon. Said he'd call my cousins and break the news."

Their steaks arrived and Walter got the hint. "Well, we'll leave you to your dinner. I'll be in touch."

The men wandered across the room and into the bar. Trevor watched them with a penetrating gaze.

"Sounds like he's interested in the will," Vicky commented, cutting into her filet.

"Don't see why. They got their cut long ago. I am curious, however, as to why Walter thinks she may have changed it. And if she did, why she'd include him or Adam. She didn't like them."

"A lot of undercurrents are swirling, which is why Rod isn't the only person with a motive."

"He had motive all right."

At any other time, the tender steak done to perfection would have melted in her mouth, but tonight she tasted little. Even the cabernet had no flavor. She excused herself and went to the ladies room. Locking the stall door behind her, she quickly checked her voice mail. Nothing. Rod still hadn't called.

Damned little shit. She dialed and left another message. "Rod, you'd better not ignore me. You're not the only suspect, so get your ass back with a sensible story."

She rejoined Trevor who gazed at her with a raised eyebrow. "What? No escape attempt?"

"Window was too small."

For the first time today, he laughed. "Okay. I've been a bore all evening. Shouldn't have been."

"Shame your relatives showed up."

"This is the best restaurant in town. Neither of them puts up with mediocre food."

The waiter cleared the table and served coffee. Vicky glanced at the bar. Walter and Adam had gone.

As if reading her mind, Trevor said, "They're over in the far corner. The fireplace blocks your view. I'm sure we're the main topic of conversation."

She added sweetener and cream to the coffee. "No need to insinuate we were living together."

"Maybe I didn't like the way Adam ogled you."

She cast her gaze into the mocha-colored liquid and blew across the surface, having no idea what he meant. She was about to investigate his comment when another voice interrupted.

"Thought I'd find you here," the sheriff said.

"Hi, Al. Have you caught him yet?" Trevor asked.

He shook his head. "Not yet. He had a big head start. We'll get him. Told you that."

"Have a seat."

Sheriff Singleton pulled out a chair and nodded in Vicky's direction.

Trevor sipped his coffee. "You just missed Walter and Adam. They're seated across the room."

Al made a face. "I'm sure if they see me, they'll be over. Don't like Adam much."

Trevor rolled his eyes. "Same here. Don't care for Walter either. Greedy, both of them."

Vicky sat silent nursing her coffee and listened. She understood greed. Maybe that's why she'd formed an instant dislike of both men. They reminded her of Rod.

"Why have you tracked us down?" Trevor asked.

"Just wanted to let you know your story checks out, although I haven't found where you stayed in Miami, Miss Denton." The waiter stopped beside him. "Coffee, black."

"I stayed at my aunt's condominium."

"I see. What's the name?"

"Oceanside Condos, I believe. I can't remember."

"I meant your aunt."

"Sullivan, Mary Sullivan." She didn't worry about lying. By the time the sheriff discovered it, she'd be history.

"And how did you and Trevor meet?"

"What's this got to do with anything?" Trevor asked in a sharp voice.

The waiter arrived with the sheriff's coffee. "No reason. Just curious."

He sipped, directing his gaze toward Vicky. Not to answer might raise a red flag and the last thing either of them needed was a curious sheriff. She hastened to explain.

"We met at a nightclub on South Beach. It was crowded, and I spilled my cocktail on his sleeve. I apologized, bought him a drink, and he asked me out to dinner. Simple as pie."

"I didn't think you liked nightlife, Trevor."

"Don't, but I was on a job. And if you must know, I was investigating a wayward husband who was supposed to be in Miami on business."

The sheriff grinned. "And was he?"

"Yeah, monkey business," Trevor replied with a laugh. "Like Vicky said, we hit it off, and when Aunt Helen said she needed a secretary, I suggested her. Why are you so interested?"

"As I said, just curious. She's beautiful and I'm trying to figure out what she sees in you."

His comment brought a laugh from Vicky. Trevor scowled.

"What? You don't think a pretty woman can find me attractive? Women consider me fascinating."

"I remember Lynn Hardesty, the bank teller. A smile and a kind word almost did you in. Her old man grabbed his shotgun and had a preacher waiting in the wings."

Trevor drained his cup and shook his head. "Lynn Hardesty was a nut case. Roland and Helen talked to the parents, and agreed Lynn needed to get out more. Why wouldn't Vicky find me charming, too?"

Her heart beat accelerated. Why indeed? She remembered the dance floor and her reactions on the plane. In some aspects, Trevor Sloane was damned attractive with sex appeal out the ass.

"I have some information you might find interesting." Al sipped more of his coffee.

"What?"

"First of all, the house will be released by noon tomorrow. You can move in whenever you want. I also had Rosa take a look around to see if anything was missing. Some of Mrs. Richardson's jewelry is gone."

Vicky tensed. Rod! The stupid son of a bitch. Apparently, Trevor thought along the same lines for he shot her a glance filled with conviction.

"What pieces are missing?"

The sheriff pulled a slip of paper from his shirt pocket. "Let's see. A sapphire and diamond necklace, a diamond cocktail ring, an emerald bracelet, several pairs of earrings all with genuine stones, and a triple strand of pearls with a diamond and pearl pendant. Her engagement and wedding rings were still on her finger, but the maid swears a large ruby ring her employer always wore was not. She also notes several other items—gold and silver—are gone."

"The ruby was the last birthday gift from Roland. It never left her finger. The son of a bitch robbed the dead. Probably would have taken the wedding stuff, but they fit tight. The pearl necklace was an engagement present from her father. I remember the cocktail ring, and the necklace, too." Anger throbbed in his voice. "What gold and silver items?"

"A pair of gold candlesticks from the mantel in the study, and several silver picture frames in the drawing room. All totaled, it was quite a haul. Oh, and Rosa also says Mr. Harvey's room is empty of all personal items."

"Of course it is. Anything else?"

Sheriff Singleton refolded the paper and returned it to his pocket. "Nope. That's all. Except for the cash and whatever was in the safe."

Vicky clenched her teeth to prevent being sick, swallowed, and offered an explanation.

"I can see how it happened. A thief was watching the house, saw the maid leave, mistook her for Mrs. Richardson, and then broke in. When he discovered the owner home, he panicked, killed her, grabbed what he could, and split."

"That's possible, but where is Mr. Harvey and Mrs. Richardson's car?"

"Perhaps he had business somewhere else, and she loaned him the car."

Trevor glared. "That car was my aunt's baby. She wouldn't loan it to anyone, not even me."

"There's a first time for everything."

"I'd still like to talk to Mr. Harvey," the sheriff drawled. "Besides, there's something else. The coroner found two distinct wounds on her head. The biggest and probably the fatal one, was made by the poker, but she had another wound above her right temple. Forensics also discovered blood on the corner of the desk in the study."

Trevor's eyes narrowed. "So, they had a fight, she fell, hit her head, and while she was down, he grabbed the poker to finish her off. Should be lots of blood splatter."

"There's enough, but the killer only needed one blow. Hit her in just the right spot with the little curved part of the poker."

Vicky shivered at the image his words evoked. She pictured the poker descending on the helpless woman shattering her skull and piercing her brain. She still didn't see Rod as a killer, but robbing the house *was* his style. Like a raccoon, the superficial snot loved bright, shiny things.

"Bastard," Trevor muttered. "What about fingerprints?"

The sheriff finished his coffee. "We lifted a lot of

65

them from the desk and the mantel. Helen, Elliot Corwin, Rosa, and Rosa's son, Carlos. And one set that remained unidentified until just a while ago. Got a hit with AFIS. They belong to a guy by the name of Roger Hart. Ever hear of him?"

Trevor shook his head. "Never. What did he do?"

"Mr. Hart was arrested last year in San Francisco for fraud, but before he could be arraigned, there was a snafu in the clerk's office, and he was cut loose by mistake. Naturally, he disappeared."

"Naturally." Trevor shot a look Vicky's way. "Fraud, huh? What kind of fraud?"

Al shrugged. "Investment fraud. The police faxed his mug shot to me. Rosa identified him as Ryan Harvey. Does he look familiar?" He pulled another sheet of paper from his pants pocket, and handed it to Trevor.

"Never saw him before," he said, handing it to Vicky.

Her breath caught. She stared at incredibly unflattering photos, full face and profile, of Rod.

"Me, neither," she said with a catch in her voice, handing the paper back to Al.

"No reason why you should." Returning the faxed mug shot to his pocket, the sheriff rose. "You know, the funny thing is, we found fingerprints on the desk, the mantel, all over the room. Found Hart's on the jewelry boxes in Mrs. Richardson's bedroom, but the poker, a picture frame, and the safe were wiped clean. Doesn't make sense to wipe off the murder weapon, but leave the rest untouched. A quick swipe with a handkerchief and he's done."

"He panicked and forgot about the other things he may have touched," Trevor suggested.

"Could be, but he had the presence of mind to steal. Had to know he was leaving his prints behind. He's alone in the house. Why not take a few extra minutes and finish the job? Lots of things about this case are odd. Can't wait to talk to Mr. Harvey or Hart or whatever his name is. See you later."

When he was out of earshot, Trevor leaned in and said in a low voice. "Kind of screws your theory of Rod never having been arrested."

She tossed her napkin on the table. "This is the first I've heard about it. I haven't talked to Rod in almost a year. Hart must be a new alias. If the sheriff's right regarding the fingerprints, then I'd have to say my brother may have robbed the place, but he didn't kill her. Rod would have either wiped down everything or nothing."

Trevor looked around, caught the waiter's eye, and motioned him over. "Check, please." The man nodded and left. "Let's get out of here. Keep this in mind. A stranger did not mistake the maid for my aunt. A stranger did not kill her, rob her, and steal her car. That, my dear, is right at the feet of your brother."

In spite of her earlier convictions, Vicky feared Trevor was right.

Chapter Five

Trevor drove up the driveway and stopped at the foot of the porch steps. He eyed the front door, half-expecting his aunt to fling it open, arms outstretched in welcome.

He exited the car, slamming the door harder than necessary, and then popped the trunk lid. Vicky also got out. She stared at the fieldstone edifice soaring three stories high.

"You must have loved playing here when you were a kid," she commented. "I'll bet this place has a million nooks and crannies for hide and seek."

He hefted the suitcases out of the trunk before answering in a terse tone, "It had its moments."

She turned to face him. "Are you going to glare at me forever? It's not my fault your aunt is dead. A little civility would be nice."

"I'll be civil when your brother is behind bars." He dropped one of the suitcases at her feet. "Since you find the place so fascinating, I'll have Rosa give you one of the turret rooms."

He left Vicky and barged up the steps. She muttered under her breath, but based on the footsteps behind him, followed. Rosa opened the door.

"*Senor* Sloane, please come in."

Trevor strode into the spacious foyer and looked around. Nothing had changed except the woman greeting him. The hanging staircase curved to the upper story and the crystal chandelier still hung over the center of the room. Even the large, round Chippendale table in the middle of the floor with its enormous Lalique vase, the last roses of the season spilling their scent into the air, remained the same. The grandfather clock in the corner struck one.

"Hello, Rosa. Wish I could say it's nice to be here."

Tears trickled down the housekeeper's cheeks. "Oh, *Senor* Sloane, I miss her so much."

He patted the woman's shoulder. "I know, Rosa. So do I." He turned toward Vicky who stood a few feet away, her gaze sweeping the foyer. "This is Miss Denton. She was hired by Aunt Helen as a secretary, but will be staying a few days to help with the arrangements and assist me with whatever paperwork is necessary."

She stepped forward, her hand outstretched to the housekeeper. "Pleased to meet you. I'm so sorry for your loss."

Rosa shook her hand, a puzzled frown on her face. "A secretary? *Senora* Richardson said nothing to me about a secretary."

"I was hired just a few days ago. I believe she planned on writing a book about Colorado and the mining industry."

"It was all very sudden, Rosa. I was in Miami. She told me her plans, and I suggested Miss Denton. Perhaps, you could set her up in one of the turret rooms?"

"*Si*, of course, *Senor* Sloane, whatever you wish. What would you like for dinner?"

"Something simple for two."

The woman nodded and reached for Vicky's bag.

"When you finish showing Miss Denton to her room, would you meet me in the study? I'd like to ask a few questions. Vicky, there's a TV in the den. It's down that hallway toward the back of the house.

I'll talk to you later."

Vicky shot him a curious glance, but followed Rosa up the stairs. He carried his bag, trailing after them. At the head of the steps, he turned right while the women bore left. His heart twisted when passing the closed door of the master suite, but he continued on toward the turret room in the northwest corner of the house. While visiting as a kid during the winter, he'd often lain awake in the large double bed snuggled warm and safe under the comforter listening to snow pelt the windows.

Aunt Helen should be warm and safe in her own home, too. Damn Rod Halston.

He dumped his suitcase on the bed, washed his hands in the large accompanying bathroom, and then headed back downstairs to the study. Trevor paused in front of the closed door reluctant to open it and view the scene of the crime. He'd seen lots of murder sites in his day, but this was up close and personal.

He shook his head, sucking in a deep breath. *Standing out here isn't going to bring her back.*

Opening the door, he entered and strode to the desk. Rosa must have worked like fiend to clean the usual forensics residue. Not a speck of fingerprint dust remained. The room looked as immaculate as when his aunt was alive. Even the painting of the house had been re-hung over the fireplace.

The first order of business was to contact his office.

"Sloane Investigations, how may I help you?"

"Hi, Pam, it me. Is Marylou in?"

"She was here when I got in this morning. Just a minute."

He waited a few seconds until his operative answered.

"Hello, boss man. Sorry about your aunt. Cops get the little bastard?"

"Not yet. Anything on Corwin come through?"

"Just the usual first layer, but don't worry, I'll peel the onion."

"I also need you to take a look into Walter Richardson and his son Adam, both live in Mineral City." He gave her the addresses of each man. "Take a gander at Richardson Mining while you're at it. It's a part of the Rocky Mountain Mineral Company. Both Walt and Adam have high paying jobs."

"Gotcha. Aren't they your uncle and cousin?"

"By marriage only, thank God. Get back to me as soon as you can."

"Will do."

Trevor hung up and lightly touched the photo of Helen and Roland on the desk, then sat in the chair and pulled the middle drawer open, riffling through the contents—his aunt's personal stationery, pens, pencils, stamps—the things found in any desk.

He closed it and opened the drawer to his right. Several folders were neatly stacked inside. Trevor selected the one on top labeled, *Trevor's Reports*, and read. Helen had kept everything organized from his last e-mail down to the first query six months ago.

He replaced the file in the drawer not needing to read further. He knew what it contained. Could Halston have snooped and found it? Had Helen walked in and caught him at it? *Of course, she did. Then the little bastard slammed her head into the desk and brained her with the poker.*

The empty safe presented a problem, but the combination wasn't all that complicated. Trevor had figured it out within minutes several years ago and told his aunt that her birth date—5-30-19-46 was too obvious. On a hunch, he rose, removed the painting, and dialed the numbers in. The metal door swung open.

Even Rod Halston could have opened the damned thing. One look at her driver's license was

71

all it took.

Trevor shut the empty safe and replaced the painting, then pulled out another folder containing bank statements. He was halfway through it when Rosa knocked and entered.

"Come in, Rosa. Have a seat."

The housekeeper complied and smiled. "I am so happy you are here again, *Senor* Sloane. Have the police captured *Senora* Richardson's killer yet?"

"No, not yet, but they will. It's only a matter of time." He leaned back in the chair, clasping his hands behind his head. "Tell me all you can about Mr. Harvey."

"There is not much to tell. She come home from Las Vegas a week ago with him. He sleep in the room next to hers. She say he was a new friend and that he be staying for a while. I did not like him."

"Why?"

"He smile a lot and always say the nice things, but I did not trust him. He come out of *Senora* Richardson's room one day. When I ask what he wanted, he say he was just looking for her."

"So he was casing the joint."

"Casing the joint?" Rosa asked with a furrowed forehead.

"Looking around to see what was valuable so he could steal it," Trevor explained.

"*Si*, that is what I suspect, too."

He fiddled with the edge of the statement folder. He didn't want to ask the next question, but had to know.

"Tell me about yesterday, Rosa."

The woman sobbed and pulled a tissue from her pocket to blot the tears. "It was awful, *Senor* Sloane. I come in at six-thirty to make breakfast."

"Did anything look disturbed?"

She shook her head. "No, I go to the kitchen, but when *Senora* Richardson didn't come down, I go upstairs to wake her. Only she no there, so I come back down calling her. I check the den first. Sometimes, she fall asleep watching TV, but she not there either. Then, I open study door."

Her gaze shifted to the side of the desk near the fireplace and away from the door. Trevor also looked. In the morning light, the faint remains of the bloodstains showed against the beige carpet.

"I try to clean it all up," Rosa whispered. "The police say I could. There was blood on the desk, the fireplace, and some on the wall."

"You did an excellent job, Rosa. We'll get new carpeting for this room and repaint soon. What did you do after you opened the door?"

"I call her name and walk into the room. I see the painting leaning against the wall, and the safe, it is open. The bottom desk drawer was also open. Then I see..." She hiccupped and squeezed her eyes shut as she sobbed again.

"What did you do then?"

"I scream and run to get *Senor* Harvey, but he not here, so I call police."

"When did you discover the thefts?"

"The police asked me to check if anything was missing. The candlesticks on the mantel were gone, along with picture frames—nice silver ones she buy in Mexico. Next, I go upstairs and find jewelry boxes open and jewelry missing."

Trevor balled his hand into a fist and lightly struck the desktop. "Everybody in Granite Springs knew about that silly cigar box. I told her it was asking for trouble." He leaned back again trying to relax the knot of tension between his shoulder blades. "I understand Mr. Corwin had dinner here a few nights ago."

"*Si, Senor* Sloane. *Senora* Richardson invite him to meet with *Senor* Harvey."

"How did Mr. Corwin and Mr. Harvey get

along?"

"Very polite, but *Senor* Corwin had angry look. After dinner, he and the *Senora* have fight in study."

"Did you hear what was said?"

The housekeeper shook her head. "No, I was in kitchen cleaning up, but when I come out, *Senor* Harvey was listening to the raised voices at the door. I stay real still until he leave to go upstairs."

So, Halston knew Corwin and his aunt had argued. Trevor would give a year's salary to know what the little slime had overheard. Enough to suspect things weren't going his way and make escape plans?

"*Senora* Richardson have a lot of visitors lately," Rosa offered after blowing her nose.

"Who?"

"*Senor* Walter and *Senor* Adam come many times in last few months."

"Together?"

"Sometimes, then *Senor* Walter came back and *Senor* Adam was here just before she leave for Las Vegas."

"Have any idea what they wanted?"

Rosa shook her head. "No, but the *Senora* was not pleased to see them, and *Senor* Adam was very angry. *Senor* Walter slam front door very hard when he leave."

Trevor drummed his fingers on the arm of the chair. What the hell did Walter and Adam want? Money? He made a mental note to see if Helen had written either of them a check in recent months. Didn't sound like it. *And why wouldn't she tell me about their visits?*

"The *Senora* was nicer to Jason."

"Jason? Uncle Ray's son? When was he here?"

"I'm not sure. Long time ago. He stay a couple of days, and then leave. He came last month, too. He only stay overnight, but the next morning, I heard

Senora Richardson say she not give him money again."

What the hell is going on here? "Was she angry?"

"Not angry. She talk like her nephew was *nino*."

"And Jason? Was he upset?"

Rosa frowned and pursed her lips. "No, he look more scared. He kiss her goodbye and leave."

The door to the study opened and a good-looking Latino entered. Rosa turned in her seat.

"Oh, Carlos, I am glad you are here. This is *Senora* Richardson's nephew, *Senor* Sloane. *Senor* Sloane, this is my son, Carlos."

Trevor had seen the man on the grounds, but never spoken to him.

He swaggered up to the desk, his manner irritating. His words even more so.

"I haven't been paid for my services. I need my money."

Rosa blushed. "Carlos," she admonished.

He shrugged. "*Mamasita,* I do not work for free."

"And exactly what is it you do around here?" Trevor asked in a cool voice.

"I cut the grass, trim the bushes, and do whatever I'm asked to do. I also like to be paid. Mrs. Richardson owed me two hundred dollars."

Rosa shot a worried glance at her son. Trevor suspected Helen didn't pay that well.

"That's a pretty high price for a gardener."

Carlos shrugged again, and lifted his lips into a smirk. "I do good work."

"As you know, my aunt's death has disrupted the usual routine. Her bank accounts are frozen for a while. Come back in a couple of days."

A scowl marred the man's handsome face. He placed his hands on the desktop and leaned toward Trevor.

"I expect to get paid soon."

Trevor glanced at the tattoos etched in the

man's hands, and then back up at his face.

"You'll get paid, when I say you'll get paid. *Comprendo,* pal?"

Carlos straightened shooting an angry look at Trevor, while his mother stared at the floor and bit her lip.

"*Si,* I understand. Just don't make it too long. I have bills to pay." He turned and strode to the door, his whip lean body tense. "I'll see you later, *Mamasita.*"

"And Carlos," Trevor added. "The next time you enter any room in this house, knock first."

He stood in the doorway and glared, his lip curling, snorted back a laugh, and left.

Rosa squirmed in her chair. "I am sorry for Carlos, *Senor* Sloane. He is sometimes impatient."

"What was he in prison for?"

Her head came up. "How did you know?"

"The tattoos on his hands are prison tattoos. I also noticed one up on his neck. A gang mark?"

She nodded. "He had some problems, but is a good boy now."

"What kind of problems?"

"He stole a car and broke into a house once."

"When was this?"

"Four years ago."

"Where?"

"In Denver."

"How much did my aunt pay Carlos for his work? It wasn't two hundred dollars, was it?"

Rosa shook her head. "No, she pay him fifty dollars whenever he work."

"Cash?"

"*Si.*"

"Thank you for being honest. I'll let you go start dinner. Did Miss Denton get settled in?"

The housekeeper stood, nodding. "Si, *senor.* I put her in the blue turret room. She say she want to take bath and a nap."

Rosa left, closing the door behind her.

Trevor picked up his cell phone and dialed his office again. Pam connected him to Marylou.

"Add Carlos Ramirez to your list. He's got a prison record here in Colorado. Probably for GTA and burglary. Check out the surrounding states along with California and Nevada while you're at it."

He hung up and leaned back in the chair, digesting Rosa's information. Walter and Adam had both been here wanting something, and last night seemed eager to get inside the house. *Why?*

And his cousin Jason begged Helen for money, apparently more than once. Why did he need it? Ray made a good living, and his aunt owned a small bookstore specializing in mysteries. To the best of his knowledge, they didn't have financial problems, although anything could happen. *And college is a budget buster.*

And then, there was Carlos. The jobs he did were the same ones Helen had lined up for Rod, which meant Carlos's services would no longer be required. Trevor was certain the fifty bucks probably came from the cigar box, meaning the housekeeper's son knew of its existence. It was also apparent the young man had free rein to come and go in the house. Did that include a couple of clandestine sojourns to Helen's bedroom?

Trevor sighed and rubbed his forehead. A nagging headache had sprung up. As much as he wanted the killer to be Rod Halston, he admitted the suspect list was growing.

****

Vicky loved the room she'd been given. Large and decorated in sky blue, bright with slashes of yellow, made it elegant yet homey. A bath in the vintage claw-footed tub was definitely on the agenda, but she had other things to do first.

As soon as Rosa left, Vicky cracked her door, watching until the woman was down the steps, and then slipped into the hallway. She wanted to take a look around, perhaps find those canceled checks Trevor had mentioned. He'd said his aunt had discovered them in a file drawer in the attic. Would she keep them there? In the study? Or maybe her bedroom?

Vicky walked softly down the corridor, pausing at the top of the stairs. From below, she heard nothing. Directly opposite stood a set of double doors, undoubtedly the entrance to the master bedroom. Without hesitation, she turned the knob. The door opened, and she entered.

A quick search revealed nothing, not even in the enormous closet. Vicky longed to stop and try on one of five or six fur coats, but refrained. She left and retraced her steps down the corridor.

Most of the doors were intricately carved, but a plain one at the end of the hall drew her attention. She opened it and flipping on the light switch, proceeded to climb the narrow steps to the attic.

Here she found several metal file cabinets against the far wall. The labels on the drawers were numbered with years, no doubt indicating tax records. She opened the drawer from six years ago. The file she sought was in front.

She hurried back to her room, locked the door, and flipped through the folder's contents. The more she saw, the madder she got. Rod had scammed the old boy for a lot more than a hundred grand. Apparently, Helen hadn't told Trevor the entire truth.

She hid the file under her mattress, and took the promised bath, not sure if the steam rising was from the hot water or her temper.

Later, Vicky descended the staircase, admiring the hand carved banister. The architecture of the house may have been over the top, but the workmanship was first rate.

She hesitated at the foot of the stairs, unsure of where to go. To her right a large archway led to a formal room. She entered, fascinated by the ceiling fresco depicting a rose garden.

"Like it?"

She whirled to find Trevor smiling from the entryway. "It certainly is dramatic."

"When this place was built, it was considered the height of elegance. Why my aunt never had it painted over, I don't know."

"Maybe, she liked roses."

"As a matter of fact, she did. We normally have the cocktail hour in the den. Would you like something?"

"A martini sounds good." She moved to stand next to him. He seemed more relaxed than earlier.

"Follow me."

The den proved to be a big room furnished with a couple of plush sofas and leather chairs. A big-screen TV hung over the fireplace. Floor to ceiling bookcases covered one wall, and opposite the TV, two portraits stared across the room.

"Your aunt and uncle?" she asked.

"Yes. Recognize Roland now?" He walked to a bar cart in the corner of the room and selected several bottles, then proceeded to mix the drinks.

"Yes. It's a good likeness. Your aunt was a lovely woman."

Vicky meant what she said. Helen Richardson had arrived at that stage of life where she was no longer slim, but neither was she stout. Her brown eyes held humor, and her strong chin said, don't mess with me.

If she'd been in Palm Springs with Roland, Rod wouldn't have seen a dime of their money.

"Was your aunt a natural redhead?"

Trevor handed her a martini, laughing. "Yes. Very proud of it, too. Flatly refused to have gray hair. Went twice a month to her hairstylist for touch-ups."

She sipped her drink and looked at him through her lashes, wondering what Rosa had told him concerning Rod. But Vicky had learned patience long ago, and bided her time. Sooner or later, he'd tell her.

"Have a seat," he said, indicating one of the sofas.

Vicky sat and let her gaze wander over him as he lowered himself into a chair. Tonight he wore jeans and a dark green polo shirt. Both fitted his body snugly. She glanced down at her silk blouse and trousers.

"Am I overdressed? Is there a dress code for dinner?"

He laughed. "No. Aunt Helen hated formality."

He sipped his martini, his gaze not leaving her face. His eyes had turned the color of milk chocolate, warm and incredibly sexy. Vicky sat mesmerized, unable to stop staring. Heat radiating from her cheeks told her she was blushing, something she rarely did.

Rosa walked into the room interrupting the moment. "Dinner is ready."

Trevor rose. "Thank you. What are we having?"

The housekeeper furrowed her brow. "You say to keep it simple, so I make meatloaf, mashed potatoes with gravy, green beans and a salad. I make apple pie for dessert."

"Sounds wonderful." He opened a cabinet next to the bar cart as she left and selected a bottle of wine.

"Wine with meatloaf?"

"Wine goes with anything," he replied. "Why the strange look?"

She shrugged. "You just don't strike me as the

wine type."

"Maybe I'm more complex than you thought."

Maybe you are at that.

Vicky followed him down the hallway and into the dining room. The table, large enough to seat a dozen people, had two places set. She took the chair on the side, leaving the end seat for Trevor. The table stretched forever to the far end of the room, and she wondered if Helen Richardson had eaten here every night. Although decorated in red and gold, the room offered little warmth.

Rosa brought in the food while Trevor opened the wine and poured two glasses. Meatloaf had never been one of her favorite dishes, but this was moist and flavorful. She was halfway through the meal before she realized neither of them had spoken.

Vicky glanced toward the kitchen door and lowered her voice. "What did Rosa have to say about Rod?"

"Enough to tell me your brother had his eyes on Aunt Helen's jewelry soon after he got here." An instant frost had entered his voice.

"He may have been curious." She wanted to slap herself for asking. His genial demeanor had changed.

"Curious my ass. He was waiting for an opportunity."

"All right, have it your way, but what did she say?"

He raised his wine glass and drank half, then told her about Walt, Adam, Jason, and Carlos.

"So, a lot of people other than Rod had a motive."

"People came to see her. We have no proof any of them robbed or killed her. Your brother's still the prime suspect."

"Maybe she was paying your cousin on a regular basis. Maybe he got pissed when she said no more."

"Jason loved Helen. He wouldn't harm a hair on her head."

"Everyone has a greed factor. It never fails to amaze me when perfectly sane businessmen like your uncle come unglued at the thought of easy money for schemes most people would find suspicious," she said.

"Uncle Roland was one of the nicest guys I've ever known. If he hadn't been the oldest son destined to inherit a company he didn't want to run, he'd have been a writer or a historian." He paused, his mouth set in a grim line. "He was an easy target for people like you and your brother. Because he was an honest, ethical man, he assumed everyone else was, too. An admirable trait, but naïve. I'm sure the words honest and ethical don't often appear in your vocabulary. You use your beauty and sexuality to lure and distract. You use, abuse, and then use again."

Her fingers tightened on her fork. "How the hell do you know what I feel or think? I am not a robot. I'm a human being."

"You, my dear, are a liar and a thief."

It wasn't the words that cut her to the quick, but the scornful tone. She blinked tears from her eyes. What he'd said was true, but she wished he thought of her in positive terms. She wanted...she fumbled for the word...what, consideration? No, respect. She wanted Trevor Sloane to respect her. And she knew respect was not given, but earned.

"It's true Rod and I take advantage of people like your uncle, but keep in mind that some of those people were not particularly honest or ethical themselves. Their greed allowed them to be used. For them, I have no remorse."

He was about to reply when the doorbell rang. A few seconds later, Rosa came into the room.

"*Senor* Sloane, the sheriff is here to see you."

"Send him in." Rosa nodded and left. Trevor sent Vicky a hard glance. "Maybe this is good news."

Sheriff Singleton entered, removed his hat, and smiled.

"Good evening, Al. Have a seat. Would you like a glass of wine? Some coffee?"

Al waved a hand. "No, thanks. Just thought I'd stop by and tell you Ryan Harvey was picked up by Utah State Police an hour ago. He'll be here by morning."

Chapter Six

Vicky's heart plummeted to her toes. Her fork slipped from suddenly cold fingers and fell with a clatter onto her plate. Rod had been apprehended in Utah. He hadn't made it back to Granite Springs. *Probably never tried.*

"Tomorrow? Why not tonight?" Trevor asked in a hard voice.

"Because he was arrested for speeding and resisting outside of Noble, Utah. They ran the license plates and caught that it was stolen."

Trevor's eyebrows rose. "He didn't ditch the plates?" He shot Vicky an incredulous glance. "How stupid is this guy?"

Vicky wondered the same. Rod must have been panic-stricken not to have done something so fundamental.

"Sheriff, exactly where is Noble, Utah?" she asked.

"It's a small town off Interstate 70 about halfway across the state." He frowned and shook his head. "Funny thing is, the sheriff over there said Harvey was eastbound."

"Eastbound? That doesn't make any sense," Trevor said.

He got my messages. He was coming back. Vicky's heart rate slowed. She breathed a sigh of relief. As soon as her credit and ATM replacement cards arrived, she'd sneak out.

"What else can you tell us? Did he say anything?" Trevor asked.

"Don't have all the details yet. They'll write up the report and e-mail or fax it to me, then transport Mr. Harvey or Hart." He rose. "I just thought you'd want to know he's been captured."

Trevor pushed back his chair and also stood. "When will he get here?"

"Kinda depends on when he leaves Utah."

"I want to talk to him."

"I'm sure that can be arranged as soon as I question him, and he's arraigned."

Vicky's mind shifted into fifth gear. She wanted to talk to her brother, too. Since he was headed back to Granite Springs, he must have concocted some kind of story. Of course, it would all be bullshit, which was why she had to get him one on one. Granite Springs may have been a small town, but the sheriff was no country bumpkin. He seemed to have his head screwed on straight. He'd be curious as to why *she'd* want to talk to Mr. Harvey.

Worry about that later.

"When will he be arraigned?" Trevor asked, bringing her back to the present.

"As soon as I'm done questioning him."

"I assume you plan on arresting him for murder," she commented.

"I'll arrest him for something, that's for sure. Goodnight, Trevor, Miss Denton."

"Let me know when I can take a crack at him," Trevor replied.

The sheriff left. Trevor turned to her, the light of victory in his eyes and a smile on his lips.

"Got him!"

"Why was he heading east?" she questioned.

"He's got a lousy sense of direction?"

"Maybe he borrowed the car for a few days."

"He heard an APB was out on the car and wants

to cover his ass."

"How would he know that?"

Trevor shrugged. "CB? Aunt Helen had one in the car."

"Why leave the license plates on?" she countered.

The smile slipped from his face. He rose, tossing his napkin onto the table. "I don't know. Maybe he's a dumb ass. I'm going to tell Rosa the news. Amuse yourself tonight. I'll be in the study making phone calls and on the computer."

He strode from the room, leaving her alone.

"He's right about one thing, Rod," she murmured out loud. "You *are* a dumb ass."

The clock struck nine as she crossed the foyer. Too early for bed, not that she'd sleep. Pausing at the top of the staircase, she leaned over the balustrade when Trevor came out of the kitchen and headed for the study. The door closed with a soft thud. Her gaze wandered to the master bedroom doors.

Without stopping to think, Vicky crossed the hall and slipped inside where she flipped on the light before entering the closet. She unzipped a garment bag holding a full length mink coat. Her fingers stroked the soft fur, then plucked it from the hanger and put it on. It was too big, but who cared? The reflection in the full length mirror next to the dressing table delighted her.

Vicky preened for a few minutes, and then replaced the coat. The next garment bag contained a silver fox stole. In front of the mirror again, she tossed the end over her shoulder admiring the effect. She repeated the process until all the coats had been modeled and caressed. These were the things she'd always longed for, and on several occasions had owned, until necessity forced a visit the pawn shop.

Next, Vicky inspected the jewelry boxes. A few

necklaces, some rings and bracelets, and a lot of earrings, mostly semi-precious stones trickled past her probing fingers. Rod had stolen the best pieces.

The sheriff didn't mention finding the jewelry. Could he have pawned it already? I can't believe he had the presence of mind to rifle through the jewel cases with Helen Richardson dead on the study floor. I'd have just beat it.

Vicky retreated to her room, washed her face, brushed her teeth, and slipping the nightgown over her head, slid into bed. She fluffed the pillows and lay down, pulling the comforter over her. The soft mattress cradled her body like a lover's arms.

It would be hours before she slept. *Wonder what Trevor's doing in the study. Calling Utah demanding a report? Informing the rest of the family?*

She rolled onto her side, burrowing her head into the pillow. For a while there tonight, he'd been pleasant. Until she'd opened her big mouth. Still, when he smiled her breath had caught in her throat. Not much, but enough to surprise her. And those eyes. Milk chocolate. *Melted milk chocolate.*

Her mind slipped back to the plane and her reactions to his touch. Awareness plucked at her again, and she rolled restlessly onto her other side.

Why do I find him so attractive? He admitted if he had his way, I'd be in jail. In spite of his obvious dislike, I can't stop staring. How does that make any sense?

She had no answers. Wary and suspicious of men, she'd always taken care of herself. Her job had been to con the guys, not fall for them.

Her heart sank at her thoughts. *Am I falling for Trevor Sloane? I've known him forty-eight hours. Impossible! How can I be falling for a man who neither likes nor respects me?*

Vicky pushed the idea away, flopping over on her back. She closed her eyes, willing sleep to come.

Right now, she was vulnerable. That's all. Tomorrow, her brother would be in Granite Springs, and with any luck, her credit and ATM cards would also be delivered.

In twenty-four hours I'll be long gone. Trevor's face flashed in front of her closed eyes. A warm sensation gnawed deep in her belly.

In a way, she'd be sorry to leave.

****

Vicky entered the dining room the following morning. A few extra minutes with the concealer and blush had softened the ravages of sleeplessness. Trevor, not looking as though he'd slept either, was already seated and eating.

"Breakfast is on the sideboard," he commented. "My aunt liked big meals in the morning, so Rosa did the same for us."

She selected a waffle, scrambled eggs, and sausage. Setting the plate on the table, Vicky returned to pour a cup of coffee, and then dug into the food.

"Have you talked to the sheriff this morning?" she asked.

"A little while ago. Your brother should be here by ten o'clock. He'll probably be arraigned later this afternoon. The questioning is a formality."

Vicky sipped her coffee. She'd spent a good chunk of the night thinking about Rod's situation and how it affected her.

"That's only an hour from now. I suppose you're going to question him as soon as the sheriff is finished."

"I'll beat the truth out of him, if I have to," he replied in a curt voice.

"I'm kind of anxious to hear his story, too. Mind if I tag along?"

"Yes."

She ate a bite of waffle, and then laid her fork

on the side of the plate.

"Rod isn't going to tell you or the sheriff jack shit, but he might loosen up with me."

"Do you think I'd let the two of you alone to concoct a story? No way."

"I still believe my brother may have been scared off by this Elliot person. Rod would react and panic. He took a few things, stole the car, and split, but he's no killer."

"I got a firsthand account of your brother from Quinn and Alex. According to both, he's a cool enough character, and he did hold them at gunpoint once." Trevor didn't look at her, but continued eating.

"Actually, I held them at gunpoint, but that's immaterial. The gun wasn't even loaded. You know, your aunt could have loaned him the car. Don't assume that just because you weren't allowed to drive it, Rod didn't convince her otherwise."

He finally made eye contact, a scowl forming between his eyes. He'd been needling her for days, why shouldn't she get in her licks, too? She forked another bite of waffle into her mouth and stared back, chewing.

"I doubt it. And I'm tired of talking about your brother." He raised the cup to his lips.

"Too damned bad, because I'm not." She leaned forward and thrust out her chin. "Admit it or not, you have a problem. Like I said, Rod'll lie to the cops and you, but only spin me half a tale. I know him and can weed out the bullshit. The only way for you to get at the truth is to make sure he does better than a public defender, and bail him out. He can stay here with us."

Trevor choked on his coffee. "What! Are you nuts?"

"It's the only way we'll get anything out of him."

"I'm sure the judge will deny bail. It'll be a

murder charge, and he's obviously a flight risk." He rose and flung his napkin onto his nearly empty plate. "No fucking way, babe. He rots in jail."

Vicky shrugged as he stormed from the room before picking up her fork to resume eating. She knew Rod. He'd tell Trevor to cram it up his ass. The sheriff wouldn't get anywhere either.

You need me, buster.

She finished her breakfast, had another cup of coffee, and then left the house for the motel. Her package should have been delivered by now.

****

Trevor paced the study. Was she serious? Bail that murdering bastard out of jail, lay out bucks for a lawyer, and then have him staying under his aunt's roof again? *No way in hell. Ain't gonna happen.*

His angry steps slowed and he stopped to stare out the window. A light frost was beginning to burn off the lawn. The occasional leaf drifted down from the shedding trees. Snow would fall in another month. Trevor closed his eyes, visualizing the falling flakes, and then opened them again. Calmer, he turned and sat behind the desk.

On the other hand, Vicky could be right. Alex Rafferty told him Rod Halston had a very convincing manner and a way with words, but was a lightweight. Did he have the guts to kill? Even a public defender would uncover other suspects, just like he had by talking with Rosa. A charge of first degree murder might be a stretch, but surely the district attorney would want to hit the killer with murder two.

But suppose the DA felt the charge iffy? Would he go for a more solid conviction on voluntary— maybe even involuntary—manslaughter?

How long do I want Rod Halston in prison? Five years? Ten? Forever? The last was the best, but

Trevor had seen a lot of plea bargains over the years.

He picked up a pencil, doodling on a notepad. In spite of his comments last night, he didn't think Rod had a lousy sense of direction. He was headed east with a purpose.

An innocent one? He flushed the thought from his mind. And why hadn't the plates on his aunt's car been changed? That's one of the first things a car thief did. It bought time. He brushed this aside, too.

Trevor didn't like that Walt and Adam had been hanging around lately either. Walt was a blustering fool, but Adam had a temper when he didn't get what he wanted. Over time he'd learned to control it, but as a kid the anger had often spilled out physically.

And why would Helen write checks to Jason? For how much? *What kind of problem did he have that Uncle Ray couldn't handle? College? Or a personal problem he didn't want his father to know about?*

Even though he had no evidence to the contrary, he added Elliot Corwin to his list. And Carlos wasn't the most trustworthy of people.

He flipped out his cell to call the office. Maybe Marylou had more information. He was ready to punch the speed dial, then stopped and put it away. Marylou wouldn't appreciate him badgering her. She'd call when she had something.

Should he call the sheriff? A glance at the clock told him that if Halston had arrived, not enough time had passed for Al to question him.

He doodled for a few minutes before tossing the pencil onto the blotter and extracting the Red Rock County phone directory from the bottom drawer. He turned to the attorney listings, marked the section, and then leaned back, closing his eyes. Didn't hurt to look.

The sudden ringing of the landline startled

Trevor out of a half-doze. He grappled for the receiver.

"Sloane here."

"Arraignment's at three in Judge Kyle Foster's court. DA may go for involuntary manslaughter."

"What? He kills my aunt with a fireplace poker and that's it?"

"Mr. Harvey's explanation, while ludicrous, has no one to refute it. I guess the district attorney figures he can always up the charges if new evidence is uncovered."

Anger and disgust roiled his stomach. "What explanation?"

"According to Mr. Harvey, excuse me, Mr. Hart, he claims Mrs. Richardson lent him the car so he could check out the Angel Mountain Ski Resort in Angel City, Utah."

"That's bullshit! My aunt wouldn't lend her car to anyone!" And considering why Helen had lured Rod to Granite Springs in the first place, the story was worse than ludicrous.

"Maybe, but only your aunt can clarify the situation, and she isn't available."

"So, it's his word against that of a relative who knew the victim?"

"Do you want to hear the rest of it?" The sheriff's voice had an edge of impatience.

"Go ahead. Maybe it'll get better."

"We found a plastic bag shoved under the front seat. It contained your aunt's jewelry."

"What's his story on that?"

"Claims your aunt wanted him to pawn it. Said she was short of ready cash."

Trevor's jaw dropped. "That's bigger bullshit! That ruby ring and the pearl and diamond necklace were gifts with sentimental value. She'd never part with them. And if Aunt Helen needed money, she'd cash a goddamned check." He ran a hand through his hair. "This guy's got the balls of an elephant. How did he explain the candlesticks and frames? Also destined for the pawn shop?"

"Haven't found them, and he says he never had them. He did, however, have twenty-two hundred dollars in cash on him."

"That's all?" The safe had contained a hell of a lot more than that.

"That's it. He claims Mrs. Richardson told him she had phone calls to make and suggested he amuse himself in town for a few hours. He had a couple of drinks at Marley's Bar and Grill, came home around ten, and decided to leave for Utah. Hart says your aunt was alive and well when she waved goodbye from the doorway."

Trevor's fingers tightened on the receiver and he clenched his jaw. Helen would never have allowed him to leave. The whole story was crap. Unfortunately, he couldn't tell the sheriff why it was crap—not yet. *And why not? Why not come clean? It would nail Halston to the wall.*

Was he silent to protect Vicky? And why do that? She was in this up to her beautiful neck. He had no answers and was pissed his logic had turned in that direction. He shook his head sharply, getting back to business.

"Look, Al, none of that makes sense. He goes to a bar, has a couple of drinks, and then decides to leave in the middle of the night?"

"I think it's a crock, too, but as I said, your aunt isn't here to refute anything he says. His attorney will find enough loopholes to raise reasonable doubt."

"I guess we need more evidence, don't we?"

"We're working on it. I'll let you know if anything turns up."

"All right, I'll see you at the arraignment."

Trevor hung up, unhappy about everything Al

had told him. Halston was covering his tracks with a silly, but plausible story. And there was still the question of why he was returning to Granite Springs.

The front door slammed and footsteps resounded across the foyer. A moment later, Vicky paused in the doorway before entering the study.

"Where have you been?" he asked.

"Walking."

"Walking? Why?"

"Why not? I had a shitty night's sleep and needed to clear my head." She removed her trench coat and draped it over a chair.

"Where did you go?" He didn't like her wandering around the town on her own. She could have used any leftover money, hopped a bus, and been gone like smoke on the wind.

She shrugged. "Nowhere in particular. Just walked. Any news?"

"Arraignment's at three."

"What did the sheriff have to say?"

He gave her the story Rod had spun. A frown marred her forehead.

"It's possible."

"Yeah, and you're a Girl Scout."

She shot him a nasty glance. "I take it you plan on talking to Rod as soon as possible."

"The minutes his ass is back in jail after he leaves the courthouse."

"I'll go with you."

"No."

"Trevor, it doesn't matter how insistent you are; he won't see you without me there."

He had to admit, Vicky was probably right.

"I do the talking. Understood?"

She nodded, turned, picked up her coat, and left the room. His gaze followed her swaying hips with a predictable reaction from his body.

"Dammit!"

****

Vicky sat next to Trevor in the back of the courtroom. Rod entered from a side door, a deputy by his side. He saw her, but was too smooth to acknowledge her presence. He stood next to his lawyer.

"How does your client plead, Mr. James?"

"Not guilty, your Honor."

"Your Honor, the people request the defendant be remanded as a flight risk. When apprehended he was driving the victim's car and had a large amount of her valuable jewelry in his possession," the prosecutor replied.

The public defender jumped in. "Your Honor, why remand? The charge is involuntary manslaughter. The deceased loaned her car to my client. I'd also like to point out he was returning to Granite Springs when pulled over. He heard about Mrs. Richardson's death on the radio."

"And the jewelry, Mr. James?" the Judge Foster said, not looking up from the paperwork in front of him.

"Mrs. Richardson asked my client to pawn it for her somewhere out of town."

"Your Honor, the victim was very well-to-do, and had no reason to pawn her jewels," the prosecutor interjected.

"Save it for the trial gentlemen. Since the defendant has no close ties to the community, and we have a dead body in the equation, bail is set in the amount of $50,000." The judge banged his gavel. "Next case."

Rod was escorted from the room, but his gaze met hers and a corner of his mouth lifted slightly.

"Judge Foster must be senile," Trevor muttered, clasping her elbow with his hand and pulling her to her feet. "Come on, let's get to the jail. I want to hear his story with my own ears."

"He's not going to change it just for you."

The walk from the courthouse to the jail took less than five minutes. It took another fifteen to go through security, and they waited twenty more for Rod to be brought into the visitor's pen. She and Trevor sat at a table on one side of a wire mesh partition, Rod on the other.

Vicky gazed at her brother with a critical eye. He wore his blond hair longer than when she'd last seen him, and although he'd put on weight, something else was different. She couldn't put her finger on it. Maybe it was the look on his face—a combination of fear and connivance. She was certain her presence gave him hope he'd wiggle out of this scrape like he had all the others.

Trevor, his mouth set in grim lines, leaned forward toward the metal grill.

"I don't buy your bullshit story, Halston. What really happened?"

"Who the fuck are you, and why should you care?" Even incarceration couldn't knock the insolent look from his face.

"My name is Trevor Sloane. Helen Richardson was my aunt, and there's no way in hell she'd lend you her car or ask you to pawn jewelry. I want the truth, or so help me I'll choke it out of you."

"I did tell the truth. Sorry, if you don't like it." He turned his gaze onto her. "Nice to see you, sis. You're lookin' good. Why are you here with this bozo?"

"Look, Rod, you've got trouble out the ass. Just tell us what really went down, and maybe you won't spend twenty-five to life in prison."

Rod smirked, but she detected the horror in his eyes the words "twenty-five to life" had wrought. He'd tell, although it would probably take several sessions of hard questions to finally wring it out of him.

A crafty look replaced the smirk. "You want me to talk? Fine. Get me out of here. I'm not saying a goddamned word in this lice-infested zoo." His gaze slid to Trevor. "And I'm not talking to anyone except Vicky."

"If you want out, you'll talk to me," Trevor said, his lip curling in a snarl.

Rod stared for a moment, and then replied, "Bail me out. I'll talk provided Vicky's there. And make it snappy. I don't look good in orange jumpsuits. I also want decent food and a nice, comfortable bed."

"Don't press your luck, Halston. You'll get what I say you get."

Rod shrugged and rose, a bored expression on his face. "Whatever, just do it. And I want a real lawyer."

He signaled a deputy who escorted him through a door into what Vicky assumed was the cellblock. She and Trevor exited the jail.

On the sidewalk, Trevor balled his fists, and said, "This better work. If I don't get anything out of him, he goes right back to the slammer."

"He'll talk eventually. Just let me handle him."

"All right. I'll go arrange bail." He handed her a hundred dollars. "My aunt's car and his clothing are still in police custody. He'll need something to wear. Go get him some clothes. Meet me here in an hour."

She accepted the money and turned, walking away. Rod had better spill his guts tonight, because by tomorrow morning, Granite Springs would be a memory.

****

Rod swaggered through the front door of the house, the self-satisfied smile back on his lips.

"Ah, home sweet home."

Trevor glowered and Vicky wanted to kick him hard. *Arrogant asshole. Always was, always will be.*

"Halston, if you don't tell me what I want to know, you'll be back with your new best buddies in no time.

"Get the stick out of your ass, Sloane. I'll talk tomorrow. Right now, I want a drink, dinner, and a good night's sleep."

Vicky handed him a bag from the thrift store. "Here're some clothes, courtesy of the man who bailed you out. It's not easy to come up with five grand on short notice."

"But he managed it, didn't he?" Rod looked at the logo on the bag. "A thrift shop! What kind of crap did you buy?"

"The kind you deserve," she retorted.

Before he could answer, Rosa came into the foyer.

"*Senor* Sloane, I have dinner..." she stopped with a gasp. "*Senor* Harvey, what are you doing here?"

"Hello, Rosa, what's for dinner?" Rod asked.

"Mr. Harvey will be spending some time with us, Rosa. Give him the smallest room you can find—one with no possible means of escape out the window."

She stared at Trevor with a shocked gaze. "I do not understand. He...he kill the *senora*."

"I can't explain it now. He won't be any extra work for you. Miss Denton will see to his needs."

The housekeeper scowled, but nodded before going upstairs. Rod strolled toward the den, the bag of cheap clothes swinging from his hand.

"Don't forget the chocolate mint on my pillow, Vicky."

She glared at her brother's retreating back, and then followed Rosa. He'd milk the situation until Trevor actually delivered him back to the jail.

My departure might be delayed, but not for long. As soon as he says something that resembles the truth, I'm on the next bus.

Dinner was not the most comfortable of meals. Rosa slammed the food on the table, glaring at Rod with every presentation. Trevor ate silently, and Vicky followed his lead since she had nothing to say either. Her brother enjoyed every moment of the tense meal, smiling, and occasionally winking at her.

The son of a bitch thinks he has it made. She wanted to slap him silly. Her fingers tightened on her fork, and she forced the food past the knot of anger in her throat.

Still silent, Trevor rose and left the room, returning a few minutes later. He tossed an object on the table next to Rod.

"Put this on."

Rod picked it up with a quizzical expression. "What the hell is it?"

"It's an electronic monitoring device worn around the ankle. I don't want you sneaking off under the cover of darkness."

"You've got to be kidding!"

"Do I look like I am? Put it on. Now."

Vicky snickered while Rod glared. "What are you laughing about? He's probably got one for you, too."

Her laughter ceased, and she shot a quick glance at Trevor.

"She didn't kill my aunt. Put it on."

Rod braced his foot against the dining chair next to him and snapped it on. "It hurts. And how am I expected to sleep with this thing on?"

"I don't give a shit if you sleep at all. You represent five thousand dollars of my hard earned cash. I'll be damned if you run leaving me holding the bag. And don't go thinking you can pry it off. The base unit is in my bedroom on the nightstand. Remove it and an alarm is raised."

"Bastard," Rod muttered.

Vicky choked back another laugh. At least that

was one problem solved.

The doorbell rang as Trevor took his seat, but before he could resume eating, angry voices filled the foyer.

Vicky looked up in surprise when Walter and Adam Richardson rushed into the room.

Walter stood with hands clenched by his side. A furious expression darkened his face, and his eyes narrowed into slits as his gaze settled on Rod.

"So, it's true! You bailed the bastard out! What the hell are you thinking!"

Chapter Seven

"Hello, Walt, Adam. I was wondering when you'd be here," Trevor replied, once again tossing his napkin onto the table and rising.

He shot a glance toward Vicky who stared across the table at her brother. Rod, in turn, stared at Walter and Adam with a blank expression. Trevor deduced he'd never seen the men before.

Adam glowered, his face reddening. "Damn right we're here. What is this...this...killer doing out of jail?"

"Let's discuss this in the study."

He left the room followed by the father-son combo. Trevor closed the door and sat behind the desk. He didn't offer either of them a seat.

"Why the hell did you bail him out?" Walter demanded in an angry tone. "Let the son of a bitch rot in jail."

"While his story is bullshit, other aspects of the case intrigue me. For instance, Rosa's ex-con son apparently has the run of the house, and knowing Helen, she paid him for his gardening services out of that stupid cigar box fund," Trevor told them.

"Are you saying he killed Aunt Helen?" Adam asked with a frown.

"I'm saying it's a possibility. Any halfway decent defense attorney will jump on it. Plus, other things can't be explained."

Trevor spent the next fifteen minutes telling the

Richardsons what the police uncovered and the story Rod had related.

"Pawn her jewelry? That's crazy," Walter said.

"Why would Aunt Helen need cash? She never parted with a dollar unless absolutely necessary, and then demanded a receipt. I'm surprised you haven't found a dozen IOUs from me dating back to my college years. This guy is full of it," Adam maintained.

"I agree, but..."

A loud knock interrupted Trevor's reply, and then the study door flew open. An angry Elliot Corwin glared from the threshold before striding toward the desk.

"Are you nuts? I can't believe you bailed the bastard out, or that he's staying here."

Elliot clenched his fists, and for a moment Trevor thought he'd use them. So far, he'd only mentioned Carlos as another possible suspect. He found it interesting that the people who'd last visited his aunt had suddenly put in appearances.

"Relax, Elliot, I have my reasons." He explained his reasoning to Corwin, repeating what he'd told the Richardsons.

"And you believe his story?" Corwin's sandy eyebrows rose. He fastened Trevor with an incredulous gaze.

"No, and tomorrow I'm going to put it under the microscope."

"I want to hear that for myself."

"Me, too," Walter and Adam replied together.

Trevor shook his head. "He refuses to say anything except to me. If he comes up with something useful, I'll tell the sheriff."

"And what prevents him from climbing down the trellis and taking off?" Adam asked.

"I have it covered." He explained about the ankle monitor.

"Where the hell did you get one of those?" Elliot inquired.

"The situation is under control." He eyed all three men. "You three heard about this fast. How did you find out Harvey was here?"

Elliot shifted from foot to foot. "Rosa called. I was with clients all afternoon. She left a message with my receptionist. I didn't read it until a half hour ago. Jail confirmed he'd been bailed out. I called Walt."

"Adam and I were in the car ready to leave for home. Came here instead." Walter ran a hand over his face.

To Trevor's eye, they all looked wary and suspicious. Of the information Halston might possess? Possibly. Hiding information of their own? Probable. He decided to probe.

"You know, from what I've heard, Aunt Helen had a lot of visitors in the last few weeks. I mean, all three of you were here."

"She invited me," Elliot was quick to answer.

"I dropped by to say hello when I was in the area one day," Adam said, sweat popping out on his upper lip.

"In the area?"

"I was on my way home from Boulder. Football game."

"I stopped in on my way to Santa Fe a few weeks ago. What are you getting at?" Walter demanded.

A funny look came over Adam's face, as if he suddenly realized the question wasn't idle conversation. "Yeah, what are you suggesting? Whatever it is, I resent it."

Only Corwin's expression remained passive and calm. "Gentlemen, before this degenerates into a lot of unfortunate things being said, I think we should call it a night. Trevor will get to the bottom of this. I trust he'll keep us informed."

Trevor rose from behind the desk not believing a word the slick-talking lawyer said. "Good idea. I wasn't suggesting anything."

He walked the men to the front door. They each shot him a speculative glance as they left. Alone, he peeked into the dining room. It was empty and the table cleared. Noises from the kitchen told him Rosa was still cleaning up. He pushed open the swinging door and entered. The woman was washing the last of the pots and pans.

"Rosa, I'd like a word with you."

"*Si, senor*." She answered in a flat tone.

"From now on, what happens or is said in this house concerning my aunt or Mr. Harvey is not to be repeated. Is that understood?"

The housekeeper's back went rigid. She didn't turn her head, but nodded. Then she whirled, soapy hands on her hips.

"I am sorry, *senor*, but my anger is great. This man kill *Senora* Richardson, yet you allow the *puerco* into her house. It is not right." Tears gleamed in her eyes.

"It might not be right, but it's necessary. Do I have your word you won't say anything again?"

"I do not understand, but *si*, I will not speak."

"Good. Finish up and go home."

Trevor left the kitchen and headed down the hallway to the den. Through the closed door, he heard the murmur of voices. He clenched his jaw and turned the knob, opening the door with a sharp movement. Vicky and Rod ceased talking and stared.

And what have they been concocting?

****

"Who the hell are they?" Rod asked when the three men disappeared from the dining room.

"Walter and Adam Richardson, Helen's brother-in-law and nephew." Vicky didn't give her brother a chance to reply, but plunged in. "What kind of bullshit story did you tell us? Not even I believe it."

"It's the truth, I swear it."

"That's crap. You wouldn't know the truth if it bit you in the ass."

"Well, it was the best I could come up with on such short notice. Thanks for the heads-up."

Vicky rose, laying her napkin beside her plate. "Let's go into the den. There's more privacy."

"I agree. I think Rosa listens at doors."

In the den, she waited while Rod poured a scotch, shaking her head when he raised the bottle toward her. Something different about him still rankled. Not only was his hair longer, but it fell forward unflatteringly over his brow.

"Why did you contact me?" he asked. "How do you fit into this?"

She reminded him of the Lost Dutchman scam six years ago.

Rod shrugged. "So what? I sorta remember the guy. Why wait all this time?"

"Because his wife knew nothing about it until a few months ago. Her husband had your Harrison alias investigated. The report was in the file. By the way, this will amuse you. Trevor Sloane is a private investigator. Quinn Rafferty was his partner."

A surge of pleasure pumped through her at the stunned expression on her brother's face.

"Quinn Rafferty! Shit! Okay, give it to me. How did this happen?"

Vicky told her brother all she knew. "If Trevor has other information, he isn't sharing at the moment. When did you get my messages?"

"Had my phone turned off for the first one. Didn't get it until later that night."

"What about the others? Did you just ignore the ringing phone?"

"I was driving and didn't take time to answer. When I did and found out Helen was dead, I headed back."

"And you're still sticking with your story?"

He smiled and gulped the scotch. "I am until I can come up with a better one."

Irritation gnawed in her stomach. "Look, dummy, Trevor Sloane is going to want answers that make more sense. He insists Helen would never have lent you her car or asked you to pawn jewelry, considering your being here was all a set up."

"So, why warn me? You knew I'd run. Why not let me be blindsided by Sloane?" He drank the rest of his drink and poured another.

"Because I was caught, too. I'll be damned if you're taking me down for a con I had little to do with. Which reminds me, you only gave me a pittance of what you stole."

Rod laughed, and then sipped the amber liquid. "So that's what this is all about. You're pissed."

She wanted to belt him in his smart mouth.

Her brother made a face. "Don't give me that look. You performed a valuable service by keeping the old boy off balance, but it wasn't worth half or even a third."

"And I find it odd Helen Richardson is just as dead as Cash Marriot—both with their heads bashed in."

"Marriot was an act of God. He had a heart attack, fell, and hit his head. I have no idea how Helen got brained."

Vicky strode over to the bar cart and poured a drink for herself. It was time to change tactics.

"I'm interested in Roger Hart. How did you get arrested?"

"I had some luck romancing a silly middle-aged woman in Chicago. She gave me spending cash, bought me expensive clothes, and even more expensive items easy to pawn. When she left for a couple of days to visit friends in Milwaukee, I grabbed some jewelry and split."

"What alias did you use?"

"I'm not sure. Might have been Rodney Hayworth of the Boston Hayworths."

"Not smart to use the name of a real family, Rod. It's too easy to trace."

He waved a hand and made another face. "Doesn't matter now."

"Where'd you fence the jewelry?"

"The usual guy in Las Vegas. Then, I headed for San Francisco with fifteen grand in my pocket. I set myself up as an investment broker, sat around in the bar at a swanky hotel, and finally latched onto a couple of older people with money to burn."

"I take it you pulled the old double-your-money-in-twenty-four-hours affair." Her stepfather had been an expert at that one.

Rod nodded. "Even spent some coin to have a fake website made: Roger Hart, Investments for a Lifetime. He cuts to the heart of the matter."

"Oh, my God." She couldn't believe people bought this nonsense, but then she also knew they lapped it up. That's what enabled her and Rod to make a living.

"Things were going fine for a while. I paid off old investors with new investor's money. At one time, I had half a million bucks in the till. Then the stock market nose-dived."

"And Ponzi schemes eventually fall apart. Why didn't you cut your losses and get the hell out?"

"I had four more fish on the hook, and thought I could add a few more bucks." He finished his drink and headed for the bar again, weaving slightly.

"In other words, you got greedy. That's your Achilles' heel, Rod. You always want more. You should never have tried a Ponzi. You don't have the talent."

He pouted and stared with a sulky expression. "I

almost made it out of town. Apparently, one investor didn't like his rate of return and had me investigated. The cops showed up as I was leaving for the airport. They booked and fingerprinted me under the name Roger Hart, but before arraignment I got cut loose. I hopped the first bus back to Vegas and tossed all the Roger Hart IDs."

"Did you kill Helen Richardson?" Vicky asked, hoping to catch him off-guard.

"No!"

Before she could ask another question, the den door swung open to reveal Trevor with a determined look on his face. He closed the door behind him and advanced toward the bar cart. He snatched the glass from Rod's hand.

"Buy your own booze. You've taken enough from my aunt."

Rod snorted and curled his lip, then ambled over to slouch on the sofa. Vicky sat in a chair, while Trevor stood, hands fisted by his sides and eyes narrowed.

"All right, you've had your drink and your dinner. Time's up. I want to know what happened, and I want to know now. No more bullshit. Why did you kill Helen?"

Rod rose, yawning and stretching. "All that liquor and food, not to mention the harrowing experience of jail, has left me exhausted. I'm too tired to answer questions tonight."

Trevor's jaw clenched and Vicky suppressed the urge to kick her brother in the shins for his insolent tone.

"You'll talk when I say you'll talk," he replied.

"Let him go," she said. "With that ankle jewelry on, he's not going anywhere."

He looked at her, and then at Rod. "You two concocting a new line of garbage?"

Rod laughed, yawning again. "Could be, Sloane.

See you in the morning."

"And don't try taking off. The further away you are from the base unit, the faster the beeps. It also has a built-in GPS," Trevor warned as Rod left the room.

"What did Walter and Adam want?" she asked.

"An explanation. Elliot joined us."

"What did you say?"

"None of your business. I'm not in the mood to talk. I'll be in the study going through Helen's files. I'll see you in the morning, and if your brother doesn't give me answers, he's back in jail. Tell him that. And don't give me your doe-eyed look. I don't care how beautiful you are, I won't hesitate to turn you over the sheriff either."

He stalked out leaving Vicky alone with conflicting thoughts.

****

After breakfast the following morning, Trevor led a sullen Rod and an apprehensive Vicky into the study. In spite of Trevor's threat to turn her over to the cops, she had chosen to dwell on his comment about her looks while she tossed and turned. Another sleepless night had left her nerves stretched. If Rod didn't come through with something for Trevor to investigate, she'd never get out of here.

Ignore all those warm sensations he provokes. Nothing can come of it, so go while the going's good. Trevor would have his hands full with Rod and never miss her.

The object of her fantasies pulled a second chair in front of the desk before taking his usual seat behind it.

"Both of you sit," he ordered.

Vicky did as told, surveying his face. He looked tired with the lines on his face deeper than yesterday.

Rod slouched in his chair, not bothering to cover his mouth when he yawned. "It's barely nine o'clock. Why get me up so early?"

"Because, I'm an early riser. Sleep well?"

Her brother scowled. "No. This thing around my leg is heavy, and it hurts."

"Like a ball and chain?" Trevor grinned with a malicious glint in his eyes.

"Take it off. You said I only had to wear it at night."

"I lied. Think of it as a fashion statement."

"And that bed is hard."

"That bed is better than you'd get in jail. The room used to be for live-in maids. Still, it's bigger than a cell, which brings me to why you're here. I'm well-rested and ready to listen to your story—again."

"Give me a break, Sloane. You heard it. Nothing's changed. By the way, who's my new lawyer?"

"I'll call one as soon as I get answers."

Vicky leaned toward her brother. "Rod, don't be an asshole. Trevor could help you. Just tell him the truth."

"That's true, Halston. Listen to your sister. If you didn't do it, then you might have information I can use to clear you."

Rod rolled his eyes and went through the same story the sheriff had given them. Trevor didn't interrupt, but listened, taking notes on a large legal pad.

"What's the name of the ski resort again, and where's it located?"

"Big Mountain in Valley High," Rod replied with a wary expression.

"The sheriff faxed your statement to me last night. You told him it was Angel Mountain Ski Resort in Angel City. Wanna try again?"

Vicky glared at her brother. He used to be a

110

much better liar.

"I was going to check out both of them," Rod answered in a smooth voice.

Trevor sent Rod a predatory smile. "I've been through my aunt's recent bank statements. She had over fifty thousand dollars in ready cash. She didn't need to pawn her jewelry."

Rod leaned forward, smiling back. "And maybe she didn't want some nosy nephew to know when she withdrew a lot of money."

Vicky cringed inwardly when Trevor's jaw flexed. She figured Rod wasn't far away from a punch in his wise-assed mouth.

"What did you do with the gold candlesticks and the silver picture frames?" Trevor asked, his voice even.

"What gold candlesticks and silver frames?"

"Gonna play it that way, huh?"

"I have no idea what you're talking about." A muscle twitched beneath Rod's right eye.

She stared hard at her brother's face. *He's lying. I'm sure of it.*

"What did you do with the rest of the money from the safe? Not even you could have spent it."

"Helen gave me a wad of cash from some goofy cigar box in the bottom drawer. Traveling money, she called it. I never even knew she had a safe, and if I did, how would I know the combination?"

Cash Marriott's safe and how she'd obtained the combination flashed through Vicky's mind. *No reason why he couldn't have used the same method.*

Her heart squeezed in her chest. Rod was digging a deeper hole with every word. His story was ridiculous.

As though reading her thoughts, Trevor said, "This fairy tale is silly. My aunt lured you here, did you know that?"

Rod's bravado ceased, replaced with a sullen

expression. "Vicky told me last night."

"Then, you must realize that Helen wouldn't have let a bottom feeder like you out of her sight."

"No need to be insulting," Vicky interjected. If Trevor continued in that tone, Rod wouldn't say a word and her departure would be further delayed.

"Did I ask for your input?" Trevor said with a growl.

"No, but you're getting it anyway." She turned her attention back to Rod. "I'm here because you got greedy six years ago. A week or two was all you needed, but you called me in and stretched it to five. Take a good look at Trevor's face, brother dear. Right now, the only thing preventing him from leaping across that desk, wrapping his hands around your scrawny throat, and squeezing until your eyes pop out, is my presence. If you don't tell him the truth, I'm leaving. You can fend for yourself."

Trevor stared, a gleam of admiration in his eyes. "She's right, Halston. I'd really like to strangle you. Why take the chance I won't?" He leaned forward, speaking in a slow voice. "What...happened?"

Rod licked his lips and swallowed, tossing her a glance before saying, "Okay, you win. That lawyer of hers, Elliot Something had been to dinner a couple of nights before. I knew he was trouble the minute he walked in the door. His whole demeanor said he didn't trust me or believe a word I said."

"Plus, Rosa told me you were eavesdropping at the door, so you knew Elliot Corwin was not your new best friend."

"I considered getting out of town."

"But you wanted a good return on your time," Trevor said.

"Why not? You charge for your time, don't you?" he answered in a droll tone.

"So, why didn't you leave?"

"Helen never mentioned being suspicious, so I

decided to go with the flow. I came downstairs that night for cocktails in the den like usual. When I passed the study, the door was partially open and I overheard Helen on the phone. She said Elliot a couple of times along with the word investments. I figured the game was up and panicked. I ran back upstairs, packed, and then joined her for drinks."

"Did she say anything to you?" Trevor persisted.

"No. But she did act distracted. The dining conversation was pretty sparse. After dessert, she said she had things to do in the study and could I amuse myself? I asked to borrow her car to go to town. She said yes. I went back to my room, rifled some stuff from the jewelry cases, sneaked my bags downstairs to the den, and left by way of the French doors to the terrace."

"Where was Rosa during all of this?"

"In the kitchen banging pots and pans."

This sounded more like Rod to Vicky—living on the edge of panic, but having enough sense to wait a couple of hours before fleeing.

"So, you stole her car and left?" she asked.

"Yeah."

"Why stop at Marley's? You should have been flying down the highway." Trevor's forehead knit into a frown.

"I wanted a drink. I was scared and had no plan on where I'd go. Las Vegas was too obvious. I stayed about an hour, worked out a story, and then left heading for Las Vegas anyway. I was almost to the Utah-Nevada state line when I heard about the murder on the radio. Grand theft auto and theft is one thing, but murder... No way. I came back."

Vicky thought most of it could be true, although if she hadn't left messages and the suggestion of a story line, Rod would have been in Vegas never suspecting a murder charge hung over his head. Her brother fidgeted in his chair, a sure sign he knew more than he was telling. Trevor was right. Stopping at a bar, while a scam collapsed didn't make sense.

"Why didn't you change the license plates," she persisted, taking a different tack.

"I did. Stopped in a small town, found a blue car in a driveway, and stole the plates. Switched them back when I was on my way here."

Why not put Helen's plates on the other car? The question nagged at her. Missing license plates alerted the owner to the theft. *He's still not telling everything.*

"That's better, Halston, but still not good enough. I could drive a semi through the holes. Let's go through this again."

Rod leapt to his feet. "Go to hell, Sloane. I've admitted to stealing the car and the jewelry, but I didn't kill Helen Richardson. If you want a suspect, try that lawyer dude. He was pissed as hell when she told him she wanted to transfer some of her money from him to me. They had one bitching dust-up. Now, if you're finished, I'll be in the den watching TV." He pointed to his ankle. "I won't be going anywhere."

"We'll talk again later."

Rod ran a hand through his hair and sighed. "Whatever."

The casual movement pulled his hair back, and Vicky now recognized why he looked different. She chuckled, the laughter building to an outright crowing.

"What's so damned funny?" her brother demanded. "You'll be next in the hot seat."

"Been there, done that." She still chortled and pointed at his head. "Your hairline's receding. You're going bald!"

Rod's face turned bright red and choking noises erupted from his throat. "Dammit, Vicky, you bitch."

"In a few years, you'll need a toupee," she said

with a gasp. "I know a guy in Los Angeles who does great work with wigs. Sean Connery's a client."

"Go to hell!" Her brother left, slamming the door behind him.

"So, how much was bullshit, and how much was truth?"

Trevor's voice quelled her mirth. She drew a deep breath. "It makes sense. Just like I said, he panicked and took what he could."

He had a thoughtful look on his face as if trying to piece together a puzzle.

"If you're more in the mood now, can you tell me what you said to Walter and Adam last night?"

"Just that there were other suspects. I questioned them a bit."

"You questioned them? Like they were suspects? Boy, do you know how to win friends and influence people."

He waved a hand. "I'll apologize later today."

"Yes, but they aren't going to cooperate with you now. Why should they? Anything they say might be turned over to the sheriff."

Trevor leaned back in the chair, his fingertips rubbing the space between his eyes.

Compassion welled. He looked tired and frustrated. "Headache?"

He nodded. "The funeral home called last night. Aunt Helen's body has been released. Funeral's day after tomorrow. I have to drop off some clothing this morning."

"Can I help in any way?"

"Do you mind taking the clothes?"

"Of course not. Where are they?"

He pointed to a garment bag lying on the sofa in front of the fireplace.

"I'll take it over right away."

She rose from her seat when a discreet knock followed by the study door opening distracted her.

Rosa entered.

"*Senor* Sloane, Sheriff Singleton in here and would like a word with you and the *senorita*."

His eyebrows rose. "Very well, show him in."

"What does he want?" she asked as the housekeeper left.

"Hopefully, he has more information."

"But why talk to me?"

"I have no idea. Maybe the woman in the airport discovered the jewelry was worthless."

She opened her mouth for a pithy retort when the sheriff walked in. The serious look on his face sent her heart racing. Something told her major league trouble was the policeman's partner this morning.

"Al, nice of you to stop by. Any new developments?" Trevor asked. "Have a seat. Can I get you a cup of coffee?"

"No, thanks. I have a couple of questions for the two of you."

Vicky perched on the edge of the chair, her stomach clenching with nerves.

"Why are you lying to me?"

Chapter Eight

Vicky struggled to breathe, the air stopping somewhere between her lungs and throat. *Oh, crap, now what? Did that idiot brother of mine say or do something we don't know about?*

Trevor raised his eyebrows and turned his palms upward, a look of confusion on his face.

"Al, what are you talking about? What lies?"

The sheriff stared, first at her, and then at Trevor. "I can understand why you'd want to talk to the prisoner. After all, the victim was your aunt. That's why I let you have access after the arraignment. So, when I asked the officer in charge of visitors if you'd been there, he said yes, *they* came. I checked the visitor's log, and sure enough, found your name—and Miss Denton's. Why was Miss Denton with you? She hadn't even met Mrs. Richardson. Got my curiosity up, so I pulled the tapes."

Trevor's gaze on the sheriff sharpened, and he cleared his throat. "Tapes?"

"We have both video and audio tapes of all non-attorney visitations."

Shit! What did we say? What did Rod say? For the life of her, Vicky couldn't remember. Even Trevor looked surprised.

"Trevor, that day in the diner you referred to the suspect as Rod. On the tape, you are clearly heard calling him Halston. And the prisoner refers to Miss

Denton, who also uses the name Rod, as sis." He placed his hands on the desk and leaned forward. "Why are you lying? Who is this guy? How does Miss Denton fit in? And why would you put up five thousand dollars bail, and then let the suspect live in your home? I want answers, and I want them now."

Vicky closed her eyes, taking several deep cleansing breaths. They'd been incredibly stupid. Trevor, wanting the truth, had been indiscreet, and she had never considered the possibility of the joint being bugged. Even Rod had let information slip. *When this interview is over, I am so out of here.*

Trevor sighed. "I didn't really lie, Al. I just didn't tell you the whole truth."

"I could arrest you for obstructing an investigation."

"You weren't questioning me in an official capacity, and I was in shock."

The sheriff took the remaining chair, pulling a notebook and pencil from his breast pocket. He flipped the pages, crossed his legs, and sat poised ready to write.

"You're no longer in shock. Consider this an official capacity. Is Rod Halston the prisoner's real name?"

"As far as I know."

The sheriff glanced at Vicky with a raised eyebrow. She nodded. He turned back to Trevor.

"How do you know him?"

"Never met the guy in my life until I saw him at the jail." He fiddled with a pen on the desk.

"Why bail him out?"

"I didn't believe his story and thought he might tell me the truth in more pleasant surroundings."

"Did he?"

Trevor hesitated and drew a five-pointed star on the blotter. "Not completely, but I'm not finished. I'll let him get comfortable, and then pull the rug from under him."

The sheriff glanced at Vicky again. Her stomach tightened. How on earth would she explain her and Rod's relationship or why she was in Granite Springs?

"And how do you fit into this, Miss Denton?"

"Rod is my half-brother."

"And?"

Sheriff Singleton's frown and sharp stare made her stomach clench more. Breakfast sat like a lump.

She folded her hands in her lap, casting her gaze downward. "Mr. Sloane found me in Miami and offered a secretarial job with his aunt."

He turned to Trevor. "Who hired you to find Miss Denton? A client?"

Trevor sighed, dropped the pen, and ran a hand through his hair. "Helen hired me."

"What? Why?"

"Six years ago, Rod Halston flimflammed my uncle. Helen recently discovered it and wanted to bring him to justice. I found him, and my aunt lured him here while I contacted Miss Denton with the offer of employment. I needed someone with knowledge of Halston's habits."

The sheriff wrote quickly in his notebook. "What kind of flimflam and how much money was involved?"

"Helen didn't say. She just said she wanted justice."

"And this happened six years ago? Statute of limitations is probably over on that."

Vicky raised her head and shot a glance at Trevor. She hadn't known. He didn't return her stare, but kept his gaze on Sheriff Singleton.

"I know, but I doubt Halston does."

Anger at being lied to and used by Trevor bubbled in her chest. She recognized the irony. *Why did I take his word for it? I never trust anyone. Damn! It's time to throw Rod under the bus. Maybe a wheel will catch Mr. Private Investigator, too.*

"Sheriff, my brother is a con artist. Always has been. He learned at an early age he could use charm and wit to get money out of people. The fact he was arrested for fraud doesn't surprise me. He has more aliases than the pound has dogs. When Mr. Sloane told me the true nature of my job, I agreed to help. And for the record, Rod has already admitted to theft of the car and jewelry, but I don't believe he's the killer."

Vicky sent a look Trevor's way. He glared back.

Al closed his notebook. "If he's admitted to theft, then I can take him back into custody, and get his bail revoked."

"Not yet," Trevor said leaning forward. "Please, Al, give me a few more days with him. He'll crack. I know it. As Vicky says, he's long on charm, but he's also short on character. I'll get the information out of him."

"Trevor, that's my job," the sheriff replied with a keen look.

"And he won't tell you a thing. He'll stick to his original story." He jerked his chin toward her. "Besides, you only have Vicky's word that he admitted any of this. Nothing's in writing or on tape. His lawyer will fight bail revocation, and he may clam up for the duration."

"Sheriff, I want my brother out of circulation, too. He's an embarrassment. And Trevor believes other people could have done it."

That ought to stick it to him. Let him explain his family for a change.

The officer turned his attention back to Trevor. "Other people? Like who?"

Vicky wanted to laugh as he squirmed in his seat. When the sheriff left, they'd have one hell of an argument.

Trevor spent the following ten minutes explaining, while she thought about the details on how and when she'd leave.

During her walk, she'd cruised through the bus station. The schedule had shown most of the departures were puddle-jumpers to smaller Colorado cities, but three had caught her eye. One left for Denver at ten in the morning. Denver had the easiest access to other forms of transportation, but would also be the first route Trevor investigated. She'd eliminated it.

A noon bus departed for Dallas via Santa Fe. That one had possibilities. Or maybe she should wait for the evening bus leaving at nine for Los Angeles with a stop in Vegas.

She'd feign a headache, refuse dinner, and while Trevor and Rod ate, leave by the terrace doors in the den. It had worked for Rod. The bus station was only ten blocks away. That one made the most sense. It would be morning before anyone realized she was gone. With a new identity, she'd set up shop as a legitimate secretary. *People are so careless and identity theft is so easy.*

The sheriff's voice brought her out of her escape plans. "Why the hell would Walter or Adam want Helen dead?"

"I'm still looking into it. The fact that they both were here in the last few weeks is suspicious," Trevor replied.

"Do you seriously suspect Elliot Corwin?"

"His actions are odd, too. It's just a feeling I have. I don't trust him."

The sheriff shook his head. "I'll check Carlos out, but he's been in town for close to a year. Haven't had any complaints. He's kept his nose clean."

"As far as you know. Any unsolved burglaries on the books? Muggings? Robberies?"

"A few," Sheriff Singleton admitted. "But I have no evidence Carlos is involved in any way. How do you know all of this?"

"I talked to Rosa. She told me about Walt, Adam, and Corwin. Carlos came by asking for back pay. I didn't like his attitude."

The sheriff snapped his notebook shut. "I still think I should take Hart or Halston or whoever he is back into custody. What's to prevent him from walking out the door?"

"He's wearing an ankle bracelet."

"Where did you get that?"

"What does it matter?"

"I'm not sure it's legal for anyone outside of law enforcement to have one." Al sent him a stern look.

"It's activated every night and he's in a room with no outside access."

Sheriff Singleton rose. "All right, you can keep him for now, but I want that damned device on full time. And Miss Denton, don't leave town. I may have more questions for you later. Where's Rosa? I need to talk to her."

"Probably in the kitchen."

He strode across the room and out the door.

As soon as it closed behind him, Trevor snapped, "Nice job! Now, he knows everything. How can I investigate with him asking the same questions? And you managed to make yourself look like Little Mary Sunshine."

"Kinda forgot to mention the statute of limitations on the Dutchman job, didn't you? I should have followed my instincts in Miami and told you to go to hell."

"But your ignorance was my reward."

Biting back a sharp retort, she rose and crossed the room to the sofa. "I'll deliver this to the funeral home. Then, I plan on taking a long walk so I won't kill you. I may not be here for lunch, but Rod makes an excellent dining companion."

She slung the garment bag over her shoulder and left, slamming the door on the way out.

In the kitchen, she ignored the sheriff who lounged at the table nursing a cup of coffee, the notebook open front of him.

"I'm taking this to the funeral home. Is there a car I can borrow?"

"*Si, senorita*, there is a big car and an SUV Carlos uses to run errands." She nodded toward a key rack hanging on the wall by the back door. "The keys are on the board."

"I don't need an SUV, so that leaves the Lincoln. I may not be in for lunch, Rosa. I have some things to do."

"*Si, senorita*."

Vicky left and walked toward the garage. She found the Lincoln Town Car and slid into the front seat, shivering at the coolness of the leather. The engine turned over smoothly. Once she delivered the clothes, she'd have lunch, stop by the bus station, and buy her ticket to freedom.

****

Trevor ripped the page of doodles from the pad on the desk and tossed it into the wastebasket.

Damn Vicky. She'd outmaneuvered him, but he refused to let her off the hook. He had both her and her brother where he wanted them. Halston would eventually crack. When he did, he'd go straight back to jail. And Vicky? He'd have to think on her punishment a while longer.

Maybe I'll tell Al about her involvement with the con, and give him a list of her aliases.

He shook his head. No, he wouldn't do that. His gut instinct told him that in this case, she told the truth. A minor involvement. Nothing more. The con had been her brother's act. *Still no excuse. Think of all the people she fleeced on her own. So, why don't I want to see her in jail? And speaking of jail, how stupid was I not to have realized the room and conversations were being monitored.*

Most jails and prisons did it provided one of the visitors wasn't an attorney, but confronting Halston had swept his usual caution aside. *Never let emotion in. It screws up everything.*

Trevor picked up one of the file folders on the desk and opened it, then closed it again, staring off into space.

Some of Halston's story made sense, but most of it didn't pass muster. The one thing that stood out, however, was the part about Helen telling Corwin she planned on investing with Rod. It corroborated what Corwin had said earlier. Why bring up something like that? Why put Corwin on guard?

Why do I think he was on guard? Is there something funny going on with Aunt Helen's portfolio?

He riffled through the stack of folders until finding the one containing her most recent financial and bank statements. It showed nothing out of the ordinary. The next several folders didn't produce anything suspicious either.

Am I letting my dislike interfere with my judgment? Maybe Aunt Helen wanted to pull his chain. Let him know he wasn't the only investment game in town.

The recent economic slide had hit everyone hard, even the rich. So, a downturn in her investments shouldn't send up a red flag. *Unless, of course, the dip was more than the average decline. And I'm assuming she was suspicious of something.*

A light knock on the door interrupted his train of thought. "Come in."

Rosa poked her head in. "*Senor* Sloane, do you want to eat lunch in the dining room?"

Trevor looked at his watch. It was almost noon.

"Where's Mr. Harvey?"

She sniffed and curled her lip. "He is in the den. The TV is on, but he is asleep on the sofa."

"Has Miss Denton come back yet?"

"No, *senor*, but she say she might not be in for lunch when she leave."

"In that case, we'll eat in the kitchen. Let me be the one to wake Sleeping Beauty."

Rosa left, and he called the funeral home. The receptionist confirmed Vicky had dropped off the clothing over an hour ago. An uneasy feeling crawled down his back. He had visions of her tooling down the highway never to be seen again. No, she wouldn't call attention to herself by ignoring the sheriff's warning not to leave town. Shame, he'd miss her conversation. He shrugged. If nothing else, he'd interrogate Halston again.

Trevor went upstairs to wash and make sure the base unit for the ankle bracelet was turned on. He carried it into the study, and then headed for the den.

Halston lay sprawled on the sofa with *Who Wants To Be A Millionaire* blaring from the television. He found the remote, turned the tube off, and eyed his houseguest. Disgusted, he kicked the ankle bracelet. Halston jerked awake.

"Ow! That hurt."

"Like I care. Get up. Lunch is ready."

He sat up and ran a hand through his untidy blond hair. "Why can't I take this thing off during the day?"

"Because I don't trust you. I've decided it'll be active twenty-four-seven, so don't get any ideas about going anywhere."

Halston glared and sulked. "Does this mean I can't even go for a walk?"

"You can walk all you want on the grounds. Go too far and it sends out an alarm. A loud one, too."

"What's for lunch?" his captive said, rising and stretching.

"I have no idea, but Rosa tends to keep it simple, which is fine with me."

Lunch consisted of vegetable soup, ham sandwiches, and a salad. Trevor questioned Halston, but got nothing in reply. He'd clammed up. Finished eating, Trevor returned to the study and Helen's files. He assumed Rod had gone back to the TV. The base unit beeped in a slow, rhythmic pattern.

****

Vicky descended the staircase at seven-forty with her stomach quivering. Her bags, packed and ready to go, sat inside the door to her room. In view of her last escape attempt, she had to make this act perfect. Trevor and Rod should already be in the den for cocktails. She slowed her sweeping stride and walked in.

Rod lounged in a chair pouting, a glass in his hand. Trevor stood near the fireplace scowling and sipping a martini.

"You're late," Rod said. "Where have you been all day?"

"I went out for some fresh air."

"Glad one of us could. Why didn't you take me?" he whined.

"She just said she wanted *fresh* air. Get you something to drink?" Trevor asked her.

"A short scotch on the rocks will do." She sat heavily on one end of the sofa, sighing and rubbing her fingers over her forehead.

"What's wrong with you?" her brother inquired.

"Headache."

"I thought fresh air helped that kind of thing."

"Well, it didn't. That's why I went out in the first place. Thank you," she said to Trevor when he handed her a glass.

"Did you take something for it?" he asked with a

concerned look.

She hardened her heart at his expression, determined not to be distracted from her goal of blowing this burg.

"Several extra strength aspirins." She gulped the liquor. "Didn't work. I may be working on a full-blown migraine."

Rod's eyebrows rose. "Since when do you have those?"

"I've always had them, but you never noticed. You never notice anything unless it concerns you. They're tension related, and the last few days have been tense."

"I don't see what you're complaining about. You don't have to wear this damned uncomfortable thing around your ankle."

"If you hadn't been an idiot, you wouldn't either," she snapped back.

"Don't preach, Vicky. Kinda looks like you got caught this time, too, so lay off."

She brushed her hand over her brow again. Rod unwittingly played into her plans.

"At least, I'm not on a wanted poster anywhere. Even if you get out of this, I'm sure the sheriff will notify the San Francisco police that he has Roger Hart in custody."

Rod jumped to his feet, his finger pointed in her direction. "I said, lay off!"

"My, what a loving family," Trevor said, a malicious smile on his lips. "I heard the two of you practically came to blows in the jungle."

"Leave Guatemala out of this," she retorted.

"What the hell did Alex and Quinn tell you?" Rod demanded. He freshened his drink before resuming his seat.

"Let's see, Quinn called you an effeminate weenie, and I believe Alex's exact words were...he's a fucking toad."

Vicky laughed. "Did she also tell you about her revenge?"

"Shut up!"

Trevor grinned. "Yeah. I'll bet you walked funny for days."

"It hurt." Rod drained his glass.

"I think that was the whole idea. You underestimated her. Served you right," she replied, amused.

"Wipe that smirk off your face. There's nothing funny about taking a knee to the nuts." Her brother's voice had risen, and his face took on a reddish hue.

Vicky finished her drink rubbing her forehead a third time, then closed her eyes and caught her lower lip between her teeth.

She set the glass on the table and stood, making sure to wobble ever so slightly. "I'm sorry, but I really don't feel well. All this arguing is making my head pound worse. I think I'll just call it a night."

"No dinner?" Trevor asked shooting her another concerned glance.

She shook her head. "No, I'm a little sick to my stomach, too. I'll take a few more aspirins and go to bed. If I'm not better by tomorrow, I'll see a doctor. Goodnight."

Vicky walked from the room, slowly climbed the stairs, and closed her bedroom door with a soft click. Inside, she sprang into action, putting on the trench coat, and making a final check of the room to see if she'd missed anything. She hadn't. The room was as neat as when she'd first entered.

She sat on the edge of the bed waiting for the minutes to pass. Rosa served dinner at eight o'clock. By eight-fifteen, the men would be eating and the housekeeper busy in the kitchen. Timing was everything. The only place she ran the risk of being seen was at the foot of the steps and from the kitchen door. She glanced at her watch. Another five minutes.

Rising, she crossed the room and flipped off the overhead light switch, then eased the door open, tiptoeing down the hallway. The murmur of voices along with the clink of silverware drifted up the staircase. Now was the time.

She slipped back down the corridor, slung her purse over her shoulder, grabbed the bags, and closed the bedroom door behind her. Walking softly, she crept down the steps.

Light from the dining room spilled into the foyer, but neither man was visible. The conversation was predictable with Trevor needling her brother, and Rod responding in a raised voice.

Vicky turned down the hall toward the den. Through the open kitchen door, Rosa stood washing dishes at the sink, the gush of water masking any noise her footsteps made on the hardwood floor. With a sigh of relief, she gained the safety of the den, and hurried toward the French doors. They opened on silent hinges. She slid through and headed around the house to the driveway where the handle to the wheeled suitcase came out. Balancing the second smaller bag on top, she set a fast pace to the street. She'd make her bus with time to spare. With any luck, no one would discover her missing until morning.

And by that time, I'll be home free.

****

Trevor forked the last bite of blueberry pie into his mouth. Dinner had not been pleasant. With every question asked of Halston, he'd received a snide reply, and then he'd resorted to snide comments of his own.

His eyes strayed to Vicky's empty chair, and he wondered if she'd feigned the headache to avoid her brother. Not that he'd blame her. But she hadn't looked well when she'd left the room with an unsteady gait.

He folded his napkin, laid it beside his plate, and stood. He didn't want to spend any more time than necessary in Halston's company either. An hour was long enough, but followed his so-called guest into the den anyway. Rod eyed the bar cart and homed in on it, pouring a generous portion of scotch. Maybe if he drank enough, the liquor would loosen his tongue. Rosa came in to gather the used glasses from earlier.

"Rosa, will you do me a favor and check on Miss Denton? See if she needs anything."

"*Si, Senor* Sloane." She left the room.

"The only thing my sister needs is the stick pulled out of her ass," Rod commented, sipping his drink.

"Must gall you to know she has more brains in her little finger than you do in your whole body. I'll bet in the long run, she banked more money over the years than you."

"Vicky has no flair."

"Vicky is careful. She analyzes what can go wrong, and considers the details. She told me your father taught her that." He found defending her bizarre.

"Harry babbled about a lot of things," Rod said with a shrug.

"I have the feeling she never underestimated a mark in her life," he replied, thinking of Alex and Quinn. "And if she did, knew when to cut her loses and run."

"Her style isn't mine."

Trevor strolled over to the bar and poured a small drink for himself.

"I still can't figure out why you'd take the chance of Helen discovering her jewelry was gone, and spend over an hour in Marley's."

"I told you already. Just drop it."

"Vegas was the first place Helen would look."

"Maybe, maybe not. I'm not talking any more, Sloane, so shut up." Halston guzzled more liquor.

Trevor clenched his jaw, resisting the urge to smack the little bastard in the mouth. He wished he could tighten the ankle bracelet, causing more discomfort.

He turned his attention to the doorway as Rosa rushed in.

"*Senor* Sloane, Miss Denton is gone."

Halston choked on his scotch. "What!"

"Are you sure?" he asked.

"*Si*, she is not in bed and her suitcases are gone."

"That bitch! She took off and left me to face the music alone!" Rod, his blue eyes dark with anger, threw his glass against the fireplace where it shattered.

Rosa screamed and flinched. Trevor grabbed Halston by the collar, tossing him onto the sofa.

"That glass was Venetian. My aunt bought it twenty years ago while in Italy."

"Who gives a shit! Vicky's gone, damn her."

"Rosa, get Mr. Harvey the broom and dustpan. He'll clean up the mess."

The housekeeper fled while he took off for the garage, breathing a sigh of relief all the cars were there. At least she had the brains not to steal one. He ran back to the house. Halston was sweeping up the glass, a sullen expression on his face while Rosa glared from a few feet away, arms crossed over her chest.

Trevor, tired of dealing with the man, entered the study. When had she split? During dinner, no doubt. Dammit. He needed to find her and haul her back. Had she called a cab to meet her at the foot of the driveway? A quick glance at his watch showed nine-twenty, which gave her over an hour's head start. Where would she go? The bus station? He didn't know if a bus was due in or out at this time of night. *But I'll bet she did. A walk to clear her head, my ass!*

He strode into the foyer intent on driving the Lincoln around town looking for her, and then stopped. Why chase her down? The sheriff had explicitly told her not to leave. All he had to do was notify Al. He'd find her and at the very least, she and her brother could compare matching ankle bracelets.

He pulled his cell from his pocket, ready to dial, when the front door opened and Vicky, complete with suitcases, walked in. She dropped her bags and stared at Trevor.

"Welcome back," he drawled. "Miss your bus?"

She didn't answer, but walked into the study where she took off her coat, draping it over the arm of the sofa. Trevor followed.

"I was all set to go. Had my ticket. Had my credit and ATM cards back. I even hid out in the john until the last minute in case you came looking for me. There I stood, ready to board, when I walked away. I couldn't do it. I couldn't leave you in the lurch to deal with Rod and this whole mess. I retrieved my bags and called a cab."

For reasons he couldn't identify, his heart lifted. She'd been gone, damn near free, and had come back—to him. He closed the door.

"Sit down. No need to let your brother know you're back yet."

She smiled and sat on the sofa. "What was his reaction?"

"Fury."

"I can imagine. How did you know I was gone?"

"I was worried and sent Rosa to check. I was about to call Al Singleton and have him haul you in."

"I can't believe I came back. I must be going senile," she muttered.

"I think you have a conscience."

"I think I'm a sap." She closed her eyes, weariness stamped on her face.

A slow heat burned in the pit of his stomach, radiating outward until engulfing his body. His breath quickened, and before he stopped to think, strode toward her. He grasped her shoulders and pulled her upright into his arms. Trevor didn't hesitate, but covered her lips with his.

The burning sensations exploded into a full blown fire. Her lips parted, and he tasted the sweetness of her tongue. His heart hammered in his ears. He tightened his arms when she moaned deep in her throat. His hand slipped beneath her sweater to caress her breast. Even through her bra, he felt the erect nipple.

Her arms snaked around his neck, her fingers tangling in his hair. When she let her head fall back exposing her white throat, he took advantage of the opportunity to nibble the delicate tendon to her collarbone.

She gasped, and while the temptation to throw her on the sofa was strong, he was also cognizant of where they were and of Halston just down the hall. He backed away.

Vicky stared with glazed eyes, trembling from head to foot. He wanted her—bad—but it was the wrong place and certainly the wrong time.

He ran his thumb down the line of her jaw, and then kissed her chin.

"Go to bed, Vicky. We'll talk tomorrow."

She said nothing, but nodded, picked up her coat, and exited. In the foyer, he retrieved her suitcases carrying them upstairs to her room. She turned, staring with wide, questioning eyes.

He leaned down, kissed her parted mouth again,

and said, "Goodnight, and thanks for coming home."

Vicky nodded again. He turned and left the room. Behind him, the door closed softly.

Trevor entered his room and stood listening to the silence. *What the hell just happened?*

Chapter Nine

Vicky opened her eyes, and then closed them again against the glare of the sun streaming through the turret windows. She rolled over, hugging a pillow to her chest, and burrowed further under the covers before daring to crack her eyelids again. She lifted a corner of the comforter and squinted at the clock on the nightstand. Eight-thirty? Surely, she hadn't slept for eleven hours.

But she had. It was her first good night's sleep since arriving in Granite Springs. Dazed from Trevor's unexpected, but not unwanted kiss, Vicky had crawled into bed, not daring to think about it. Now, in the light of day, she did.

Unable to banish Trevor from her mind as she'd waited for her bus, a thousand questions pummeled her brain. In the end, as she hurried from the smelly restroom, one final question lingered...would he miss her? She hesitated. *Will he miss me as much as I'll miss him?*

Vicky rolled onto her back, still clutching the pillow. He could have told the sheriff the truth, but didn't. She wondered why.

She could no longer ignore the burning, the deep gnawing inside her every time they came into physical contact. She'd welcomed his lips and his arms. The smoldering heat had erupted into fire. His hand on her breast fanned the flames, and she'd wanted him—needed him—like a drowning man needed a life preserver. His arms represented a safe haven from all the fears of the world.

She, Victoria Denton, who neither wanted nor needed any man, now wanted and needed this one. The kiss last night had shattered the carefully crafted shell in place for years.

Never get involved with a mark. And never, under any circumstances, fall for him.

She squeezed the pillow and bit her lips. *Is that what's happening? Am I falling for Trevor Sloane? I must be. Why else would I have come back?*

Or maybe, she of all people was confusing lust with love. Vicky had no idea. She'd never been in love, had never allowed it to happen.

Thanks for coming home, he'd said last night. Home. It sounded comforting. It spoke of permanence. It implied a sense of belonging.

Her stomach grumbled reminding her she hadn't eaten since a hurried lunch at Marley's Bar and Grill yesterday. Sighing, she threw back the covers, and tossing the pillow aside, headed for the bathroom.

Showered and dressed, she paused at the top of the stairs, and then turned toward Trevor's room. The door stood open and she entered. The room had the same layout as hers, but while she slept with the colors of summer, Trevor made do with the light greens of spring.

The room was neat with nothing out of place. Even the comforter had been pulled up over the sheets. She liked neatness in a man. Her stepfather and Rod had been pigs.

Leaving, Vicky descended the staircase. The study door was closed, so she aimed for the dining room, hoping breakfast was still available.

It was. She filled a plate, poured a cup of coffee, and pulled out a chair. Rosa appeared wiping her hands on a dishtowel.

"Good morning, *Senorita* Denton. Did you have a good sleep?"

The woman had a questioning look in her eyes, probably curious as to why she'd bolted. Vicky refused to satisfy her curiosity.

"Wonderful, thank you. Sorry, I'm late this morning. Thank you for holding breakfast."

"*Senor* Sloane said you would be hungry. When you are finish, I will clean up. He say *Senor* Harvey can do without if he is not up by nine."

She laughed. Rod up before nine? Preposterous.

"I won't take long, Rosa. Go ahead and start. Just leave the coffee, please."

The housekeeper smiled, nodded, and whipped away a couple of containers from the chafing dishes on the sideboard.

Vicky forked fluffy scrambled eggs into her mouth and made the decision to help Trevor, although how, she didn't know. Rod wasn't being cooperative. Maybe she could assist. It was her job to be convincing and not even her brother was immune to her persuasion. Plus, Trevor hadn't been the most diplomatic of people with Elliot, Walt or Adam.

She pushed her plate away and sipped at a second cup of coffee, an idea forming in her mind.

****

Trevor sat behind the desk, flipping through an open folder in front of him, not seeing what was there. He'd tossed and turned all night, trying to forget the taste and feel of Victoria Denton. It had been an exercise in futility. Her scent encircled his head, clinging as though magnetized. He had no idea what time he'd drifted off, but had risen, tired and confused.

Why did I do it? He had no answer. He never did things on impulse, but kissing her seemed natural. His hormones had leaped from hot and bothered directly to insane desire. It was a sensation not experienced in a long time, and he wasn't sure how to handle it.

Strange, when she'd tried to charm him at the airport, he'd laughed it off, been immune, but now, when she no longer tried to use her obvious attributes, he bit like a hungry fish.

She was still a great actress—the fake headache crap from last night proved that. He'd swallowed the bait, even been concerned. If Rosa hadn't checked, her disappearance wouldn't have been discovered until morning. Hell, Halston, who must have seen the act before, had bought it. Yet, he'd wanted her back, and not necessarily because she'd outsmarted him.

I want her. I want to strip her naked, touch her, kiss her, and bury myself deep inside. I want to stroke that soft skin until she's sobbing and begging for me.

Even thinking about it tightened his groin and made him twitch. He shifted in his chair and slapped the file closed.

Dammit! Quit thinking about her. I have the main suspect living under my roof. Go grill Halston again. He knows a lot more than he's telling.

Trevor grabbed a notepad, making a list of questions to throw at Vicky's brother when his cell rang. Caller ID showed Marylou was on the other end.

"About time," he said with a growl.

"Well, somebody woke up on the wrong side of the bed this morning, didn't they?"

"Never mind my sleeping habits. What have you got?"

"It's been my experience that when men wake up grumpy and out of sorts, it's because they aren't getting any."

His irritation deepened when she ignored his question.

"Marylou, if you weren't such a close friend and a damned good operative, I'd have canned your ass long ago. Now, cut the bullshit. What do you have?"

She laughed. "All right, all right, don't have a stroke." Papers riffled over the phone. "I got back the preliminaries on the names you gave me. Nothing's detailed. I'm still searching."

"Just give me what you've got."

"Okay, Elliot Corwin is pretty much what he seems—a successful attorney with no blips on his record with the bar. He was arrested for DUI five years ago, did some community service, and has been clean ever since."

Damn, this wasn't what he wanted to hear. "So, he's clean on the lawyer side. What about the investment angle?"

"Everything was fine until six or seven years ago when he was sued by a client in Salt Lake City."

Finally, meat and potatoes. "For what?"

"I'm still digging, but apparently the investor needed money and tried to cash out some of his investments only to find the reality was not what Corwin's report claimed."

"He doctored the figures?" *Now we're getting somewhere.*

"Corwin said the reports were accurate, but the fund had gone down in the last two or three months, and the next report would have shown the decline."

"Damn, perfectly plausible explanation. What happened?"

"They settled. Corwin paid the man half of what he'd lost in exchange for his silence. Needless to say, the client pulled the rest of his portfolio."

"Any idea which funds or stocks were involved?"

"Not yet."

Trevor scribbled notes wondering if they were the same ones his aunt had in her portfolio.

"What about Walter and Adam Richardson? Get

anything on them?"

"Walter is nearing retirement and spending less and less time at the office in Mineral City. Turned the actual running of the company over to Adam several months ago. He's staying on in a transitional role. Rumor has it he's leaving at the end of the year." She paused, and then said, "He recently forked over a huge down payment on a condo in—get this—Los Angeles."

"What? Why the hell would he retire to California? It's expensive, congested, and not retirement heaven right now."

"I don't know, but he's in the process of buying a two thousand square foot condo in Brentwood."

"How big a down payment?"

"Three hundred grand."

Trevor dropped his pencil. *What the hell is going on?* "Three hundred thousand dollars? How much was this place?"

"According to the real estate agent, he talked the desperate-to-leave California owners down to one mil."

"That's a bargain basement price for a place that big in Brentwood."

"The owner was about to go into foreclosure. It was sell or else."

"So, he's still going to need a loan of seven hundred thousand to close the deal."

"And he's been stalling the paperwork. My guess is to buy time. He can't get a loan that big and needs an outside donor."

"I'd guess the same."

Trevor's suspicions shot into the stratosphere. If Walt needed money to close the deal, who else would he ask but his sister-in-law? And if she refused... But would that lead to murder? Something didn't sound right.

"Marylou, dig deeper into this. Why would

Walter and his wife, Marge, retire to California? Marge would hate it. And what about the mortgage? Taxes and insurance will guarantee a sky high monthly payment even with a good interest rate. He must have a hell of an investment plan. See if he's one of Corwin's clients."

"Got it. By the way, all this has taken place in the past two months."

The same time he started showing up here. "Got anything on Adam Richardson?"

Marylou cleared her throat. "Yeah, he's an asshole, if you'll pardon my French."

"I know. In what ways?"

"He's got a reputation in Mineral City as a womanizer. Plus he's garnered three DUI arrests in the past three years, but wiggled out of all of them. He's got one hell of a good lawyer."

"Name's not Corwin, by any chance," Trevor asked in a hopeful tone.

"No. His mouthpiece's name is Hardy." She paused as more papers being shuffled came over the phone. "Adam Richardson is also in deep personal debt. He recently bought a condo in Vail, and signed the papers on a beach house in Miami last winter. He drives a Hummer 2 in Mineral Springs, but six months ago purchased a Porsche to troll for women in South Florida. He's living very high on the hog."

Adam flashing money wasn't any surprise. "How high?"

"He charges all the law allows and then some, on the corporate credit card, plus last January, he negotiated a huge bonus for himself. And, you're going to like this—he is currently fighting a personal lawsuit brought by a woman who says he raped her."

Trevor sat back in astonishment. "Rape? Are you serious?"

"Rape and assault. I don't have all the particulars yet, but the charge was filed two months ago. He's claiming it was consensual rough sex."

"Oh, brother," he muttered, writing fast.

Lawyer fees must be skyrocketing. Would he have had the nerve to ask Helen for money? Helen, who didn't like Adam in the first place, forking over God knew how many bucks to keep him out of jail on a rape charge? No way in hell. And if she told her nephew to go to hell... He remembered his cousin's short fuse, and even visualized the poker in his hand.

"And for the last nail in this suspicious coffin," Marylou said. "Richardson Mining, a subsidiary of Rocky Mountain Mineral Company is not doing so hot. It's underperforming on all levels. I'd say Walter's lost interest, and Adam's a jerkoff who doesn't have an ounce of business sense."

This news didn't surprise him in the least either. "What's the head office's take on this?"

"Mum at the moment, but I'll find a way in."

If Rocky Mountain Mineral shut down Richardson Mining or fired Adam, his slick cousin would be out of luck. Maybe he came to Helen asking to help save the company. And if she said no... He placed another black mark next to Adam's name. He hated to admit it, but Rod Halston might be innocent of murder. *Always look to family first. They have the most to gain.*

"Marylou, drop everything and get on this. I need results in a few days."

"Drop everything? I have two divorces, an insurance fraud, a runaway, and more skip traces than I can count. Who's going to take up the slack?"

"Put Bob or Rudy on them," he replied with a trace of impatience in his voice. "And let Pam investigate some of the skips."

"Pam is already doing more than her fair share. She comes into the office at six and doesn't leave until nine. Bob is threatening to quit. He hasn't seen his wife and kids in weeks. I'm not sure, but I think Rudy is living in his cubicle. There's way too much for three people to handle, and I'm not counting Pam who's doing this because she's a nice person."

Trevor ran a hand through his hair. Damn, a year ago, he was wishing for increased business.

"Marylou, I promise I'll get on it as soon as I can. Put up a notice on our website for resumes. Now, e-mail all these reports to me ASAP, and keep digging. There's got to be more, especially on Corwin."

His hassled operative sighed. "I'll do my best."

He hung up and rubbed his temples. No sleep and bad news made his head ache. Someone knocked, and then opened the door. Vicky stood hesitating on the threshold. Marylou's reports disappeared from his mind, replaced by memories of last night.

His gaze swept her from head to foot. Her blonde hair hung in soft waves past her shoulders. Today, she'd dressed in jeans, tight in all the right places, and wore a bright purple, long-sleeved t-shirt, the material clinging to her torso, emphasizing her breasts. This was the first time he'd seen her in truly casual clothes. She looked sexier than when dolled up.

The sensations his body had experienced the night before returned. He felt like a high school geek about to ask the homecoming queen on a date knowing he'd get shot down in flames. It made him vulnerable, and he didn't like being vulnerable.

Her blue eyes held wariness even though her face remained impassive. "May I come in?"

Trevor cleared his throat, determined to keep their conversation impersonal. "By all means. Did you get a good night's sleep?"

Smiling, she advanced to the desk and took a seat in front of him. "Yes, thank you. Must be the clean mountain air."

"Did you have breakfast?"

She nodded. "I just finished." She fidgeted for a moment and licked her lips, an action that had him squirming in his chair. "I want to talk to you about last night."

"I'm not going to apologize, if that's what you're thinking," he began when she held up a hand.

"I'm not asking for one. We can discuss that later. Rod is withholding information."

"I know. I intend to turn up the heat. He's not got much substance. He'll crack like an egg."

She shook her head and leaned forward. "Not for you, he won't. Look, he robbed your aunt, but he didn't kill her. I'd stake my life on that. But something else happened that night. Something he's not going to part with unless he gets compensation."

"Like what?"

"Removal of the bracelet, you letting him go, or dropping the charges."

He inhaled a deep breath, not sure what she was asking. "The chances of any of that happening are slim and none. What are you getting at?"

"I know my brother, his weaknesses and fears. I saved his bacon on more than one occasion. Let me talk to him some more. I can push his buttons, and then give him a few days of boredom. By then, he'd do anything to get out of this house."

"Including lie." He didn't want to give Halston a few days of rest and relaxation at his aunt's expense.

"When it suits him, Rod will tell the truth."

"And you think you can accomplish this?"

"I know I can." She sat back and hesitated. "Are you investigating the lawyer, and your uncle and cousin?"

"Yes."

"I can help there, too."

"How?"

She smiled, those kissable lips widening across her face. "You all but accused them of being suspects. They won't talk to you now. But, given the right opportunity, they may to me."

"Why would they do that?" The possibility intrigued him. He *had* antagonized the men.

"Because as far as they're concerned, I'm a neutral third party—the secretary with no axe to grind. They don't know about my relationship with Rod and won't as long as the sheriff doesn't say anything."

"He won't."

"Trevor, I can do this. I've invited confidences all my life. It's how I made my living. Have you found out anything in your investigation?"

He hesitated, unsure if this was the right thing to do. Could he put Vicky in a position of having to get close to Adam? Adam with the rape and assault charge hanging over his head.

"I don't know..."

"Yes, you do. I see it in your eyes. You know this is the only way. Now, is there anything in the reports I can use?"

He caved. He didn't like using her, but knew the Richardsons and Corwin wouldn't open up to him. He turned to the computer and pulled up his e-mail until finding Marylou's message with the attachments he'd requested. With a decisive click of the mouse, he printed, handing them to Vicky.

"Here. Not too pretty, are they?"

She rose and walked to the sofa, reading. He also stood, strolling over to gaze out the window. The morning sun had disappeared under a light overcast. A chill swept through the old sashes. Snow wasn't far away, if not in the valley, then in the mountains.

"Assault and rape?" she asked. "Does your cousin have a temper?"

"Yes. He's learned to keep it in check most of the

time."

"And your uncle wants to live the good life in Southern California. Is that unusual?"

"Not the good life part, but Los Angeles, yeah."

"Have your office check out Walter's trips to Southern California over the last year or so—where he stayed, where he dined, that sort of thing. Follow the paper trail. I'll bet he wasn't dining alone."

"Another woman?"

Her eyebrows rose in a mocking look. "Isn't there always?" She stood and walked back toward him. "Okay, no time like the present. The funeral's tomorrow, so I imagine everybody's in town, but I need you to make sure. Call them. Give them a song and dance about meeting early at the funeral home for a family moment of meditation or something."

"And then what?"

"Just make the calls."

He shrugged and did as she asked, while she paced the room, her forehead furrowed.

He finished and hung up. "Corwin and Adam are still in town, but Walter's in Mineral Springs to pick up Marge. They're due back later tonight. What's your idea?"

"We'll go to dinner at the steakhouse. Corwin might not be there, but my guess is Adam will. You said he likes good food."

"What will you do?"

She told him. He didn't like it, not one bit, and argued with her. Vicky stood firm.

"I know what I'm doing. I can handle myself."

"I don't like it. I don't like leaving you alone with an accused rapist."

****

Vicky descended the stair case at seven-forty-five wearing the low-cut black cocktail dress she'd worn when first meeting Trevor. A double strand of pearls graced her throat. Semi-precious gems glittered in her ears and on her wrist. All had come from Helen's jewelry boxes. The silver fox stole settled around her shoulders.

Trevor stood at the bottom of the steps, his jaw unhinged and his eyes wide. She let her hand rest on the balustrade as she slowed her pace allowing him to take in the full effect. His eyes darkened and her stomach tightened in response.

"You look fabulous, too good for Adam Richardson. Where'd you get the fur?"

"From your aunt's closet. I also borrowed her jewels."

"Oh?" A frown marred his brow, and a strange expression flitted across his face.

"Borrowed is the operative word. Your cousin is easily impressed. Furs and jewels are impressive."

"What if he recognizes them?"

"He's a man. All he'll see is me in them. Trust me on this. Where's Rod?"

Her brother had been so relieved to find her back he'd almost done the impossible—hug her. She'd let him stew for another day, and then hammer away, threatening departure again if necessary.

Trevor grinned. "In the den sulking. I called Al and said we'd be out for a while tonight, so he sent over a deputy to keep an eye on him and the monitor. Your brother isn't a happy camper. He didn't like the *pollo con arroz* Rosa made for dinner or eating it in the kitchen."

Vicky laughed remembering his bitching about the food in Guatemala. "He'll get over it. Did you eat, too?"

His grin faded. "Yeah, but I'm still not happy about leaving you with Adam."

Vicky finished her walk down the staircase, and reached up to pat his cheek. "I'll be fine. Now, shall we go?"

The ride to Campbell's took less than ten minutes. When they walked in heads turned as she wound her way into the bar. Trevor chose a small table in the center of the area. She sat, looking around before making eye contact with Adam perched on a stool at the end of the bar.

"He's here," she said in a low voice.

"Can't see him. He's behind me. What's he doing?"

"At the moment, ogling me and guzzling a glass of something."

"That would be bourbon, and I don't like the ogling part," he said. "I want to hit him."

A waitress stopped by and they ordered—a martini for her and scotch for him. Alone again, she gazed over Trevor's shoulder toward Adam. He smiled and raised his glass in a salute. She nodded in reply.

"You just smiled. Why?" Trevor's voice had a hard edge.

"To show how friendly I am."

"Don't be too friendly."

"It's all part of the game, and I've done it a thousand times before. Now, try to act natural."

He scowled. "Natural would be me beating the crap out of him if he lays a hand on you."

She loosened the stole, allowing it to slip further down her upper arms and reveal more skin. Another glance at Adam showed him still smiling and gazing at her chest with hooded eyes. The bait dangled and the fish nibbled.

Vicky opened her evening bag removing her lipstick and compact. In the mirror, she daubed at her perfectly pinked lips, and then adjusted a curl in the topknot on the crown of her head.

Primping and preening, she allowed her gaze to drift frequently to the man at the bar. His captivated stare urged her on. She stifled a laugh at Adam's reaction when she stroked a perfume wand in her cleavage. He choked on his drink and ran a hand through his hair, then licked his lips. She could almost see the sweat beading on his forehead.

This is going to be a piece of cake. His tongue is practically dragging on the bar.

"Why the smug look?" Trevor's brows drew together. "What's he doing?"

"Drooling."

Their drinks arrived. She sipped. He gulped half his scotch and drummed his fingers on the table top.

Vicky leaned forward, and said in a low tone, "Do you remember your part?"

"Yeah, I remember. I don't like it, but I remember."

"Good. Now, finish your drink as though angry."

He drained the glass and banged it on the table. She slid her gaze to the end of the bar where Adam watched the action with narrowed eyes.

"I'm not sure I can do this," Trevor muttered.

"Why not? You're a private investigator. You playact all the time when prying information out of people. It's not all that different from a con."

His brows drew together again, and he replied in an indignant tone. "May I remind you that what I do is entirely legal?"

"Good, you're getting pissed." She placed her fingertips on his arm. "Now!"

He jerked away, raising his voice. "Dammit! Don't give me those big, blue eyes, pretending you don't know what I'm talking about."

Several people at nearby tables turned to stare.

"But, Trevor, it's just not true. I swear it."

"You expect me to believe that? You disappear for hours, and then refuse to tell me where you were or what you were doing. Who'd you meet?"

"No one! If this is the way you're going to act, I'm leaving."

Trevor rose, tossed some money onto the table, and glowered. "No, I'm leaving. Do you take me for a chump? Find your own way back to the house."

The conversation had risen in volume. Now, the entire bar focused on them. Adam Richardson, she was pleased to note, stared with keen attention.

"Fine," she snapped.

Trevor strode away as rehearsed while Vicky bit her lip in feigned embarrassment, and cast her gaze around the room blinking her eyes rapidly. Richardson was off the stool and headed in her direction before Trevor had left the building. She fumbled in her bag for a handkerchief.

"Are you all right, Miss Denton?"

She patted her eyes with a delicate motion. "Yes, I'm fine. Trevor's just upset."

"No reason to embarrass you like that. But then, he always was an arrogant so-and-so. May I join you?"

"Yes, of course." He sat, and she laid her fingers on his hand. "Please don't worry. His aunt's death is stretching his nerves something awful."

"Then he shouldn't have bailed out the killer and invited him into Aunt Helen's house."

"Yes, I think that was a bad idea, too. He's also rather possessive."

"So, are you two an item?"

She shrugged and sipped her martini. "Not really. I met him in Miami. He seemed like a nice guy."

"Will you allow me to buy you dinner?"

Vicky leaned back in her seat, sipped again, and batted her eyelashes.

"Why, thank you, Mr. Richardson. I'd like that very much."

He leered and squeezed her hand, then signaled the waitress asking for another bourbon on the rocks.

"My father is Mr. Richardson. I'm Adam," he said with a wink.

"Adam, I'm Vicky."

His gaze slid down to her partially exposed breasts. Licking his lips again, he rattled the ice in his glass and raised it to his mouth, a lascivious look in his eyes.

Vicky sipped her drink. *You're mine, all mine.*

Chapter Ten

Trevor called upon all his self-control not to look over his shoulder as he left the restaurant. Once outside, however, he whirled, peering through the window toward the bar. He craned his neck for a better view, and finally saw Vicky. Adam stood next to her. A vicious dart of worry tinged with jealousy stabbed him in the chest. He understood the worry, not the jealousy, and chose to ignore it.

This is business. Keep your eyes open.

The temptation to remain was strong, but Vicky had been adamant when they'd rehearsed their movements and lines earlier.

"You've got to leave. If someone overhears the argument, and then sees you skulking in the parking lot or behind the bushes, they may think you're up to no good and call the cops."

"Might reinforce the fight."

"No cops. Just leave, and let me handle it."

He'd reluctantly agreed. In the restaurant, Adam seated himself in the chair Trevor had vacated. He'd give his last paycheck to overhear their conversation.

A couple leaving the steakhouse paused under the canopy. He turned his head and locked gazes with them. The woman whispered something to the man who nodded. They returned inside.

Damn, Vicky was right. He moved toward the parking lot. He'd have to wait this one out at home.

Back at the house, he relieved the deputy of his duties. The monitor on the desk beeped softly every ten or fifteen seconds. The blaring TV told him Halston hadn't moved a muscle since dinner.

Determined to ignore his racing heart and churning stomach, he opened one of Helen's files, and then gave up after reading the same page three times.

This is ridiculous. I've never been nervous about an operative doing her job. Calm down.

What he wanted was a drink, but to get one meant talking to Halston. On the other hand, he belonged here and owed no one an explanation.

Trevor exited the study striding down the hallway to the den. Rod lounged on the sofa watching a reality show. Ignoring his unwanted houseguest, he crossed to the bar, and picked up an empty scotch bottle.

"You're out of scotch," Halston said. "I'm making do with vodka."

Anger, quick and hot, clogged his throat. "You fucking parasite. Starting now, you're on the wagon."

"What?"

Trevor gathered the remaining bottles in his arms and marched toward the door.

"Hey! You can't do that!"

"Watch me! There's soft drinks and bottled water in the kitchen. And don't ask Rosa to serve you. Get it yourself."

He took satisfaction in the surprised look on the man's face before storming from the room. Back in the study, he set the bottles on the desk, and then returned to the den. Ignoring a sulking Halston, Trevor grabbed the ice bucket. In the kitchen, he filled it, snatched several glasses from the cabinet, and stomped back to the study where he poured Grey Goose over ice and gulped.

The liquor burned all the way down, but did little to settle his stomach or his temper. Damned weasel. Tomorrow, the wine would join the liquor.

Two shots later, Trevor paced the room like a caged tiger, checking his watch every few minutes, his mind moving at a frantic speed.

What was Vicky doing now? Had Adam put the moves on her yet? How would she handle it? Would Adam's temper get the better of him?

If he lays so much as a finger on her, I swear I'll kill him.

Time lagged. He picked up another file, forcing himself to read slowly, before glancing at his watch again. *An hour and a half? How the hell long does it take to eat?*

The phone rang and his heart jumped in his throat. Vicky? Was she all right? He stumbled across the floor and answered.

"Hello?"

"Trevor, its Uncle Ray."

He sagged against the desk in relief. "Hi, Uncle Ray, are you in town?"

"Sylvia, Jason, and I got in a few minutes ago. We're at the motel. Caroline won't be able to make it."

"Motel? You can stay here. There's plenty of room."

His uncle paused. "I don't think that's a good idea."

"Why not?"

"Helen's attorney called last night. He told us you'd bailed out the suspect and he's staying with you. Is it true?"

Trevor closed his eyes. *Damn Elliot Corwin. What business is it of his?*

"Yes, it's true, although why Corwin decided he needed to butt into a family affair, I don't know."

"Why'd you do it? Helen would have a cat if she

knew."

Trevor explained his motivation for springing Halston, but stopped short of Helen and Vicky's involvement. *Save that for later.*

"I still don't like it, Trevor, but I'm too tired to deal with it tonight. We're going to grab something to eat, and then go to bed. I'll see you tomorrow at the funeral home. What time is the viewing?"

He gave his uncle the information and hung up. He resumed pacing, but this time his focus was on Corwin. The lawyer had overstepped the boundaries. Ray and his family would have found out soon enough. Trevor resented being put on the defensive. Maybe it was Corwin's way of evening the score, of reminding him Helen had good friends she considered family.

The front door opened and closed. The bubble of anxiety pressing in his chest deflated at the sound of high heels on the oak flooring. A moment later, Vicky entered the room.

"Welcome home. How'd it go?"

She removed the fox stole, draped it over the arm of the sofa, and sat in the chair beside the fireplace.

"God, I'm exhausted. Is there anything to drink?"

He poured vodka on the rocks and handed her the glass. "What happened?"

Vicky sipped, and then sighed. "How long did you stay outside peeking in the window?"

Heat burned his cheeks. "Not as long as I wanted. How did you know?"

She shot him a glance through her lashes. "Just figured."

"What happened? Did you learn anything?"

"For starters, he'd been drinking long before we got there," she replied, kicking her shoes off and rubbing her toes. "That made my job easier. I

155

wanted him drunk, but not too drunk. I began with a trip down memory lane of his aunt and uncle. He rambled on about his childhood, you, and a bunch of things that didn't matter.

"Then, I commented on how glad I bet he was to have seen his aunt just before she died."

"What was his reaction?" If he'd made the comment, Adam would have told him to go to hell.

"He admitted he'd been in town a few days before the murder. I pumped him concerning the company during dinner and wine. He said things had been rough for a while, but would soon turn around."

"Must be counting on an inheritance. What else?"

"He let it slip his aunt refused to lend the company money. By this time, he was sloppy drunk and not making much sense, so I backed off and changed the subject."

Vicky sipped more of her drink, and curled her feet under her, allowing the hem of the dress to creep past her knees. She had damned fine legs, and for an instant, Miami and the bikini crowded his memory. He shook his head to clear the image. *Get rid of these stupid fantasies.*

"It wasn't until he killed the last of the wine with dessert that I got around to personal problems. I lamented the economy being bad and how I'm having to cut back on expenses, yadda, yadda." She paused to sip the last of the vodka.

"And?" He tried to keep the impatience from his voice.

"He agreed with me and intimated he had made some bad investments over the last couple of years." She smiled and leaned forward. "Want to guess with whom?"

"Elliot Corwin?"

"Bingo. He is not happy with your aunt's

attorney and investment counselor."

Trevor stared at her triumphant face and nodded. "I wonder if he said anything to Aunt Helen about Corwin."

"I don't know, but he did say he wanted to corner Elliot soon and discuss the situation—whatever that means."

He sat on the arm of the sofa, his fingers stroking the soft fur of the stole, and being careful not to make eye contact with her. The vision of a few moments ago still slipped in and out of his mind. "How'd you get home?"

"Taxi. Adam was too drunk to drive. When I left, he was sitting at a table in the back of the restaurant with a coffee cup in front of him and half passed out."

Trevor admitted she'd elicited more information in two hours than he would have in two weeks. It wasn't much, but confirmed most of what Rosa had said, and reinforced Marylou's report. As a bonus, he learned about Corwin's involvement. He wondered again if Walter had also invested with the lawyer and lost money.

"Nice job, Vicky." He buried his fingers in the fur stole. "You have good people skills. Why con? The last time I asked, you gave me the story of your childhood. What's the rest? A good executive secretary can earn plenty of money. I don't get it."

She sighed and set her glass on the end table. "You were right, you know—about hating my life. No matter how successful, I was always scared. Scared that one day the axe would fall and I'd get caught. After the Guatemalan fiasco, I tried to go straight. I lived with my Aunt Iris until she died a few months later. She left me a small inheritance. I sold the house, but by the time the debts were paid, I barely broke even.

"I also discovered my sketchy work history

wasn't an entry into a high paying salary. The most I made was fifteen dollars an hour. It was dog shit compared with what I could make from a scam. I gave it a year, renting a crummy apartment, scrimping to buy a better grade of hamburger, and then said the hell with it. I went back to what I did best. At least, I lived and ate better."

She looked at her watch and rose. "I'm tired, and tomorrow's going to be a long day. May I come to the funeral or would you rather I didn't—considering the circumstances."

"Come, by all means. I'd like to have you observe the mourners, give me your opinion."

"What about Rod?"

"I'll call Al and have another deputy baby sit."

She nodded and yawned. "Goodnight, Trevor." Vicky picked up the stole and smiled. "I'll put everything back where I found it."

Trevor stared at the empty doorway after she left. Funny, his whole attitude had changed the instant she'd returned last night. And tonight, he'd been worried sick about her with Adam. Add to that the surreal fantasies he'd been having, and the whole thing constituted total confusion.

He rose and picked up the vodka, then paused setting it back down. *No, no more. Tomorrow's going to be rough. Go to bed.*

He turned out the lights and mounted the stairs, his thoughts on Vicky. *What's happening? And how can I prevent it from consuming me?*

****

Trevor sat next to Vicky in the front row at the mortuary. His Uncle Ray, Aunt Sylvia, and Cousin Jason filled the rest of the seats. Across the aisle, Walter, Marge, and a very hung over Adam occupied those chairs along with Corwin. Behind him, much of the town had turned out to pay their last respects.

The minister droned on eulogizing his aunt's

life, but he heard little. His mind was back thirty years remembering the good times whenever he and his parents had visited Granite Springs. Memories choked him. Grief tightened his chest and he swallowed the ever-increasing lump in his throat. God, he would miss Helen. She'd had a down-to-earth, no nonsense outlook on life, not to mention a wicked sense of humor.

Trevor jerked out of his thoughts when Vicky's hand covered his. She squeezed lightly, interlocking their fingers. He turned his head. She stared straight ahead at the minister, her face calm and serene. Then, her head also turned, and her lips curled in a small smile.

She understands. A woman I called a liar and a thief a few days ago is giving me comfort and understands my grief better than family.

He inhaled a shaky breath and squeezed back.

When the service ended, the mourners filed past the casket for a final farewell before heading to their cars and the processional to the cemetery.

"Did you notice anything unusual before the services began?" he asked when they were alone.

"Your aunt and uncle were nice, but Jason seemed uptight."

"I noticed that, too. Ray isn't happy with me for bailing out your brother. And I'm surprised he's leaving tomorrow. I'd thought he'd stay longer."

"Walter fidgeted from the moment he came through the door. He's anxious about something. I had a chance to chat with his wife, mentioning I was originally from Los Angeles, how much I missed it, had she ever been there—that kind of thing."

Trevor shot her a quick look. "What did she say?"

"Said she'd only been there once and didn't like it. Too many people and lousy air. She prefers Colorado."

"And Walter's buying a million dollar condo in a city his wife hates?"

"I told you, he has another occupant in mind. She also said she and Walter are leaving for Mineral City as soon as the will is read. She didn't seem all broken up by your aunt's passing."

The hearse pulled away from the funeral home, and Trevor followed. "She and Aunt Helen weren't close."

Vicky turned her gaze onto him. "Did you notice anything?"

"You mean other than Adam looking like he'd spent the night in a gutter?"

She laughed. "I avoided him. He must remember something from last night. He seemed surprised to see us together." She paused, and then said, "I suppose there's the usual after-funeral get together with food and drink."

He nodded. "Of course."

"What did you notice?" she asked again.

"Walter crassly requested the will be read when the guests leave. Corwin looked impassive and disinterested during the service, like his mind was miles away. Rosa sat in the back with her son, Carlos."

Vicky shifted in her seat. "She introduced us. He leered and made a comment about how he had a weakness for blondes. Total creep. No wonder he was in prison."

"Carlos was all over the funeral home spreading his charm. I saw him talking with Adam and Corwin. He even cornered Jason."

He turned into the gates of the cemetery, parked, and walked hand in hand with Vicky across the grass to the gravesite where the final words of praise were mercifully short. Trevor was the last to leave. He stared at the casket with the spray of crimson roses spilling across the lid and made a vow.

I swear I'll find the killer and bring him to justice.

****

Vicky closed the door behind the last of the guests, and rolling her eyes, sagged against it with a sigh.

"God, I thought they'd never leave. I can't understand how people can intrude on a grieving family, eat tons of food, and drink copious amounts of booze for hours on end. It's damn near five o'clock. Four and a half hours is enough already."

Trevor massaged the back of his neck. "I told Rosa to keep it simple, but forgot she's Latin. Her idea of simple and mine differed."

Elliot opened the study door and poked his head out. "Trevor, whenever you're ready, I'll read the will."

"I'll be with you in a moment. Is everybody in there?"

"Yes, we're waiting for you." He turned, closing the door behind him.

"Didn't take long for the vultures to flock," he muttered. Trevor wished he was anywhere but here.

Vicky pushed herself away from the door. "While he's dispensing the good news, I'll go check on my brother. Being locked in the bedroom damn near all day has probably put him in a lousy mood." She entered the study, returning a second later with a bottle and two glasses. "You're right about the vultures. They are impatiently awaiting your arrival." She glanced at her full hands. "Good thing you replenished the scotch. It'll put him in a better frame of mind."

"I put him on the wagon."

She held up the bottle. "Which makes me a savior. He might talk."

He chuckled as she climbed the stairs. Damn, she was good. Today, he meant it as a compliment.

161

His mirth vanished when he entered the study. Corwin sat behind the desk flipping through the pages of the document in front of him. Walter and Adam stood by the fireplace, drinks in their hands. Adam's still shook. Marge occupied one of the chairs, while Ray and Sylvia sat on the sofa. Jason slouched in the other chair, legs crossed, his foot tapping in the air. Rosa sat stiff and upright near the desk.

Adam diverted his attention from his glass to Trevor. "Good, you're here. Let's get this show on the road. I have a long drive tonight."

Ray frowned and Sylvia sent him a disgusted glance. Trevor walked to the window, staring into the deepening dusk.

Elliot heaved a sigh. "Very well. I guess there's no reason to delay. The will was presented for probate earlier this week."

"What's that mean?" Jason asked, his foot tapping faster.

"It's a process by which the court proves the will, appoints or approves an executor, and eventually settles the estate after taxes."

"Taxes?" Adam asked.

"Taxes. The federal government and the state each get a cut."

"Who's the executor?" Ray queried from the sofa.

Trevor turned to gauge the reactions.

"Up until a few weeks ago, I was," Elliot replied in an even tone. "But a week or so before her death, Helen made a change requesting Trevor be put in charge."

"Why him?" Walter said, his voice hard, his expression suspicious.

"Said she wanted family to have the responsibility. Now, may I proceed?"

"Please do," Marge said. "Let's get this over with."

His Uncle Ray and Aunt Sylvia didn't seem too

surprised by the announcement. Jason and Rosa looked as if they didn't understand the term executor. Other than Walter's comment, the rest of the Richardson clan said nothing, but Adam scowled, and Marge had a bored expression on her face.

Corwin read down the first page silently before raising his head. "She leaves approximately a ten million dollar estate, which includes this house, numerous investments, and personal property like jewelry, furs, bank accounts, and such."

Adam whistled. "Wow, I had no idea she was that well-off, did you Uncle Ray?"

"I didn't concern myself with Helen's worth. If a family member needed help, she was always there." His tone held a hint of censure.

"Yeah, right," Adam replied, guzzling the liquor in his glass.

Jason shifted in his seat and frowned. Trevor eyed his two cousins. They'd both begged his aunt for money.

Elliot returned to the will. "She left a quarter of her estate to three local charities. Next, she leaves Rosa Ramirez one hundred-thousand dollars."

Rosa gasped, burst into tears, and made the sign of the cross. "The *senora* was too generous."

"I agree," Jason muttered. His mother sent him an angry look, kicking him in ankle.

"A hundred grand for a goddamned servant?" Adam blurted.

Walter made a rude noise, while Marge glared.

Trevor moved toward the housekeeper, placing his arm around her shoulders. "Rosa, you attended Aunt Helen every day for over fifteen years. When Uncle Roland died, you gave her companionship. She considered you more than an employee and left you the money as thanks. Enjoy it however you want." He kissed her temple. "Now, why don't you go home for the evening?"

The woman nodded, wiped her eyes with a tissue from the box on the desk, and left.

"Her ex-con son will worm the money out of her," Jason said in a sullen voice.

"Then that's Rosa's affair."

"Family money shouldn't go to servants," Walter muttered.

"Go on, Elliot," Trevor said, suddenly tired to the bone. He rubbed the knot of tension in his neck. A small dart of pain slashed behind his eyes.

"'To my nephew Jason Hamilton and his sister Caroline Hamilton, I leave the sum of five hundred thousand dollars each in a trust fund to be administered by their father, Raymond Hamilton, until they reach their thirtieth birthdays, when all funds shall revert to them outright.'"

Jason thrust his body upright in the chair. "What? A trust! I'm planning on law school. I need the money now." His gaze darted from the lawyer to Trevor.

"Jason, your mother and I can pay for law school," Ray said in a firm voice.

His cousin sat back, a frown on his face and a worried look in his eyes.

"'I bequeath my remaining two hundred shares of Richardson Mining Preferred stock to be split evenly between Walter Richardson and his son, Adam Richardson.'"

Adam opened his mouth, but Walter cut off the words with a quick wave of his hand. His son's mouth grooved into a sharp downward slant.

"'To my brother, Raymond Hamilton, I leave the sum of four million dollars.

"'The remainder of my estate, including all personal property, the house and its furnishings, goes to my nephew Trevor Sloane.' The will was duly signed by Helen H. Richardson and witnessed by Cora Duncan and Jessica Marshall on October 8th of this year." Elliot looked up. "Any questions?"

"How soon do we get the money?" Jason asked.

"Jason!" his mother said with a gasp.

"As soon as the probate court says you will. Ray, let me know if you need any help setting up the trusts."

"Thanks, Elliot. I'll talk with my lawyer in San Diego."

"Ten million bucks and all we get is some stock worth less than five grand? Dammit, we're family, too." Adam's shaking voice rivaled his trembling hands.

"I don't understand," Walter said, perspiration popping out on his forehead. "Why would she cut us out of the will?"

"Undue influence is my guess," Adam said with a curled lip, shooting a hateful glance Trevor's way.

"It's not fair," Marge commented.

"Since the will was signed so recently, I have to assume she made changes," Walter said.

Elliot nodded. "That's true, but I'm not at liberty to discuss those changes with you."

"We'll sue. Helen was obviously not of sound mind."

Elliot rose and shuffled papers together. "Walter, when Roland died, all but those last two hundred shares of Richardson Mining were transferred back to you. At the time, that represented close to five million dollars. The sale of his half of the company took place twelve years ago. That money went directly to Helen upon his death. As far as she was concerned, you'd already gotten your inheritance." He shoved the papers into the briefcase. "The will is legal. Suing will not break it. Trevor, I left a copy of the will on the desk. If you have any questions concerning the executor's duties, give me a call. Goodnight."

Elliot strode quickly from the room. A moment

later, the front door opened and closed.

"I think it's time for us to go, too," Marge said in frosty tones as she rose.

For once the Richardsons had nothing to say. Trevor breathed a sigh of relief as they stomped through the foyer and left.

His Aunt Sylvia walked over and hugged him. "Don't let them make mischief, Trevor. Helen never liked any of them. Greedy and unscrupulous, she said."

Ray shook his hand. "Being executor is a time consuming pain in the ass. If you need any help, let me know, but I don't think you will. Now, how about a quiet dinner at the steakhouse for all of us."

Trevor almost accepted, and then changed his mind. He needed time to put everything into perspective. Becoming an overnight millionaire and handling the estate was another rock on his already heavy load.

"No thanks, Uncle Ray. I have things to do here, and it's been a long day. If I don't see you, have a good trip back to California."

The Hamiltons left and silence descended on the house. He picked up the will, and then put it down again. Tears blurred his eyes. For a moment, he was tempted to give in to grief. Trevor swallowed hard. *Not now. Later, when this whole mess is behind me.*

Footsteps tapped on the hardwood floor of the foyer. A second later, Vicky appeared in the doorway.

"I take it everybody's gone. I heard cars leaving."

"Yeah, they're gone, thank God."

"Was it bad?"

"It was bad, but not unexpected." He gave her the gist of the reading.

"Are you going to keep the house?"

"I don't know. It's probably worth a couple of million, but with real estate in the tank, who knows?" He eyed the depleted bottle of scotch in her hand. "How's your brother? Drunk?"

She grinned. "A little, but antsy as hell and bitching up a storm. He's ready to crack."

"Why don't we have dinner here, just the two of us? Take a tray up to your brother. I can't stomach eating with him tonight. Later, maybe you'd like to help me go through some of Helen's papers. She had a lot of files."

After a quick dinner and with Rod ensconced back in the den, they adjourned to the study. He poured them each a glass of wine, and hauled out several files.

"These are mostly canceled checks going back seven years. See if you can find any that look out of the ordinary."

Vicky took the files, selected one, and settled on the sofa, her jean clad legs curled under her, while he kept his distance behind the desk. Sitting next to her on a plush sofa was asking for trouble.

It wasn't long before she waved a check in the air, "Here's something odd."

"To Corwin?"

"No, to your cousin, Jason. It's dated two years ago for ten thousand dollars."

"Ten grand! Why the hell would Helen give him that much money? What could he have needed it for?"

"A car?" she replied, lifting her eyebrows.

"Uncle Ray would have coughed up the money."

"He's a college student. Maybe he got into trouble with credit cards. It happens to kids on their own for the first time."

Trevor rubbed a finger across his lips. "I guess it's possible. He might not want his father to know he'd blown the budget."

Vicky riffled through different folders for several minutes. "Whoa, wait a minute. This ain't good."

Unable to stay seated, he rose and joined her.

"Corwin?" God he hoped so.

She handed him a check. "No, Jason again. It was written eight months ago—for twenty grand this time."

Shock reverberated through his body. Jason? He snatched the slip of paper from her hand and read with his own eyes. Twenty thousand big ones with Helen's name on the dotted line. He turned it over. Jason's signature was on the endorsement.

"What kind of a spendthrift is your cousin?" she asked.

"When Rosa said he'd been here asking for money, I visualized something along the lines of a few hundred dollars—a grand at the most. But this..." His mind went back a few hours ago and Jason's reaction to the contents of the will.

Vicky's gaze skewered him. "And Rosa said your aunt told him no more. A refusal might pose a problem for someone used to getting big bucks. Trevor, we could have another player in the game."

Chapter Eleven

The following morning, Trevor pulled a file from the cabinet, and then returned behind the desk to read. Vicky sat in the corner of the sofa with another folder in her hand. She reached for the coffee cup on the end table and sipped.

After his second sleepless night in a row, he finally arose at six-thirty, showered, grabbed a pair of jeans and a t-shirt, and came downstairs. Vicky joined him for breakfast an hour later. Halston didn't put in an appearance, which was fine with Trevor.

Now, on his third cup of coffee, he glanced at her. "Find anything of interest?"

"Not in her correspondence. Most of it's a combination of giving and denying donations to charities."

"Denying?"

"Hmm." She shuffled the papers lying on the sofa. "In this letter to the American's for American Relief Fund, she says she'd be happy to make a large donation as soon as the fund ceases giving its president, board of directors, and chairman of the board salaries and bonuses that amount to almost half the donations received last year."

Trevor chuckled. "That sounds like Helen. The less taken by the people who run a charity, the more likely she was to donate."

"I wish I'd known your aunt. I think I could have

169

liked her."

He didn't comment, but thought his aunt might like the new and improved Vicky, too.

"Is there anything else?"

"Not yet. How about you? You have the financials."

"Her portfolio is a pip. She kept every report from every investment for seven years." He shook his head. "Wading through this mess will take forever."

"I'd eliminate the reports prior to your uncle's death. If you're still looking to nail Corwin, I'd start with a grieving widow putting herself in the hands of someone she trusted."

"You have a point. Which reminds me, Corwin said he'd drop off the latest reports around noon. I invited him to stay for lunch. Should be interesting. Your brother can eat in the kitchen by himself."

Vicky closed the file, drained her cup, and rose stretching her arms over her head. "I can't believe your aunt wrote so many letters. Most people nowadays use e-mail."

"Aunt Helen wasn't comfortable with a computer. She'd write, print, and snail mail most of the time. Wasn't real fond of cell phones either. Had one anyway."

Vicky picked up her cup again and made a face. "I need more caffeine. How about you?"

"I could do with another cup. Rosa probably has a pot still on in the kitchen."

She nodded and left. Trevor ran a hand through his hair. Today was going to be a ball buster.

As if to confirm his suspicions, his phone rang. It was Marylou.

"Got anything?" he asked.

"What? No hello, how are you?"

"Hello, how are you, what have you learned?"

"You're becoming downright sarcastic, you know

that?"

He slumped in the chair and sighed. She was right.

"I'm sorry, Marylou, but it wasn't the best of nights."

"Again, huh?"

"Not for the reason you think. My aunt was buried yesterday, and the vultures gathered for the reading of the will."

"My turn to apologize," she replied, her tone sympathetic. "Since Carlos has the easiest information to check, I started with him."

"I'm all ears." Vicky returned and he nodded as she placed a cup of steaming coffee on the desk, the aroma alone doing wonders for his state of mind. He motioned for her to close the door.

"Carlos Ramirez was a member in good standing with the Los Gatos gang in Denver. They were into damn near every illegal activity from drugs and prostitution to burglary and extortion. According to his file, your man was arrested for grand theft auto and burglary five years ago. It was pretty much an open and shut case. He plea bargained and did four years before being released a little over a year ago. He petitioned for permission to move to Granite Springs to live with his mother. He's kept all of his appointments with is PO in Denver."

Vicky sat in the chair facing him, raising the cup to her lips.

"That confirms what Rosa and Sheriff Singleton told me. If he got out on parole, he must have kept his nose clean in prison, too."

"There was nothing to state otherwise, although it's noted he'd acquired several tattoos supporting the in-house Hispanic gang."

"That's to be expected. Anything new come through on Corwin? How about the Richardsons?"

"I'm still digging on Corwin. He's a lawyer and

knows how to cover his tracks."

Suspicion and doubt crept into his mind again as he sipped his coffee. "Has he been doing that?"

"Hard to tell. Things got a lot tighter about three years ago. More security.

"Walter and Adam? Anything new there?"

"I'm not sure. I touched base with the woman who brought the rape and assault charges against your cousin. Turns out she works at Richardson Mining."

"You're kidding."

"Nope. Her name's Anne Parker and she works—or rather, worked—as a receptionist. Walter fired her last week."

"How could Walter be that stupid? He's asking for a wrongful termination lawsuit."

"Which the lady and her attorney will file in a few weeks. However, she did have some interesting news. Three weeks ago, Adam had a visitor. She said the young, Hispanic male hit on her big time while waiting for admittance to Adam's office."

Marylou paused and Trevor could almost see her victorious smile.

"Carlos Ramirez?"

Vicky shot him a sharp look.

"That's the name he gave."

"I don't suppose he also gave up why he wanted to see Adam."

"Personal business. He and Adam went outside to talk. Adam returned alone a few minutes later."

Trevor made notes on a pad, writing fast, but not half as fast as his mind worked. Why the hell would Carlos drive to Mineral City to see Adam? Just because Carlos hadn't been arrested in Granite Springs, didn't mean he was staying out of trouble.

If Adam had a drinking problem, maybe he had a drug habit as well. Could Carlos be his connection? And had his cousin missed a couple of payments?

Drug dealers don't deliver the goods that far from home turf. They come to collect money or deliver ultimatums.

"Thanks, Marylou, you did great. Can this woman add more to the situation at the mine?"

"I think she has a ton of crap to tell, but wants to clear it with her lawyer first. I have a lunch date with her later in the week."

"Terrific. Keep working on Corwin, and I need you to add another name to the list—Jason Hamilton."

He shot a glance toward Vicky who raised her eyebrows while sipping her coffee.

"Isn't he your cousin, too?"

"Yeah." He relayed the pertinent information Vicky had uncovered the night before.

"Got it. E-mail me his address and everything. I'll get to it as soon as I can. I have to testify in court this afternoon on the Cardwell divorce."

"Thanks, Marylou. Call me when you get something."

He hung up and finished jotting notes before raising his head and staring into Vicky's eyes.

"Marylou?" she asked.

"My best operative. She digs through the bullshit and finds the diamonds."

"Has she worked for you long?"

"About five years."

He shifted his gaze to the folders on the table next to her, and then picked up another from his pile on the desk. He didn't have the heart to tell Vicky the first assignment Marylou ever worked on was tracking down Victoria Denton for Quinn Rafferty.

****

Vicky freshened her lipstick and ran a comb through her hair, then fluffed the strands around her face. Standing back from the bathroom mirror, she viewed her reflection with a critical eye. She'd exchanged her jeans for a pair of navy blue slacks. An aqua sweater, just snug enough to draw attention to her breasts, deepened the blue of her eyes. She wanted alluring, not cheap. Elliot Corwin was due any minute, and with luck, by the time he left, she'd have a dinner invitation.

Satisfied with her appearance, Vicky descended the staircase to find her brother and Trevor in the foyer.

"Why do I have to eat in the kitchen?" Rod whined.

"Because I'm expecting a guest and don't want to spoil his lunch." He shifted his gaze toward her. It was impossible to miss the appreciation in his eyes. "You look nice."

"Thank you. I thought I'd make an effort to look good for Elliot."

"Corwin's your guest?" her brother asked.

"That's right, Halston. The man who had you pegged as a third-rate bullshit artist from the get-go."

Rod glared before shifting his gaze to her. "Well, why can't Vicky eat with me? Why should I be all alone? Rosa hates me and doesn't talk. Not even my damned lawyer has been to see me. All he does is call and not that often. And why do I still have this public defender? Where's that super-lawyer you promised?"

"I'll discuss it when you finally tell the truth. Now, be a good boy and go eat your lunch."

Rod's brows drew together in s deep scowl. "I'm bored. Why can't we go out to eat for a change? I'd kill for a burger and fries. How come Vicky gets to eat with you?"

"If I were you, Halston, I wouldn't use that terminology, and Vicky is invited to the party." The doorbell rang. "My guest has arrived. I suggest you go eat. Rosa won't keep the food warm long."

Rod turned and ambled down the hallway, muttering, "Yeah, just like she never has breakfast when I get up."

Vicky waited until he disappeared, and then said in a low voice, "He's about to crack. Give him one more night of boredom and bad TV. I'll work on him in the morning. Maybe exchange a lunch at Marley's for information."

"What's wrong with getting him liquored up tonight? The sooner we know more, the better."

"I may have plans for tonight," she answered in a smooth voice.

The doorbell pealed again and Trevor hurried to open it with Vicky behind him. A dark gray car was parked at the foot of the steps.

"Come in, Elliot. Glad you could make it."

Elliot Corwin entered. Neither man offered to shake hands. Vicky did.

"Mr. Corwin, how nice to see you again."

He smiled, swept a quick gaze up and down her figure, and then clasped her hand in his.

"Miss Denton, you look lovely." He held on a few seconds longer than necessary before allowing his hand to slowly slide free.

"Thank you, and its Vicky."

His smile widened. "Please, call me Elliot."

Like a bug to the zapper.

Trevor didn't smile. Instead, he shot her a look that clearly said he knew what she had in mind and didn't like it.

"Would you care for a drink before lunch?" he asked.

Elliot shook his head. "No, thanks, I have to be in court this afternoon. But I do have those reports you wanted."

Trevor led his guest into the study where Elliot placed his briefcase on the desk and extracted a large manila envelope.

"The last one is incomplete. It only deals with the first half of the year. I won't get the third quarter results for another week or so, and of course, the year end in January or February. I'll get them to you as soon as I can."

Vicky leaned against the doorjamb observing the men. Both were tense and the atmosphere crackled with their dislike. It skittered along her skin, raising the hair on her arms. They stared at each other like mongooses would a snake—intense and unwavering.

Trevor stood straight, his back rigid, while Elliot's voice was cold. Neither face revealed what they thought or felt. She wondered why the lawyer had bothered to accept the invitation. He could have dropped off the information, or Trevor could have picked it up at the office.

To break the tension, Vicky stepped forward. "Trevor, would you like me to file those with the others, or do you want to read them after lunch?"

Both men relaxed their postures. Trevor tossed the envelope on the desk.

"I'll read them later, Vicky." He smiled and gestured toward the sofa. "Shall we have a seat?"

At that moment, Rosa appeared in the doorway. "Lunch is ready, *Senor* Sloane."

"Thank you, Rosa." He smiled again and nodded. "I don't know about anyone else, but Rosa's lasagna is not to be missed."

"I thought I smelled something Italian when I came in. I always said Helen had the best cook in Colorado."

"Only Colorado?" Vicky said with a laugh. "Rosa will be insulted."

Elliot grinned and offered his arm while Trevor heaved a deep breath, leading them to the dining room.

Trevor seated himself as Elliot pulled out her chair and stared at three place settings.

"Where's the houseguest?"

"In the kitchen. And he's not a guest. Think of this as a medium security prison. He has privileges, but eating with me is not one of them," Trevor replied unfolding his napkin.

Rosa entered with three salad plates. A boat of salad dressing and a bowl of garlic bread already sat on the table. The housekeeper disappeared, and then returned a moment later with an uncorked bottle of Chianti. She poured everyone a glass before setting the bottle in front of Trevor.

Vicky speared a piece of radicchio, noticing that while Elliot may have declined a cocktail, he had no problem with the wine. His first move was to drink half the glass.

"Have you had any luck with your investigation of Mr. Harvey?" he asked Trevor.

"Not really. I'm letting him get good and bored. Tonight I may ply him with liquor and see if he opens up."

"His story was nonsense. Helen would never have pawned jewelry for ready cash," the attorney agreed. "I found the reading yesterday revealing."

During the salad course, the men discussed the events of the previous evening. Perhaps that's why he had accepted the luncheon invitation—to get Trevor's reaction. Eventually, Elliot must have realized she'd been silent.

"I'm sorry, Vicky. I forgot you weren't present. How rude of us."

"That's all right. I was just thinking how lucky Mrs. Richardson was to have Trevor, and such a good friend like you. I remember you from that first day. You looked so shocked."

"I was. I'd been in the diner and heard one of the waitresses say something about all the police cars at the house. So, I came right over. Horrible, absolutely horrible." He shot a quick glance in Trevor's direction, and then back to her. "I still think harboring the number one suspect in Helen's house is crazy."

She recognized dangerous territory and jumped in before Trevor could answer. "Maybe, but you know the saying about catching more flies with honey than vinegar, although why anybody would want to catch flies is beyond me."

She laughed as Rosa entered, whisking away the salad plates and replacing them with lasagna, the aroma making her mouth water.

"I admit I'm a complete moron when it comes to lawyers and such. How is it you're an attorney and an investment counselor at the same time?" She forked a morsel into her mouth. *Heaven, sheer heaven.*

Elliot reached for a slice of bread. "The two aren't all that different. Both involve advice. In fact, I majored in economics. I was investing and giving advice while in law school. Did well at it, too. Later, I had a client who knew of my degree and asked about a certain mutual fund. He made money, and eventually turned his portfolio over to me. Got most of my clients by word of mouth."

"Do you have financial clients outside of Granite Springs?" she asked.

"I have several in Denver, Colorado Springs, Boulder."

"Any outside the state?"

She cut off another piece of lasagna and gazed toward Trevor. He ate, but kept his narrowed eyes focused on his guest.

"No. I don't like to spread myself too thin. After all, I'm a lawyer first. I'm considering backing off from the investment part of my life."

"Don't blame you what with the stock market in the condition it is," Trevor commented. "Don't suppose there's much lawyering to go around here in

Granite Springs either."

"You'd be surprised. Someone's always arguing over property lines or mineral rights, and everybody has to have a will. The ones people can do online are fine if kept simple, but the more you have, the more complicated the dispersal. I also do a lot of business in Denver and other cities regarding contracts and such."

"I imagine you'll charge a fee for doing the probate work." His voice may have been even, but his eyes held a hard expression.

Elliot stiffened. "Of course. I assume you charge for what you do, too."

"I enjoy catching scum and making them pay."

Vicky leaped in with another question fast. "Have you always lived in Granite Springs? I find the town charming."

She breathed a sigh of relief when Elliot turned and smiled, relating his life history from his birth in St. Louis to his choice of practicing in a small town.

"Small towns offer a less frantic lifestyle, but I still have the option of a big city a few hours away."

The rest of the meal passed with small talk between them, Trevor chiming in on occasion. Still, she was glad when Elliot left, thanking his host.

"And please tell Rosa I enjoyed it very much." He hesitated in the front door. "Vicky, would you be free for dinner tonight?"

Trevor turned and stalked into the study.

"Why, yes, I am." *Zzzzzap! Nailed.*

"Good. Shall I pick you up at say seven o'clock? We'll have dinner and drinks at Campbell's."

"Sounds wonderful."

He smiled and exited. She closed the door, and then wandered into the study.

"Did you have to bat your eyes at him throughout lunch?" Trevor asked in a tight voice.

She laughed. "Careful. You sound jealous."

"Don't mess with me. I don't like him."

Her laughter died. "He's all right, but did you notice he lied?"

"I noticed. He came steaming up the driveway that morning saying he'd heard Helen had been murdered. Rosa called it in at seven-thirty. We arrived about an hour later. Now a waitress at the diner may have seen police cars, but no way would anyone know why that quickly."

"Which means he had another information source. The sheriff?"

"No. Remember Al's reaction? Told him he'd wanted to talk to him. Besides, Al doesn't leak information."

"Someone else in the sheriff's office?"

Trevor frowned, wrinkling his forehead. "I doubt it, which leaves me with a whole lot of questions."

"You think *he* killed her?"

"As of now, I can't find a motive."

"I'll work on him during dinner. He also lied about having clients outside the state. Didn't your office unearth someone in Salt Lake City?"

"Yes, but that was years ago." He stabbed her with a sharp gaze. "I still don't trust him. Are you sure you want to dine with him?"

"I'll be fine. He's more refined and sophisticated than Adam."

"And will be a tougher nut to crack. At least he doesn't have a rape charge hanging over his head." He pulled her into his arms, kissing her hard before stepping back. "Just be careful, okay?"

Her heart pounded and her lips burned from his touch.

"I will." Her voice came out in a throaty whisper.

Vicky left the room on wobbly legs. The kiss had been brief, but effective. Her insides quivered and the ever-tightening spring of desire churned her core. She climbed the stairs to plan her ensemble for the evening and considered substituting a cold shower for a hot bubble bath.

****

In a replay of a few nights ago, Vicky descended the staircase wearing Helen's jewelry and the fox stole draped over an ice blue cocktail dress. Trevor stood at the foot of the steps with a dour expression.

"You certainly have enough fancy clothes."

"Didn't expect me to vamp Ed Williams in the same basic black every time, did you?"

His brows slid together in a scowl. "Do you plan on vamping Corwin?"

He really is jealous. The knowledge sent a shiver of delighted satisfaction up her spine.

She was excused from answering by the sweep of headlights flashing through the window signaling Elliot's arrival.

Flinging the end of the stole over her shoulder, Vicky brushed past Trevor whose feet appeared anchored where he stood. The doorbell pealed and she opened up.

Elliot made no motion to enter, but looked her up and down from the top of her upswept hairdo to the tips of her crimson polished, silver sandal clad toes with an appreciative gaze.

"You look fabulous."

"Thank you. I didn't expect to get a chance to dress up in Granite Springs."

He laughed and crooked his arm. "We aren't all bumpkins. Shall we? Your chariot awaits."

She laughed along with him and tossed a, "See you later," to Trevor as she took Elliot's arm. He opened the car door and she slid into the soft leather seat of his BMW. At Campbell's, he valet parked and escorted her in.

"Reservation for Corwin," he told the maître d' who immediately showed them to an intimate table for two not far from the fireplace.

Vicky slipped the stole off and draped it over the back of her chair revealing the low cut bodice of her dress. The firelight danced and refracted off the beading and sequins.

The look of appreciation in his eyes deepened as he pulled out the chair.

"You are a vision." He glanced at the fur. "Isn't that Helen's?"

She sat and moved the place setting a fraction of an inch while he took his seat across from her, surprised he noticed.

"Yes, it is. Coming from Miami, I didn't have any cold weather clothes, so Trevor was kind enough to suggest I wear it." She laughed lightly. "I'm glad he did. Evenings are quite chilly."

A waiter approached handing them menus and taking their drink orders—martinis for both.

"I understand you and Trevor were here the other night," he said when the man had gone.

News travels fast. "Yes, but not for long. I guess you heard."

"A friend was here with his wife and told me." He frowned and fiddled with the stem of a water goblet. "Trevor never liked me. Not sure why."

"Forgive me, but you don't appear to like him either."

A young man filled her water glass, and she lifted it to her lips, gazing at him from beneath lowered lashes.

"I don't. He was possessive of Helen, especially the last six months or so. His visits to Granite Springs used to be once or twice a year, but suddenly it's every few months."

"I've heard it said that close relatives sometimes sense when a loved one is about to die."

Elliot snorted. "Trevor Sloane is not psychic. If he were, he'd have nailed the killer or warned Helen before she was murdered. He shouldn't investigate any of this. He's too emotionally involved."

The waiter brought their drinks, and took a moment to inform them of the specials for the evening.

"Let us finish our drinks first," her companion said.

The man nodded and left.

Vicky renewed the conversational thread. "She was his aunt. He loved her, so emotion is expected, and I didn't mean he was psychic, more like intuitive. If only you had been there that evening instead of in the afternoon. You may have deterred the whole thing."

Elliot's hand stopped with the martini glass halfway to his mouth. "Who said I was there?"

Vicky sipped her drink and slid an olive off the spear with her teeth. "Rosa. Just think, other than Rosa, you were the last one to see her alive—besides the killer, of course."

He frowned and sipped. "I guess that's true. She asked me over to discuss the transfer of funds to that leech Harvey. I still argued against it, but in the end, it was her money and she could do what she wanted." He shook his head. "Thank God all he got was the measly ten grand in the safe and whatever petty cash she had in that silly cigar box."

So, Elliot knows how much money Helen kept in the safe and about the cigar box. Interesting.

Vicky leaned forward allowing him a better view of her cleavage.

"But how could he have known the combination?"

"It was easy, she used her birth date. A slick fish like Harvey would figure that out."

And he knew the combination to the safe. Even more interesting.

"But what happened to the money? I heard he only had a couple of thousand when the state troopers caught up with him."

Elliot shrugged and drained his glass in an abrupt move. "Who knows? Maybe he stashed it in a safety deposit box along the way."

He signaled the waiter for a refill, turning his gaze onto her glass with lifted eyebrows.

She shook her head. "Why should he do that? Why not wait until he got to where he was going? And what about the rest of the safe's contents? Trevor said all her papers were missing, too."

"How should I know?" His voice grew testy.

Vicky backed off casting her gaze down to the table. "I'm sorry. I didn't mean to upset you. It must be hard talking about the murder of a close friend."

"It is. I feel like I'm being interrogated." She raised her head. He said it in a lighter tone, but his eyes held a wary expression.

"Goodness, I certainly didn't mean that! How rude of me. I'm sure you and Trevor are both right in blaming Mr. Harvey. He doesn't look trustworthy to me." She reached out and let her fingertips stroke the back of his hand. "Please, forgive me for being too curious."

Trevor was right. He's harder to manipulate than a drunken Adam and a weak Rod. Time to call it quits. At least I got a few morsels of information.

He smiled, the wary look gone. "I guess it's only natural what with being in the house and all. Let's change the subject."

The waiter returned with his drink and they ordered—a strip steak, rare, for him and a filet, medium, for her, both with baked potatoes and salads.

Elliot smiled and raised his glass, asking about her life. She gave the standard, sure to make a mark sympathetic, answer.

"I was born and raised in Michigan. My parents died in an automobile accident when I was ten. Since

I had no aunts or uncles to take me in, I spent the next eight years in foster care."

She rambled on with the old pulling herself up by the bootstraps story ending with, "And I found myself in Miami. The job market was good at the time and the weather fabulous, so I stayed."

"How'd you ever hook up with Trevor?"

Vicky latched onto the explanation she'd given the sheriff.

Their food arrived, and when they were once again alone, she said, "Your turn. You said you're originally from St. Louis. I've never been there. Tell me about it."

She feigned interest, tuning out most of his words, and wishing she could enjoy the meal. As it was, her mind tucked away the information she'd gleaned. Trevor would grill her when she got back to the house.

They pulled into the driveway, surprised to see the sheriff's car parked in front.

"What's he doing here?" Elliot asked.

"Oh, he comes and goes on a regular basis. I think he keeps Trevor up to date on things."

"Or maybe he's questioning Harvey."

"Perhaps."

Elliot walked her to the front door, dropping a light kiss on her lips.

"Thank you for coming. I enjoyed it."

"So did I," she lied. "Thank you for asking me."

"I've got a busy schedule for the next few days, but I'd like to do this again soon. I'll call."

"By all means."

He stalled as though expecting her to ask him inside. The last thing she or Trevor needed was Elliot Corwin participating in a discussion with the sheriff. Finally, he nodded and turned.

Vicky slipped through the entryway and rested her back against the closed door. Voices drifted into the foyer from the study. Curious, she entered. Trevor sat behind the desk reading a slip of paper. The sheriff sat in a chair.

"Excuse me, I didn't mean to interrupt, but I heard voices and saw the car in the driveway."

Trevor set the paper on the desk and looked up. "You're not interrupting. How was your date?"

"Fine, thank you."

He cleared his throat. "Good. Al came by with a list of the jewelry recovered from Helen's car when Halston was arrested."

The sheriff rose and nodded to her. "I also have other news."

"What's that?" Trevor asked with raised eyebrows.

"Forensics has examined both the car and Mr. Halston's clothing. The car had his fingerprints all over it, but they also discovered blood on the right knee of his navy blue slacks. We don't have DNA on it yet, but the blood type matches that of Helen Richardson."

Chapter Twelve

Vicky's heart rate slowed, and then sped up again. Black specks dotted her peripheral vision, and for a moment, the room tilted. Jumbled thoughts flitted through her mind.

Don't faint. Don't look at Trevor. Damn you, Rod. What did you do?

By taking a deep breath, she staved off fainting, but couldn't help looking at Trevor. He stared at the sheriff with an angry, yet satisfied expression before shooting her a smoldering glance.

"So, he did kill her."

"There has to be an explanation," Vicky said in a low voice. "He could have gotten blood on his slacks at any time."

"My aunt had a rare blood type—AB negative."

"The type on the trousers is the same," the sheriff confirmed.

"I don't think he knelt in a pool of AB negative on the side of the road while changing a tire. He could only have gotten it from Aunt Helen." He spat the words out and glared.

Vicky's stomach turned over. She needed a drink and headed for the bottles on the credenza behind the desk. Grabbing a glass, she poured a generous shot of scotch.

"Any blood splatters in the car or on the rest of his things?" Trevor asked.

The sheriff frowned just like he had when

informing them Rod had been driving east when apprehended.

"No, not a speck."

"Doesn't matter. He could have tossed the shirt, but kept the pants not realizing they had blood on them. What about his shoes?"

"He was wearing Gucci loafers when apprehended, and they were clean, just like the other two pairs of shoes in his suitcase."

Vicky tossed the scotch down her throat. The liquor burned all the way down, but settled her queasy stomach and jangled nerves.

Gucci? The little rat was living high.

"Also doesn't matter. I'm sure he had more. Probably chucked the bloody pair."

"All of this is speculation," she said, pouring another drink.

"He lied," Trevor said, his lips setting into a hard line.

"Which is why I'm re-arresting. I don't care what steps you're taking to pry information out of him, he comes with me."

"Wait a minute, Al. He doesn't know about this new evidence. Let's get him in here, hit him with it, and turn the screws."

The sheriff paused. "All interrogations will be done under controlled conditions at the police station. I don't want his lawyer coming back at us months from now with some procedural bullshit. Pardon my language, ma'am."

Vicky nodded and set the glass back on the credenza. Things did not look good for her brother. His lies had caught up with him.

Trevor rose and walked toward the door. "Works for me. He's in the den. Let's see what he has to say."

At the den door, Trevor stepped aside allowing the sheriff to enter first. Vicky trailed in behind the men. Rod lay on the sofa, channel surfing. A surprised expression replaced the boredom when he saw his visitors. The surprise quickly gave way to bland.

"Good evening. I don't often get visitors back here. What can I do for you?"

"On your feet, Halston," Trevor ordered.

"Why?"

"Because you're coming with me to the station," the sheriff said.

Rod frowned and rose, shooting a glance her way. "What for?"

The officer reached behind him and unclipped his handcuffs. "I want to talk to you, that's what for. Turn around and put your hands behind your back."

"Hey, you can't do this."

Trevor smiled. "Sure, he can. He's a cop, and you're out on bail."

The sheriff snapped the cuffs on Rod who sent her another pleading look.

"Vicky, help me."

"Rod, they just want to talk. Cooperate. Please."

"I won't say a word unless my sister's there."

"I'd think you'd prefer your lawyer," Al said, leading Rod away.

Trevor gazed at her in triumph. "This is going to be good."

No, it wasn't. It was going to be messy. She tightened the stole and followed him through the kitchen to the garage. Neither of them spoke, and at the jail a deputy ushered them into a small enclosure with a two-way mirror while the sheriff escorted her brother into an interrogation room. Trevor flipped a switch on the wall.

"Where's my sister?" Rod's voice carried through a speaker above the mirror.

"Your sister is not an officer of the court, and you aren't a minor." He released the handcuffs. "Sit down."

"Then I want my lawyer."

Sheriff Singleton nodded and left the room. The moment he was alone all bravado on her brother's part disappeared. His face crumbled into fear etched lines, and he whimpered like a child. He stared at the mirror.

"Vicky, what am I going to do? Why am I here? Dammit, why didn't you warn me?"

"Is he being recorded?" she asked Trevor.

"I don't think so. The questioning hasn't begun and he's asked for his lawyer."

She hesitated not wanting to go over old ground, but did anyway. "As I said before, Rod is a lot of things, but not a killer. There has to be an explanation for the blood."

"Yeah, like he did it. I don't understand why you're defending him. You don't even like the bastard."

"He's the only family I have, and dammit, he wasn't always this way. Blame Harry, blame my mother, but every once in a while I remember a little boy who came to me with his scraped knees. Yes, he was a greedy brat, but my mother spoiled the hell out of him. He was her favorite. I spent years trying to please her. After her death, I wanted to please my stepfather. I never succeeded because Harry was a self-centered egotist who didn't give a damn about anyone but himself."

Trevor's harsh expression softened. "I'm sorry, Vicky. Being an only child, I never had to compete for affection. Must have been hard. I see decency in you. I see none in your brother."

"He's Harry's child." She shifted from foot to foot wishing she'd taken the time to change out of her high heels. "My feet hurt. Is there a chair around?"

"I'll go find one. Would you like something to drink? Coffee? It'll be out of a vending machine."

"God, no. Make it a soft drink, no caffeine."

He left the room and she turned her attention back to Rod who now paced, fear and uncertainty on his face. Every couple of seconds, he paused to stare into the mirror, but said nothing.

You'd better come clean this time or I swear I'll throw you to the wolves. As of now, I'm done pulling your chestnuts out of the fire.

Trevor returned with the chair and two caffeine-free Cokes, handing her one. She sat, eased off her shoes, and popped the top, tilting the can to let the cold fizz slide down her dry throat. The snap and hiss from behind told her he'd done the same.

They waited another twenty minutes until Rod's lawyer arrived. The sheriff followed him into the interrogation room.

"All right, Sheriff, this had better be good. Why is my client here?"

"We found new evidence. I contacted the district attorney's office and am re-arresting your client. I imagine the DA will up the charge to second degree murder. He'll go before the judge first thing in the morning."

"He can't do that!" Rod said, a frantic look on his face.

"What new evidence?" his attorney said with a frown.

"We found blood matching Helen Richardson's blood type on a pair of slacks rolled up in the trunk of the victim's stolen car."

"So what? He could have worn them anytime in the last week. And Helen Richardson could have had a nosebleed."

"Which bled only on the right knee of his slacks?"

The lawyer conferred with a clearly frightened Rod, and then addressed the sheriff again.

"Do you have a DNA match?"

"Not yet, but Mrs. Richardson had an unusual

blood type—AB negative."

"Rare, but not exclusive."

"Exclusive enough."

"You can't do this to me!" Sweat rolled down Rod's face. "I didn't kill Helen! I swear it!"

"Just tell us what happened. Might buy you a lighter sentence." The sheriff's voice took on a threatening tone. "But it has to be the truth. No more lies."

In the observation room, Vicky bit her lip and shivered. Tears welled in her eyes. Her brother was going down and he probably deserved it, if not for Helen Richardson's death, then for a lifetime of deceit. *This could so easily have been me. I can't do this anymore. I just can't. I'm too scared, too tired.*

Rod licked his lips before answering in an emasculating whine.

"Okay, the truth. Helen said she had some things to do after dinner, and why didn't I go have some fun in town? Fun in Granite Springs...right. At any rate, she gave me the keys to the Lincoln, and I ended up at Marley's."

"What time was this?" Sheriff Singleton asked.

"I don't know...eight-thirty or so. We had an early dinner. She said she had some business to conduct."

Vicky glanced at Trevor.

He frowned. "What business? What was my aunt up to? And why would she send your brother out of the house?"

She had no answers and turned back to Rod's grilling.

"So, you were at Marley's. When did you leave?"

"I can't remember. Eleven maybe? I'd had a few, so I drove back to the house slowly, parked the car in the garage, and came in through the kitchen. I started to go upstairs when I saw the lights on in the study. I was curious. Helen was usually in bed or catching the late night news on TV in the den."

He leaned over to whisper in his attorney's ear. The man nodded.

Rod licked his lips again. "Can I have something to drink? I'm parched."

When the sheriff left, he asked, "He can't really toss me back in jail, can he? I'm out on bail."

His lawyer sighed, giving his client a stern look. "Yes, he can. This new evidence puts you at the scene of the crime. If the DNA's a match, you're toast."

"But I didn't kill her!"

"Convincing a jury otherwise may be tough. Our best bet might be a plea bargain on the theft charge with reduced charges on the death. I'll work on it."

The sheriff returned with a bottle of water. Rod cracked the cap and drank half of it in three gulps.

"Okay, let's get on with this. You came back to the house, saw the light on in the study, and then what?"

"I went in. At first I didn't see anything, and then saw her feet sticking out from beside the desk. My first thought was that she'd had a heart attack or something, but when I got closer, I saw the blood. It was all around her head. Scared the piss out of me. I knelt down to feel for a pulse, but there was nothing. Guess that's how the blood got on my slacks."

"Why didn't you call 9-1-1? Just because you didn't feel a pulse doesn't means she was dead."

Her brother shivered, and emptied the bottle of water. "She was dead all right. Cold as ice."

"What happened next?"

"I panicked. I knew I'd be the number one suspect, so I grabbed the cash out of the drawer, hauled ass upstairs to her bedroom, and rifled the good stuff out of her jewelry boxes. I packed my bags and took off."

"Why'd you take her car?"

"I'd been seen driving the Lincoln on a couple of occasions. I thought the Mercedes might buy me more time."

"I think you took the Mercedes because it would fetch a pretty price."

The lawyer jumped in. "Don't answer that. Are you about finished, Sheriff?"

"If you were so panic-stricken, why were you eastbound? What about the candlesticks and picture frames from the study, and the money in the safe?"

Rod shot a quick look toward the mirror, and then shook his head. "I didn't take them. And I never knew she had a safe in the house."

Vicky's chest constricted. *Eastbound. Those calls. Those damned calls.*

"And you saw no one in or around the house?"

"No." He paused. "Wait a minute, there was a car."

"What car?" Al leaned in close, his eyes narrowed.

"I told you I was taking it slow coming back even though traffic was light. I'd just passed the stop sign when this car sped past with its headlights off."

"What kind of car?"

"I don't know. It's a dark stretch of road. I figured the driver was more loaded than me."

"How about a color? Can you identify the driver? Man, woman, chimpanzee?"

"No need for sarcasm, Sheriff. My client's cooperating."

Rod furrowed his forehead. "I don't remember anything about the driver. I just assumed it was a man. Seems to me the car was dark. Can't be any more specific than that."

Sheriff Singleton straightened and re-handcuffed the prisoner. "Okay, Mr. Halston." He opened the door. A female deputy carrying shackles entered. "This is Officer Daniels. She'll take you to your cell."

Rod rose and planted his right foot on the chair. "Do I still have to wear this thing?" he asked, pointing to the ankle monitor.

"No. Trevor, if you've got the key come on in and unlock it."

Trevor left the enclosure for the interrogation room where he removed the device. The shackles were snapped around his ankles, and Rod was led through the door to the cellblock.

"Do you think this is the truth?" Trevor asked.

The sheriff shrugged. "If it's not, it's damned close. Still don't know why he was eastbound."

"He was returning because he didn't kill her and didn't want a murder charge hanging over his head," the attorney said.

Sheriff Singleton made a face and waved his hand in dismissal. "He avoided answering that question. There's a reason, and coming back to clear his name is crap."

Vicky sat on the hard chair, her hand clenching the empty soda can so hard it crumpled. She'd observed her brother's face and body language with a sharp eye. The little bastard was still lying.

****

Vicky strode into the study, flinging the fox stole over the arm of the chair. The short drive home had been mercifully silent, giving her time to think.

"I'm sorry, Vicky. I wish you could have gotten this information out of your brother before the police did." He sat on the sofa, brushing a hand over his face.

She was too tense to sit, preferring to pace instead. "At least he's out of our hair for a while. He's where he belongs."

"Do you believe this version of his story?"

"Not all of it, but we're getting closer. I watched

his facial expressions and how he fidgeted. He's still hiding things."

"Like what?" Trevor questioned.

"That business about the candlesticks and picture frames for a start. If he'd spent any time in the study or drawing room, he'd have scoped them out. Plus, the police said the painting was leaning against the wall, and the safe partially open. He couldn't have missed seeing that. Rod would have looked inside, and left his prints behind."

"So, you don't think he took them?"

Vicky shook her head and leaned against the desk, arms folded over her chest.

"No. Let's assume he's telling the truth, which means the killer took them, perhaps to make it look like robbery," she suggested.

"Why not go whole hog and take the jewelry, too?"

"Time maybe? And if Rod's guilty, why take the papers in the safe?"

Trevor stared at the fireplace, lines grooving into his forehead. "If your brother panicked, he may have grabbed without thinking."

Vicky rubbed her temples. "I'm too tired to think clearly. It's been a long night."

"Did you learn anything from Corwin?"

"He wasn't nearly as forthcoming as Adam." She gave him the details of Elliot's replies to her questions.

"So, he knew how much money Helen kept in the safe, the combination, and all about the cigar box. Knowledgeable man." He paused, and then bolted upright. "Holy shit!"

She turned to stare. His face bore a stunned expression. He looked at her with a raised right eyebrow.

"What?"

"Vicky, you told him Rosa said he'd been here

that afternoon, but that's not true. She said he and Helen argued the night of the dinner when she caught your brother eavesdropping. She said nothing about the *day of the murder*."

She caught her breath. "He answered the wrong question. If he weren't here the day of the murder, he'd have said so. I made a mistake, and he didn't correct it."

"I'll talk to Rosa first thing in the morning. See exactly who came and went that day."

He rose from the sofa and walked toward the desk where he picked up a sheet of paper.

"What's that?" she asked.

"It's the list of jewelry recovered from the Mercedes." He read silently for a moment, frowned, and then read it again. "That's funny. The ruby ring isn't listed. If he didn't have it, where could it be?"

"Let's see, no candlesticks, no picture frames, and now no ring. It might not be a bad idea to check pawn shops between Granite Springs and beyond where he was picked up. He had a lot of cash on him. It may not have all come from the desk drawer."

"I'll get on it first thing in the morning. I know a guy in Provo who might help. I'll fax him a picture of your brother, and he can check." His lips curved into a lopsided smile. "It's been a long one. I suggest we go to bed."

For a moment, she wondered if he had just propositioned her. God knew his smile was killer, and his crinkling eyes sexy as hell. That throb of awareness pulsated deep in her core.

"I know I've said this before, but you did a good job with Adam and Corwin. You were right. I'd have never gotten half that much information. I'm good at questioning people and spotting lies, but you have the ability to invite confidences. You're a good listener, and know when to make the right comments."

"Years of practice," she answered in a slightly breathless voice.

His praise lifted her spirits. His eyes took on a sleepy, sexy quality. The man oozed sex appeal, stabbing her in all the right places. All of a sudden, the room grew much too hot.

The list of jewelry fluttered from his fingers to the desk. Two quick strides brought him in front of her where he pulled her into his arms. Before she could think, his lips crushed hers.

Heat erupted, turning her body into a blast furnace. With a low moan, Vicky wrapped her arms around his neck. His grasp tightened until a slip of paper wouldn't fit between them. She couldn't distinguish her body heat from his. Her lips parted, allowing their tongues to tangle and taste. A tiny portion of her mind noted the many flavors of Trevor. Fingers played a sensual symphony along her nerves as he ran them up her back. The zipper of her dress parted, the rush of cool air doing little to tame the warmth radiating from her skin.

The ice blue silk drifted from her shoulders to pool around her feet, leaving her semi-naked and shivering with anticipation. The strapless bra joined the dress on the carpet.

Trevor's lips traveled from her mouth and down her neck where he nibbled delicately as though sampling a new hors d'oeuvre. Like slivers of hot steel, the fire raced through her blood blotting all meaningful thoughts from her mind.

His hand slipped around her rib cage to settle over her breast. He squeezed gently, his fingers rolling the center of her nipple until it was diamond hard. Bending her over his arm, he took the sensitive bud into his mouth.

Vicky gasped and cried out. Her core throbbed, and for a moment, she wondered if she'd climax standing up. Her hands fumbled and yanked the polo shirt from his jeans. Eager fingers ran through the hair on his chest and along sculpted muscles to his back before plunging under the waistband to massage his firm derriere. His hand found its way inside the thin strip of silk encasing her warmth.

She cried out again and pulled at his belt until it opened. The fastening and zipper on his jeans followed a second later. Her hand slid into his boxers to encircle the erection in her hand. Hard and hot, it scorched her palm.

A strangling gurgle erupted from Trevor's throat. He raised his head and stepped back. Her ears buzzed and her breaths came in short, tortured gasps as if she'd run a marathon.

He kicked off his shoes, muttering in a hoarse voice, "Slow down. I want this to be in a bed, not on a goddamned sofa or the floor."

He grasped her hand, towed her up the staircase and into his room. Yanking the covers back, Trevor reclaimed her lips, stripped off her panties, and in slow motion, lowered her onto the crisp sheets. He shoved his jeans and the rest of his clothing to the floor before climbing into bed.

His hands and lips roamed her body stoking the flames to new heights. She oozed heat from every pore and writhed when his lips and teeth once again captured her nipple. He nibbled, licked, and sucked until she sobbed.

His hand trailed down her body to caress her very essence. With soft cries and thrusting hips, she invited more. Vicky's hands smoothed down his body until finding the shaft of burning steel. Together, they stroked and massaged, their moans louder and more demanding.

The incredible tightening in her gut wiped out all other sensations. She wanted him and couldn't wait much longer. Her panting breaths threatened to strangle her.

"Trevor, please, please."

He murmured something incoherent, nestled between her legs, and plunged inside filling her in one swift, smooth motion.

Vicky's hands clutched the sheets, her head whipped from side to side on the pillows as she locked her legs around his waist. Rational thought no longer existed. She reacted like an animal, matching his powerful thrusts. Her hands released the sheets to tangle in his hair. His breath seared the skin of her neck.

Her climax erupted with little warning. The fire peaked, crowned, and exploded. She screamed and pumped, prolonging the gut wrenching contractions a few seconds longer, her fingernails scoring his back.

With a shout, he lunged one last time. He twisted his body from side to side as if trying to bury himself deeper. She tightened her legs and raised her hips, grinding her pelvis against his.

Then, it was all over. Her arms and legs fell onto the bed, limp and useless. Trevor rolled onto his back. Both gasped for air. Vicky opened her eyes when the world had ceased spinning.

"Oh, my God," she whispered. She'd never ever had an orgasm like that.

His fingers intertwined with hers. "Yeah, I know." He sucked in several breaths. "I didn't mean for this to happen, but I guess it was inevitable."

"Why inevitable?"

"Because you're too damned beautiful, and too damned sexy for it not to occur." He raised her hand, his lips brushing her fingers. "I knew I was in trouble on the plane."

"I knew it on the dance floor." She spoke the truth. Even though scared to death, she'd felt the attraction the instant he'd touched her.

He turned his head to gaze at her. "Where do we

go from here?"

Vicky drew a deep, trembling breath. "Don't ask me that now. I'm too keyed up."

It was a good question, though. *Where do we go from here? We've crossed the Rubicon and can't go back.*

He sighed. "I suppose you're right. I should have had more self-control, at least until this business with your brother is cleared up, and Helen's murder solved."

She disengaged her hand from his and rolled over, nestling her head on his shoulder, her hand splayed across his chest. Her fingers played with the hair.

"Don't talk about Rod. Not tonight. No Rod, no Elliot, no Adam. I'm tired, so tired of all the drama and the intrigue. Tonight is for us."

His hand smoothed her skin from shoulder to waist pausing to caress her breast along the way.

"All right, tonight is for us." His tongue traced a path down her jaw.

The banked fires rekindled into small flames. Warmth spread to every extremity. The tightening in her core left her breathless and wanting again.

Trevor leaned over crushing her breasts against his chest, and took her lips in a kiss that curled her toes.

The night spiraled away into heat and pleasure.

Chapter Thirteen

Vicky awoke savoring the relaxed indolence after a night of unrestrained passion. She finally opened her eyes. The clock on the nightstand read eight-thirty. Time hadn't been much of a consideration while making love. Her hand stroked the cool sheets next to her. Trevor had risen quite a while ago.

She burrowed deeper under the covers. Last night had proven the most satisfying of her life. She'd always presented a cool demeanor, but Trevor's hands and lips had melted the glacier. The heat that had seared her skin and churned her body still remained.

Rolling over, Vicky stared at the ceiling. *Is this love? I don't know. The question is; does he feel the same?*

They were so different, so night and day, and yet...

No sudden light bulb glaring forth, no loud banging of a drum heralded the epiphany. Even if Trevor didn't care enough to commit, and sent her away when the murder was solved, her old life had ended. Never again would she con.

Maybe it was seeing herself through Trevor's eyes, and not liking the view. Maybe it was seeing Rod, frightened and weak, with jail time in his future. No matter. It was finished, done with.

A weight lifted from her conscience, freeing her

from years of rationalization. Tears welled in her eyes and trickled down her temples. She wiped them away. Victoria Sedgwick, Victoria Grayson, and all the other alter-ego Victoria's disappeared. Victoria Denton had been reborn.

A tantalizing whiff of coffee and frying bacon told her Rosa had breakfast well in hand. She laughed, tossed the covers aside, rose, and realized she was stark naked, reminding her where she'd left her clothing the night before. Then, she glimpsed her cocktail dress draped over the arm of a chair. She slipped it over her head and hurried down the hall to her room where she found the rest of her things.

Showered and dressed, she performed the first task of her new life. Vicky slid the folder purloined from the attic files from under her mattress and returned it. If the damning evidence it contained relegated Rod to prison, then so be it.

****

Trevor forked another bite of French toast into his mouth. He hadn't been this hungry in a long time. This was his third helping and he craved more.

Or perhaps what he craved was Vicky. Scam artist or not, she had wormed her way under his skin and into his blood. For some reason, he didn't mind. How had it happened? He didn't have a clue, but from the first moment he'd seen her bikini-clad body romping on a Miami beach, he'd known she was dynamite. Apparently, he was the match. Last night, he'd been blown off a precipice into an unknown abyss. He didn't seem to mind that either.

I've been careful with relationships. No other woman held a candle to...

Rosa entered the dining room interrupting his thoughts.

"More coffee, *Senor* Sloane?"

"Yes, bring in another pot. I don't know when Miss Denton will be down, but I'm sure she'll be

203

hungry. By the way, I have some news."

He told her of Halston's re-arrest and of the new evidence discovered by the police.

"That is wonderful, *senor*." She smiled and clasped a hand over her heart, her eyes brimming with tears. "I know that stinking *puerco* killed my *senora*."

"After breakfast, I'd like to ask you a couple of questions, if you don't mind."

"Of course, *senor*. What about?"

He shook his head and rose to refill his plate. "Later. Just a few questions about the day of the murder."

Rosa nodded and left. He had resumed his seat when Vicky walked into the room.

His gaze immediately took in the black wool slacks, crisp, form-fitting white blouse, and red, flat-heeled shoes. Her hair was held in the nape of her neck by a large clip, also red. She looked good enough to eat. He chomped on a piece of bacon instead.

She pulled out her chair and sat, her gaze never leaving his face. He'd been staring, too.

"Good morning," she said.

Funny, he'd never noticed the musical lilt to her voice. His breath stopped. Then he swallowed, and gulped his lukewarm coffee.

"Good morning. Did you sleep well?" *Did she sleep well? What the hell kind of silly question is that?*

A smile brought her face to life as she poured a cup of coffee. "Who slept?"

He had to laugh. "Touché. It was a stupid question."

She eyed the sideboard, and then rose, filling her plate. Reseated, she said, "Thanks for bringing up my clothes."

"I woke up about seven and realized I needed to

get them out of sight. Rosa doesn't normally go into the study except to clean, but I didn't want to leave everything lying on the floor." He reached over and laid his hand on her arm. "Vicky, I may not have intended for last night to happen, but I'm not sorry it did."

She smiled again. "I'm not either, but I think of the eight hundred pound gorilla thing. It'll be hard to ignore."

He sighed and resumed eating. "We'll deal with the consequences later. The problem will be avoiding a recurrence."

Her gaze pinned him with a curious look. "Do we want to avoid making love again? I enjoyed it."

"So did I, but it could complicate things."

"Things are already complicated."

Rosa returned with a fresh pot of coffee. He chewed another bite of bacon thoughtfully. She'd nailed it. The simple delivery of a con artist to his victimized aunt had turned into something that dug deep into his soul.

"Do you mind if I ask a personal question?" she asked.

"What is it?"

"You know all about me, but I know little about you. How old are you? Where were you born? Did you go to college?"

He put his fork down and refilled his cup with fresh coffee.

"I was born and raised in Los Angeles, and next February 26th, I'll be forty-two." He shook his head. "Guess that must sound ancient to you."

"Not at all. I turned thirty-six last June."

"I know. It's in your file."

She laughed softly. "Did you have a good childhood?"

"I suppose. I mean, I did the usual boy things. I remember Christmases were the best. The entire family used to congregate here between the holidays. The house was full of friends and neighbors."

"Where did you go to college?"

Trevor's gaze locked onto her lips sliding over the fork to take a piece of French toast into her mouth. *God Almighty, she's sitting at the breakfast table, and I'm having fantasies about those lips on...*

He struggled to suppress the surge of heat racing through his body before answering.

"My college of choice was Colorado in Boulder, close to Uncle Roland and Aunt Helen. I came to Granite Springs on a regular basis."

Vicky sipped her coffee. "What about women? Forty-two and no one's snapped you up?"

His gaze focused on his plate, and then he picked up his fork, but didn't spear any food. *I should have seen this coming.*

"Uh-oh, I can see I asked an awkward question. Did she break your heart?"

He hadn't talked about Rebecca in a long while. Even now, almost twenty years later, the memories hurt, but he wanted Vicky to know.

"Yes," he replied, his voice low. "Her name was Rebecca, and she was my wife."

She set her cup down with a hard click, her face impassive. "I'm sorry, I shouldn't have asked."

He sat back in his chair, his gaze settling on the wall over her shoulder. "We met my senior year in college. Dark hair, dark eyes, she had my heart the minute she smiled. We were married a month after I graduated. I majored in Criminal Justice and had been accepted into law school at UCLA. It was a hard grind. Becca worked, insisting I go full time so I could thrust her into living the good life sooner. It was a standing joke."

Trevor paused as he thought about those days—carefree, happy, and unsuspecting. He shook his head. It had been a long time ago. Vicky remained silent, but her gaze told him she was prepared to listen.

"I finished my first year at the top of my class. On our anniversary a few weeks later, I splurged on a bottle of champagne, New York strips, and a dozen red roses figuring to surprise her. Then came the knock on the door. It was the police. Becca had been killed, run down in a crosswalk by a drunk who ran the light."

The impassive expression vanished, replaced with shocked sympathy. "Oh, Trevor, I'm so sorry. You must have been devastated."

"For three months, I couldn't function. I quit law school and joined the army volunteering for front line duty. I expected to die—hoped I would. When I didn't, I realized that's not how things work. It wasn't my turn."

"How long were you in the army?"

"Eight years. Served in Kuwait and Kosovo. I returned to L. A. after my discharge, got my P. I. license, and worked for an established firm before teaming up with Quinn and starting my own. I met Quinn in the army." He paused, thinking not of his former partner, but of the policeman at the door. "She'll be dead nineteen years this summer."

Vicky shifted in her chair, her gaze directed to the liquid in her cup. "That's a long time. You must have had relationships. I refuse to believe last night was an eruption after nineteen years of celibacy."

"I'm only human, and yes, I've been with women, but things never progressed."

She blinked her eyes, not lifting her gaze. "No one ever measured up, right? Have you considered marrying again?"

Funny. Twenty-four hours ago, he'd have said no, but now, he wasn't so sure. It dawned on him he was lonely, and for the first time in years, thought about the things he and Becca never enjoyed—a home, children, even growing old together.

"I haven't thought about it," he said slowly. "Her death was the low point of my life."

Vicky lowered the cup to the saucer. "I understand low points. My whole life has been one. I couldn't see a way out until Quinn's damned map showed up. To me, the treasure at the end was my ticket to something better."

"Quinn told me. Must have been hard to find out it was non-existent."

"Crushing. My life was being wasted. I may not have had money while working legitimate jobs, but I felt a whole lot better about myself when I did."

He folded his napkin and pushed his plate away shrugging as if a huge weight had lifted from his shoulders. Becca's image, forever young, flashed through his mind. She smiled before fading away. Trevor clenched his fists to hide the sudden trembling. Had he just let go of the past?

"You finish eating. I have to ask Rosa those questions we discussed last night. Come into the study when you're done." He rose and walked from the room aware his life had changed.

Trevor detoured to the kitchen. "Rosa, when you're ready, come into the study."

"*Si, senor.*"

He entered the room and sat behind the desk and tucked the disturbing breakfast conversation into the back of his mind. Time to get down to the business of Helen's murder.

Rosa entered, closed the door, and sat in the chair in front of him, her gaze darting from place to place.

"Please relax, Rosa, you're not in any trouble. I just need some clarification about the day of the murder."

She frowned. "Clarification?"

"I need to know what happened that day. Begin

at the beginning. Did my aunt eat breakfast?"

"*Si, senor*. She eat, and then went into the study. The door, it was not closed, and I heard her talking to you. She sounded happy."

"That's right, I called about eight-thirty. Was Mr. Harvey here?"

She snorted and made a face. "*Si*, he came down, but didn't eat. He had coffee and read the newspaper. I was making lunch when he took the car keys and left. I asked the *senora* if he would be in for lunch and she say no, *Senor* Harvey running errands for her in town and that I should just make her a salad."

"Did she have any visitors that morning?"

"No. She spend a lot of time on the phone and on the computer. Carlos cut the grass and came in for his money, but she told him to come back later. She was busy."

"Did she owe him anything other than from that day?"

"No, *senor*, not that I know of."

He picked up the letter opener, testing its point with his fingertip. So his aunt spent time on the computer, an instrument she hated. And Carlos had been here.

"Did he come back in the afternoon?"

The housekeeper shifted and clasped her hands in her lap. "I do not know. I leave at two o'clock to do shopping for dinner."

"When did you return?"

"A little after four. The *senora* request an early dinner. She did not say why."

"So, you have no idea if anyone visited while you were gone." Damn, he'd hoped to hear Corwin's name dropped.

"No, *senor*. *Senor* Harvey, he was in the den when I come home." She lifted her gaze from her hands to his face. "Do you think someone came?"

He shrugged. "It's possible."

"It was not Carlos, *senor*. He say he had business in town and would come back the next day."

"I'm sure it wasn't, Rosa." *Could Carlos have returned that night? Had an argument taken place with disastrous results?*

"You took a cab home after serving dinner?"

"*Si*, my car did not start."

"Did Carlos come by later to fix it?"

"*Si*. He say he and a friend come by after work. They fix and Carlos drive it to me."

After work or during work? Which means Carlos could have been at the house alone with Aunt Helen.

"Thank you, Rosa. You've been very helpful. I wish I had been here to protect her."

The housekeeper nodded, wiping a tear from her eye.

"Take tonight off. Miss Denton and I will eat out."

She rose, nodded again, and left.

He let his gaze wander to the painting over the fireplace. *Corwin was here all right, and I'd bet good, old Carlos put in an appearance, too.*

In spite of the lawyer's slip of the tongue to Vicky, he had no proof of anything. And he'd love to get a gander at his aunt's e-mail and computer, but the police had confiscated it.

With a sigh, he turned on his laptop and checked his e-mail, glad to see a lengthy message from Marylou.

****

Vicky pushed a piece of French toast around her plate. Trevor's revelations had sent her appetite into the great beyond.

I was right. No one will ever measure up to his dead wife. She laid down her fork and raised the cup to her lips with trembling fingers. *Okay, he's not interested in marriage. I can live with that. Perhaps marriage isn't for me, either. Doesn't matter. I'll survive. I always do. But no backsliding. Go legit.*

She picked up her plate and carried it into the empty kitchen setting it beside the sink, and then grasped the edge of the countertop blinking tears from her eyes.

Don't dwell on it. Find something to do. Keep busy.

She returned to the dining room and removed the dishes from the sideboard. Next she scraped the meager leftovers into the garbage, squirted liquid soap into the sink, and ran the water. Grabbing a scrubber, she plunged her hands in and washed the plates and cups. Physical labor was therapeutic, transferring some of the emotional stress to her task.

She didn't hear Rosa enter over the sound of the water.

"*Senorita*! What are you doing? That is my job. You are a guest."

The poor woman sounded upset. "I haven't been pulling my weight the last week or so."

Rosa shooed her away from the sink. "You are big help to *Senor* Sloane. That is enough for me. You will help him keep that killer in jail."

Vicky dried her hands remembering the housekeeper did not as yet know of her relationship with Rod.

She hung up the dishtowel and made her way into the study where Trevor was printing out something from his computer. Gazing at his profile, her heart twisted, and more than anything, she wanted to hear something from him that would give her hope for the future.

Get a grip, dumb ass. Ain't gonna happen.

She straightened her shoulders and called upon the ice maiden to bring back her cool demeanor.

He looked up from the pages he collected as the printer spit them out. "Done with breakfast?"

"Yes. Did Rosa give you any information?"

He told her of his conversation with the housekeeper.

"About what we expected. What's on the agenda for today?"

"You might be interested in this." He handed her the papers. "It's the results of my search on Walter and Adam."

She read, struggling to keep her mind on business. The eight hundred pound gorilla had gained weight.

"Those are credit card receipts. Both Walter and Adam were in Granite Springs the week of the murder."

"But apparently on different days. According to this, your uncle was here on Tuesday, but your cousin showed up on Thursday."

"Walter had dinner at a place called Dirty Dan's just south of town. I've been there. It's a honky-tonk. Not the place he'd choose to eat."

"He might have been coming to see your aunt, or was on his way home," she offered.

"Wrong direction. Look at the amount. A beer and a burger would cost fifteen bucks."

"It says here, the bill was thirty-seven fifty." Vicky squinted at the receipt scan. "He's a lousy tipper."

Trevor waved a hand. "I don't think he was alone."

"Who was with him? Adam?"

"If Aunt Helen wanted to meet someone away from the house or her usual haunts like the Foothills Diner, she'd go to Dirty Dan's. I think they had a meeting right after she came back from Las Vegas with your brother in tow."

He steepled his fingers under his chin and

smiled. The lines around his eyes deepened. Even with the subject matter, he leaked sex appeal like a sieve. She gave the mental gorilla a swift kick in the ass and forced herself to concentrate.

"I wonder if anybody at this place remembers them," she said. "A few questions might be in order." She riffled through the pages. "What about Adam?"

"The receipts show him getting gas in a small town twenty miles north on Thursday afternoon."

"We have no proof he was actually in Granite Springs."

"Look further. Adam was arrested later that day in Grayson, where the mine is located, on a charge of DUI and road rage. He pulled a gun on some hapless woman who drifted into his lane."

"So, let's assume he met or talked with your aunt. Maybe he asked for money and she refused. He leaves, gets wasted, and the motorist bears the brunt of his pent up fury."

"That's my guess. Read further and you'll see Marylou made some headway with Rocky Mountain Mineral Corporation headquartered in Greeley."

"Where's the mine?"

"Richardson Mining offices are in Mineral City fifteen miles from Grayson where the mine is located."

"How far is Granite Springs from Mineral City?"

"Fifty miles."

"How did your Uncle Roland run the business from so far away?"

"He didn't. He left the actual running of the mine to Walter, preferring to make an appearance once a week. His father did much the same."

Vicky whistled. "No wonder Walter was pissed about the sale. He had little input. What did the books look like all those years your uncle was absently in charge."

"According to the reports, the books were in

order, but the head accountant retired shortly after the sale twelve years ago. He's since died. If he knew or fixed anything, he took it to the grave."

Trevor ran a hand through his hair, a worried expression on his face.

"Read further. Rocky Mountain Mineral is not happy with the way things are being run. Walter's on the road to retirement, and Adam's attention is focused on wine, women, and song. He's about to get the axe."

"I wonder if he knows."

"I'm sure the handwriting's on the wall."

Vicky took a deep breath and stared out the window marshalling her thoughts.

"Let's assume Adam knows, or at least suspects, he's about to bite the big one. His life is unraveling fast—the drinking, the womanizing, the rape and assault charge hanging over his head. Maybe he comes to ask his aunt to intervene, save his job, that sort of thing."

"To which my aunt would say no."

She sifted through the papers again, reading the credit card receipts, and then straightened.

"Trevor, did you see this one?"

"Which? There are a lot of them over the two weeks prior to Helen's death."

"This one." She singled out a sheet and placed it in front of him. "There are four receipts crammed on this page. Check out the third one. It's a bar bill from The Wrecking Ball."

Trevor picked up the paper, frowning. "That's a dive on the west side of town. It's popular with bikers, and prostitutes. What the hell would Adam be doing there?"

"That isn't important. Look at the date."

His eyebrows rose and he sent her a sharp glance. "It's the day of the murder, and the time is listed as nine-fifteen p.m."

214

"Suppose Adam got drunk, came to the house, and killed your aunt when she refused his request for money or intervention." She paused as another thought occurred to her. "Rod could be telling the truth. He said a dark-colored car raced by him on the road. What color car does Adam Richardson drive?"

Trevor sucked in a deep breath and exhaled so hard the papers on the desk fluttered.

"He drives a black Lexus."

Chapter Fourteen

Vicky's heart raced at the news. So, Adam had more of a motive for murder than they first thought. Motive and opportunity—a powerful marriage.

"Are you going to tell the sheriff?"

"Yeah, but first I want to have a talk with the bartender at The Wrecking Ball. If Adam was drunk, he may have let something slip."

"It's barely ten. Are they open this early?"

"The dump's never closed. They stop serving at curfew, but the door is always open. Al's been trying to close them down for years. He thinks the after hours business is drugs."

"And Adam was there." She rose. "I'll get my coat."

Trevor shook his head. "No way. This place is rough at any time of day. Your presence will add gas to the fire. Stay here. I'll be back for lunch."

Her first reaction was to argue, but then decided against it. He had a look of determination on his face. If the bartender didn't answer the questions, things could get rough.

"All right, but please be careful."

He smiled and rose from behind the desk, stopping at her side. She stood facing him. He planted a swift, hard kiss on her mouth.

"I'll be fine. I can look damned nasty when I want. Besides, Tiny won't want any trouble this early in the morning."

"Tiny?"

"The bartender. Stands six feet, six inches and weighs in around three-fifty. Don't worry, I can handle him."

"Not if he belts you one."

He laughed and kissed her again. "I'll be all right."

Vicky tidied up the desk when he left the room. With nothing to do but wait, she wandered into the kitchen seeking another task.

"I'm at loose ends, Rosa. Can I help with lunch?"

"*Si, senorita*, if you want. I am making chicken salad."

She busied herself with cutting up cooked chicken breasts into bite-sized chunks, all the while worrying about Trevor. Her hands may have been busy, but her mind refused to rest. *Is he there yet? Please God, don't let him antagonize anyone.*

Maybe conversation would help. "I'm not sure Mr. Sloane will live on the premises when this is all over. What will you do? If you invest your inheritance wisely, you can live very well here in Granite Springs."

"I am so grateful to the *senora* for thinking of me, and I have great use for the money—not that I am happy she's dead," the housekeeper hastened to add.

"Of course you aren't. I know you were very devoted to Mrs. Richardson. What do you plan to do? Buy a nice car?" She figured Carlos had plans, too, and hoped none of the money was earmarked for her worthless son.

"Perhaps. That would be nice, but I want to bring my sister and her family to the United States. They live in Chiapas province. It is *muy* bad. The *federales* and the rebels are everywhere and kill for no reason. Here, they will be safe."

"That's a wonderful idea. Good luck."

Vicky worked in silence, thinking how to question Rosa about Adam Richardson and his possible presence in Granite Springs the night of the murder.

"I want to apologize for the day of the funeral."

"*Senorita?*"

"About the nasty things Jason and Adam said about Helen leaving you money. Mr. Sloane told me."

The housekeeper shrugged as she mixed mayonnaise and chopped celery in a small bowl.

"I am not family, so I do not mind."

For a woman with Latin blood, she's remarkably impassive. Vicky tried another tack.

"Jason is young, but Mr. Richardson was rude. I had dinner with him the other night. He had too much to drink and I had to come home in a taxi. I'm glad he didn't get any of your employer's money."

"He is a bad one. He argue with the *senora* the last time he was here."

"When was that?"

Rosa halted mixing and stared out the kitchen window, her face screwed up in thought. "It was after she come back with *Senor* Harvey. He come by one morning. The *senora* called him a stupid donkey." She returned to mixing.

"Stupid donkey? You mean a dumb ass?"

"*Si,* that is it."

"Rosa, could Mr. Richardson have been here the day of the murder?"

"I tell *Senor* Sloane, no one come here in morning. I was gone in afternoon."

"Someone could have come while you were gone or after you left that night."

Rosa shrugged. "It is possible."

"I'm sure you would have noticed any cars heading for the house that night."

"I do not remember. I was tired."

The woman turned to stare with a frown.

Instinct told Vicky the time for questioning had run out.

"Chicken's ready. Shall I add it to your bowl?"

"*Si, senorita*. Thank you for your help. I will finish now."

I've been dismissed. She nodded and headed for the study to await Trevor's return.

****

Trevor drove home frustrated. Tiny remembered the well-dressed man, but that was all. Tiny evaded all questions with a simple, "Don't know."

He'd been about to leave when Carlos walked in. They'd stared at each other in surprise. Trevor recovered first.

"Carlos, what are you doing here?"

"I might ask you the same. I work here. Little early to be hitting the sauce, isn't it?" The brash Latino pushed by. "By the way, I'll be over after I eat for my money."

Getting Carlos one-on-one sounded like a good idea. "I'll be there. One o'clock?"

Carlos nodded, and Trevor had left, remembering Marylou's information about Carlos and Adam meeting. *And now, we find out Adam was not only in town the night of the murder, but probably talking to Carlos in the bargain. Was he paying off an old debt or running up a new one?*

Now, he entered the house and walked into the study. Vicky waited, curled up on the sofa with a file in her hand.

"Thank God, you're back. How did it go?"

He told her the little he knew, and mentioned Carlos.

"Carlos gives me the creeps."

"What are you reading?"

"More files. These are her paid bills for August. Nothing exciting, unless you count the overpayment of six dollars to the water company."

Rosa appeared in the doorway to announce lunch. He ate quickly with little conversation, anticipating his meeting with Carlos. Even though he loathed doing it, Trevor decided to pay the two hundred Carlos had demanded earlier for services rendered. It might loosen his tongue.

He's the kind of guy who makes it his business to know things—and profit from them.

He ate the last of his chicken salad and finished the iced tea.

"What are you going to ask Carlos?" Vicky asked in a low voice, casting her gaze toward the kitchen door.

"Haven't decided yet."

"Want me to stay?"

He shot a look toward her smiling face. He didn't want Vicky anywhere near that predatory vulture.

"No. Not this time. I want him *mano y mano.*"

"Are you sure?"

"Absolutely."

She drained the last of her tea and patted her mouth with a napkin, her lips curling into a smile. A surge of warmth spread throughout his body.

Trevor took a deep breath and rose. "I'll be in the study."

A few minutes later, Vicky entered. "I'll just take a couple of files to the den." She picked up several folders. "Good luck."

The front door opened, and then slammed shut. Heavy footsteps crossed the foyer. Before Vicky could leave, Carlos appeared in the doorway, and sauntered in, giving her a sweeping look from head to toe. His gaze lingered on her breasts.

"Hello, *chiquita,*" he said in a drawling voice, his lids half-shuttering his eyes. "You look beautiful. Suppose we go out to dinner tonight?"

Vicky stared back at him, replying in a frosty

tone, "I don't think so. I don't plan on being hungry."

Trevor wanted to punch the smirking Latin. Carlos watched Vicky's swaying hips leave as she closed the door.

"Sit down, Ramirez."

He sat in one of the chairs, and propped his booted feet up on the desk, his sculpted mouth drawn up in a suggestive smile.

"Whew! That is one damned fine secretary you have, Sloane. Tell me, do her services include more than taking dictation?"

A hot river of anger flowed from his stomach to his chest. Trevor forced his hands not to clench.

"Never mind Miss Denton, and get your feet off my aunt's desk. I want to talk to you."

Carlos removed his feet, still smirking. "I want my money. Your aunt owed me two hundred dollars."

"My aunt owed you fifty dollars, but I may pay what you ask in return for some information."

Carlos clasped his hands behind his head. "Yeah? What kind of information?"

"When did you last talk to my aunt on the day of the murder?"

"Around noon. I did my work and asked to be paid. She said to come back later."

"Did you?"

The young man grinned. "No. I was busy."

"Doing what?"

"Business transactions that are none of your affair."

"Your mother said she was out in the afternoon running errands, yet she called a cab to go home that evening."

"Her car didn't start. A simple problem. A buddy dropped me off after work, I fixed it, and drove it home."

"What time?"

"I don't wear a watch, Sloane."

"And you weren't here at all that afternoon?"

He shrugged. "I can't remember."

Trevor eyed Carlos. The man was a smooth liar, but a liar just the same. He knew more.

"Sure you didn't come into the house to ask for your money and overhear my aunt and someone arguing in the study?"

"Someone? You mean like Elliot Corwin or this Harvey guy?"

His stomach tightened. He was right. Carlos had seen and probably overheard one or the other of the men.

"Did you see either of them?"

"I saw them plenty of times. I just can't remember when." He grinned. "Now, how about my two hundred bucks?"

Trevor was tempted to ask about the man's relationship with Adam, but didn't want to reveal he knew. Instead, he stood and reaching into his hip pocket, extracted his wallet. He peeled off two fifty dollar bills and tossed them onto the desk.

"That information was only worth a hundred. More information, more money."

Carlos snorted and unclasped his hands, before rising. He snatched the money and shoved it into his front pocket.

"I'll think about it." He sauntered from the room, his boots clomping on the hardwood as he headed toward the kitchen.

"Damned little twerp," he muttered out loud. "I'll bet he eavesdropped on Corwin and Aunt Helen that afternoon. Probably did the same with anyone else who stopped by. He knows exactly what went down."

Vicky entered the room and closed the door. "Did you get anything out of the creep?"

He gave her the gist of the conversation and

spied the folder clutched in her hand. "Did you find anything?"

She sat in the recently vacated chair and opened the file.

"I'm not sure, but look at this. It's an invoice dated September 29th from a detective agency in Seattle. I found it not in accounts payable, but in this folder labeled with a question mark."

She handed him the sheet of paper. "Puget Sound Private Investigations? What the hell?"

The invoice itemized a background check, a financial check, and an investigation into an investment firm. No specifics were given, but the bill was a whopping fifteen hundred dollars.

·"Did she pay it? I don't remember seeing anything in her canceled checks," he said.

"It might not be there yet if she paid it just before the murder."

"I don't get it. Why would my aunt call in a P. I. in Seattle? Why not use me? I told her I'd investigate anyone she wanted." He ran a hand over his face. "Is anything else in the folder?"

She laid the folder in front of him. "Several printouts from various websites of other detective agencies, but that's it. If she got a bill, wouldn't the work have been completed?"

Trevor re-read the invoice. "Definitely. Didn't your brother say my aunt told him she had business to conduct?"

"That's why he was at Marley's." Vicky frowned and flipped through several folders on the corner of the desk. "If the invoice is dated at the end of September, then where is the report? Wouldn't she have received that first?"

"She certainly would."

He stood and strode to the file cabinets in the corner, searching the contents. Several minutes later, he closed the bottom drawer and rose from a crouch.

"Nada. No folders labeled P. I. reports or anything along those lines. Damn, Helen, what were you doing and why didn't you let me handle it?"

Vicky perched on the edge of the desk. "Maybe she was investigating a family member—someone she didn't want you to know about."

"Jason?"

"Or her brother, or even you." She crossed her arms over her chest.

"Me?" His voice rose in surprise with a touch of outrage. "She had no reason to investigate me."

"Don't give me that look. She recently changed her will. She could have been making sure you were capable of being the executor."

Trevor sank into the chair behind the desk and pinched the bridge of his nose. Would his aunt investigate him?

"Trevor? Suppose your aunt *was* investigating someone in the family. Suppose the report she received was less than favorable. *Suppose* she planned on showing it to you when you returned to Granite Springs. Where would she keep it?"

"In a file drawer, the desk, the..." He suddenly understood the direction of Vicky's question. His gaze swung to the fireplace. "And the safe was empty. Elliot Corwin admitted he'd been here on the afternoon of the murder."

"Adam Richardson was in Granite Springs that night."

"And Carlos was at the house to fix his mother's car. Who else could have shown up? Jason?"

Trevor reached for his cell phone and dialed in the number of the Seattle detective agency.

"Puget Sound Private Investigators, how may I help you?"

"My name is Trevor Sloane with Sloane Investigations in Los Angeles. I need to talk to someone regarding one of your clients."

"One moment, please." He listened to canned music, tapping a pencil in time to the beat until a voice came on the line.

"This is Tom Schiller. How can I help you?"

Trevor repeated his request, adding, "The lady in question was my aunt. She was murdered last week. I found your invoice in her files, but no report. Can you help me? Why did she hire you?"

"Mr. Sloane, as a private investigator you must know I can't reveal any information about clients, not even to relatives."

"How about the executor of her will?"

"I'm sorry, but those are the rules."

"Thank you for your time."

Trevor hung up, his pencil still tapping. It had been worth a shot.

"Didn't tell you anything, huh?" Vicky asked.

He shook his head. "I wouldn't either if I got a call like that."

"What's next?"

"I'll try the legal angle and get a court order." He tossed the pencil onto the blotter. "That report has to be at the heart of the matter."

"Did your aunt have an address book?"

"Sure. Police took it. Why?"

Vicky frowned and chewed her lower lip. "I once played a mark who kept a second address book in her bedroom."

He rose. "Let's go check her bedroom."

He searched the closet while Vicky rifled through drawers.

"Got it!" she said, standing next to the nightstand.

"Let's take a look."

They trooped back down to the study. "You read the names, and I'll see if they ring a bell."

Vicky opened the book, and riffled through the

pages with a frown. "There's nothing under A, B, or C. The first entry is Detective Agency with a 206 area code."

"That's Seattle. I just called them. Nothing under C, like in Corwin?"

"Nothing."

"I guess she might not include him since she knew his number. Same with her best friend, Marlene Babcock. Keep looking."

She flipped pages, shaking her head. "Here's something under M. It says Michaels Accounting. Area code is 303."

"That's Denver. Why would she contact an accountant in Denver? Bob Palmer is her accountant in Granite Springs. Been with him for years. What's the number?"

Vicky gave him the number, and he dialed. The phone was answered on the third ring.

"Michaels and Sanford, how may I help you?"

"Are you a CPA firm?"

"Yes, sir."

"My name is Trevor Sloane, and I'm the executor of the late Helen Richardson's estate. I found your number in her files and need to talk to whoever handled her account."

"That name again, sir?"

"Trevor Sloane, calling on behalf of Helen Richardson of Granite Springs."

"Please hold." Once again he listened to a pop diva for several minutes before anyone came on the line.

"This is Jeff Sanford."

Trevor repeated his request.

"I'm sorry to hear of Mrs. Richardson's death. She was a nice lady."

"I'm confused, Mr. Sanford. Mrs. Richardson's CPA is located in Granite Springs. I just read his latest monthly report in her files. Can you help me?"

"She came by one day a month or so ago. She wanted us to perform an independent audit on an investment company out of Denver. When I explained we'd have to have the corporation's permission, she requested we hold. Then, she called about a week or so ago asking if we could do the same with an investment firm in Granite Springs."

Trevor's nerves hummed. An investment firm in Granite Springs? There was only one—Corwin Investments.

"She said to get whatever I needed from the companies."

"And did you?"

"Mr. Corwin called a few days ago refusing permission. Colorado Land Investors gave the okay."

"Can you audit one without the other?"

"Yes, but we haven't begun as of yet. Do you want us to continue?"

"Absolutely. Could you please shoot me a letter confirming all of this with times and dates included?"

"Be glad to."

"Thank you." He hung up and relayed the information to Vicky.

"I wonder when they contacted Elliot with the request." Her eyes held a speculative look.

"I wonder if he refused because Helen was dead or because he's a crook."

Trevor stood and walked to the window, staring at the lengthening shadows. He'd bet the farm Helen had Puget Sound investigating Elliot Corwin. A surge of satisfaction washed over him. His aunt had taken his advice. He just wished she'd let him know.

He turned back toward Vicky. "I think we're getting closer to the answer. How about we go to Dirty Dan's tonight? It's not too far, just south in Alpine on the other side of the ridge."

She raised an eyebrow, giving him an arch look.

"And we just might have a discussion with the bartender and waitress regarding two patrons a few weeks ago?"

He laughed. "Why not? They also have a jukebox and a decent dance floor. Feel like going low-brow?"

A corner of her mouth curled. "Let me get changed. Jeans and a t-shirt all right?"

"Perfect."

Trevor couldn't keep his gaze off Vicky as she left the room. Tight jeans and a t-shirt. Add a pair of high heels and he'd salivate.

****

Dirty Dan's didn't look any different from other honky-tonks Vicky had patronized. Her watch read seven o'clock, yet a sizable crowd guzzled beer and chowed down on wings.

Trevor led her through the maze of tables, snagging one next to the large dance floor.

A short distance away, a waitress balanced a tray laden with beer bottles over her head. A stage behind the dance floor held the biggest jukebox she'd ever seen.

A waitress stopped next to them, wiped the varnished wooden table top with a damp rag, and slapped a couple of menus down.

"Name's Kathy. I'll be back in a couple of minutes to get your order. You want a pitcher?"

"Yeah, make it Bud," he said.

Vicky opened the menu, read for a few minutes, and then closed it again.

"This place won't make the American Heart Association's list of healthy eating establishments."

Trevor laughed. "If it ain't burgers, it's fried."

"What would you suggest?"

"Any of the burgers or the chicken tenders."

Trevor sent his gaze toward the bar. "Looks like a lull. Think I'll go have a chat with the bartenders. If the waitress comes back order me a Giant Double

Bacon Cheeseburger and fries." He rose and winked. "No bathroom windows, now."

She wanted to laugh, but sent him a look of mock outrage instead. "Maybe you should handcuff me to the table."

"I might handcuff you, but not to the table."

He winked again and moved off as she fought to control the gush of heat rolling through her. That big bed of his was a four poster, and her mind immediately conjured up a vision that sent sparks racing along her nerves. Handcuffs, huh? She'd never done it with handcuffs. She inhaled a deep breath and blew it out.

Slow down. The night is still young.

The waitress brought the pitcher and two mugs. Vicky poured and cast her gaze toward the bar. Trevor was at the end talking with the bartender. A movement out of the corner of her eye caught her attention. A big, beefy cowboy type a couple of tables over had pushed back his chair as though ready to rise. He grinned and saluted in her direction with his beer bottle. She froze him with the ice maiden look. He ceased grinning and frowned.

Hurry up, Trevor. I don't want to fight him off alone.

The waitress returned, sparing her from further unwanted attention.

"Made up your mind yet?"

"Yes, my friend will have the Giant Double Bacon Cheeseburger with fries, and I'll go with the chicken tenders."

"How do you want the burger cooked?"

"Uh, medium-rare, I guess." Vicky shifted in her seat. "Have you got a second?"

The waitress tossed a glance around the rapidly filling room. "You're kidding, right?"

"I have a couple of questions to ask. It won't take long, I promise."

"Oh, all right, but make it snappy."

"Were you working on a Monday night two weeks ago?"

"Nope. That's my day off."

"Do you know who might have been here? I'm trying to locate the mother of a friend of mine. She sometimes gets it in her mind to take little trips without telling her family. They worry." Vicky spoke in a pleading voice and forced tears to her eyes.

The girl's face softened. "Let me ask. Monday's aren't too busy as a rule."

She left and Vicky once again allowed her gaze to travel to the bar. Trevor was now at the other end talking to a different bartender.

A shadow fell across the table. She looked up to see the cowboy next to her.

"How about some company, little lady?"

"I'm here with someone." Her frosty voice formed icicles in the air.

"Well, now, he don't look too attentive. I call that unforgivable. What say we do a little dancing when they crank up the music?"

"I only dance with the guy what brung me." She mimicked his accent, drawling in a deliberate mocking tone.

The arrow found its mark. The cowboy scowled. "Ain't no call to get uppity."

"Beat it."

The man sneered, and muttering something under his breath, strode back to his table.

Vicky gulped half the contents of her mug, casting a glance back to the bar. Trevor still stood in the same place.

Come on, come on. I'm sitting here in skinny jeans, a tight red t-shirt, and red stilettos—a magnet for every weirdo in the place.

She hadn't minded Trevor ogling her as she'd walked down the stairs earlier. The look he'd given her spoke volumes even though his words had been, "Looking good."

Someone tapped her on the shoulder. She twisted her head ready to send another cowboy on his way. A woman stood next to her.

"I'm Jenny. Kathy said you're looking for someone?"

Vicky relaxed. "Yes, thank you. Can you have a seat?"

Jenny pulled out a chair. "I'm on break. How can I help you?"

She gave the newcomer the same story, including a detailed description of Helen and Walter, and then added, "And he'd be a lousy tipper."

"Yeah, I remember. Gave me two bucks. Cheap bastard."

"Can you remember any conversation they may have had while you served them?"

"Not specifically, but I do remember the woman seemed pissed about something. She ate and left real fast. I saw him later at the bar." She shrugged. "I'm sorry. That's the best I can do."

"That's all right. At least she isn't with the cheapskate." She reached in her pocket and slipped the woman a ten.

"Thanks." Jenny left as Trevor returned. "Any luck?"

"Walter was into several bourbon and waters by the time Helen joined him. He was nicked they had to meet here and made a comment to Aunt Helen who said if he wanted to talk, he'd have to do it where she wanted. Then they left to get a table. Later, Walter bellied up to the bar and sucked down several more drinks. What were you and the waitress talking about?"

She gave him the information Jenny had passed on.

He took a long pull of beer. "So, the two tally.

Both were pissed."

Their food arrived. Trevor dug into his enormous burger with gusto, while she eyed the chicken tenders in front of her. She dipped one in the ranch sauce, and bit in. For cheap fried food, it wasn't bad.

"So, do you think Walter was asking for money?"

"Of course, he was," Trevor replied, wiping his mouth with a napkin. "He must have wanted that condo bad."

They finished their meal and ordered another pitcher. One of the bartenders mounted the stage and turned on the jukebox. The first song was a slow, sexy ballad.

Trevor grinned. "Shall we?"

He led her onto the floor, and took her into his arms. As the crowd thickened, their feet ceased moving, and they stood swaying to the music.

Vicky laid her head on his shoulder and wrapped her arms around his neck while his hands slid around her waist occasionally straying to her derriere. Her heart thumped in slow beats keeping time with the music. If she raised her head, they'd end up necking on the dance floor like a couple of teenagers. The warmth of his body seeped into hers fanning already glowing embers.

The song ended and a faster, more toe-tapping selection played. They continued to sway as though to a different tune. Then a gruff voice interrupted.

"Cutting in."

Vicky raised her head. It was the bothersome cowboy. He also swayed, but the odor of his breath told her it was beer induced. His face bore an ugly expression as though daring her to refuse.

"Not you again," she snapped.

Trevor tightened his grip and whirled her away, saying over his shoulder, "Not tonight."

The man stomped off the dance floor, back to his table and laughing buddies.

"Has he been bothering you?"

She told him of the earlier confrontation. "Maybe I should have danced. He looks pissed."

"He'll get over it."

Trevor kept her on the dance floor for ten dances before taking a break. The cowboy glared. Vicky ignored him.

Two hours later, her feet called a halt to the evening. Trevor paid the bill, and she was relieved to note the cowboy and his friends had left.

In the car, she laid her head against the headrest.

"Tired?" Trevor asked.

"Yeah, but I had a great time."

He laughed. "I knew you weren't all furs and diamonds."

"Don't get the idea I'm a cheap date. I like the good life, too. Remember?" Funny, she never thought she'd make a joke out of her former life.

The road was dark as pitch. He negotiated a hairpin turn, the guardrail reflecting in the headlights. Vicky sucked in an apprehensive breath. The crest of the ridge loomed ahead. A car going in the opposite direction passed them, the lights blinding her. She shivered.

A pickup roared up behind and pulled out to pass.

"Goddammit! Is he nuts?" Trevor swore.

The double yellow line glowed in the high beams. Then without warning, the truck swerved into them.

"Look out!" he yelled, twisting the wheel.

Another sharp curve was dead ahead. The guardrail advanced with frightening speed. Vicky gasped when the passenger side wheels left the road. Gravel spit up under the fenders like bullets. The truck hit them a second time sending them into the barrier. The shriek of metal against metal drowned

out her scream. She braced her arms in front of her
face. The airbags deployed, and then the world
turned upside down as the Lincoln barrel rolled
down the steep hillside.

Chapter Fifteen

Trevor closed his eyes and held onto the steering wheel with a death grip as the car continued its wild tumble. The seat and shoulder belts dug in painfully, but kept him from being flung around the interior. Metal screeched against rock. Glass shattered.

The dizzying gyrations finally slowed and came to a halt, the car resting right side up at a sideways forty-five degree angle. Steam billowed from the engine. Stunned, his mind worked in staccato, disjointed thoughts.

Dizzy. Get out. Get help.

He released his clenched hands from the steering wheel, pushed the deflated airbag out of the way, and cautiously moved his arms and legs. Nothing broken, thank God. His torso hurt like hell from the restraints. A low moan next to him wiped the cobwebs from his brain.

"Vicky!" Fear churned his stomach and rasped in his throat. He unsnapped his seatbelt and slid down the seat toward her. "Vicky, honey, are you all right? Come on, talk to me."

She moaned again and moved her arms to bat the airbag from her face.

"Trevor?"

"Are you all right?"

"I...I think so. Nothing seems to be broken, but my head hurts like hell."

The trunk of a small sapling bulged through the

shattered window.

"Are you bleeding?"

She raised her hands, feeling her face. "A little. I feel sick."

"So do I. Dizziness. We rolled down the hill." He released the mechanism on her seat belt. "We need to get out of here. I don't smell gasoline, but who knows?"

Using the steering wheel, he pulled himself back to his side of the car and tried opening the door. It didn't budge.

"Probably jammed. Maybe I can get out the window."

He yanked his polo shirt over his head and wrapping it around his hand, punched out the remaining jagged glass from the frame, and then eased his body through. The road loomed a good seventy-five yards away. In spite of the well-defined path from their tumble, the hillside was strewn with rocks and small trees, along with bits and pieces of the Lincoln. The headlights still functioned and stabbed the inky darkness with its beams. *It's a miracle we're still alive.*

"Come on, Vicky," he said, sticking his hand inside. "Hold on. I'll pull you out."

She clasped his wrist and crawled up the seat. Within seconds she stood next to him.

Trevor pulled on the tattered remains of his shirt, and reached for the cell phone clipped to his belt, breathing a sigh of relief it still worked. Now, if only this ravine didn't block the signal.

Vicky, attempting to climb to the road, slipped and skidded back down with a cry.

"Honey, wait. Don't try it alone."

He dialed 9-1-1, grateful when he got through. After giving the operator the pertinent information, he turned his attention to Vicky. She sat clutching her knee.

"Did you hurt yourself?"

"Banged my knee on a rock. I'll be okay. Let's get out of here."

"I think you'll have a tough climb in those," he said, pointing to her stilettos.

She kicked them off, and then laughed, holding one heelless shoe up for inspection. The laugh bordered on hysterical.

Trevor grasped her elbow, pulling her upright. "Calm down, honey. That hill's pretty steep. We'll wait until help arrives."

Her laughter ceased, but she shook like a nudist in a snowstorm. Tears flowed down her cheeks. He wrapped his arms around her, holding her close to his body heat.

Shock. She's in shock.

"Guess, I should have danced with that fucking cowboy," she said, her words muffled against his shoulder.

Sirens blared in the distance. He relaxed. Help was on the way. A few minutes later, the flashing lights halted at the top of the hill. In the multicolored glow, Trevor gazed at the section of missing and damaged guardrail.

"Are you all right?" a voice called.

"More or less, but we can't get back up the hill."

Thirty minutes later, with the help of the police and paramedics, they were each placed on gurneys. Trevor had a deep gash on the back of his hand, probably incurred when exiting the car. Vicky had one on the right side of her forehead just above the hairline. The bruises would show up later.

Sheriff Singleton strode over. "What happened?"

Trevor gave him the information about where they'd been, the cowboy, and the pick-up.

"Any idea who this guy was?"

"None. Just a cowpoke who had too much beer and wouldn't take no for an answer."

The sheriff flicked his flashlight down into the ravine. "That is one badly totaled car. You guys were damned lucky."

"We're ready to transport," one of the paramedics said.

At the hospital, he received eight stitches in his hand and a box of pain pills. Vicky boasted four sutures along with a box of pills to call her own. It was two in the morning before they were released.

Trevor unlocked the front door and the two of them limped across the foyer and into the study. He tossed the pills onto the desk and made a beeline for the liquor on the credenza. Vicky eased herself onto the plush the sofa.

"Forget pills. I need a drink. You?"

"Scotch."

He poured two glasses, handing her one before sitting next to her. "Are you in much pain? You had me worried there for a moment."

"My head's banging like a bass drum, but I'm all right. Sorry, I came apart on you like that."

"Don't apologize. I was damned scared, too."

She gulped half the contents of her glass. "Trevor, what if it wasn't the cowboy?"

"What do you mean?"

"We've done a lot of investigating. Asked a lot of questions. Ruffled a lot of feathers. Someone at the mine could have tipped off Walter and Adam. Maybe they discovered your operative was nosing around. And Carlos wasn't real thrilled with you this afternoon."

Trevor hadn't thought of that. He'd assumed the cowboy had followed them from Dirty Dan's. On the other hand, any one of the men she mentioned could have followed them to the bar.

He finished his scotch in one long swallow. "You could be right. I'm sure that when Al finds a pick-up with heavy damage on the passenger side, it'll come back as stolen."

Vicky finished her drink as well and yawned.

Trevor brushed a lock of hair from her face, tucking it behind her ear. "Come on, let's go to bed."

He rose and helped her to her feet, then taking her into his arms, kissed her. In spite of his injuries, her soft lips kindled a fire in his gut.

Tearing his mouth from hers, he held her tight. "I'm sorry for involving you in this. I understand the possible dangers of my profession and had no business exposing you."

Her hand smoothed down his cheek. "I offered. Besides, I'm doing it to help for a change."

She yawned again. Trevor kissed her forehead, led her from the study and up the staircase, turning right toward his room. Inside, she offered no resistance when he undressed her and settled her under the covers.

Within seconds, he lay next to her. "Go to sleep, honey. You won't be alone tonight."

"Thank you." Vicky rolled onto her side.

He followed suit using his arm to spoon her close. Her skin scorched his, and a flame flickered inside him.

No, not tonight. Sleep. Let her sleep.

She moved with a sleepy sigh. He tightened his arm across her body and suppressed a shudder. Her moan in the car was the sweetest sound he'd ever heard. Still, he'd feared she'd been badly injured.

I couldn't go through that again. When did Victoria Denton become so important in my life? And what do I want to do about it?

****

Trevor eased his way down the staircase early the next morning. While sore, no stabbing pains crippled his progress. In the bathroom, he'd inspected the bruises on his shoulder and across his chest and hips from the seat belts. Another had

239

formed on the left side of his forehead, probably from banging it against the frame when the car rolled. A hot shower helped relieve the stiffness. As he left the room, Vicky moaned, rolled over, and drifted back to sleep.

Sleep hadn't been much of an option. His dreams consisted of tumbling cars, steep hillsides, and of what might have been—like fireballs from exploding gas tanks.

Noises from the kitchen and the eye-opening aroma of fresh-brewed coffee told him Rosa was on duty. He entered the room.

"Good morning, *senor*, you are..." she turned as she spoke and gasped. "*Senor* Sloane, what happened?"

Not wanting to frighten the woman, he told her a drunk had run them off the road.

"*Senorita* Denton, she is all right?"

"Yes. Just some bumps and bruises. She's still asleep. Keep it simple this morning." He poured a cup of coffee. "I'll be in the study. Give me a call when breakfast is ready."

Trevor fired up his laptop and logged onto his e-mail. Thirty-seven messages popped up, most from the office. He was halfway through the list when Rosa paused in the doorway.

"Breakfast is ready. I have scrambled eggs, *senor*, with those little sausages you like."

"Thanks, Rosa. Would you make me up a plate and bring it in here?"

The housekeeper nodded and left. He absently scratched the bandage over his wound. Damned stitches itched already. He'd applied an antibiotic ointment after his shower, and hoped they healed fast. *I hate stitches.*

He replied to another e-mail before Rosa returned with a tray bearing his breakfast and a small pot of coffee. He thanked her, and dug in.

When finished, Trevor poured another cup before pushing the tray away and returning to his laptop.

Midway down the remaining list a message from Marylou had come through at three-fifteen in the morning. Didn't the woman ever sleep? As close as he could tell, his best operative survived on caffeine, cigarettes, and an over-active metabolism.

He opened the e-mail and read, and then groaned at the report on his cousin Jason Hamilton. Marylou had dug deep, and Jason was no whiz at covering his tracks. This was worse than expected. It also brought up a whole new set of questions, not the least of which was, how did he tell his uncle?

The ringing desk phone made him jump. Who the hell would be calling at eight o'clock in the morning? Al? He fumbled for the receiver and answered.

"Trevor, are you all right? Was Vicky with you?" Corwin's voice hammered in his ear.

"Vicky was with me, and I'm fine. We're both fine. How did you know?"

"I stopped in the Foothills Diner for breakfast this morning and saw Ken Jacobs. Said he'd just pulled Helen's Lincoln out of a ravine. What the hell happened?"

News travels fast in small towns. Ken Jacobs owned one of the towing services in Granite Springs. Al must have called him.

"We were coming home from Dirty Dan's. A drunk ran us off the road."

"Any idea who?"

"Not yet. Sheriff's working on it. You're up with the birds this morning."

"I have business in Boulder today. Won't be back until afternoon. I'm glad you and Vicky are okay. If there's anything I can do, just name it."

"Right. Thanks for calling."

Trevor hung up and drummed his fingertips on

the blotter. Something about the conversation had sounded off. Corwin's voice was tight, nervous. Trevor found the tone strange, unless his worry had been for Vicky. Or he was behind the wheel. Trevor shook his head. He didn't picture Elliot Corwin in a pick-up. He was strictly flashy import.

A movement at the door caught his attention. Vicky stood there wearing jeans and a turquoise t-shirt, her hair loose around her shoulders. The bandage reminded him about the close call last night. She looked fragile and very desirable. His nerves hummed.

****

Vicky stared at Trevor happy to see he didn't look too bad. His bruised forehead was a mirror image of hers. Stiff and sore, she'd made it downstairs with a minimum of effort.

"Good morning. How do you feel?" she asked.

He cleared his throat. "Not too bad considering. Would you like breakfast? Rosa can make you a tray."

She came forward and sat in the chair in front of the desk. "That sounds wonderful, but I need coffee first."

He grinned and rose. "I'll be right back."

Trevor removed his tray from the desk and left, returning a few minutes later with a cup of aromatic Folger's in his hand.

"Here you go, complete with fake sugar and lots of cream. Rosa will be in shortly."

She accepted the coffee and sniffed, then sipped. Her stomach warmed.

"What are you doing?" she asked, motioning toward the laptop.

"Catching up on my e-mails." He resumed his seat with a frown.

"What's wrong?"

"I got the report back on Jason."

242

"I take it from the look on your face, it wasn't good."

"Worse than expected."

Rosa entered bearing Vicky's tray and set it in front of her. "*Senorita*, I am so happy you are all right. I hope the sheriff catches this man soon."

"Thank you, Rosa, so do I." The housekeeper left and Vicky, pleased to see a fresh pot of coffee on the tray, dug into the fluffy eggs. "So, what did the report say?"

"Jason should never have gone to school in Las Vegas."

She looked up. "Gambling?"

"Big time. Marylou talked to his former girlfriend. She said he signed a couple of markers at the Wild One Casino in downtown Vegas, and when he couldn't pay, goons roughed him up."

"The Wild One?"

"You know it?"

"Only by reputation. I didn't troll there for marks. It's a dump owned by Vito Marcelli, a scumbag reputed to have mob ties."

"That's what Marylou reported. So, his next stop was Granite Springs. Aunt Helen wrote a check, and he paid up."

"Only it didn't last, and he started the cycle all over again," she ventured.

"Wrote him another check, and when he came back to the trough a third time, she said no."

"Oh, God, now we've got the mob involved in this?"

Trevor shook his head. "This wasn't a mob hit. Too messy. Besides, they'd go for Jason, not Aunt Helen." He picked up a pen and twirled it between his fingers. "No wonder Jason was dismayed to get his inheritance in a trust."

"How much does he owe this time?"

"Around fifteen grand."

"And his parents don't know?" she asked, finishing her meal and pouring another cup of coffee.

"No, Ray and Sylvia would have dealt with Jason and the situation right away. I just don't know how I'm going to tell them." He looked up and smiled. "You taking it easy today?"

"More or less. I plan to visit Rod this morning. A couple of nights in jail might have loosened his tongue."

"Will you be back for lunch?"

"Probably." She emptied her cup and set it on the tray. "Trevor, are we getting anywhere with this?"

He sat back and sighed. "The noose is tightening. Wish I knew around whose neck."

****

Vicky pushed through the doors of the Granite City Jail and hesitated, then strode toward a large desk manned by a female officer. The woman looked up and smiled.

"Good morning. How may I help you?"

She inhaled a deep breath before answering. Jails made her nervous. It could just as easily have been her on the other side of those bars.

"I'd like to see my brother, Roderick Halston."

The officer's smile widened, the corners of her brown eyes crinkling with the effort. She pushed a lock of mousey brown hair behind her ear.

"I didn't know Rod...I mean, Mr. Halston, had a sister."

"I'm afraid he does and I'm it..." she let her gaze wonder to the nameplate on the desk. "...Officer Daniels."

The woman slid a clipboard toward her. "You'll have to sign in, and then step over to the table."

Murmuring a thank you, Vicky signed her name with the pen attached to the clipboard by a length of string, and then eyed a long table off toward the left.

A metal detector rose like a jailhouse arbor beyond. The last time she'd gone through had been after Rod's arraignment. Then, she'd been too distracted to pay attention to the routine.

Officer Daniels glanced at the clipboard. "Thank you Ms. Denton. If you'll just step this way."

She rose and walked to the table. Vicky followed.

"May I have your purse, please?"

She handed it over while the woman took every item out, and then inspected the inside and along the handle before replacing them. She handed Vicky another clipboard and a visitor's badge.

"You will be separated from the prisoner by a wire mesh screen. There is to be no touching. Neither are you allowed to give the prisoner anything. Duration of the visit is one hour maximum. An officer will be present in the room with you. When you're finished, he or she will accompany you back to the lobby where you may retrieve your belongings. Please sign on the line at the bottom signifying you understand all the rules, then step over to the metal detector."

Vicky signed and did as told. She stood with arms outstretched and legs wide while Officer Daniels passed a wand over her body, then walked through the metal detector.

"This way, please."

She followed the policewoman down a long dingy hall.

"I hope you don't mind me saying this, Ms. Denton, but I feel kind of sorry for Mr. Halston. He seems so lost and confused. I know all prisoners claim to be innocent, but in this case, I believe it. I hope everything works out."

Oh, Jeez, another one.

She took a second look at the woman, pegging her age at somewhere between forty and forty-five.

The khaki uniform pants stretched across her wide hips and ample rear end. Excess flesh muffin topped over the waistband. Only the gun and radio showed she wore a belt.

When she didn't answer, the officer looked over her shoulder, and said, "I really mean it. He's very polite. Never gives me any trouble. Not like some of them."

Vicky wanted to tell the poor woman to beware, but held her tongue. She'd find out Rod was a user soon enough. "Thank you for the support. I'm sure the real killer will be found soon."

They stopped in front of a steel door with a mesh covered window. Her escort pressed a button. A second later an answering buzzer opened the door with a soft click.

Vicky stepped through, and the door closed behind her. The officer on duty directed her to a cubicle. She pulled out the chair and sat. A minute later, Rod was escorted in, wearing handcuffs, through another door in the back of the room.

Under the harsh glare of the overhead lights, she gazed at her brother. Jail did not agree with him. His hair was long, stringy, and his face puffy. His once trim waist had thickened. Rod looked forty, not thirty years old.

He ambled over and took a seat. "About time you got here."

"You're lucky I came at all."

"This place sucks. Get me out."

"No bail, remember?" She hesitated and said in a low tone, "I'm sure you have more than your fair share of creature comforts. I met Officer Daniels out front."

Rod smirked and leaned toward the partition, his voice dropping to a whisper. "Ah, yes, the ever helpful Anne. Thanks to her, I have a couple of extra pillows, another blanket, and she sees to it I'm well-informed by slipping me the newspaper. Did you know the county commission is thinking about road improvements in next year's budget?"

"Oh, brother," she muttered.

"She also buys me little things like magazines, and sneaks in the occasional candy bar." He settled back, his voice returning to normal. "Did you bring me anything?"

"No. Why should I? You seem to be doing just fine without me."

His smirk stretched into a grin. "I wouldn't mind clean underwear and fresh socks. It's the least a sister can do for her brother." He eyed her head. "What the hell happened to you?"

Vicky waved a hand. "Nothing important. A little fender bender."

"Tell my lawyer to get me out of here."

Typical Rod. Not even a how are you? She leaned forward, her fingers gripping the edge of the board serving as a desk. "I might just do that, but first you have to come clean about the night Helen Richardson died."

Her brother stared, and then burst into laughter.

****

Vicky strode through the front door, slamming it behind her. The drive home hadn't eased the anger Rod created.

"Vicky, is that you?" Trevor called from the study.

She made her way into the room. "Yeah, it's me."

He looked up with raised eyebrows. "I take it your visit didn't go well."

"If you mean, did my brother unload anything new, the answer is no. He refused to talk and demanded we do something to get him out of jail, which included a high-powered attorney. I told him to make do with is PD."

"Point is *does* he have anything new to impart?"

"Probably, but he's in full bargaining mode."

Trevor shrugged with an amused smile. "Then he'll sit in jail. Bargaining time is over."

The doorbell rang. A few seconds later, Rosa walked past to answer. The murmur of voices carried through the foyer followed by footsteps across the floor.

"Oh, God, I can't face visitors now. You expecting someone?" Vicky asked.

"Nope."

The housekeeper paused in the doorway with the sheriff a few steps behind.

"*Senor* Sloane, Sheriff Singleton would like to see you and Miss Denton."

Trevor waved him in. "Come on in, Al. Anything new?"

The sheriff entered, draping his long frame into a chair by the desk as Rosa disappeared back toward the kitchen. He set a file folder in front of him.

"Close the door, will you?"

Vicky complied and returned to perch a hip on the corner of the desk.

"Find the pick-up yet?" Trevor asked.

"We will. Wouldn't be surprised if the driver wakes up hung over as hell and gives us a call about someone damaging his car. Happens all the time. No, I'm here for another reason." He opened the file and pulled out a sheet of paper. "One of the things we confiscated from Mr. Halston was his cell phone. He received three calls, complete with voice messages, the night of the murder and the next day."

Vicky's heart sank to her toes. Damn, she knew those calls would come back to haunt her.

"God bless fancy cell phones. They store all kinds of good information. We traced the calls to a cell number in your name, Miss Denton. Care to see?"

"That won't be necessary, sheriff. I made the calls." She didn't dare look at Trevor.

"The first call came in about eight o'clock from Miami the night of the murder. The voice message said something like, get the hell out of town, it's a set-up."

"That's right. I wanted to give my brother warning he was about to be pinched." What else could she say? She could feel Trevor glaring a hole in her.

"I see. The other two messages originated here in Granite Springs. They both suggested he turn around and come back. Your brother accessed the first message at eleven-ten the night of Helen Richardson's death, and the other two just prior to his arrest. Guess we know why he was eastbound."

Vicky licked her lips, the glaring hole growing bigger by the second.

"I knew my brother was in trouble, and that running away was no solution. He obviously agreed."

"So, there was no phone interview for a job, right?"

"No. I came to help my brother."

"His story still has holes," Trevor said in a tight voice.

"So does yours," the sheriff replied sending him a look. "We checked Mrs. Richardson's phones, too. You made a call from Miami at eight twenty-two Granite Springs time the morning of the murder that lasted seventeen minutes. You also contacted her again later that evening and left a message. You told me you hadn't talked to her in two weeks."

Vicky finally looked at Trevor. He scowled, but told the sheriff, "I wanted to let her know we were on our way home. She said something like, good, I need to talk to you about a lot of things. That was it. By the time we got here, she was dead."

Sheriff Singleton's cell rang. He crossed to the

other side of the room before answering.

"Kinda forgot to tell me you called your brother, didn't you?" he said in a low tone.

"I thought I'd escape at the airport."

"Why call him? You don't like the son of a bitch."

She cut a look at the sheriff who still talked. "I couldn't let him be set up."

"Bullshit. You wanted something to hold over him. He stiffed you out of a lot of money from Uncle Roland. You wanted your share."

"All right, so I wanted my share, so what? The situation has changed."

"When you didn't escape, you called and told him to get his ass back here. Good strategy. Why go down alone?"

"I called because I knew Rod wasn't smart enough to come up with a decent story."

"Plus, once he was in custody, you could skip out and leave him to his own devices."

"That was the plan, but I came back. Remember?"

The stern expression softened, and his lips curved into a tiny smile. "Yeah, I remember. I suppose there's something to be said for even misplaced loyalty."

The sheriff snapped his phone shut and strode back to them. He replaced the paper in the folder before raising his head.

"Where's Mrs. Ramirez?"

"In the kitchen. Why?"

"That was Deputy Carlyle. He found a pick-up with heavy right side damage parked along the side of an isolated road up near the old Happy Jack Mine. Carlos Ramirez was inside. Dead. Shot in the head at close range."

Chapter Sixteen

"Carlos ran us off the road?" Trevor exclaimed.

Vicky gasped and plopped into the chair.

"So it would appear," the sheriff replied. "Why would he want to run you off the road?"

"We had an argument yesterday afternoon," Trevor admitted.

"What kind of an argument?"

"He claimed my aunt owed him two hundred dollars for yard work and such. I know she didn't pay him any more than fifty. I gave him a hundred, but he wasn't happy."

"So, he felt you owed him money." The sheriff frowned and wrote in a notebook.

"Yes, but is an extra hundred bucks worth killing over?"

"Depends on how badly he needed the hundred bucks. Don't suppose you saw him at Dirty Dan's last night, did you?"

Trevor shook his head and tapped his fingers on the desk. "No, can't say that I did. How about you, Vicky? Did you see Carlos last night?"

She licked her lips, and ran a shaking hand through her hair. "No, but then I wasn't looking for him either.

Trevor ceased tapping his fingers, and sent a penetrating stare at the officer. "Can you give me any details about the crime scene?"

"A hunter found him. According to Deputy

Carlyle, he thought the guy was sleeping one off. Then he got a good look at the blood and called it in."

"Where was he shot?"

"Took one in the neck and another to the head. He was still behind the wheel, which means he never had a chance to get out of the truck."

"What about the gun?"

"Still searching. There's a lot of ravines with heavy underbrush in that area. The shooter would have to be a moron to keep it." The sheriff frowned. "It's a narrow, gravel road. We'll check for evidence of a car turning around, but from the information I received, my guess is the killer was waiting." He snapped the notebook shut. "I need to tell his mother. Damn, I hate this part of the job."

Trevor glanced at Vicky sitting like a statue, and decided this needed a woman's touch.

"Vicky, would you ask Rosa to come in? Don't mention Al wants to talk to her. Just tell her I need her."

She nodded, rose, and left. Neither man said anything during her absence. The sheriff paced, while Trevor stood, and walked to the window where he stared at the landscaping Carlos had pruned only weeks ago.

Carlos ran them off the road? Why? The hundred dollars wasn't important—especially if the ex-con was into numerous illegal activities in Granite Springs. A C-note was a drop in the bucket, so taking a whack at them didn't make sense. Unless...

Vicky returning with Rosa interrupted his line of thought. He turned to face them.

Al ceased pacing and smiled at the housekeeper. "Mrs. Ramirez, please have a seat."

The woman sat and looked up, puzzlement and fear on her face. Vicky stood behind her, tears welling in her eyes.

"Rosa, the sheriff has something to tell you," Trevor said, trying to ease the situation, but finding it impossible.

"*Si, señor,* what is the problem?" Suspicion throbbed in her voice.

How do you tell someone there's been a murder in the family? In Mexico, a visit from the police was an occasion for fear and suspicion.

Al didn't mince words, but gave the woman the bad news in three short sentences.

Rosa screamed, clenched her fists against her chest, and fell out of the chair onto the floor. She thrashed from side to side, tears rolling down her face, and shrieking in Spanish.

Trevor knew enough of the language to decipher "my baby, my angel, my only child." He rushed forward, but Vicky beat him to the Rosa's side.

She clasped the woman in her arms and rocked her, murmuring soothing words.

Unsure of what to do, Trevor poured a glass of scotch from the credenza and approached his sobbing housekeeper.

Vicky continued to comfort. "I'm so sorry, Rosa. There, there, try to get a hold of yourself. You're not alone. Mr. Sloane and I are here for you. You won't face this alone. I promise."

Several minutes passed before the hysterical sobbing diminished to shuddering breaths. Vicky helped the poor woman into the chair and reached for the glass in Trevor's hand.

"Here, Rosa. Drink this." The housekeeper complied, taking a couple of tiny sips.

"Mrs. Ramirez, can you answer a few questions?" the sheriff asked in a gentle tone.

She nodded and hiccupped, sipping again from the glass clenched in tight fingers.

"Do you have any idea who'd want to do this to your son?"

"No, no!" Her high-pitched wail bounced off the walls of the study.

"Has he had any arguments with anyone lately?"

She cast a quick glance at Trevor, but shook her head.

"I know he got out of prison last year. Did he have any problems adjusting?"

"No, no. Carlos is a good boy. He no longer do those bad things. He work at the Wrecking Ball."

"Doing what?"

"Cleaning tables, serving drinks, sweeping the floor." She screwed up her face and bit her lip before taking another sip of scotch.

"And he lived with you?" the sheriff continued.

"*Si*, but he rent apartment, too."

Trevor glanced at Vicky, who shrugged.

"An apartment? Where? When?" he asked.

"Last month. It is over on Grandview. Apartment D."

Trevor knew the area—a run-down section of town. The word apartment was being kind. Most of the structures resembled motels on the exterior, and the clientele was transient. It was rumored to have numerous comings and goings, as in the drug trade.

"Why did he rent it?" Al asked.

"He say he needs his space, but he no stay all the time. He still has things at my house. He say he didn't want me to be alone."

Rosa reached for the tissue box on the desk as fresh tears flowed. Vicky massaged the woman's shoulders and murmured consoling words again.

"Can you give me the names of his friends?"

"He did not have many friends. Only the bartender and a few other people at his work." Her voice rose. "Who do this? Who would kill my *nino*?"

The sheriff closed his notebook, and crouched in front of the woman.

"Mrs. Ramirez, I know this is rough, but I need you to come down to the morgue to make a positive identification."

She wailed louder, her shuddering sobs threatening to push her from the chair.

"I can do it, Al," Trevor hastened to say.

"No, no, I want to see my son. Perhaps you make mistake," Rosa interrupted casting a glance full of hope toward the sheriff.

Before he could answer, Trevor stepped in. "I'll come with you."

Al nodded. "We should have things ready in a while. I'll give you a call. Mrs. Ramirez, can I run you home?"

"I think Rosa should stay here," Vicky cut in.

"Absolutely," Trevor said in agreement.

"*Gracias*, but I want to go home."

"We'll take her in a while," he said to the sheriff. "Let her get herself together."

"All right. I need to get out to the..." he broke off, cast a glance in Rosa's direction, and then continued. "I have to be somewhere. I'll stay in touch."

The sheriff left. Trevor crouched in front of the housekeeper and pried the empty glass from her fingers.

"I'm so sorry, Rosa. If there's anything I can do, I will."

She lifted her head, her eyes red and swollen. "Find the *bastardo* who do this. Please, *Senor* Sloane." She bit her lip and clutched at his shirt. "I do not tell the sheriff the whole truth. But Carlos was a good boy. You believe me, don't you?"

"Of course, we do," Vicky answered for him. "What didn't you tell Sheriff Singleton?"

"I worry about Carlos the last week or so. He buy lots of new clothes and gold necklaces. I see the bags in his room. He also say he would buy me a good car. One that does not need so much repair. I do not know where this money comes from."

"Did you ask?" Trevor wanted to know.

She nodded. "He say he got big tips at work, and won a small pay from the lottery."

The mention of a car brought another question. "Rosa, what kind of car did Carlos drive? What color? I never noticed."

"I do not know what kind. Only that it is American. It is not new and has many colors."

Sun fade? Primer? Rust? Winter in Colorado could play havoc with cars.

"Rosa, why don't you go upstairs and lie down for a while? Are you sure you don't want me to go to the morgue?"

She rose, swaying slightly. "No, *senor*. If this is my *nino*, I want to see. I want to hold his hand, and put a curse on the man who did this."

Vicky led the woman from the room. Trevor poured a scotch and sat behind the desk, sipping slowly. So, Carlos had money. Enough to buy new duds and bling. Plus, he must have had expectations of more if he planned on buying his mother a car. *Drugs? Blackmail? Or both?*

Carlos Ramirez was street smart and prison smart, but not smart enough. *Especially if the person being blackmailed has already killed.*

The front door opened and closed. Trevor rose and tossed the scotch down his throat. Walter appeared in the doorway.

"You know, Walter, there's a marvelous invention called the doorbell. It's located to the left of the door just above the doorknob. Try using it."

Walter hesitated, a small frown furrowing between his eyebrows.

"Sorry, Trevor, but Helen never stood on such formality." His eyes narrowed. "What the hell happened to you?"

Trevor waved his hand dismissively, tired of explaining, but watching the reaction. "A little accident, that's all. What are you doing here? I have to tell you, this hasn't been the best of days."

No shit. Hell of an understatement. He sat back down and scratched at the bandage on his hand. *Goddamned stitches.*

Walter, showing no curiosity, took the chair in front of him. "I'm sorry. Look, Trevor, I need a favor." He licked his lips and ran a hand over his face. "I...I need a loan."

That didn't take long. Less than a week after the funeral and he's here with hat in hand.

"A loan? Why?"

"I'm trying to buy a piece of property, and could use some help. Economic times are bad. Two years ago, this wouldn't have been a problem, but now..." He didn't finish, but shrugged his shoulders.

"What piece of property?"

Walter spoke, but didn't look him in the eye. "It's a condo. Retirement is just around the corner, and I wanted something smaller than the house."

"Where? In Mineral City?"

Sweat popped out on the older man's forehead. He daubed at it with his sleeve.

"No. In..." he cleared his throat. "...In Los Angeles. Brentwood to be exact." When Trevor didn't answer, he rushed on. "It's a steal at a million. I put down a sizable chunk of dough, but the bank is balking on lending the balance. Things have tightened up. It's a good buy. The real estate market will come back and the place will sell for double, maybe even triple what it's worth now."

Trevor sat back, enjoying his aunt's brother-in-law's discomfort.

"Los Angeles? That's quite a switch. Why not Denver? I'm having a hard time visualizing Marge in California."

"We like diversity, and we'd keep the house in Mineral Springs for summers."

"That's an awful lot of money for a part-time home."

"True, but like I said, it'll appreciate. I've always got my eye on turning a profit."

Walter's jaw clenched, and suddenly Trevor was sick to death of the nonsense.

He leaned forward abruptly. "Walter, what's really going on? I talked to Marge at the funeral. She doesn't even like Los Angeles. And you're not retiring—you're about to get canned. No wonder the bank won't loan you seven hundred thousand big ones."

Shock rolled across the man's face. "You...you investigated me?" he asked in a voice barely above a whisper.

"Walter, why are you so gung-ho on buying a condo in an upscale suburb?" Remembering Vicky's supposition, he took a shot in the dark. "Got a girlfriend?"

The man slumped in his seat. "Yeah. She demanded something better than her apartment. Has her heart set on this place. And don't give me any kind of moralistic bullshit. I've put up with Marge for over forty years. Denise is only thirty, and makes me feel young again. I'm not dumb enough to get a divorce. All I want is a place to stay when I visit."

"Walter, you're a chump. Denise will suck the money out of you like a vacuum cleaner, and then dump your ass for someone richer and younger."

He shrugged. "Maybe."

"And trust me, your wife *will* find out about it. By the time she's finished, you'll be living in the trailer park, and sitting on the back steps in an undershirt sucking on a beer can. Forget it."

"You're right, Trevor. Everything you say is

true, but I can't help myself. Your report is right on. I'm leaving Richardson Mining at the end of the year. Adam's probably gonna get canned, too. I...I admit I gutted the company." He leaned forward tears welling in his eyes. "Been doing it for years. Padding the expense account, borrowing money and not paying it back. It started about the time Roland died. At first it was just a couple of hundred, then a few thousand, and finally, the sums reached into five figures. I knew the shit would hit the fan some day."

"And has that happened?" He tried to drum up sympathy for the man, but came away dry.

"Last month. A surprise audit found the discrepancies. Rocky Mountain Mining gave me until the end of the year to pay it back and resign or face charges."

Trevor snorted and eyed the man with contempt. "You don't want a loan for a condo. You want a loan to stay out of jail. The girlfriend dump you already?"

Walter hung his head and nodded. "Three weeks ago." He took a handkerchief from his pocket and blew his nose. "I thought maybe Helen would lend it to me, but she refused. I asked several times. Then she died, and I hoped there was something in the will. Please, help me. I'm begging."

"Did Helen know why you wanted the loan?"

He shook his head. "I told her I needed it for a retirement home in Palm Springs. She and Roland used to winter there. Thought she'd do it for nostalgia's sake."

Trevor wanted to crawl across the desk and shake the man until his head rolled off.

"Tell me, am I the only one you've hit on?"

"No, I asked Elliot Corwin for a loan when I found out Helen hadn't left me anything. Son of a bitch laughed and refused. I thought he might feel obligated after all the money I lost with him."

"You invested with Corwin?"

Walter nodded. "Half a million dollars. Some mall to be built near town. It never materialized and the venture went belly up. I'm still pissed about it. The little weasel had plenty of time to warn his investors of the coming crash, but didn't. He's the only one I know of who didn't take a bath."

So, both Walter and Adam lost money with Corwin.

He shot a quick look at Trevor. "I assume you've also investigated my son."

"Yes."

"Then you must know he has problems. He's an alcoholic with a temper, and deep in debt. Helen turned his requests for money down, too. I know what you're thinking, but he's no killer. He hasn't got the guts."

I'm not so sure about that. Given the right set of circumstances, anyone can kill.

"Are you going to lend me the money?"

"No, Walter, I'm not going to lend you seven hundred thousand dollars. But I will talk to Rocky Mountain Mining and ask them to go easy on you. In the meantime, I suggest you get yourself a good lawyer. You're gonna need one."

Walter slowly rose, looking old, beaten. He shuffled from the room. The front door opened, and then closed with a soft click.

He'll be dead within a couple of years.

He buried his face in his hands, angry and wondering why he cared.

****

Trevor entered the foyer and slumped against the front door, relieved to be home. The clock chimed seven. The sun had long since set, and the chandelier, its light dimmed to low, cast shadows into the corners. Another light source and the sounds of pots and pans clanging told him Vicky was

260

preparing dinner.

The past ninety minutes had been one of the worst in his life. The sheriff had called to say Carlos was ready to be identified. Keeping his promise, he drove Rosa to the coroner's office and stayed by her side during the process. He'd spent his fair share of time in morgues, but this visit ranked at the bottom of the barrel.

He pushed himself away from the door and walked down the hall, pausing in the kitchen doorway. Vicky turned from the stove.

"How did it go?"

"Awful. I never had to stand back-up for a relative before. Not pleasant."

"Where's Rosa?"

"At home. She refused to come back here. Said she wanted to be alone. Guess I don't blame her."

Vicky nodded. "I can understand. She wants the familiar around her. I take it there was no mistake—it was Carlos."

"Yeah, the coroner had cleaned him up, but cause of death was only too obvious. Rosa had hysterics again. Took an hour to calm her down. She refused to view the video. Insisted on a face-to-face. At least in a tape, things like bullet holes can be masked." He shrugged out of his windbreaker and tossed it on one of the chairs at the table already set for dinner. A large salad bowl sat in the middle. He walked over to the stove, and then sniffed. "Smells good. What's for dinner?"

"Chicken alfredo, salad, and garlic bread."

"Didn't know you could cook."

She shot him a sidelong glance. "There are lots of things you don't know about me."

Vicky turned back to the stove, wooden spoon in hand, to stir a pot. She'd changed clothes from this morning. Tonight she wore skin tight black slacks that hugged every curve as though painted on her body. The leg part stopped at mid-calf. Black shoes, rounded at the toe, graced her feet. A long-sleeved, low-cut white blouse with ruffles cascading down the front stirred his inner fires.

He was tired, dispirited, and glad to see her. Trevor wanted nothing more than to kiss her senseless and run his hands over those black clad curves.

Moving behind her, he clasped her waist, and buried his nose in her floral scented hair.

"Forget chicken alfredo. You look good enough to eat. Those slacks or whatever are giving me impure thoughts."

She laughed, set the spoon on the stovetop, and turned in his arms, her hands on his shoulders.

"They're called Capri pants." She stuck her foot out, wiggling it back and forth. "Like the shoes?"

"Love the shoes." He nibbled at her neck.

"Ballet flats. Supposed to be sexy."

"They are. But this ruffled thing has them beat." His teeth found her ear lobe, while his fingers roamed through the ruffles.

She sucked in an audible breath, and then emitted a sound not quite a moan. Her fingers tightened.

A timer on the stove dinged.

He stepped back as she laughed. "Saved by the bell. Wine's in the fridge and the corkscrew's on the table. Why don't you make yourself useful?"

"I'm very useful. Oh...you mean opening the wine."

"Ha-ha." She sent him a glance along with a half-smile.

Chuckling, he opened the bottle, pouring two glasses of Pinot Grigio, while she drained the noodles and filled the plates, adding grated cheese on top of the mixture.

Vicky sat, smiled a wicked smile, and twirled

fettuccini before popping it into her mouth. A string escaped from the fork, and she sucked it in slowly between pink tinted lips.

Trevor wanted to leap across the table and do some sucking of his own. Heat enveloped him, and the stirring in his groin proved the stove had nothing to do with it. He gulped half of his wine to put out the fire.

Vicky continued smiling and sipping from her glass. At the same time, her slipper clad foot slid up and down his leg. His internal thermometer rose.

"Naughty girl," he said in a choked voice.

"You're not eating. Don't you like it?" She smiled wider and lowered her foot.

"I love it." He picked up his fork and dug into the best tasting chicken alfredo he'd ever eaten. At least, he assumed it was the best. His taste buds had ceased working, unlike other parts of his body.

She did the noodle thing again, smiling and licking her lips. A few minutes later, she bit into a slice of garlic bread, licking the butter from her fingers, the tip of her tongue curling around each.

She was driving him nuts—and she knew it. With his libido sky high, he somehow got through the meal resisting the urge to drag the little she-devil up the stairs and make wild monkey love until she begged for mercy—or he did.

Vicky rose, collected the plates and sashayed toward the sink, her hips swaying. Like Pavlov's dog, Trevor followed. He brushed the hair from her neck and nuzzled it with his lips.

"Forget the dishes. Let's go upstairs."

"Can't do that," she murmured in a husky tone. "A good cook always finishes what she starts."

To punctuate her words, she squirted dishwashing liquid into the sink and turned the taps on full force.

"Lady, you turned on more than an oven

tonight."

"I'll finish that, too." She flung a towel over her shoulder, hitting him in the face. "I'll wash, you dry."

He managed to keep his hands off her while she filled the dishwasher with plates and glasses, and then scoured the pots and pans. When she flicked the bubbles from her fingers, he wanted to plunge his hands into the froth and smooth them up and down her body.

Just when he thought he could stand it no longer, she dried her hands, and turning, said, "I believe you mentioned something about an oven?"

"You're damned right I did!" He grasped her wrist, led her from the room, and up the staircase.

In his bedroom, Trevor wasted no time, pulling her into his arms and kissing her until they both were breathless.

With little finesse, he unbuttoned the blouse and pushed it from her shoulders, then unclasped her bra. Both hit the floor. Her fingers yanked the polo shirt from his waistband and over his head, joining the clothing already by the bed. She kicked off her shoes.

He found the zipper of those sexy slacks and peeled them, along with a thong, down her legs. His jeans and boxers followed. Naked, they staggered into the bed.

Trevor's lips slid down her cheek to her throat, nibbling along the delicate tendon before trailing to her breasts and the erect centers. He laved and sucked, Vicky's moans music to his ears. His hands smoothed her trim waist and flat stomach, and then caressed the junction of her thighs. Panting, she opened, allowing his fingers to massage.

Her soft moans escalated into sharp cries as his lips brushed her navel. The cries increased when his mouth replaced his fingers. She clutched his hair, her body undulating like a ribbon in the wind. He gripped her hips and moved his tongue to her rhythm.

She climaxed with a shriek, pumping her hips and pulling his hair. Finally, she ceased movement. Her panting breaths echoed in the darkened room.

Trevor lay on his back beside her, aching with need, but curbing his desire until she regained control. With gritted teeth he reached up and turned on the bedside light, and then propping himself up on an elbow gazed at the blonde hair spread across the pillow in a silken tangle. Her blue eyes had darkened to cobalt, and her breasts still heaved with every breath taken between parted lips. She looked like a goddess.

"You're beautiful."

"And we aren't finished yet."

Quick and lithe as a cat, she pushed him onto his back and straddled his hips. Her teeth nipped and her tongue soothed the bites from his neck to inner thighs. His fists gripped the bedspread, and he twisted from side to side, ready to burst. The blood boiled in his veins, and when she took him into her mouth, he damn near exploded. It required every ounce of strength to hold back. He wanted to bury himself inside her, to feel her moist heat surrounding him.

"Vicky! God, baby! Slow down. Can't hold it much longer."

He didn't recognize his voice. The words had come from a tortured throat in rasping tones, barely coherent. His hips pumped and his groin tightened. Then, as the point of no return approached, she pulled away, and moved over him.

"Vicky!"

With a diabolical smile on her lips, she lowered her hips, sliding onto his burning erection an inch at a time. He groaned, grasped her hips, and moved.

She slid up and down, increasing the speed with

each stroke. Trevor groaned and shook. Then, Vicky clasped his shoulders, her nails digging into the skin, threw back her head, and screamed. The contractions of her orgasm pulsated around his shaft. He fell from the precipice, releasing with the power of a volcano. Guttural noise burst from his throat. He rammed her hips down to his, keeping her prisoner until he had nothing left to give.

Spent, he let his hands drop to the covers, and lay sucking air while she kissed her way up his chest before crashing beside him.

Trevor had no idea how long they lay not speaking. Eventually, he rolled toward her and brushed damp strands of hair from her forehead.

"Vicky, I...I..." He couldn't find the words.

She kissed the palm of his hand. "I know. You don't need to say anything. I feel the same."

He cradled her, his lips brushing her cheek. Everything had changed. This was not the Victoria Denton of Miami. He could have had sex with Victoria, but with Vicky, he made love.

Love. Is that what this is all about?

He never considered falling in love again. Oh, the thought had crossed his mind from time to time, but no one piqued his desire to that degree. Until now.

Was it just sex? No. It was more. He needed her as much as she needed him. He jerked with surprise.

Vicky sighed in his arms and settled deeper into the pillow.

Need. That was it. He'd sensed vulnerability in her on the dance floor the first night they'd met. She tried to mask it, but he'd seen it in her eyes and heard it in her voice. He'd ignored it, concentrating on the matter at hand instead. More astonishing, he admitted vulnerability, too. Becca's death had left a hole in his heart—a wound he thought would never heal.

It's not there anymore. Vicky healed it. I can live again.

He closed his eyes tight. He'd been blindsided by this whole thing, but there was no getting around the fact he loved Victoria Denton.

Chapter Seventeen

Vicky awoke alone in the bed. She stretched her satiated body like a sleek cat, but didn't quite purr. Last night had been fabulous, because she'd given herself without ulterior motives. She'd done it out of love.

Even the word sent a shiver racing along her skin. Love. She'd fallen, and fallen hard, for the most unlikely of men. She'd suspected it a couple of days ago, but last night had sealed her heart's fate. Victoria Denton, thief, liar, and con woman, was head over heels in love with Trevor Sloane, a straight arrow.

I never thought it would happen. But it has, and there's no getting around it. Then the same doubts of earlier resurfaced. *Does he feel the same about me? And if he doesn't, can I do anything about it?*

It was a troubling thought, but could Trevor make love as passionately as he had last night without feeling a spark of something to say he cared?

If he didn't love her, could she walk away? Leave without putting up a fight? Could she tell him the truth, hold up her head, and maintain her dignity if rejected?

And does one maintain dignity or pride with a declaration of love? She had no idea.

The aroma of frying bacon tickled her nose. Her stomach rumbled. A glance at the bedside clock encouraged rising. It was after eight.

Vicky dressed and hurried downstairs. Not only did breakfast sound good, but she wanted to look into Trevor's eyes, praying she'd see an expression other than indifference.

Trevor stood at the stove, turning strips of bacon in the frying pan. His jeans hugged his slim hips, and she wanted to laugh. He'd put his shirt from the night before on inside out.

"Good morning," she said from the doorway before strolling behind him. "What's to eat?"

He turned and smiled, the corners of his brown eyes crinkling, and the expression in them soft, a hopeful sign.

"Good morning." He leaned down and brushed his lips over hers. "Bacon and pancakes. Hungry?"

"Ravenous," she replied. Her fingers played with the bumpy shoulder seam in his shirt.

The smile deepened, and his gaze dropped to her lips again. "Yeah, me, too."

"You know, sexy talk at dinner led to a very pleasant evening."

"So it did. I've heard, however, that breakfast is the most important meal of the day. Shame I'm not serving fettuccini."

She laughed. "I'll see what I can do with pancakes and syrup."

He chuckled, and then jumped when a loud snap from the pan sent grease splattering. He stabbed the offending slice of bacon with a fork, and set it on a paper towel to drain, throwing her a sidelong glance.

"I see you know your way around the kitchen, too," she said in a low voice.

"I have hidden talents."

"And some that aren't."

"A man who's handy in the kitchen is an asset."

"I wasn't thinking about the kitchen."

He laughed and removed the remaining strips

from the pan. "Why don't you get a cup of coffee and set the table? These won't take long."

Vicky poured, grabbed a couple of plates from the cabinet, and silverware from the drawer. Within a few minutes, Trevor slid three pancakes onto her plate, and four onto his. She spread butter on each one, covered them with maple syrup, and then inhaled the aroma.

"This smells good enough to eat."

He cut off a piece and popped it into his mouth. "It is."

They ate in silence concentrating on the food. Then, the imp inside Vicky demanded release. With deliberation, she dipped her finger in the pooled syrup and licked it clean. She repeated the action, this time slowly sucking the digit into her mouth.

Trevor stared, his pancake laden fork halfway to its destination. He lowered it to his plate, and grinned.

"You know, I've never ravaged a woman on the kitchen table before." He glanced at the table top. "I imagine the maple syrup will make a mess."

Vicky dipped her finger in the sweet topping again, and licked, then leaned forward.

"I love maple syrup—and chocolate sauce."

He smiled, dipped his finger in her plate, and popped it into his mouth.

"I'm partial to butterscotch and caramel. And whipped cream."

"Oh, definitely whipped cream."

The visions their conversation evoked made her squirm. She'd never in her life indulged in that kind of sex or this kind of sex talk. It was a turn on beyond belief. A flame deep inside flickered into life.

Trevor laughed and shoved another forkful of pancakes into his mouth.

"Let's explore certain culinary possibilities later. Business first, then pleasure."

Okay, so we won't make it on the table. But, my gut instinct says he's not indifferent.

She scraped her plate, set it in the sink, stretched, and said, "I think I will be totally decadent and take a long, hot bubble bath."

"Holler if you need company," his voice teased.

Vicky climbed the stairs, chuckling at the image of highly masculine Trevor Sloane covered with bubbles. In the bathroom, she stripped off her clothes, tossing them into the corner, and then turned the faucets on full blast. Steam billowed, fogging the mirror and window. She shook a generous amount of bubble bath under the gushing stream and waited until the froth lipped the edge of the tub before turning off the taps. With a contented sigh, she stepped into the liquid heat and reclined, the vintage claw-footed tub a perfect fit.

With the bubbles caressing her chin, she let her mind wander to Trevor, their relationship, and the murder that had brought them to this point. She closed her eyes against the seductive heat.

The bathroom door opening brought her out of a semi-doze. The object of her daydreams stood next to the tub. Her heart rate accelerated and her breath stopped somewhere between lungs and throat. A throb from deep within stoked the banked fire.

Trevor smiled lopsidedly with a devilish glint in his eyes and drew his finger down the condensation on the mirror.

"It's like a sauna in here."

"A sauna is dry heat. This is more of a steam bath."

"Damned perfectionist."

He shed his clothes and stepped into the water, kneeling between her outstretched legs. Grasping the edges of the tub, he leaned over, kissed her, straightened, and sat back on his heels.

His hands stroked her shoulders, and then

271

glided to her breasts, the slippery soap acting as an erotic toy. In spite of the heat, her nipples hardened. When his fingers pinched the erect centers, Vicky sucked in a shaky breath, biting back a moan.

Her gaze locked on his and she wondered if her eyes had darkened, too. The chocolate brown had turned nearly black.

Unable to control herself, she reached out to caress his chest, and then plunged her hands underwater grasping an erection of monumental proportions.

"H-m-m, somebody ate their Wheaties this morning."

"Breakfast of champions, although technically, I had pancakes." His voice had a ragged tone.

"Damned perfectionist."

He laughed and slid his hand lower. She gasped when his fingers found, and then massaged, that pinpoint of desire. Those internal fires burned hotter coiling the sexual spring tighter.

"What happened to the ice maiden?" he whispered.

"She melted. She was only there to protect," she answered with in breathless tone.

"Protect from what?"

She stroked in time to his massage. He groaned.

"Hurt and fear."

He ceased his motions, braced both arms on the edge of the tub, and kissed her.

"You'll never know hurt or fear again, honey, I promise."

Her heart beat in heavy thumps as she read her own meaning into his words.

Closing her eyes, she murmured, "I want you. Now."

She heard the desire and the desperation in her voice, but didn't care.

He slid his knees to the sides, forcing her legs

wide. Vicky flung her calves over the rim of the tub inviting him inside. She cried out when he accepted. Water splashed, cascading onto the floor as they rocked. Her fingers clenched on his shoulders, the fire growing, spiraling outward until she was consumed with need.

The blood pounded in her ears. She wanted this to last forever, yet at the same time, her body demanded satisfaction. She strained, thrusting upward in ever-increasing speed. The spring tightened. It was both pleasure and pain.

"Now! Now! Oh, God, yes, yes!"

Had she spoken or were those Trevor's words echoing in the room? It didn't matter. She shrieked. Spasm after spasm ripped through her. He lunged with a gasp and cry, his panting breath scorching the skin under her ear.

Gradually, reality returned. The air chilled her exposed legs, and the steady drip of water confirmed a large portion of her bath had spilled out. The water barely covered her breasts.

Trevor lifted his body in slow motion, bubbles sliding from his shoulders to his waist. She chuckled.

"What?"

"You have bubbles in your hair."

"So do you." He leaned forward and kissed her. "I've never made love in a tub before."

"Neither have I. What's next—caramel?"

He laughed, rose to his feet, and grabbed a towel from the rack next to the tub, drying his body. Then, wrapping the oversized terry cloth around his hips, he removed himself from her bath.

"We'll see." The laughter died, replaced by a serious expression. "Vicky, I..." He hesitated.

"What?"

"I..." he stopped again. "Nothing. We'll talk later. Need help?"

She took his offered hand and stood. He kissed her and left the room, closing the door behind him.

She stared at the raised panels, consternation clutching her chest at his abrupt exit. No little touches, no downtime caresses. He'd just left. Of course, they couldn't have stayed in the cooling water much longer, but still... Doubts rose. She let the water out of the tub and dried off. Clean up required six more towels, but the deed had been worth every one.

****

Back in the study, Trevor sat behind the desk, one hand fiddling with a pencil. He felt guilty at running out on her like that, but confusion had overwhelmed him.

He'd gone upstairs to shower and dress when the sound of the running water made him pause at the top of the stairs. He'd stood like a sentinel, unmoving for long minutes, his mind a kaleidoscope of visions, all involving chocolate and whipped cream.

In spite of the silly sex talk, he'd never indulged in sex aids. *Is that what food used during sex is called?* He doubted Vicky had participated in something like that either, but she talked a damned good game.

Unable to stop himself, he'd turned toward her bathroom, and the most erotic sex of his life. He came close to uttering those three words he hadn't said in twenty years as he adjusted the towel, but stopped. Somehow, making a monumental declaration in a bathroom after having made love in a bubble bath, didn't seem quite, well, right.

He shook his head. *Later. Think about it later. Time to get to work.*

He turned his attention to his laptop, his mind instantly focusing when he saw Marylou's e-mail. He read the attached report. Anger bubbled in his chest along with the satisfaction he'd been right all along.

Vicky poked her head into the room, a smile on her lips. "I'm going to clean up the kitchen. Would you like more coffee?"

"I'd love some. Just got a report from Marylou. I was right, Corwin was up to no good."

"How so?"

"She talked to somebody at the investment firm in Denver."

"The one dealing with the mall property?"

He nodded. "Corwin personally invested close to a million and a half bucks in the venture."

Vicky's eyebrows rose. "That's a powerful lot of money. Where'd he get it?"

"*That* is the big question. He wasn't worth that much." He paused. "You know, Walter said he lost a bundle. And we know Adam took a hit, too. I wonder if Corwin borrowed from clients who said no."

"Like your aunt. But wouldn't they notice if money was missing?"

"Not if the reports were doctored to cover up the shortfall. In order to make the one point five million, he could have borrowed fifty thousand here, a hundred grand there, and then, when things went south, couldn't pay it back. I'll have Marylou nose around his other investment clients. See what turns up."

Vicky yawned. "Guess I'd better get that coffee."

She turned to leave when the doorbell rang. Her footsteps echoed across the foyer, and a moment later he heard the murmur of voices. Then, Sheriff Singleton entered the room.

"I was just going to make some more coffee. Can I get you a cup, too, Sheriff?" she asked.

"That would be nice. Thanks."

Vicky left and Trevor motioned to the chair. "Have a seat. Anything new?"

"Plenty. First of all, the pick-up is the one that

hit you. Cream-colored paint on the passenger side matches the Lincoln, but the lab boys will check to make sure."

"I assume it was stolen."

The sheriff nodded. "From the parking lot at the Wrecking Ball. Customer came out at three in the morning and called it in."

"The Wrecking Ball? Not very original." Trevor paused, tapping the pencil on the blotter. "How did Carlos know where to find us?"

"Maybe he waited along the side of the road and followed you."

"But how did he know we were going out? He could have waited for an eternity." Trevor shook his head. "It's a loose thread, but I'll work on it later. Find the gun?"

"Not yet, but the area's honeycombed with ravines. We'll find it. Searched his apartment. Found drugs and money."

"Not surprising. Carlos wouldn't deal out of his mother's house. What kind of drugs and how much money?"

"Cocaine, crack, heroin, marijuana, and close to ten grand along with a list of phone numbers, but whether customers or suppliers, we don't know yet."

Trevor's gaze strayed to the painting above the fireplace. "Aunt Helen had ten grand in the safe."

"The money we found was mostly twenties and very used."

"Nope. Aunt Helen kept her money in neat stacks."

Al paused, shifting in his seat. "We're also searching Mrs. Ramirez's house."

"Poor Rosa. How's she holding up?" Trevor mentally slapped himself. He should have called the housekeeper first thing.

"All right, I guess. Had a man and another woman with her. Said he was a cousin."

"At least she has some family to help."

The sheriff opened the file folder that always accompanied him these days and withdrew several sheets of paper stapled together.

"We also have the results on the calls to and from Mrs. Richardson's land line and cell. Her cell had a lot of activity in the week prior to her death. A couple to Seattle, some to Denver, a lot to and from your cell." He paused as if waiting for Trevor to speak. He didn't. "We're most concerned with the calls the day of the murder. She called Elliot Corwin around ten-thirty that morning. I never did get a chance to talk to him. Always said he had court dates or meetings with clients. I need to know what they talked about. A deputy is on his way to Corwin's office now."

Trevor sat back, his mind working in fifth gear. *God Almighty! What if Helen confronted Corwin with her request for an audit, demanding he give permission? And what if Corwin knew the audit would reveal...what? Embezzlement?*

Had his aunt signed her own death warrant? Had Corwin come to the house and killed Helen? Was Halston telling the truth after all? Had he walked in just minutes after the murder?

Vicky returned with a fresh pot of coffee and three cups on a tray. She set it on the credenza behind the desk and poured, then turned to leave.

"If you'll excuse me, I'll leave you two alone."

"No, that's all right," Trevor said, taking a sip. "Have a seat. Al has news."

He brought her up to date on the searches.

"Why would Carlos try to kill us?"

"I'm not sure he intended to kill you, maybe just scare you, and it got out of hand."

Trevor shook his head. "If that's the case, why's he dead?"

The sheriff shrugged. "A drug deal gone bad?"

"Out there? In the middle of nowhere? When it's obvious he used his apartment?"

Sheriff Singleton gulped half his coffee. "Look, Trevor, I don't know. We're still working on it." He set the cup on the desk and leaned forward. "I have another question for you. Last week you said your aunt was your client, and that she was checking out Mr. Halston. Then I discover Miss Denton is his sister. I gave you some slack at the time, but another murder has used it up. What gives? Why were you in Miami?"

He shot Vicky a glance, and then turned toward the sheriff. "I told you. Helen thought Vicky might be able to help us deal with her brother. She said to bring her along."

"Are you a con artist, too?"

"No," Trevor hastened to answer. "She had a legitimate job in Miami."

He didn't dare look at Vicky. Finally, unable to resist, he looked her way. Her face bore neither surprise nor gratitude, just a curious mix of relief and fear.

The notebook snapped shut. "All right, I'll buy it for now." He pointed a finger at her. "But if your name pops up in any complaints anywhere in the country in the last couple of years, you'll see a cell."

Vicky relaxed and Trevor breathed easier. He knew Victoria *Denton* wouldn't show up. Marks had never known her real name.

"You might be interested to know we found the candlesticks and silver picture frames."

Trevor jerked. "Where?"

"In a pawnshop fifty miles north of here—Prescott to be exact."

"So, Halston went out of his way to dump them? Why not unload the jewelry, too?"

"We showed the owner a picture of Mr. Halston. He said that was *not* the man who pawned them.

Gave a description of a male Hispanic."

"Carlos?" Vicky said with a gasp.

"Let's not jump to conclusions. We're getting a photo array up to Prescott as we speak."

A knock sounded on the front door. Vicky rose to answer, returning in a couple of seconds with a deputy.

The sheriff stood and met the man near the doorway. "Yes, Carlyle, what is it?"

He passed a baggie to his boss. "Thought you might want to see this."

Al turned his back on them and examined the bag, talking in soft undertones.

"Wait here." He walked back to Trevor, tossing the object on the desk.

He picked it up, and stared at the contents. "It's Aunt Helen's ruby ring. The one that's missing. Where did you find it?"

"Tucked inside a drawer in Carlos's room at Rosa's."

Trevor sat back with a thump, the implications staggering. Anger worked its way from his chest to his throat.

"The only way he could have it was if he'd ripped it from her dead body," he exclaimed in a hoarse voice. "Which means the son of a bitch was inside the house that night."

"What about the maid?" Deputy Carlyle asked. "Could she have snatched it that morning when she found the body?"

"No way!" Trevor snapped. "Rosa loved my aunt. She wouldn't do something like that. Anything new with Carlos's murder?"

"Tire marks further up the road at the crime scene showed a car had parked. We made an impression and are checking it now. Also found marks next to the pick-up indicating someone accelerated fast. The bullets entered the body almost dead even with a slight upward slant for the head shot. Whoever killed him stood next to the driver's side window."

"So, the killer waited for Carlos, got out, fired, and hauled ass."

"That's the way I see it," the sheriff said.

Trevor drummed his fingers on the arm of his chair. *This was no drug deal. This was a payoff for taking care of me. Vicky was collateral damage.*

"How would Carlos know the safe combination to steal it in the first place?" Trevor ran a hand over his face. His brain reeled from an overload of information and new suppositions.

"Unfortunately, Carlos isn't around to tell us."

"Someone else was here that night," Vicky said. She sucked in a sharp breath. "Remember the funeral? Carlos sidled up to a lot of people."

Trevor nodded. "Blackmail." He sat up straight. "Carlos found the body, but didn't know who had done it. That's when he took the ring. Probably the other stuff, too. The safe was open and empty. Or he saw someone, but it was dark and didn't know who. He may have been feeling out the suspects at the funeral"

"And that same someone didn't like you asking questions and making insinuations," Singleton said. "So, whoever it was decided to kill two birds with one stone."

"Kill me, and then kill Carlos. Problem solved."

"Only we didn't die," Vicky added.

"Who did Carlos talk to at the funeral?" the sheriff asked.

"Walter, Adam, Elliot, my nephew Jason Hamilton."

"I need to talk to all of them. And this time I want alibis for night before last. Carlyle, contact the Richardsons and Jason Hamilton. Deputy West should be at Corwin's asking about that phone call."

The sheriff had barely finished speaking when his cell rang. He answered, walking across the room, and waved Deputy Carlyle on his way.

Vicky she gazed at Trevor with soft eyes. "Thank you for not giving me away. You could have told the sheriff what I was really doing in Miami. Why didn't you?"

He shrugged. "Water over the dam. It's not relevant now. Besides, I don't want to see you in jail."

She lifted the corners of her mouth in a warm smile and sighed. Her eyes went a shade bluer.

"I have close to a half a million dollars in a Caymans Bank. It won't begin to cover all the money I've stolen over the years, but I'd like to make restitution."

He wanted to hug her. This was the final capitulation. In his heart, he knew she'd never go back to conning.

"We'll work on it."

The sheriff snapped his phone shut and returned, a frown digging deep lines into his forehead. "We have a problem."

"What kind of problem?" Trevor asked.

"My deputy went over to Mr. Corwin's office. It was locked, and he had to wait a while until the secretary showed up. Deputy West had a seat while the woman gathered papers. When she opened Corwin's office door, the room had been tossed. The drawers were dumped on the floor, and the safe stood wide open."

"What does Corwin have to say?"

"That's the problem. The secretary can't get a hold of him. He doesn't answer his home or cell phones. And Deputy West says his car isn't at either his office or house." Sheriff Singleton removed his hat and wiped his forehead before settling it back on. "Elliot Corwin is missing."

Chapter Eighteen

Vicky's mind raced. *Missing or running?*

Trevor rose, a frown furrowing his forehead. "Are you sure?"

The sheriff nodded. "Looks that way. Don't know yet if his disappearance is voluntary or a kidnapping."

"What does the secretary say?"

"Heading there now." He crammed his hat on his head, marching toward the door.

"Mind if we come along?" Trevor asked and shot her a questioning glance.

She nodded. Her money was on Corwin running.

The attorney's office was chaotic. The secretary stood off to the side answering questions and wringing her hands.

"I don't understand any of this. Who'd want to kidnap Mr. Corwin?" she wailed.

The sheriff walked over to the woman and his deputy, notebook out and ready. "Mrs. Jeffries, start at the beginning. What time did you leave last night?"

"A little after six. Mr. Corwin had business in Boulder, but came back around three. I stayed to clean up some old paperwork."

"Was he still here when you left?"

"No. He'd gone home maybe fifteen or twenty minutes earlier. He said he was expecting company for dinner at seven. New clients, I think."

The sheriff wrote fast, but not half as fast as Vicky was thinking.

Suppose he came back to the office in the dead of night, made it look like a break in and burglary, then skipped town?

She tossed a glance at Trevor who casually walked around the reception area, inching ever closer to Corwin's office and the yellow tape across the open door.

"Carlyle, get out to the Corwin house. Ask the maid if he was home last night and for how long? Get the names of his guests." The man nodded and left. Sheriff Singleton resumed his questioning. "Right, Mrs. Jeffries, then what happened?"

She took a deep breath. "Last night, he thanked me for staying, and said I didn't need to hurry in this morning, that he wanted to work from home, so I took my time getting here. When I arrived, your deputy was waiting to see Mr. Corwin. I told him to have a seat, gathered up some files needed for the day, opened the office door, saw the mess, and..." The secretary left the sentence unfinished.

Trevor stood outside the doorway to Corwin's office, gazing inside. To distract the sheriff, Vicky dared a question.

"Did you happen to notice if any messages had been left on your machine? What about faxes? I'm a secretary, and those are the first things I check."

"I...I didn't notice any flashing lights, but I think there is a fax." She walked toward the machine behind her desk. "Yes. It came in at nine this morning. It's from some accounting firm in Mineral City asking about an audit for Walter Richardson."

"I'd better take that," the sheriff said reaching for the sheet of paper. "Can you access Mr. Corwin's e-mail?"

"No."

Vicky wondered if Richardson had given Corwin any warning of the audit request.

Trevor had ducked under the tape, entering the lawyer's office. The sheriff looked up.

"Trevor, get out of there."

"I'm not touching anything."

"Out, now."

Trevor obeyed. "How much of a head start do you think Corwin has?"

"We don't know he's running or if he's even been kidnapped. He may have simply gone out of town."

"For what reason?" Trevor's tone held a hint of exasperation. "My aunt and Carlos Ramirez were murdered. He's lying about a lot of things."

"I'm not going to make accusations against a solid citizen with no proof. We have to take this one step at a time." He turned to the secretary. "Thank you, Mrs. Jeffries. Why don't you go home? Can't do much of anything with us around. If we find Mr. Corwin, we'll let you know."

She shot a hard glance at Trevor. "Mr. Corwin wouldn't hurt a fly, and I think you insinuating he did is awful. It's ludicrous. He and Mrs. Richardson were good friends."

On that note, she gathered her coat and purse, and sailed out the door.

The sheriff eyed Trevor. "She's right. Keep your suspicions to yourself."

Vicky took a deep breath. She just might have the solution. "Sheriff, you may have a witness."

"What do you mean?"

"I think my brother knows a lot more than he's telling. Given an incentive, he might open up."

"What kind of incentive?"

"Other than the blood on his clothes, you don't really have much for a murder charge. To a jury his explanation might raise reasonable doubt. And you've recovered the jewelry, again with an explanation, however lame. If he talks, drop the charges or reduce them to a misdemeanor."

"That's not up to me."

"Then call the district attorney's office," Trevor said. "As much as I hate to say this, I think Rod Halston may hold the key to what happened."

Sheriff Singleton sighed and pulled out his cell.

While he made arrangements, Trevor crossed to her. "Do you think Rod will cooperate?"

"To get out of jail? Yes."

"But will he tell the truth?"

"At least ninety-nine percent of it." She fudged on that figure. Rod would tell as much as he needed to make himself look good, but that was all.

The sheriff snapped his phone shut. "We meet in an hour. The DA was going to offer a deal anyway."

"Must have agreed with the reasonable doubt theory. We want to be there," Trevor said.

"You can use the observation room again."

"Good." He cupped Vicky's elbow in his hand, leading her from Corwin's offices. "Let's grab a quick lunch, and then see what your brother has to say."

****

Vicky stood close to the two way glass window in the observation room. Rod's defense lawyer sat at one end of a long table. The prosecutor sat at the other. Both played with papers in folders rather than speak. A pitcher of water along with a small stack of paper cups graced the space between them.

"I hope this works," Trevor said, flipping the switch to activate the speakers.

"My brother will do anything to get out of jail."

"There's still that outstanding warrant in California. He'll be extradited."

Before she could answer, Sheriff Singleton entered the interrogation room from one door, while a deputy escorted Rod through another. Shackled, he shuffled across the floor and sat next to his attorney.

The sheriff lounged in a chair near the assistant DA and spoke first.

"Mr. Halston, it's time to fish or cut bait. We want the truth about what happened at Helen Richardson's the night of the murder."

A crafty look crossed the prisoner's face. "Yeah? What's in it for me?"

The prosecutor riffled through the pages in his folder, his expression impassive. "I'm Assistant District Attorney Mark Winters. We might be able to offer a deal."

Vicky's gaze swept over her brother. He still looked like hell with a bloated face and a greasy sheen to his hair. She wouldn't be surprised if he smelled.

Rod's lawyer, Bob James, leaned forward. "What kind of a deal?"

Winters shrugged and stared at Rod. "I can go man two, he does the max."

Rod laughed. "Drop dead. It only takes one to hang a jury."

"There's still that outstanding warrant," the sheriff said in a soft voice.

Rod and his lawyer put their heads together.

"Drop the charges," James countered. "You don't have enough to convict. He explained why the jewelry was in his possession, and how the blood got on his slacks. He'll deal with the warrant in California."

"Never knew a warrant was out," Rod said, his tone silky smooth. "After all, they cut me loose. Why should I question it?"

"I'll petition for eighteen months, not including time served."

"Drop the charges, and he won't fight extradition," James told the others in the room.

"That's as low as I'm going. Take it or leave it. If you don't, I'll see you in court on a murder two charge. Do you really want to take a chance on that jury?"

Take it Rod, you dummy. Take it and tell the truth. Beside her, Trevor stood rigid. *God help you if you did it. Trevor will make your prison life a living hell.*

The defense attorney conferred with his client again. Rod shook his head, but James made a cutting motion with his hand.

"Take it dumb ass," Trevor muttered, echoing her thoughts. "It's the best deal he'll ever see. He doesn't deserve this slap on the wrist."

"I know," she said. "But it's the only way he'll talk."

"All right, you have a deal," James said.

The prosecutor glared at her brother. "Give it to us straight. If I find out you've lied, you'll be back here facing the maximum."

Rod leaned back in his chair, crossed his arms over his chest, and smirked. "Where do you want me to start?"

"The night of the murder," the sheriff said. "What time did you leave the house and why?"

"The part about Helen having business to conduct is true. I was getting stir crazy, so I left. It was around eight-thirty when I pulled into Marley's." He raised his eyes to the two way mirror as though knowing she stood behind it, and grinned. "I had a few drinks, flirted with one of the waitresses, and then headed back to the house."

"What time was that?" Winters asked.

"I don't know...eleven, eleven-thirty. I parked the car in the garage, and came in. The house was dark, except for a light in the foyer.

"The old girl always went to bed early and got up at the damned crack of dawn. I went upstairs to my room. When I took my phone out of my pocket, I saw Vicky had called telling me the jig was up and to get the hell out. Helen knew who I was and had jail on her mind."

"Bet that gave him a turn," Trevor said.

"He doesn't react well to bad news."

She refocused her gaze on her brother, who now clasped his cuffed hands behind his head. Sweat stained his underarms. He looked seedy—a small time grifter working for peanuts, whose time was running out. At least Harry had never looked like an unmade bed.

"We already know about the phone calls. Your sister told us. What did you do then?" Sheriff Singleton asked.

Rod shot a sullen glance at the mirror. "I packed real fast and snuck down the stairs. I figured on taking one of the cars to the closest city with an airport, and getting the hell out. Unfortunately, I didn't have much cash, so I went into the study, flipped on the light, and grabbed the cigar box."

"You knew about that?" the sheriff said with raised eyebrows.

"Yeah, I was in there one day when she paid off Carlos. Now, there is a slick operator. He was always hanging around outside the windows or skulking near doors trying to listen."

"Could he have been doing that when your aunt was talking to Elliot on the phone or during their meeting in the afternoon?" Vicky asked.

"Could be. May have heard enough to blackmail Corwin."

"Go on, Mr. Halston," Winters said.

"I took whatever was in the box, and then noticed two files sitting on the desk. The top one had my name on it—my real name. I opened it and saw a full dossier on my activities for the past several years."

"And the second folder?" the sheriff prompted.

Rod laughed again, tilting his chair on its two

back legs. "It was from some private eye company, and the name on the file was Elliot Corwin."

"Son of a bitch!" Trevor swore loudly. "She did it. She had him investigated. God, I hope she didn't tell him what she'd done."

"Since we didn't find a file, I'd have to say she did, and that Elliot was in that room at some time in order to take it," she said.

"Or Carlos found it and used it for blackmail purposes."

"We have no idea what was in it."

"Do you really think it was anything good?" he asked in an exasperated tone.

Vicky shrugged and turned her attention back to the room and Rod.

The sheriff and the attorneys looked at each other. "Did you read it?"

"Some."

"What did it say?" Winters wanted to know.

"The gist of the report was Corwin was embezzling."

The Sheriff rose and left the room.

Winters wrote quickly on a legal pad before saying, "Go on."

"I was standing by the desk when the old gal appeared in the doorway. 'What the hell do you think you're doing?' Scared me to death. So, I told her I was leaving."

"What was her reaction?"

Rod leaned forward, setting the chair down on all four legs. "She said something along the lines of 'wanna bet', walked over, and snatched the file from my hand. Then she reached for the phone. I asked, 'What are *you* doing?' and she said, 'Calling the cops like I should have earlier. Had other things on my mind.'"

"Yeah, I'll bet," Trevor said in a low tone. "Like nailing her thieving lawyer to the wall."

"Compared to that, Rod and I were small potatoes," Vicky commented. "She took a chance confronting him. When cornered, Rod can get nasty."

Her brother had poured a cup of water, and took his time drinking it before continuing. The sheriff reentered the room and resumed his seat.

"So, Mrs. Richardson was going to call the police. What happened next?" Winters demanded.

"I tried to grab the phone out of her hand. We fought over it for a few seconds before I got it free. I pushed her away intending to rip the cord out. She was wearing a long nightgown and robe along with a pair of goofy shoes—a bunch of feathers on top."

Mules. Backless slip-ons, usually with a small heel. Vicky had often worn them when vamping a mark.

"I don't know what happened, maybe her heel caught in the bottom of her robe, but she stumbled backward and fell, hitting her head on the edge of the desk. I mean, the old girl dropped like a stone, face down. Blood gushed. Never been so scared in my life."

Cash Marriott flashed through Vicky's mind. Another mark with the same injury? A tremor rippled up her spine. *Rod, is this the truth or are you grasping at old memories?*

Beside her, Trevor stiffened. "My aunt and Quinn's grandfather? Kind of convenient, isn't it?"

She didn't answer, because she had her doubts, too.

"Why didn't you call 9-1-1?" the sheriff asked.

"I was scared, I tell you. I put the phone back on the desk, and knelt beside her. I'm not real good with shit like that. I don't know anything about pulses. I lifted her hand and let it drop." He shuddered. "Flopped like a dead fish. I figured she was a goner. I remembered the jewelry I'd scoped out earlier, ran upstairs, crammed the things into my pockets, and took off. Grabbed my bags, my file, the first set of car keys I touched, and high-tailed it out the back door."

"What about the candlesticks, the picture frames, and the safe?" Winters inquired.

"I told you, I didn't even know she had a safe, and why the hell would I grab candlesticks and picture frames? They're bulky and hard to hide. I had the keys to her car, and took it. The file hit the first rest stop dumpster on the Interstate. Vicky left another couple of messages later saying to get my ass back with a plausible story. I figured she knew what she was talking about. Vicky always watched my back."

He shot a snide look at the mirror. The sheriff did the same, frowning before jotting something in his notebook.

Vicky wanted to kick her weasel of a brother. Rod had no intention of going down alone. Trevor's arm stretched around her shoulders, giving her a light squeeze.

"Don't worry." His lips briefly touched her temple. "You won't go to jail. I promise."

The heat of relief and gratitude radiated from the pit of her stomach. He wanted to protect her. He *did* care. But how much?

"What time was this?" the sheriff asked.

"How the hell should I know? I didn't pay any attention. I was shaking like a leaf. Had to pull over to the side of the road to calm down."

"Where?" Al wrote in his notebook again.

"Right before the stop sign at the foot of the hill."

"Let's see, it's about midnight in a residential section of town with few street lights, and even less traffic. Pass anybody along the way?"

"While I was sitting there, this dark-colored car blew the stop sign and barreled up the hill at a good lick. And before you ask, no I didn't see the driver."

"Corwin," Trevor said.

"Or Adam. Don't forget, he was in town that night, too."

"Maybe. Whoever it was found her dead, and stole everything he could. Your brother left out the part about bashing her head in."

Vicky had a sinking feeling he was right.

"How long did you stay on the side of the road?" Winters asked.

"Not long, maybe five minutes, ten tops. Someone else passed me, too."

Sheriff Singleton raised his eyebrows and shot her brother a stern look. "Yeah? Who and where?"

Rod curled his lips into another one of his patented smirks. "I was just coming into town when Carlos passed me. I watched in the rearview mirror. He turned left at the corner, like he was on his way to the house."

"And how do you know it was Carlos Ramirez?" Winters asked.

"I recognized the car. He parked at the house when he did yard work. All that rust and primer wasn't hard to miss."

The prosecutor frowned. "Mrs. Richardson died from a blow to the back of the head with the fireplace poker."

"Well, I sure as hell didn't do it," Rod said in a petulant voice.

"I think my client has cooperated long enough," James said, speaking for the first time since Rod began his story. "Are you finished?"

The assistant DA rose, gathering his files and papers. "For the time being, unless, of course, his story turns out to be a crock. I'll talk to my boss. See what he wants to do. He'll want to hear Corwin's story first."

The sheriff closed his notebook, and signaled

toward the door. A deputy came in and escorted Rod back to his cell.

Trevor flipped the switch off, and turned to Vicky. "Do you believe it?"

"Yes. Rod doesn't react well in a crisis situation. He did exactly what he's always done. Take what he can and get the hell out."

"You think Corwin bashed her head in for good measure?"

"Rod was scared. He wouldn't remember to wipe his prints off the poker. And if he had the money from the safe, where is it?"

"God, I hope the cops catch up with Corwin soon. Come on, let's talk to Al."

They left the tiny room, and met the sheriff in his office.

"Do you believe him?" Trevor demanded.

"No reason not to at this point." Al flipped through his notebook. "There may be some holes in a few of his explanations, but I think he's leveling with us."

"What about Corwin?"

"I sent out an APB on him. He's a person of interest in the death of Helen Richardson. I'll also contact the Mineral City police. See what color cars Walter and Adam Richardson drive."

"Walter drives a silver Jag. Adam, a black Lexus," he told him. "My money's on Corwin, though. How would Adam know the safe combination?"

"You said she used her birthday," Vicky replied. "For that matter, your cousin Jason could have known it, too. Doesn't sound like it was a big secret."

"No, it was Corwin. Shit, the little bastard could be anywhere." Trevor ran a hand through his hair. "If he gets out of the country…"

"The closest international airport is Denver. We've already alerted them. Take it easy. Corwin's running scared. He'll make a mistake."

"If he did steal the money from the safe, he'll play hell getting it past security at an airport," Vicky said. "Even if he packs it in his checked luggage, the x-ray machines will show something."

"I hadn't thought of that," Trevor replied. "Stacks of money could resemble C-4 explosives."

"If it was me, I'd drive to the nearest large city, open an account, and then transfer the money once I was in a safe haven," she commented. It was the way she'd always operated.

The sheriff shot her a keen glance. "Know a lot about that, do you? Your brother made it sound like you were a partner."

"My brother says a lot of things."

"And most of it malicious," Trevor cut in. "Corwin might be driving to Mexico or Canada."

"Not Mexico," Al said, shaking his head. "Too much political turmoil. While I was out of the room, I talked with Deputy Carlyle. The maid at Corwin's confirms he had dinner guests. We found their names in his appointment book and called them. They said they left his house around midnight."

"So, he got in the car and went to my aunt's."

"Not necessarily. Just because Halston said he saw a dark car pass him, doesn't mean it was Corwin's. Please, let us handle this when we catch him."

"*If* you catch him, Trevor rejoined.

"*When* we catch him." The sheriff paused, frowning. "Maybe you should stick around the house for a while. Don't expose yourselves. If Corwin had one crack at you, he might try again."

"Naw, he's long gone. Why stay and risk capture?"

Vicky placed her hand on his arm. "He's right, Trevor. Elliot's scared and probably not thinking straight, especially if he's on the hook for two murders."

"He's smart enough to have gotten away with embezzlement for years. He may have panicked and killed Aunt Helen, but Carlos was premeditated. He hired Carlos to kill us, and then killed Carlos in cold blood. He's come a long way."

She silently agreed. Elliot Corwin looked better and better as the killer. Of course, Carlos's death could have been the result of a bad drug deal. She thought about Adam Richardson, his possible drug use and money problems. Could he have kidnapped Corwin in desperation? She rubbed her forehead where a nagging headache throbbed behind her eyes.

I can't think about this any longer. I just want it over. I want to live a normal life.

"Why don't the two of you go home? We'll get Corwin. In the meantime, I'll be out at his place asking questions. If he's scared and desperate, he'll have made mistakes."

"Yeah, the first of which was killing my aunt."

Trevor grasped Vicky's hand and pulled her from the room. At least, her brother was finally getting his. Jail time was too good for him.

She cast a quick glance at Trevor. His face was set in a frown. "What are you thinking?"

He shook his head. "Just a feeling that Corwin's not done yet."

Chapter Nineteen

Vicky cleared the dishes from the table. Dinner had consisted of soup, salad, sandwiches, and very little conversation. She glanced at a subdued Trevor. His reticence to discuss anything about Rod's story or Corwin's disappearance had her worried. She'd prefer angry outbursts.

"The sheriff will get Corwin," she said, attempting to draw him out.

"Maybe."

Trevor frowned and doodled designs in the condensation on his iced tea glass with his finger. He drained the glass, rattling the ice with an angry gesture.

Vicky bit her lip and loaded the dishwasher.

"Want to talk about it?"

"No," he said, his reply sharp and his eyes hard.

"I'm sorry, I didn't mean to nag, but you've been so quiet..." she let the sentence fade.

He finally turned his gaze to her, the expression softening.

"No, I'm sorry. I didn't mean to snap. I have a lot on my mind." He rose and walked toward her. Cupping her face in his hands, he brushed his lips over hers. "When this is finished, we'll talk. We *need* to talk, but not now, not tonight."

Her heart thumped, and for once she couldn't read the expression in his eyes. Talk? Saying "Vicky, I love you," or "Thanks for helping, see you around?"

She swallowed hard and closed her eyes.

"I understand." Her voice caught, destroying any attempt to sound cool and in control.

Trevor sighed, and rubbed his thumbs along her cheeks. He then walked to the fridge and refilled his tea glass.

"Why don't you watch a movie or read a book? I have a lot of Sloane Investigations work to do. I've been neglecting it. I'll see you in the morning."

He disappeared from the kitchen leaving her with a sinking feeling in the pit of her stomach. She clenched her jaw to keep tears from welling. While he hadn't said it in so many words, the implication was clear. Sleep in your own room tonight.

Her shoulders sagged, and she let the tears flow.

****

In the study, Trevor slumped into the chair behind the desk. His emotions had been in turmoil ever since leaving the jail. If only Halston had called 9-1-1, his aunt would be alive today. Corwin wouldn't have gotten the chance to kill her. He hoped the DA tacked on deprived indifference to the charges against Vicky's brother. Disgust at Rod Halston, anger at Elliot Corwin, and fear Vicky would walk out the door, never to be seen again, churned in his gut. He needed her, loved her, but didn't know how to express it. What had he said to Becca all those years ago? God, he couldn't remember.

Maybe it gets harder with age. Maybe we lose the ability to express our emotions. Maybe it's more cut and dried.

Would Vicky leave? He'd seen the confusion, the almost desperate look in her eyes. Did she love him? He'd wanted to ease her mind, but other more pressing events crowded out his personal life.

Later, deal with it later. Assuming later wasn't too late.

297

He was on edge, the hairs on the back of his neck rising and falling with each unexplained sound in the house—sounds he'd heard a dozen times before. He resented the feeling. Over the years, he'd staked out and investigated dozens of lowlifes, and he'd be damned if Elliot Corwin would disrupt his thoughts and actions.

He rose and walked toward the window, cupping his hands around his face and peering into the darkness. The full moon had risen throwing the lawn into a series of sharp black shadows.

Trevor backed away and pulled the drapery cord with an abrupt motion, closing out the view. He rubbed the back of his neck and the little hairs that stood at attention.

Knock it off. There's nothing out there. Let business occupy your mind.

Determined not to allow his nerves get the better of him, he strode back to the desk and turned on his laptop.

****

Vicky sat on the sofa in the den not paying attention to the sitcom on TV. For unknown reasons, she was nervy, unable to sit still for more than a few minutes. Her gaze flickered to the terrace doors for the umpteenth time during the past hour. She'd checked and re-checked the locks after dinner, but now, she rose and checked the French doors again.

Why am I so jumpy?

She put it down to her less than settled future. Trevor's reticence and ambiguous words kept running through her mind. Vicky tried to push the thoughts away. She couldn't deal with the situation right now.

Once again, her gaze strayed to the terrace. The beveled and carved glass was decorative, but provided little in the line of privacy. She felt on display to anyone who cared to look.

Oh, for Christ's sake, quit thinking this way.
With an abrupt move, she grabbed the remote and
jabbed the off button. *Make tomorrow's coffee, and
then get the hell to bed.*

She rose, tossing the remote onto the table and
left the room. Maybe tomorrow she and Trevor could
talk, clear the air. Whatever he wanted—good or
bad—she had to know. She couldn't take this
uncertainty much longer.

Vicky entered the kitchen, flipping on the light
over the stove. As she reached for the coffee pot, a
movement wavered in her peripheral vision. She
turned her head and froze, struggling to breathe.
Her heart stopped, and then pounded away at
ramming speed. Elliot Corwin stood near the cellar
door, gun in hand. For a moment she stared, unable
to move or think.

"Put it down, real easy," he said in a low, hoarse
voice.

She did as told, her gaze never leaving his face.
He had a wild, desperate look about him. His head
jerked from side to side as if expecting to see ghosts.
The scent of fear rolled off of him.

"How...how did you get in?" She intended her
voice to be strong, but it came out as a breathy gasp.

"Key. Helen gave it to me years ago. Where's
Sloane?"

"In...in the study."

He motioned with the gun. "Come on. Let's
invite him to the party, too."

Vicky swallowed hard and tried to contain her
runaway heart, while forcing her wobbly legs to
carry her across the kitchen.

"What do you want?" she asked in a normal
tone.

"Keep it quiet. Understand?"

She nodded, even though her mind raced to find
a way to warn Trevor. *Keep him talking. Maybe*

Trevor will hear. But what then? He won't be expecting this.

She slowed her step. Corwin, right behind her, ground the gun into the small of her back. She gasped at the pain. Surely, Trevor would hear two sets of footsteps crossing the floor. She walked as noisily as possible. The study door loomed, the light within spilling into the hallway with a bright slash. Corwin pushed her through. She stumbled and fell against a chair.

Then Corwin leveled the gun at Trevor's chest.

****

Trevor looked up at Vicky's undignified entrance, and then saw Corwin. He leapt to his feet. Corwin grabbed Vicky's arm and slung her toward him. She crashed into the desk with a cry. He ran around the mahogany antique and gathered her close. His arms tightened around her trembling body, while trying to suppress the tremors rippling through his. He never suspected Corwin would show up here.

"Don't be stupid, Corwin. The sheriff knows everything. Whatever you're planning, ain't gonna work."

"We'll see. Sit down, both of you. I gotta think."

He motioned them toward the sofa where they did as instructed.

Trevor needed to think, too. *Get him talking before he uses that gun.*

"How much did you embezzle from Aunt Helen?"

"About two hundred thousand. I'd have gotten away with it, too, if you hadn't put the bug in her ear about trusting me."

"Why kill her? What happened that night?"

"It all started with that damned mall property—a sweetheart deal. The land was in a prime location, but the price was high. Minimum buy in was one and half million dollars. Real estate was going through the roof at that time, and I saw a way to make a bundle."

"But you didn't have the funds," Vicky said.

"I had about half, so I suggested investing to several of my clients."

"Including Aunt Helen."

"She was first on my list. She refused. I moved on to others."

"Like Walter and Adam," Trevor said in the calmest voice he could muster.

"Yeah. A month later, I was still short by half a million, so I borrowed it from a couple of accounts."

"Embezzled, you mean," Trevor replied in a sneering tone.

"Figured we'd build, lease, and I'd get the money back before anyone was the wiser."

"But it didn't work that way, did it?" Vicky remarked.

Corwin shook his head and wiped sweat from his forehead with his free hand.

"There were problems getting clear title to the land, and the construction company was so busy they couldn't begin for almost a year. Then real estate tanked. The consortium bought me out for pennies on the dollar. I took a bath."

Trevor hoped the longer Corwin talked, the less attentive he'd be. "How did you keep your clients in the dark?"

"My accountant, Ben Jacobs over in Boulder. He was looking to retire, so I offered him five grand a month to make things look right. Unfortunately, I had to shuffle other accounts to pay him off."

"Which meant you dug a deeper hole every month," Vicky said.

"I have no idea what Helen saw in that final report to make her ask for an independent audit."

"I'd been after her for a couple of years to do it," Trevor replied, unable to keep the satisfaction from his voice. "Maybe the returns were too good to be true in the current market. Aunt Helen was smarter than she let on about a lot of things."

"Shocked the hell out of me when she came by the office and said she'd initiated the audit. Said we'd talk more when she got back from Vegas. When she and Harvey started talking investments, I panicked."

"We know she called you at ten-thirty on the morning of the murder." Trevor forced himself to sound conversational, non-threatening.

"She wanted to talk to me privately at the house. I came a little after two. She had a report by a private investigator, and knew I'd lifted funds from her portfolio. Claimed to have evidence. She gave me forty-eight hours to replace the money. If I did, she wouldn't press charges given our long history together, but if I couldn't replace the funds, she'd call the police."

"Which, of course, you couldn't, so you came back and killed her."

His voice rose allowing the anger to break through the calm façade. It brought Corwin out of true confessions and back to the present. The gun, which had momentarily sagged, now refocused.

"And Carlos?"

"The son of a bitch was blackmailing me. I had to get rid of him."

"And our accident?" Vicky asked in a wavering voice.

"Never send a boy to do a man's work. Egotistical, incompetent little shit. I should have done it myself. I knew I'd goofed that night at dinner when I answered your question about being here in the afternoon. Took me until the next morning to realize Rosa couldn't have seen me. She wasn't around. Then, I got to wondering if you'd set me up, flashing your smile and obvious charms to get information. Decided I needed to do something about the two of you." Corwin paused, frowning. "I can right that mistake at any rate. On your feet."

He poked and prodded them back to the kitchen, where he grabbed the SUV keys from the board.

"Outside."

"And then what?" Trevor asked.

"I'm still working on it," he said with a snarl, pushing them out the door into the cool Colorado night. The moonlight illuminated the courtyard. Shadows, stark and hard, dappled the cobblestones.

Trevor clasped Vicky's cold, trembling hand and squeezed, trying to reassure her. She squeezed back. Ahead, one of the shadows moved behind the bushes next to the garage. Another slithered from tree to tree off to his left. He breathed easier. They weren't alone.

"Open the garage door, Vicky, and no funny stuff. I'll drop him like a stone if you try something."

Vicky hauled the door up. Corwin's BMW was parked next to the SUV.

"How long has that been here?" Trevor asked. Over his captor's shoulder one of the shadows moved closer.

"Since about four this morning. As good a place as any. Who'd think to look for me in your garage? Figured if you went anywhere, you'd use your rental parked along the side of the house."

Keeping his gaze glued to his captives, Corwin pulled another set of keys from his pocket and hit one of the buttons, popping the trunk lid of the BMW. He reached in and yanked a cable free.

"Get in."

"And then what?" Trevor asked again. He had an inkling of what Corwin had in mind. The cable he'd disconnected was probably to the inside trunk release. "You turn on the engine and we die from carbon monoxide poisoning?"

Beside him, Vicky trembled harder, sucking in a sharp breath. "You won't get away with this. The sheriff is looking for you. My brother saw your file on the desk and read it."

His lips curved into a not so pleasant smile. "Who cares? No one's going to miss you for a while. By the time they discover the bodies, I'll be long gone, living the good life under a new name."

Corwin motioned Vicky toward the car. When she didn't move, he jerked her forward, putting her between him and the shadows in the bushes. He ground the gun into her ribs until she cried out.

"Ladies first, honey."

Fury clawed its way from Trevor's gut to his chest, and then hammered in his head. If the cops rushed now, Corwin could shoot her before they'd gone two feet. Without stopping to consider the consequences, Trevor gave him a different target.

"You bastard. Leave her alone."

He charged. Corwin swung the gun in his direction. At the same time, Vicky smashed her elbow into his stomach. His grip loosened, and she flung herself to the stones, half dragging him with her. The gun fired. It was answered by another shot, a sharp cry of pain, and Vicky's scream. Trevor hit the killer like a freight train, sending them both to the ground.

The next few seconds were a cacophony of shouts, rushing footsteps, and sobs. Vicky crawled to him.

"Trevor, are you hurt?"

"No, he missed me." He looked up at Al and Deputy Carlyle. "Thanks, guys."

The sheriff nodded. "My pleasure. I had Carlyle keeping an eye on the place. Something told me you were in danger. He called when he saw someone sneak out of the garage and into the house."

Deputy Carlyle was on the radio requesting an

ambulance. On the ground, a handcuffed Elliot Corwin writhed and sobbed.

"Did you shoot him?" Vicky asked.

"Just grazed his arm," Al said. "You took a hell of a chance, Trevor."

"When he put Vicky into the line of fire, I had to do something. Did you hear that half-assed explanation of how he was going to off us?"

"I heard. Sticking around town to settle a score was nuts. I guess when you're desperate, the mind blows a fuse."

Sirens blared in the distance.

****

Hours later, after giving their statements, including Corwin's confession to them in the study, they arrived home from the police station, exhausted, but alive.

They had tumbled into bed, too tired to do anything but sleep, not rising until close to noon. While Vicky made lunch, Trevor called the sheriff.

"He was treated and released last night. I arrested him on attempted murder charges. DA may up it to murder two after we hear his story."

"Think he'll tell the same thing to you he confessed to Vicky and me last night?"

"I doubt it. However, the fact he tried to kill the two of you makes anything he says suspect. I've gotta go. I'll drop by as soon as I can with any news."

Trevor hung up and wandered back into the kitchen where he gave Vicky the latest news.

"So, what do we do now?"

He ran a hand through his hair, and then over his face, the stubble scratching his palm.

"I'm going to get cleaned up. Then, I guess I'll get back to work on Sloane Investigations."

Her gaze flickered from his face to the sandwich in her hand.

"Oh, I see. Your aunt's files are all over the

house. I'll re-file them."

Can't talk love while looking like a bum. Get cleaned up first. Then, wait until after you hear from Al.

He trotted up the stairs, his heart pounding with anticipation. And for once, his aunt's case had nothing to do with it.

****

Vicky wedged another file in a drawer. She avoided looking at Trevor. If she did, she ran the risk of bursting into tears. His answer to her coy question of what they'd do had not been encouraging. Dispirited, she filed another folder.

From the desk area, Trevor swore under his breath before typing on his laptop. He'd been answering e-mails and on the phone for the past two hours.

He leaped to his feet when the doorbell rang and exited the room. The sheriff? She clutched a file to her chest. Did the officer realize her future hung in the balance by what Corwin had said?

Sheriff Singleton followed Trevor back into the study.

"Afternoon, Miss Denton."

She nodded, too keyed up to answer with words.

"What happened?" Trevor asked in a raspy voice.

"Mind if I sit down first?"

"I'm sorry, but what did Corwin have to say?"

The sheriff sat, and heaved a deep sigh. "You ain't gonna like this, but at the arraignment a while ago, he pleaded not guilty by reason of mental defect."

Trevor's jaw dropped, and he stared for a moment before blurting, "You've got to be kidding."

"Wish I was. Claimed he didn't have any memory of what happened last night."

"He sounded perfectly sane while holding us at

gunpoint. What about Helen?" Vicky asked, stunned by this revelation.

"Admits to 'borrowing' from her account and discussing it with her that afternoon. Says he went back to the office, and then home where he got stinking drunk. The rest is a blank."

"Lying bastard," Trevor muttered. "And Carlos?"

"Denies killing him or being blackmailed."

"That's all?" Vicky couldn't believe Elliot Corwin might get out of this on a diminished capacity plea.

"Forensics is still working on a few things, and we're searching his house." The sheriff rose. "He's not as smart as he thinks. He'll have made a mistake or two along the way."

"That ten grand is still missing and what about the gun?" Trevor asked.

Al smiled, but didn't answer. "What are your plans now?"

"I'm meeting with a lawyer about Helen's estate tomorrow morning. I may turn over some of the executor duties to her. I'll clean up things here, and then head back to L. A. My business misses me."

"And you, Miss Denton?"

Vicky laid the folder on top of the cabinets, bit her lip, and shrugged. "I...I'm not sure."

Trevor sent her a smoldering glance, sending her heart rate up a few beats.

"I am. I'll be in touch, Al."

The sheriff chuckled and left.

Trevor moved toward her. "Vicky, let's talk."

Vicky's legs trembled, and her nerves rasped raw. *I am.* At best, the words were ambiguous. At worst, decisive.

"It's almost over. No reason why we can't get on with our lives."

Still ambiguous. He can mean anything.

"Yes, I suppose so." She tucked a strand of hair behind her ear.

Trevor pulled her into his arms and kissed her breathless, then stepped back. Her heart pounded, sending hope surging along her singing nerves.

He ran a hand through his hair. "Aw, hell. I don't know how to say any of this."

Her heart now plummeted to her toes. Pain gnawed in the pit of her stomach.

I'm getting dumped. I should know the signs. I did it myself once I had what I wanted from a mark. She swallowed the lump forming in her throat. She pulled away, stepping a few feet to the right. *Keep your chin up. Be cool. Don't let him know he's ripping your heart out. Beat him to it.*

"I understand. I helped a little, and we had a good time. Now it's over. You don't need me anymore. You go back to Los Angeles, and I go...wherever the wind blows me." She'd meant to sound cool and composed, but her voice wavered.

He sent a sharp glance her way. "Is that all it was to you, a good time?"

She tried to keep her composure, but failed. Her chin trembled and her eyes filled with tears. To avoid looking at him, Vicky turned and walked with an unsteady gait to the window, staring out at, but not seeing, the manicured lawn. The sob broke from her throat.

"No, it was more—much more. You'll get a good laugh out of this, but I love you. Isn't that a hoot? Me, the thief and liar, falling for the private investigator that captured me. Has to be a movie or a book in there someplace. Please, don't laugh, at least not so I can hear it. I'll pack and be out of your hair in an hour."

She clapped a hand over her mouth, embarrassed at the silly words pouring forth. Tears trickled down her cheeks.

He crossed the room, and placing his hands on her shoulders, whispered against her ear, "Why would I laugh? I'm trying to say the same thing. Don't believe for a moment that I don't need you. I love you."

Vicky whipped around, her heart in her throat, her gaze searching his face. The chocolate eyes, soft and smiling, said he told the truth, yet she had to ask.

"You...you mean it?"

He folded her into his arms, close to his heart.

"I mean it. I almost told you yesterday, but making such a declaration in a bathroom didn't seem right." He smiled. "I was too unsettled to discuss my feelings last night. I was afraid you didn't feel the same. I'm not sure I could have taken rejection. I was scared to death you'd tell me to get lost."

"Never. And I thought you wanted me to leave."

"No way, baby. I want you forever."

Her breath caught in her chest. Good grief, did he mean...

"For...forever?"

"Forever. I'm asking you to marry me."

"What about your wife? You've held onto her memory for a long time."

He drew in a deep breath, and then released it. "A part of me will always love Becca, but that doesn't mean I can't make room for another love. I think you'd have liked her. She was warm, funny, and certainly wouldn't have wanted me to grieve the rest of my life." He snatched her close again. "Vicky, I love you."

"What about my past? What if we meet up with someone I swindled?"

"Then we'll deal with it. The night you came back, when you could have hopped a bus to anywhere, convinced me you'd changed. And while the loyalty to your brother may have been misplaced, it was there just the same. I liked to think you can transfer that loyalty to me. It took a while longer to admit you'd gotten under my skin and into my heart." He paused. "You haven't said yes yet."

Delicious warmth spread from her stomach, radiating out to the tips of her fingers and toes. He loved her. He was asking her to spend the rest of their lives together.

"Oh, God, yes!"

His mouth crushed hers, and when she parted her lips, their tongues danced. Her arms snaked around his neck and tightened. Heat, deep and searing, melted her insides. She wanted to show him how much she loved him. Not the hot animal love of yesterday, but a slow loving guaranteed to drive even the most level-headed of men crazy with desire. He finally raised his head.

"Do you have visions of a long white gown, a church full of people, and all the traditional trappings? Or will a justice of the peace do?"

"I want you." Her fingers yanked the shirt from the waistband of his slacks. "The sooner, the better."

He swatted her gently on the fanny. "Took you long enough to admit it."

"You beast!" she exclaimed, laughter mixing with desire.

"Beauty, I'm all beast when it comes to you."

He groaned, threaded his fingers through her hair, and then kissed her to within an inch of her life. He raised his head, eyes glittering with love, desire, and amusement.

"I have always wanted to do this."

"Do what?"

"Me Tarzan, you Jane!"

He laughed, and clasping her waist, lifted, and then tossed her over his shoulder.

"Trevor!" she said, gasping.

He laughed again and strode from the room. Her

hair hung down, brushing his calves. Vicky didn't know whether to laugh or protest the caveman act. On the whole, she liked it.

He carried her up the staircase and into his bedroom.

Chapter Twenty

Vicky sat cuddled in her husband's lap. The huge double chair in the den had turned into her favorite piece of furniture—other than the bed.

"Happy?" he asked.

"Delirious."

"The bloom hasn't faded after a week?"

"It's your job to maintain that bloom."

"Goodness, a honey-do list already."

She laughed and kissed his chin. This was the usual evening routine. The teasing led to caressing, then kissing, and finally to making love. Sometimes, they even made it upstairs.

"I talked to Marylou today. Broke the news I am now a married man."

"What was the reaction?"

"She and Pam are furious they missed the big event, and insist on a party when we get back."

"Are we going back? What about this house?"

"I discussed that with the lawyer who's doing most of the executor work. I think I'll offer it to the Granite Springs Historical Society. I have great memories of the place, but without Helen or Roland, it's not the same. We don't have to live in Los Angeles. There are a lot of nice areas nearby, including Palm Springs. After all, technically that's where this all began."

"Very funny." She paused. "But what about the business? Living there means commuting."

He shrugged. "So, we commute."

"We?"

"We."

"Are you offering me a job?"

He raised his eyebrows, his eyes filled with amusement. "I'm not going to pay my wife."

She punched on the arm. "Wanna bet? What do you have in mind?"

"A partnership. Vicky, what's mine is yours, and Marylou read me the riot act again today about getting another operative."

She quit cuddling and sat up. "You want me to be a private investigator, not a secretary?"

"Darling, have you ever wondered why you couldn't go straight after Guatemala?"

"Because I couldn't make as much money from legitimate work as I could from conning."

"You hated conning."

"I know, but what else was I going to do?"

He shook his head and smiled, kissing the tip of her nose. "You also hated being a secretary. It was boring taking dictation, typing letters, and answering a phone eight hours a day, five days a week. Conning presented a challenge, a thrill. I figured that out when you pulled information from Adam and Corwin. You weren't setting them up as marks, but as sources. You even made the comment that PI work is nothing more than a legal con. So, will you do it?"

"Become an investigator? Don't I have to get a license? What about my past?"

"You never conned under your own name."

"Can we go on stakeouts together?"

"I insist."

"Can't wait to sit in the back seat with you."

"I see innate problems with that. We'd better stay in front."

Vicky laughed and resumed her cuddle position.

"Who'd have thought the one talent I have could be turned into something positive?"

Trevor lifted her chin with his finger, and kissed her. A tendril of heat coiled in her stomach, and she tightened her arms around his neck.

"Hmm, God, I love you," he murmured against her lips.

Before she could answer, the doorbell rang.

"Damn, who the hell can that be? It's after ten." He kissed her again, removed her from his lap, and rose. "Hold that thought."

His footsteps echoed down the hallway and across the foyer. A moment later two sets of treading feet came back. She sat up, smoothing her hair. Trevor re-entered the den followed by the sheriff.

"Sheriff Singleton, this is a surprise."

"I decided to drop by. I've got several things to tell you."

Trevor gestured toward the bar. "Care for a drink?"

"A short scotch wouldn't be bad, but I'm still on duty. It's been a long day."

He poured two tumblers of liquor, handing one to his wife. "What's new?"

"Plenty, but let me start with the least important, First of all, we talked to Adam Richardson. He's been canned from Richardson Mining. Told us he's entering rehab for alcohol and cocaine addictions. He also admits to being at the house that night around ten o'clock begging Helen for money. She told him no. Said she was madder than hell."

"We knew he was in town," Trevor said.

"I stopped by Rosa's this afternoon. She's moving to Santa Fe," the sheriff said.

Trevor nodded, a saddened look on his face. "She gave notice last week. Without Aunt Helen and with us not living here, she didn't want to stay."

"Too many memories. I guess the murders and finding out her son was responsible for our accident made it impossible," Vicky added.

"Anything more on Carlos's death?"

Al smiled a predatory lawman smile and nodded. "Corwin wasn't as smart or thorough as he thought. We found a duffle bag with ten thousand dollars in it along with all the missing reports from Mrs. Richardson's safe hidden in the attic, including the report your brother saw that night."

"He didn't get rid of them?" Vicky asked.

"Told you he wasn't as smart as he thought. We recovered the gun from a ravine a couple of days ago. Also found a box of forty-five caliber shells in a kitchen drawer covered with his fingerprints. The gun had been wiped clean, but the shells remaining in the cylinder had his prints all over them. Criminals forget they leave fingerprints on the bullets."

Trevor leaned forward. "Did you tell him yet?"

Al grinned. "This morning. That combined with over a week in jail did it. He crumpled like a cheap house in an earthquake. Cut a deal with the state, and told us everything."

"And?" Vicky and Trevor asked in unison.

"Confirmed what you said the other night. He came back later that night, found your aunt, and thought she was dead. She came to while he was rifling the safe. Said he panicked, grabbed the poker and hit her. Meanwhile, Carlos arrived to have a look at his mother's car. Remember? It wouldn't start. Corwin was so panicked and still half-drunk, he never heard Carlos arrive."

"So, Carlos saw him kill Helen?" Vicky asked.

"No, saw him leave. Carlos told Corwin he went in, found the body, grabbed the ring, candlesticks, frames, and then proceeded on to blackmail. Adam and Walter Richardson said he tried to pry money out of them about things he'd overheard. They told him to cram it."

Vicky sipped her drink. "But Elliot paid because he was guilty."

"And us?"

"Corwin admitted your investigation was cutting close. He still hoped to get out of the embezzlement mess. So, he asked Carlos to keep an eye on you."

"He contracted Carlos to kill us, making it look like an accident, and then later when meeting him for the payoff, killed him," Trevor mused.

"That's about it," the sheriff agreed.

"But how did he know we'd be going out?" Vicky asked.

Her husband shook his head. "I told him."

"What? How?"

"Finally remembered. I told Rosa to go home early, and that we were going out to eat. After our discussion that afternoon, Carlos went back to see her. When she quit, she told me she mentioned it."

"So, he informs Corwin who gives him the green light, follows you, does his thing, and heads for the rendezvous point," the sheriff said.

"Where Elliot waits and bang, bang, kills him," Vicky finished.

"That's the way it went down." The sheriff shook his head. "Doesn't make sense. Corwin had everything going for him—a good practice, a decent investment business, respected in the community."

"Greed," Vicky murmured. "Greed does it every time."

"What kind of deal did Corwin cut?" Trevor asked.

"Your aunt was a solid murder two charge, but both Mrs. Richardson and Corwin are prominent citizens. There was the possibility he might use the mental defect theory. Plus, juries are unpredictable. Carlos could have bought him the death penalty, although he could say he killed Ramirez under duress using the same defense. He and his lawyer agreed to aggravated assault against you, and two counts of murder two, twenty-five to life with no possibility of parole, served consecutively. We won't be seeing Elliot Corwin again."

Trevor slammed the rest of the scotch down his throat. "Serves the son of a bitch right."

"Uh, I have one other piece of news," Al said, shaking his head again, an embarrassed look on his face. "It involves Mr. Halston."

Vicky looked up, taking a sip of her drink. Had the sheriff uncovered more cons? And did any involve her?

"Oh, no. What?" she said with a groan.

"He's escaped."

Now Vicky choked on the scotch. "How?"

"When?" Trevor barked.

"Around six this evening at shift change. He had help."

"Oh, my God, I should have known," she said.

"How could you have known he'd escape?" Trevor asked.

"Anne Daniels."

"How'd you guess?" the sheriff inquired with raised eyebrows.

"He charmed her into giving him little extras—another blanket, a pillow, God knows what else. He always finds a desperate woman. Any clue where they went?"

"Nope, but we'll get him. First time anyone's ever escaped from my custody."

"How'd it happen?" Trevor asked.

"Deputy Daniels was on duty in the visitor's pen. A few minutes before six, she entered the cell block and escorted him out. Tape shows her uncuffing him. He stripped off the jumpsuit, and left in jeans, a t-shirt, and sunglasses. She escorted him right out the front door. Had a couple of misdemeanors being brought in at the same time. With all the activity, no one noticed. Discovered it at the nine o'clock bed check." He shook his head. "It was well-planned, right between shifts. Her car is missing, but we have the license plate number and make and model. We'll get them. She probably brought the clothes into the jail over the last couple of days. My guess is, he dressed after lights out the night before and put the jumpsuit on over them."

"He'll drag out an alias and set up shop again." Vicky shook her head. "He's living on borrowed time. His looks are fading, and I'm not so sure about the staying power of his charm either."

Trevor threw his arm around her shoulders, giving them a squeeze. "He'll make a mistake and get caught."

Al moved toward the door. "I've still got work to do. When are you returning to Los Angeles?"

"Tomorrow, maybe the next day. I have a few more things to settle here, but that shouldn't take long. Thanks, for all you've done."

"My pleasure, and thank you, too. You pissed me off a couple of times, but in the end, you came through. Have a safe trip home." He nodded and left.

When the front door closed, Vicky turned to Trevor. "Do you think the sheriff will catch up to my brother?"

"He hasn't got you covering his ass anymore."

"Knowing Rod, he's already got a scheme in mind."

"Can't believe a deputy helped him escape. She must know what's coming."

"My brother's good. Made her think she was the love of his life. Sooner or later, he'll dump her."

Trevor took her into his arms. "I'm tired of talking about Rod. Let's get back to our discussion before Al interrupted us."

"We weren't discussing anything. We were kissing."

"And doing it very nicely, I might add. Damned perfectionist. Let's go upstairs."

"You want to discuss something?"

He pinched her bottom lightly. "No, you little devil. I want to make mad, passionate love to you until you scream for mercy or beg for more."

She wrapped her arms around his neck, and whispered, "Damned perfectionist."

****

Los Angeles, three weeks later

Vicky shoved a file into the drawer, and then admired the gold band on her finger glinting in the sunshine coming through the window. Trevor offered to buy her a diamond engagement ring and wedding band, but she'd refused. Too many diamonds over the years had left her jaded. Married a month now, the thrill never ceased.

Pam and Marylou welcomed her in grand fashion. Her first day in the office saw no work done. She, Trevor, and the office staff had partied all day. Already, Vicky considered the two women friends, a first for her. She couldn't afford friends during her conning years.

"Are you going to stand there admiring that ring all day? Work, woman, work. That's what I pay you for. I'd hate to can your ass," Trevor said with a grin.

She stuck her tongue out at him. "Some paycheck. A cup of coffee, a stale bagel, and an occasional lunch."

"Guess who I talked to this morning."

"Who?"

"Quinn."

She ceased admiring, and stared. "You're kidding. What did he want?"

"Wanted to know if I found you. I told him I not

319

only found you, but caught you, and then decided to keep you."

"You make me sound like a fish. I assume you told him we're married."

He nodded. "Damn near shocked him to death. He told me I was nuts and to keep a close eye on my wallet."

Vicky slipped behind the desk, and wrapped her arms around her husband's neck, laying her cheek against his hair.

"I promise you'll never have to do that."

"I know. Told Quinn that, too. Come here, you wench." He pulled her into his lap and kissed her. "Can't believe how happy I am. Never thought I'd find that quality again."

She traced his lips with a fingertip. "I always hoped I'd find that knight in shining armor to carry me away from a life I hated. I found him in you."

"That sounds like something out of a novel."

"Believe it or not, I often read romance novels. They represented something clean and hopeful in contrast to the life I led. I wanted so badly for that world to exist."

She kissed him deeply. Just when things began heating up, her cell rang.

"Damn." There was only one person other than Trevor and the office staff who had that number. She extricated herself from Trevor's lap, crossed the room, and fumbled in her purse to find the phone. Caller ID confirmed her suspicions.

"Hello, Rod."

"Sis, you gotta help me. I'm in trouble," he said, his frightened tone easy to hear.

She glanced at Trevor who said in a low voice, "Find out where he is."

"What do you want, Rod?"

"Sis, I'm in jail in Palm Beach."

She glanced at her husband. "That's your

problem. What are you doing in Palm Beach, Florida?"

Trevor pulled out his cell phone and dialed.

"Setting up old farts with too much money." His voice rose an octave.

"And that's why you're in jail?"

"No, no! Look, sis, haul your ass down here from wherever you are. I need help."

He's scared to death and running to me as usual.

"I'm in Los Angeles. I married Trevor."

"That cop?"

"Private investigator. I'm getting my license and joining his firm."

"You're nuts!"

"No, I'm happy for the first time in my life."

"But I need help."

"Too bad. At least you'll be in jail in Palm Beach."

"But they'll find out about my escape! They'll send me back," he whined.

He never changes. No congratulations, not a word about anyone except himself.

"You deserve it. What happened to Anne Daniels?"

Trevor was speaking softly to someone.

"I don't know. I ditched her in Dallas and came here."

"What did you do to end up in jail?"

"I got caught on a DUI."

All those cons, and he gets nailed for drunk driving. What a moron.

"Rod, you're on your own."

His vice turned wheedling. "Aw, don't say that, Vicky."

"I'm sorry, Rod. I mean it."

"You always help!"

Panic replaced wheedling. She wondered when the sniveling would start.

"I cannot and will not help you. Ever again."

"No! Sis, you can't mean that! I'm your brother, for God's sake! Please, Vicky...please, don't do this to..."

Disgusted, Vicky snapped her phone shut, and turned to Trevor. It rang again. She ignored it.

Trevor finished his call at the same time. "I told Al."

She told him the gist of the conversation.

"Al will get in touch with the Palm Beach authorities. It's over for him. He'll do plenty of jail time in Colorado and California."

"I know," she said with a sigh.

"Honey, I wish I could say I'm sorry, but I can't. He's a narcissist, unable to see anybody but himself—a bad seed. He's getting what he deserves."

"And when he gets out, he'll go right back to conning, only by then he'll be an old man." The phone rang again. Vicky opened it and broke off the receiver, then dropped the pieces in the wastebasket.

"A part of me will always wonder if he told the complete truth."

"About what?" Trevor asked.

"About Helen's death."

"Corwin killed her."

"But did she trip like he said, or did Rod slam her head into the desk attempting to kill or knock her unconscious? I never thought he could deliberately kill someone. Now, I'm not so sure. The older he gets, the more his desperation grows."

"Perhaps, but he's no longer your problem. We may never know the complete truth, but I'm satisfied. Aunt Helen can rest in peace."

"'Oh, what a tangled web we weave, when first we practice to deceive.'"

"Tennyson?"

"Sir Walter Scott. Ironic, huh?" She glanced into the trash can. "I need a new phone." She turned to

Trevor with tears in her eyes. "I swear you'll never regret marrying me."

He rose and held her close. "I know. You are *not* your brother."

She sniffed. "You're the only person in the world I've ever trusted. I'll never stop loving you."

"Thank goodness, because that would scare the crap out of me." He smiled and wiped her tears with his fingertips. "Let's get you a new phone—one with an unlisted number."

Vicky gathered her purse, thanking God for sending Trevor Sloane to Miami. Her life had taken a massive turn, and for the first time her future looked bright. They'd even discussed children.

I'm safe, secure, and married to a man I adore.

She lifted her chin, and followed him out the door.

A word from the author...

I was born in Indianapolis, Indiana, but lived for many years in Memphis, Tennessee, which I now consider home. I have two adult children and four grandchildren. At present, I reside in Ft. Lauderdale, Florida, with my husband, Bruce, and two dogs, Lucky and Liza.

I've been a serious writer for six years and belong to RWA, Florida Romance Writers, River City Romance Writers, the special interest chapter of RWA, Kiss of Death, and Mystery Writers of America, including the Florida chapter. I achieved PRO status in 2004. I also co-chaired FRW's 2007 Fun In The Sun Conference.